Symphony on Sand

KATRINA JEWETT HAMMONS

Publisher Anne Alvin

Copyright © 2012 Katrina Jewett Hammons.
All rights reserved.
No part of this book may be used or reproduced in any manner whatsoever without written permission except in the case of brief quotations embodied in critical articles or reviews. For information, contact kjewett@annealvin.com.

ISBN: 978-0-9850019-0-2

www.annealvin.com

For information on Reading Group Guides, as well as ordering, please contact the Anne Alvin Marketing Department at 602.368.9980 or E-mail: Anne@AnneAlvin.com.

This book is a work of fiction. Names, characters, businesses, organizations, places, events, and incidents either are the product of the author's imagination or are used fictitiously. Any resemblance to actual persons, living or dead, events, or places is entirely coincidental.

Written, manufactured, and printed in the United States of America.

We the People...

THREE FRIENDS, ONE YEAR, three events—Reagan Hamilton is a teacher and a die-hard Democrat. Alexandria Giroud is an attorney and a staunch Republican. Taylor Ray is a corporate executive and an Independent. These women take on the highs and lows of life together until betrayal, deceit, and tragedy strike in a heated election year. Suddenly, the friends must make tough choices. Can friendship triumph over the zero-sum game of politics? Only the journey tells...

Chapter One
The Break of Dawn

*D*AWN BREAKS EQUALLY for all daily.
Not for me today, Reagan thinks. *Daybreak betrays!*

Reagan escapes the new day and the chances sunlight brings in exchange for darkness. She creates night in day.

She sits in bed, alone, white t-shirt and jeans worn days before still on. Her usual charging thoughts are halted. Inside her mind is a vacuum with space for sorrow only, nothing else.

Her typically lavender-scented, neat, shabby-chic bungalow home smells like death. A thick and musty stench mixes with her home's usual floral scents.

Any other day Reagan would declare a house like hers a natural disaster, unfit for living, too unclean to dwell.

She'd counsel any person who found their home like hers to clean thoroughly and often, citing cleanliness is next to Godliness while rolling up her sleeves and helping clean.

Yet, today Reagan resides in filth, and surprisingly she does not care. She sinks; she succumbs. Her soul dies as she resides in a foul-smelling, disorderly home. Fear controls and completely overcomes her here. She is anxious about everything and thankful for nothing. She is numb, in a coma-like state.

She fell into a deep depression three days ago when she learned her husband was not coming home. Hearing her new reality, she grabbed onto panic and tightly held. She abandoned everything and everyone, even herself. She left space in her mind to think only about the one, her spouse, Jackson Hamilton.

– 9 –

Now, on day three, at the break of dawn, she sits balled up in her bed in complete night. Darkness envelops her eyes. She closes her mind.

She cannot comprehend why she is sitting alone in bed. *How did we get here?* she begins to question, when suddenly a loud ring startles her.

Identifying the ringing bell as the one she set for Jackson, she starts to act. She numbly stands and walks.

Feeling her way to her dresser where her lamp and telephone sit, she consciously takes time to make a quick request, half to God and half to Jackson, maybe even half to herself. *Please bring us back together.*

Reaching her dresser, she quickly turns on her lamp and answers the telephone.

She tries to speak, but her voice is weak, her mouth is dry, her words are faint. She is unable to express the anticipation she feels.

"Jackson?" Her voice is almost silent, like a whisper, even though she is saying the word with all her might, full of hope.

"Reagan, hi, listen, I've—"

Reagan cuts off a cacophony of bloated, meaningless words after identifying the caller as her *so-called friend*, Alexandria Giroud. She hangs up the telephone and internally rants. *You untrustworthy scoundrel! Don't call my house!*

Lifting her disappointed eyes, Reagan catches a glimpse of herself in the large, faux antique mirror affixed to the wall above her dresser.

Reagan sees herself for the first time in three days and is shocked. Her mind jarringly shifts to herself. She looks so different. Her shoulders are sunken, as if the burden of her ordeal is too heavy, too weighted. She cannot lift her shoulders up; they sink into her chest.

Her eyes are swollen and red from days of crying until she had no tears left. Her eyes look like a drought-ridden, desert riverbed. Seeing her body, she realizes her slim frame is thinner than it was three days ago. Her collarbone leaps from her descending shoulders.

She looks dead.

𝄢

SHE STARES AT HERSELF and reminisces back to her last meal, three days ago—smoked salmon, steamed asparagus, a loaded baked potato, and grape juice. On that sunny day, she remembers sitting in her kitchen, waiting on her husband. Hours pass. The sun sets. Jackson doesn't come home. She patiently waits, reading *Faulkner, As I Lay Dying*. She isn't alarmed.

Her husband is a political columnist. He writes for a startup, e-political website. She knows he is working on the latest, breaking story, so she waits.

More hours pass.

Jackson still doesn't come home or call.

Weird! He usually calls. She picks up the telephone to call his cell. His voicemail picks up on the first ring. *Is his cell battery dead? Probably so, oh well.* Shrugging her shoulder, she begins to eat alone. Biting into her salmon, she smiles as the perfect mix of sun-dried tomatoes and herbal seasonings blend with the salmon and arouse her taste buds. *Delightful! Mmmm—the asparagus! I've hammered this recipe!* She tastes an impeccable balance of sesame, ginger, and soy on her smoked asparagus tips. *Delicious.* She licks her lips.

Returning to her book, *As I Lay Dying*, while dining, she reads. Just as she eats her last asparagus tip and then the last bite of her meat, she rethinks a line in the book in her mind. *"Life was created in the valleys. It blew up onto the hills on the old terrors, the old lust despairs. That's why you must walk up the hills so you can ride down."* Chewing while pondering, she begins to think, *Interesting, but*—when her telephone rings.

Recognizing the ring tone as her husband's, she glances at his cold but scrumptious looking meal while answering the telephone. Smiling and picking up the receiver, she speaks. "Hi Jackson! I have great dining and a terrific book, so stop working and why don't you come home?"

Realizing the caller is not Jackson but someone else, her smile fades. Hearing the words on the other end, she drops her book onto her plate. The news hits her like a ton of bricks.

He's not coming home?

The news takes her appetite.

That was her last meal in three days.

She has only sipped on a few drops of water all while feeling no hunger and no thirst. And his plate still sits in the same place, on the table, albeit the salmon is obviously rotting.

— ✹ —

RETURNING TO THE PRESENT, and now, looking at her sunken eyes in the mirror, she does not see herself. She ogles at these eyes, locked in a trance, until her telephone rings again.

Please be Jackson. Please. She shifts her eyes this time before answering. Identifying the caller, ALEXANDRIA GIROUD, she realizes the CALLER ID betrays. *Again, stop calling me!*

RING, RING, RING—Reagan frowns and ignores the call. The rings sound out and bounce off her tiny bungalow unacknowledged until the ringing ends in exchange for a pre-recorded salutation, which begins.

"We aren't home. Leave a message please after the beep."

BEEP..........

Speak to my answering machine, traitor! Reagan holds up her hand—the talk to the hand motion—while the answering machine intercepts the call.

After the beep, Reagan hears Alex bolt out a full and bloated sigh through her answering machine recorder, as if she is frustrated, as if she knows Reagan is avoiding her calls.

Reagan expects to hear Alex apologize, but she doesn't. Instead, Alex is uncharacteristically silent.

Lost for words—not you, not the woman of many words, Reagan thinks, until the answering machine cuts off Alex's silent message.

Reagan closes her eyes and rolls her shoulders. She is relieved Alex is gone.

RING, RING, RING—

Go away!

RING, RING, RING—*I don't hear you. I'm not answering!* The answering machine salutation answers again. Alex recommences her silent message through the answering machine.

Dog got your tongue? Guess— Reagan is cut off by frantic pounding sounds vibrating through the walls.

Bracing her hands on her dresser, Reagan tries to un-fog her brain so she can discover the source of the racket.

Scrunching her gaunt face and slightly tilting her head to the left, she follows the sound with her ears.

Holding onto the dresser still, Reagan tightens her grip and leans her body forward. It feels like the noise is pulling her head in two different directions, as if in a tug-of-war.

Listening closely, Reagan discerns that the sounds are coming from her left, but then they are also coming from her right.

Is the noise coming from the porch, the backdoor, both, what? And why, why is that sound echoing—the noise is everywhere!

Searching with her ears, she realizes that the sound begins on her porch, but the noise is also coming through her answering machine. *Is Alex on my porch?*

— ♪ —

Standing on Reagan Hamilton's front porch with a cell phone to her ear, Alexandria Giroud knocks, paces, and thinks. *Reagan, I've been calling you for three days with no luck! I even used Jackson's cell phone, but you hung up in my face! Maybe now you'll answer me if I'm calling you while knocking on your front porch!*

"Come on, open the door!" Alex mumbles, still pacing back and forth on the porch while occasionally stopping to pound on the front door.

Reagan does not answer.

Seeing curtains move from inside her friend's home, Alex pounds harder and yells louder, "I know you're home!"

No answer.

Deliberating on how to get inside the house, Alex sways her body from left to right and intermittingly adjusts her long, bob-layered brunette and honey-highlighted hair. She eventually stops swaying and stands rigid, motionless. She inhales deeply and then exhales before she begins to knock again at the door, pleading with Reagan. "Open up! I know you're in there, please!"

Again, there is no response.

Alex huffs loudly, as if her fiercely exhaled breath can open the door, but no chance.

"Reagan!" Alex yells into the telephone. She tries to reach her friend, who she believes is on the other side of the door.

No answer.

Cradling the telephone in between her shoulder and ear, Alex crosses her arms and grits her teeth. Annoyed, she is at a loss for words. She is unable to talk her way inside the door. She does not know how to reach a friend in the midst of a crisis when that friend feels that she is the cause.

She knocks on the door again.

"Reagan, p – l – e- a- s-e? I can explain!"

More knocking.

Alex's pleas go unacknowledged.

— 𝄢 —

REAGAN STARES AT HERSELF in the mirror, like a zombie, listening to Alex and thinking, *Jezebel, get away from my door!*

Chapter Two
Nine Months Earlier

Taylor Ray, Whitfield Ray, Reagan Hamilton, Jackson Hamilton, and Alexandria Giroud dance in a cozy circle of friends when suddenly, "Celebrate good times, come on," blasts out loud.

Taylor Ray, the hostess, smiles.

Alexandria Giroud yells, "Kool & The Gang, that's the cue," before jumping and screaming, "*10-9-8-7-6-5-4-3-2-1*—Happy New Year!"

Happy New Year cheers fill the room in unison as friends celebrate at the home of Taylor and Whitfield Ray. . . .

Alex dances from side to side with a glass of merlot in hand.

Reagan and Jackson Hamilton dance in each other's arms.

Taylor Ray also dances with her husband, Whitfield Ray, but while her feet and body sway, her mind shifts to her party accommodations . . . *Dandy, my timer worked. Celebration's playing on time! But fiddlesticks, what about the resolutions? Shouldn't we be raising our flutes or something? So here goes!*

"Prosperity!" Taylor lifts her glass and shouts her resolution, but seeing the goblet of merlot in front of her, her mind shifts. *We have goblets in hand, not champagne glasses! You can't toast at a Ray party with wine! Oh fiddlesticks!*

"I'm faithful and thankful!" Reagan proclaims in her husband's arms.

Dancing solo, Alex mischievously grins, raises her wine glass, and resolves, "New Beginnings!"

Great, everyone's said their resolutions and while Alex may be thinking sneaky she didn't say anything risqué but wait, what about the diamond-confetti?

Diamonds, where are you? You're supposed to fall from the ceiling at countdown!

Come on! Come on!

Yes! The diamond-like confetti is falling! Check!

Hope they like the diamonds, but wait, the champagne!

How do I get champagne in everyone's hands, especially when Alex won't put down that darn Merlot!

Oh but wait, the food. Is the filet minion still hot? Are the lobsters still warm? Oh fiddlesticks, Whit move over!

Unable to see the food on the marble countertop, Taylor gently coaxes her husband's body so that he moves slightly to the right. With the countertop where the food sits in clear view now, she confirms. *Yes, check, the flames are blazing underneath the chafing dishes.*

But wait, what about the exotic cheeses and dessert wines and the chocolate covered strawberries? Is the chocolate fondue still— Taylor's thoughts are finally interrupted when her husband abruptly stops dancing.

Pulling away from her body, Whitfield stares into her eyes for a few seconds before drawing her close to him again.

Gently kissing her earlobe, he whispers, "Tay, everything's perfect!"

Shrugging her shoulders, trying to resist her weak spot—him speaking in his deep voice while nibbling on her ear with luscious lips—she tries to reconnect.

Taylor Ray is a public relations executive. Her husband, Whitfield Ray, is an executive management consultant. As career heavy hitters, the Rays host many events each year, with Taylor Ray setting the stage for each event.

While she is a perfect hostess, her husband often tries to get her to enjoy the events she hosts. And this New Year's Eve party is but another example of him knowing her so well and trying to get her to relax.

9

RESTING HER HEAD ON her husband's chest, Taylor feels his body next to hers. Popping her hips in beat with the song *Celebration*, she smiles. *My par-tay's a hit!*

Reagan, an elementary school teacher, dances and shouts, "C- e- l- e- b-r- a- t- i-o-n!" She annunciates each syllable in the word—celebration—as if she is teaching phonics. Jackson, her husband, focuses mainly on his wife as he steps from side to side, slightly off beat.

Taylor claps to the beat of the music. Seamlessly, she stops clapping and changes posture. She begins to sashay her hips while her husband of three years grabs her waist and holds her with his hands and his locked eyes. She controls his hands and his eyes with her sultry sway. He latches on as she rotates her hips and reigns with her body, her buttocks, her gyrations, her motion, her posture, and her eyes.

C – e – l – e- b – r – a – t – i – o – n, bounces off the walls and fills the room as these friends get together on a crisp night, under stars that shine through the windows. New year air creeps into the open sliding glass panel door. Just as a breeze tickles the corners of a Happy New Year banner that hangs between two of the eight methodically placed Roman columns that decorate the second floor loft, Alex steps from side to side, sips Merlot and slurs, "A MAN!"

"Stop, we're not doing the man talk." Taylor immediately cuts her off, trying to keep her party on course.

"Why not?" Alex asks.

"Not that kind of party!" Taylor explains.

Reagan nods as if in agreement and keeps dancing.

"Quite naturally, you'd say not here! But Reagan I listened to you cry about your first crush in high school! And Taylor, I heard about all your men in college! So yep, we're doing the man thing!" Alex demands, still dancing.

"Really, Alex? I mean, can't we—" Reagan begins.

"Move the dialogue!" Taylor quickly finishes the sentence, trying to hasten the conversation.

"No! This is a New Year, and I'm officially resolving to find a man," Alex adds, as she raises her glass.

"Let him find you," Reagan whispers.

"No, I can't wait. I'm searching!"

"If you insist, let's get to the point! You're too bossy, inconsiderate, and unaccommodating!" Taylor explains, popping her hips with each word.

Instantly, Whitfield drops his hands from Taylor's waist and shoots them up in a stick-'em up position, as if to say he is not a part of the conversation Taylor is having with her words or hips.

The women continue.

— 9 —

WHITFIELD SENDS JACKSON A non-verbal cue. *Escape!* Simultaneously, both men head to the large outdoor balcony, except Whitfield turns back and grabs scotch and shot glasses from the well-stocked bar, which is snuggled in a nook in the loft.

Cradling the bottle under his arms while holding the shot glasses in hand, Whitfield returns to the outdoor living area and sees Jackson standing, obviously taking in the immaculate view. Whitfield lets out a loud, exaggerated exhale. Breathing in again, he takes in his hiatus from the indoor chitchat and walks over to Jackson, handing him his scotch.

"Thanks," Jackson says, leaning against a column.

Whitfield downs a full glass of liquor. Gritting his teeth once done, he gasps and asks, "Who psychoanalyzes women on New Years?"

"No one in their right mind," Jackson responds. He sips the scotch and discretely swirls the liquor against his tongue.

Pouring another shot in his glass, Whitfield catches a glimpse inside and cautions, "Don't look back! Alex is like Medusa!"

"When she starts her man quest, you don't want to look. She turns the atmosphere into stone," Jackson says, adjusting his lean.

Whitfield broadens his shoulders, causing his back to squarely face the glass pane wall, trying to block and save Jackson from seeing or hearing the scene transpiring inside before he states, "She's easy on the eyes, but she has issues—serious problems."

"What?"

"She's trouble!" Whitfield pauses and chuckles before adding, "But I want her to fix a dude and make him stick, turn some gullible dude into stone."

"Why? So our wives will stop the man search madness?"

"Exactly."

"Yeah, Reagan, she's anxious over Alex's drama."

"Nah, not Tay. She's her friend, but she doesn't play the drama game. She gives her advice and then moves on."

"And so shall we."

"I hear you, so moving on, how's the scotch?"

"Hits the spot."

"Good, and the view?" Whitfield asks.

"Breathtaking. The mountains, the sky, man, you're living large!" Jackson answers.

Gulping another shot of liquor, Whitfield leans over the wrought-iron rail and says, "Honestly, I agreed to buy this house because the view is amazing! You can see Camelback Mountain, the McDowell Mountain Preserve, and even city lights!"

"Yeah, the view's nice, but man, you've got a chandelier outside—that must have set you back!"

"I wouldn't know. That's Tay. I'm a minimalist, but I do like the view. The view and the sex sold the house!"

"Sex?"

"Yeah, man. Tay walked into our old house sexing me, trying to get me to buy this new house when our old house was perfectly fine."

"I was wondering why you moved. The old house had five bedrooms, with upgrades, in a nice gated neighborhood, right?"

"Yes, but nice wasn't good enough for Tay. She likes grand! So one day, out of the blue, she came home with sales brochures and sex! She was cute, hot and bothered! She was begging and sexing me, which you know didn't work."

"But you bought the house. Her sexing did something?"

"Nah, again, the view," Whitfield declares, and pauses. An image of his wife hanging from the indoor-chandelier flashes through his mind before he adds, "But I'll admit, her sexual-convincing was enjoyable!"

Jackson laughs before the men fall into silence underneath the crystalline New Year sky. Lit by thousands of stars and a full moon, the sight is spectacular.

— 9 —

TAYLOR FROWNS AS THE debate continues inside.

"I'm young, single, successful, and happily so," Alex proclaims.

"What about Genesis?" Reagan asks.

"What?" Taylor and Alex both snap back in unison.

"Adam & Eve, that's the intent," Reagan replies, as if she's explained everything, biblically speaking that is.

"Who's Adam?" Alex asks.

"Please tell me you're kidding." Taylor half-chuckles before adding, "Even I know Adam."

"In the beginning, God created Adam and Eve, remember?"

"Ha! Why do you always end up in the Bible?" Alex asks, and then adds, "Who cares, I can't wait on a so-called 'Adam!'"

Reagan sighs.

Taylor offers another option with a sarcastic smirk and a raised voice, trying to completely change the subject—get the conversation off the Bible, knowing Reagan could stay here and talk religion all night. "Alex, try FindAMan.com!"

"Online dating?" Reagan inquires, as if in shock, before answering her own question. "Never, ever, no online dating!"

"Desperate!" Alex exclaims.

Silence falls between them.

Breaking the silence, Reagan speaks. "You never know who you'll meet online, so be careful." Reagan looks genuinely concerned, as if she is talking to her elementary school students and telling them not to walk out into the street without looking.

"You watch too much LIFETIME!"

"I watch news and spiritual shows, too, and speaking of the Spirit, Alex, why don't you try the church?"

"Please don't go there," Alex says, frowning.

Taylor throws her hands up in the air before she shakes her hips again.

"You can find a good man in church," Reagan explains.

"I don't need church dating!" Alex barks back.

"Desperate times require desperate measures, but can we change the subject? Again, this is a party, remember?" Taylor says.

Moving close to Alex, Reagan gazes into her eyes before patting her on the back and saying, "He'll come. He'll find you. Be patient."

Alex brushes off the encouraging words and says, "I'm not waiting! Who cares if I find the one?"

Reagan tilts her head slightly to the left. Lines of worry frame her face. After a while, she speaks. "Alex, live God's way and the perfect guy will find you."

"Why does everything turn to religion with you?" Alex asks.

"She's super-religious, but anyway, stop, please!" Taylor pleads.

"Who said I'm not living right?" Alex questions.

— 𝄢 —

Taylor frowns, realizing she is not able to redirect the conversation. She feels frustrated because her party is completely off course. *Maybe Whit can call someone, anyone—a date for Alex so we can change the subject.*

Suddenly, Whitfield walks in, surveys the room, and then passes a puzzled, enough already look to Taylor.

"Ladies . . ." Jackson pauses to cough. "Aren't we celebrating?"

"Absolutely! This is a party, right babe?" Whitfield adds, walking towards his wife.

Taylor's eyes lock on her husband's. She gladly refocuses her attention on him. She smiles and recommences her sultry sway, except her steps and gyrations are determined, purposeful. She seductively draws near to her husband until she is close enough to clasp his hands. Pressing her body against his, she looks squarely into his deep brown eyes.

Whitfield smiles and draws even closer until their lips touch. They share a sensuous kiss. As soon as their lips part, Taylor whispers, "I'm hopeful this year!"

Whitfield whispers into her ears, "Tay, we'll get what we want."

Yes, please let this be the year we have a baby.

Chapter Three
Alexandria Giroud, Esq.

The ALARM SOUNDS!

"All right, A-L-L R-I-G-H-T," Alex says, before she sits up, rubs her eyes, swings her feet out of bed onto the floor, and begins her morning rituals without a thought, a pulse set by routine.

Exactly NINETY MINUTES LATER, she is in play, striding through the law firm foyer. Her heels strike the marble floors; the sound mixes with rustling papers, beeping pagers, striking typist, and whispering chatter—all office thunder in full roar by 7:16 a.m.

Her quick steps suddenly stop. She has a cramp in her leg. She stops and massages her aching leg when she hears her assistant, Heidi Martinez, ask in a concerned voice, "Are you okay?"

Not wanting to let anyone, not even her trusted assistant, know that she is hurt, Alex lies and says, "Snag in my pants."

"But your leg?" Heidi asks.

"Don't be silly, I'm perfect," Alex answers, and hastens her steps to support her lie. CLICK, CLAT, CLICK, CLICK, CLAT.

Ouch! Façades hurt! Alex walks briskly, feigning strength in the midst of discomfort. Her leg hurts because she strained her muscle this morning during her daily thirty-minute, four-mile run. Yet, she acts like she isn't hurt because she doesn't want to appear weak in an environment boiling over with testosterone.

Finally! She walks into her 10x12 urban, colorless, contemporary office and closes her glass door.

I hate all this glass! She knows she has no privacy. She can see everyone outside her office, and they can see her. She wants to close the seamless, electronic blinds that could shield her with one touch of a button, but she surmises that if she acts perfect but then walks into her office and conceals herself by letting down her ceiling to floor black shades, she'll look suspicious.

Maintaining appearances, perfection at work, she sits in her white leather office chair and rests her hands on her glass, contemporary, clean-lined desk. Readying herself to dive into work, her escape, she catches a glimpse of the only pop of color in her sterile-looking white office. *Duncan Anderson.*

Staring at the photo of her ex, Duncan Anderson, the only photo in her office, she wonders, *Why aren't we still climbing?*

The photo is of the two of them hiking together near Mount Rushmore. To her, it's like they are standing on top of the world.

She stares at the photo and sees herself with him, hand-in-hand, wearing parkas, gloves, hats, and carrying hiking sticks, *in love!*

She gets goose bumps remembering climbing Mount Rushmore with her ex years ago. *We were meant to tackle a lifetime of summits!* She feels the emptiness of his absence. *At least I feel the warmth of your body every once in a while.*

She sighs because while the photo is a trophy piece to others, the photo means so much more to Alex. To others, the photo says, *I've climbed to the top of the world with wealth, have you?* But to Alex, this photo is as close as she gets to The One, or the person who should have been The One—Duncan Anderson.

— ❊ —

"Marshall needs you!" a voice on Alex's intercom belts out loudly, interrupting her thoughts.

Hearing the name of her boss, and the voice of Judy Carpentar, her boss' assistant, Alex quickly awakens from her trance and stands. *Ouch!* She grabs a pen and pad and walks towards her boss' office.

"Good morning, Mr. Hanes," Alex says, stepping into his office.

"We've got to control the media!" Marshall Hanes barks. He extends his arm to hand Alex a newspaper.

Walking close to his desk, she takes the paper and reads the headline.

HMO KILLS YOUNG MOTHER AND WIFE

Wow, that's a stretch, Alex thinks. "Where's fair and balanced journalism these days?" she inquires.

"They're selling papers; I don't care."

Alex nods. "Of course."

"I'll control the message, regardless of the papers they're trying to sell."

"Absolutely."

"Get Lisa Martin on board. We must prepare her public relations people."

"We'll get ahead of the story," Alex says, taking her pen to pad.

"Issue a press release, short and to the point, clearly stating our position."

"Saying HealthSolutions did nothing wrong?"

"Obviously, but we'll say her procedure wasn't insured."

"Explaining the bone marrow transplant was experimental and not covered under her insurance policy?"

"No, that's a court room battle! We're controlling public opinion!"

"Right, of course," Alex says, thinking, *Sometimes, the hats we wear are so confusing. Are we a public relations firm, lobbying firm, law firm, or all of the above?*

"We'll tell the public the case is frivolous."

"Blame the plaintiff's lawyers, say they're greedy."

He nods. "You're catching on. And tort reform, use the usual tag lines."

"Make the victims the guilty."

"You got it. We've got to control public perception; make the public feel we're right and the plaintiffs wrong."

"What's our timeline?"

"As always, before the end of the news cycle—and also have somebody ready, an internal HealthSolutions person, a likeable person, a woman, nurturing looking and easy on the eyes. She must be ready and available, 24-7, and able to act as our media contact, a spokesperson."

Alex begins speaking. "How about—" but Judy Carpentar chimes in via office intercom and says, "Richard Riley, line 2."

"Got it." Marshall presses a button on his telephone and speaks while shooing Alex off with his other hand, pausing to mouth the words, "Go away!"

Alex quickly stands and exits his office, knowing Richard Riley is a political party heavyweight and fundraiser.

Wonder what's up? Richard Riley only calls when he has a political favor to call in, money he's trying to raise, or a political scheme or plan. *Wonder which one this time?*

Chapter Four
Reagan Hamilton: The Class

REAGAN STANDS BEFORE her classroom with heavy thoughts. She begins a mental tirade. *Why must I teach the test? Teaching rote standardized test taking skills isn't education! Why teach kids to memorize answers to multiple choice questions? Why can't I challenge these kids and make them great thinkers?* Tossing thoughts around in her mind, she rants until the school bell rings, interrupting her thoughts. Her fifth grade students tumble through the door, some pushing, some shoving, some out of line, some yelling obnoxious things, but all entering and walking to their assigned seats.

"Shut up, stupid!" Clifford yells.

"I know you are but what am I?" Charlie shouts.

Chatter fills the room until Reagan begins to speak to the children. Though small in stature, they are deafening in volume, creating chaos all about. After a few minutes, all forty-two are quiet, and Reagan resumes her search. She inspects the desk until she finds what she is looking for—"Ah, great, the test!"

Turning her back to her students, she faces the chalkboard with the standardized test in hand. She scours the test and tries to think of a new way to teach the items on the exam.

She canvasses the ins and outs of her brain, the full circumference of her knowledge bank. She simply does not know how to creatively teach standardized test questions. Trying to ignite passion in standardized test taking stretches her so she is oblivious to the beginnings of a stewing brew.

— 9 —

Meanwhile, it boils . . . . .

"I did it!" Tyler gestures across the street and speaks.

"No, me!" shouts Jefferson, as he points to the same thing.

"No you didn't, I did!" Haxley blurts out.

Tyler, Jefferson, Haxley, and a host of other characters in the back of the classroom proudly claim authorship of the graffiti on the bridge immediately across the street from the school. Hearing the commotion as she begins to write 2 + 5 = on the chalkboard, Reagan turns back around and immediately grabs the reins. "Stop the chatter Tyler, Jefferson, Haxley, and Bailey!"

"Ms. Hamilton has eyes in the back of her head," Haxley giggle-sings.

"I do, so that's two demerits for you," Reagan snaps back.

Flipping his bangs back, he pouts. "Awe man, Ms. Hamilton."

"Remember the rules…sit quietly, listen carefully, focus, and participate!" Reagan says and then stares at her students, giving them a cold, threatening look, a technique she learned from her principal, Mr. Lee. She holds this posture for what seems like a full minute before she transitions back to the test. Setting up another math equation on the chalkboard, chatter interrupts her mid-calculation.

"Not again!" Dixon says out loud.

"Ms. Hamilton and that dumb test!"

"PBS teaches more than 6 + 2!"

"I hate tests! Can you say lackluster?"

Did she say lackluster, meaning boring, uninteresting? I'm limiting these children. "Listen, students, test prep is great!" Reagan authoritatively ends the noise immediately with her statement.

Placing her hands on her hips, frustrated, she adds, "Test mastery will prepare you for a bright future!" *Liar!* Her stomach turns. *This test is the bare minimum.* The knot in her stomach grips and tugs. She feels stuck. She has been told repeatedly that she must teach the test and nothing else. She tries to motivate her students to eagerly embrace test preparation as their core curriculum, but she doesn't even believe in what she is preaching.

"I understand test prep isn't exciting, but you can excel!" Reagan smiles as she examines her class, trying to see if she has persuaded her students, even if she can't convince herself.

Reagan quiets their words, but the children loudly speak with non-verbal communication. Some students have sunken eyes; others have bored faces. Studying the faces of her students, the knot in her stomach tightens, pulls her in, and holds. She sinks. *They're right, but my hands are tied. I can't teach more than the rote standardized tests. That's what Mr. Lee says.*

– 9 –

STANDING AND STARING INTO the unengaged eyes of her students, she thinks back to the last time she tried to do more. Weeks ago, she was standing before her classroom using an exciting method to teach mathematics.

Her students were singing and laughing and learning multiplication when suddenly Mr. Lee, the principal, walked into her classroom.

With deep frown lines fixed on his face, he summoned her into the hallway for an impromptu principal/teacher conference. . . .

"Ms. Hamilton, a commotion you're causing I see students laughing. That's wrong; explain. I'm perplexed," Principal Lee said.

"I'm using an MIT methodology," Reagan said.

"With laughter?" Principal Lee probed, crossing his arms.

Reagan nodded. "Yes, the MIT teacher's conference, last summer. We learned how to teach math using music. And look, Mr. Lee, it's working!" Reagan paused and gazed at her students from the hallway and saw them solving mathematical equations in her absence. She marveled, turned back to Mr. Lee, and added, "Wow, the music and math methodology really works! I'm teaching addition, subtraction, and multiplication even. They'll excel! Come in and observe," Reagan said, with obvious enthusiasm.

"MIT? You're in a regular school, Reagan, not MIT," the principal scolded.

"What's the difference? They're learning, even critical thinking skills."

"Critical thinking here? Why, Ms. Hamilton, that's preposterous."

"Mr. Lee, I'm sorry, I don't understand."

"Ms. Hamilton, stick to the test only. These kids can't handle more. You must comprehend, if you travel on unknown journeys, far off course, away from our plans, you'll drop our scores. Can't let that happen; and hence stick with what we know."

"I know the MIT method. I spent six weeks learning the method," she said, defending herself.

"Great-grand, yes, your training, great-grand but irrelevant, comprehend, recall, understand, realize, our school motto explains our method."

She nodded, thinking, *Please, don't go there!*

"Ms. Hamilton, repeat after me! 'Test regularly, test often, test always!'" he said, in a chant she couldn't stand. She frowned, stood there, and watched the middle-aged man ridiculously simulate his infamous cheer routine, with fake-pom-poms, too!

— 𝄞 —

RETURNING TO THE PRESENT, still staring at her students, Reagan hears the "test always" chant ringing in her ears, but she also feels she must engage her students beyond mere test focusing. *Maybe I can turn the test into a game,* Reagan decides. She is inspired by Rita, Sonya, and Marvin, students who sit with their hands clasped in the middle of the desk with wide eyes and slight smiles. Rita, Sonya, and Marvin accept anything taught, but Reagan thinks, *I can turn test prep into a fun game!*

"Class, separate into teams," she says, before explaining the rules of the game.

"All right!" Lizzy jumps up and readies herself to play with her team.

If the test is their best chance, I'll make sure they grasp the test fully and completely at least! Reagan begins to teach Standardized Testing *Who Wants To Be A Millionaire Style.*

Chapter Five
Taylor Ray Deals

"YOU'VE GOT A DEAL!" Taylor announces, before hanging up the phone. She swivels in her chair and locks her eyes on her assistant, Joseph, through the glass wall. "Joseph! I've closed another one!" she says, via interoffice teleconference.

"What did you sell?" he asks, leaning in towards the intercom.

"I've sold advertising inventory for the TV shows *News & Action, Compassionate Conservatism v. Conservative Democrats*—oh, and *Political Sports!*"

She smiles as Joseph leaps up from behind his oak executive desk and walks the few feet to her office door. "You're a winner, Ms. Taylor. That's what you are!" He grins and moves inside. "Tell me the good part! What products are we selling?"

Thumbing through her notes, she answers, "We're selling the usual—diapers; maxi pads; birth control pills, particularly the ones that promise four periods a year; and lots of clothes, jewelry, and shoes."

"Ugh, ESTROGEN!" he exclaims, holding his chin.

"Oh, no! Hormone management sells both ways!" she says, wagging her finger to the right and left.

"Really?" he asks, leaning back.

"Consider *Political Sports*, the show where the anchors talk about sports and make analogies to political plays."

"Yes, that's the one where the anchors wear jerseys but talk politics."

"Precisely," she says, nodding. "That show sells male enhancement drugs, sports cars, and other male stuff."

He smiles, raising an eyebrow. "What's wrong with VIA-MAN?"

Before she can answer, her cell phone rings. She swirls in her chair and answers without looking at the CALLER ID, thinking, *Could be the fertility center!*

"Taylor Ray." She pauses, then frowns. "I'm sorry, but not a good time!" The call continues even though Taylor tries to end the conversation. Her facial lines deepen as she listens.

"I'll get rid of that caller!" Joseph whispers.

Taylor shakes her head and mouths, "No!"

Joseph's frown matches her own. He crosses his arms and fixes his gaze on her until suddenly, as if fed up, he mouths the words again. "I can get rid of telemarketers in a jiffy!"

"No!"

— 𝄢 —

JOSEPH WATCHES TAYLOR AND wonders, *Why's she so secretive? Odd!*

Joseph knows Taylor always dodges unwanted calls by delegating to him. Like last week. Joseph remembers sitting with Taylor in her office when suddenly the telephone rings. Looking at the CALLER ID, Taylor says, "Aunt Frieda," under her breath. She cuts her eyes at Joseph and delegates. "Handle it!"

He does.

"Taylor Ray's office," he answers.

"Hi baby," Aunt Frieda coos, since formalities aren't her thing.

"Hello, Ms. Frieda. Taylor's not available."

"She never is, baby. I know, I know, busy blah, blah, blah. Baby, take note! This call is important! See the lottery jackpot is $23,000,000! Did you know?"

"No, I didn't," Joseph answers, thinking, *Who cares?*

"See, y'all don't know everything in those ivory towers. You've got to take some time to relate to the people, and then you'll know these things."

"Ms. Frieda, sorry—" Joseph begins, but Aunt Frieda cuts him off.

"Baby, tell Tay about the jackpot and let her know that I'll stop by and pick up her portion. We can buy huge lots of tickets together and triple our chances!"

"Ms. Frieda, Taylor's in a meeting."

"I can wait."

"Out of town."

"Oh really, she didn't tell me."

"Sorry, maybe next time, Ms. Frieda."

"How 'bout you go in half with me! We can win big! Get your portion together. I'll swing by and pick up your money."

"No thanks." He ends the call shortly thereafter.

— ♪ —

JOSEPH SMILES BECAUSE HE is proud of his skills. *I'm the perfect assistant!* At least this is his thought until he turns his attention squarely back on Taylor. His mouth drops. *She's squirming in that seat!*

Taylor is not very good at ending unwanted calls quickly or easily on her own. Abrupt endings are her weakness and Joseph's strength. *Listen to her. She only gets a few words in from time to time.*

"Listen, I can't talk."

The caller obviously continues to talk because Taylor still sits with the phone to her ear.

"Okay, okay, but—"

The caller must have cut her off.

"I see, well, but we—"

I know the caller didn't cut her off again.

This call goes on for minutes more until Taylor finally scribbles down information and says, "Mm-hmm, bye!" It's clear that the caller ended the conversation, not Taylor.

— ♪ —

TAYLOR LOOKS UP FROM her notepad and eyes Joseph.

"Everything okay?" Joseph asks.

Faking a smile, Taylor quickly answers, "Yes, sure."

Seeing Joseph's concerned frown, she realizes that she is not doing a good job of sounding convincing.

Deciding to end the inquiry, she hands Joseph a manila folder and says, "File these, please."

Chapter Six
Control the Message: The Media

ALEX HANGS UP the telephone, having advised and controlled the Selena Cox media story. Feeling confident that the media correspondent will turn the focus from Selena Cox's death to greedy lawyers, she begins her courtroom defense strategy.

Yes, Selena Cox had cancer.
Yes, the HMO denied a bone marrow transplant to treat her cancer.
Yes, Selena Cox had a Health Solutions' HMO insurance policy.
Yes, Selena Cox died while insured.

But, the HMO isn't responsible for her death because Selena Cox's insurance policy specifically excludes experimental bone marrow transplants. Case closed and dismissed, which is good! Alex picks up her pen and pad and begins to write when suddenly, her mind trails off. She begins thinking about the lawsuit. *I don't understand why these whiny plaintiffs think HMOs pay for everything! HMOs don't cover every medical need! HMOs insure the masses by making tough decisions. HMOs must cap insurance policies, exclude costly treatments, and cut corners to provide insurance to more people. Besides, HMOs focus on preventive care. If a person wants insurance to protect against costly, experimental treatments or catastrophic events, consider a supplemental policy!*

Alex begins to refocus on the case and put her thoughts to pad. Just as she writes out her arguments to dismiss the lawsuit, a voice comes through the intercom.

"Marshall needs you immediately!" Judy Carpenter says in a loud, urgent voice.

Heartbeat racing, Alex jumps up and rushes into his office. Arriving within seconds, holding a pen and pad in hand, she enters.

"Mr. Hanes, how—"

"Get out!" he shouts, shooing her away with his hand.

I thought you said immediately! She steps outside his office and waits.

Fifteen minutes later, her heartbeat is steady but her blood boils. *Why do I feel like he's constantly saying jump, and I'm like, how high?* But she knows the answer. *Because you are! He's the jump commander, and you're the how high jumper. Why do I put up with him?* She wants to return to her office. *But NO! If I leave, he'll have a FIT! He expects me to wait here so as not to inconvenience him with needing to call Judy to have Judy call me to tell me to come to his office.* She waits.

– 𝄢 –

WASTING TIME WAITING, ALEX begins to reminisce about her first encounter with Marshall, six years ago. *Should have known then,* she thinks sarcastically, as her mind goes back to that day when he walked into her office and introduced himself.

"Marshall Hanes, founding partner, head litigator, national reputation—and you are?"

"Alexandria Giroud."

"And?" he asks in a harsh tone, as if her name alone is meaningless.

"Alexandria Giroud, law student, ivy-league, summer associate, future internationally renowned litigator." She tries to match his ego.

As the words leave her lips, she watches him. *How did I do?* She can't tell because he doesn't say a word. Instead, he raises one eyebrow and curls the edge of his lip, smirk-like. He looks like he is impressed or maybe even threatened by Alex's ambition. Alternatively, he might be thinking that she's unrealistically optimistic, naïve even. She isn't sure.

He grins and stares into her eyes for what seems like an eternity to Alex. Finally, he speaks. "Follow me."

She eagerly walks behind him, except his pace is too swift for her to keep up.

Leading Alex into the firm's grand foyer, he holds up his hands and says, "Examine closely. Here's success!"

She sees that he is pointing to an oil canvas portrait of himself and two other men, and her internal thoughts race. *Okay, life-sized portraits of the named partners. What should I say?*

Posing close to his portrait, he says, "Intriguing?"

Words, words, I need words.

Marshall continues to hold his pose, waiting for her response.

How can I miss these life-sized portraits! I see them daily!

He bats his eyes.

What is this fool doing? Alex wonders. *Law school didn't teach us anything about this. College Psychology maybe, but not law school.*

Marshall is now smiling. He has a huge grin. It seems to spread across his entire face.

Biting her tongue because no appropriate words come to mind, she thinks, *What do I say? Let's see, nice teeth, great hair, fabulous shirt, or handsome tie? Is that a toupee on your head, or are the photos enhanced to fill in your receding hairline?*

Lucky for Alex, Marshall finally puffs air into his chest and talks. "I know you're in awe of my greatness!"

Seeing his posture and hearing his words, she struggles to keep her jaw from dropping to the floor, her natural reaction to his shenanigans.

Like bullets, he begins rolling out his resume-vitae figuratively, not literally.

"Alexandria, *I AM* a senior named partner of Richardson, Davis & Hanes."

Should I tell you kudos, congratulations, or really? Good thing she doesn't have to say a word. He continues.

"I started the firm with Davis and Richardson in '92. Have you met them?"

Good! A question I can handle! "Yes, Mr. Davis interviewed me."

"Of course, I knew that. Anyway, when we started the firm, I only had experience and drive. I worked hard and pulled us all up.

I led the firm into greatness. I pushed this law firm straight to the top!" He emphasizes the word "I" each time he says it.

Awkward. That's not my understanding.

"I carry this firm! Clients pay hefty retainers to have access to me—to my excellence!" His words about himself—the I, the me, and the my—last a beat too long.

Okay, silence is golden here! I know politics and this IS a zero-sum game. If I agree with you, Davis and Richardson will question my loyalty and judgment. Yet, if I disagree with you, you'll probably go ballistic! Therefore, to safely navigate this awkward situation, I'll let you talk and I'll listen!

"We're the top HMO law firm in the country because I get results!

"I am the lead defense litigator. My client's demand my leadership and talents!

"I've won thousands of cases, usually at the summary judgment stage. Did I mention I get results?"

"You did," she says, nodding while thinking, *If I work here after law school, I hope I don't end up working with you.*

— 9: —

UNFORTUNATELY, WHEN SHE JOINS the firm after law school graduation, full-time, she is assigned to work exclusively with him.

So today, she finds herself dealing again with a person she knows requires excessive attention, and part of that means she must respond to his beck and call and wait when he says wait—another forty-five minutes, in fact.

"Alex!" he barks out, even though the door is partially shut and he cannot see her on the other side of the door. He knows she is there waiting.

"Mr. Hanes." Alex enters his office.

"We've got to get ahead of health care reform."

"Yes, absolutely," she says, nodding.

"We've got to guarantee results, one way or another."

"Absolutely," she answers, putting her pen to pad.

"Focus closely!" he adds, raising his hand for emphasis. "Primaries are stampeding ahead, and 2008 is an election year."

"Right." She nods again. *Everyone knows this is an election year!*

"We've got to get ahead of the game—the Republicans will lose, and the Democrats are running super liberals this year."

Alex is confused. *How does he know the Republicans will lose? It's only January. The election's months away!* She feigns agreement only to appease him because she knows he doesn't react well to disagreement.

"You've got Democrats with lofty plans for America." Rolling his eyes, he adds, "Obama wants to increase competition, reduce underwriting costs and profits, and improve the quality of health care."

"I hardly find his plan relevant," she says. "He's not a frontrunner, but anyway, Senator Obama's plan is an oxymoron. Frankly, universal health care is contradictory to improving the quality of care. You can't do both."

Not responding to her thoughts, he says, "And Hillary Clinton's on her soap box nagging about 'mandatory health plans, universal coverage, and limiting premiums to income levels.'"

"She lost that war the first time," Alex says.

"We'll make sure she loses again if she wins the Democratic nomination," Marshall adds, pounding his fist into his desk.

She nods.

"So that's where you come in," he explains, smiling.

Sensing his assessment, she says, "Absolutely. You know my political ties. What do you need?"

"We'll get ahead of the game." He hunches close to his desk. "You'll lobby so we win even when we lose."

Win even when we lose? How? "Sure," Alex says, with a quick, sharp nod.

"So here's the plan. Take notes," he begins, gesturing to her notepad.

Don't you see my pen to pad, control freak?

"We'll stay quiet in '08 and make nominal contributions to the Republicans."

Why?

"We'll contribute to the Democrats so they'll owe us."

Why do we want them owing us?

"We'll let the Democrats clobber each other, and we'll stay under the radar. We'll strategize and develop business plans when everyone else is sensationalizing over the election."

"Won't we develop a message?"

"Of course, but we'll let the Democrats win, enter office, push for health care reform, get health reform, and wait."

"Why let them do anything?"

"Because that's our plan. We'll let them reform health care, but we'll make sure the reform fits our business model and maximizes our profits."

"Why not help the Republicans win?"

"Whoa—wait—hold up," he says, holding up his hands as if he's halting a train. "Sweetheart, listen closely."

I'm all ears, you condescending jerk!

"Understand dear, to get results, we won't worry about elections. We'll concede to the Democrats. This is their year. They're due a win. Consider history, and frankly, who wants to clean up the mess that's out there? Let them deal with the chaos."

Concede this early? And what chaos?

"So here's the deal. We'll control public opinion."

Why not a public relations firm?

"When the time is right, we'll work with a team to leak stories about death beds, rationed care, increasing costs. We'll create confusion. We'll muddy up the landscape so much, no one will be able to get their hands around health care policy."

"I can do that. I actually think that's a great strategy, and not too far-fetched. Universal care could cause death beds."

He smirks before adding, "Alex, focus. We don't care about the truth. Your goal is mass confusion."

I was just agreeing—

"We'll make sure no one can get their arms around policy."

Okay?

"We'll have people lost. They'll all want and need the same thing, but they'll be clawing and fighting at each other not knowing what they want or need."

"Like crabs in a barrel."

"You got it!"

"And to thicken our genius plan, we'll be there at the ready when the law is passed."

"Is that when we'll roll out the leaks?"

"Yes, or perhaps before the law is passed, so we look like we're putting up a fight."

"All right, and if the law is passed."

"No, WHEN the law is passed, we'll evaluate the landscape. If we don't like the law as implemented, we'll talk about death beds and rationed care again. We'll have people scared to death so that they're urging their policymakers and governors to attack the law, repeal the law, end the law."

"Why? Aren't we going to make sure the reform works for our clients?"

"Yes, but we also want to try the law out first, see how our clients like it. If they aren't pleased, we'll tell the people they don't like the law, and they'll fight like hell to repeal it. Then we'll tweak the law or start over. Of course, if we're pleased with the law, we'll change public opinion in a heartbeat. We'll tell the people to like the law, and they'll comply."

"I see," Alex says, but she is still unsure.

"Hell Alex, we'll have the people scurrying around like rats in a maze, going down different paths molding road blocks, making sure nothing gets done, unless we want results."

"I understand, but I'm not sure why you're so sure," she begins, but pauses, staring at him, trying to gauge whether he can accept a contradictory view. Understanding that this view must be one he'd be glad to hear, she says, "I wouldn't rule out a Republican win. We're not even through the primaries yet. And besides, who knows which Democrat will win."

"You're articulating fiction, aren't you?" he asks, smirking.

"I'm not," she says earnestly, leaning forward. "If the Republicans shift the focus to taxes and foreign policy, we win!" She lifts both hands, a voilà pose.

"We'll shift, but there's something else coming down the pipeline."

"Which is?"

"The weary middle class. That middle class welfare bubble is about to burst. When that happens, people will be looking for help."

"You're thinking the middle class will turn into needy citizens, almost like welfare recipients?"

"Absolutely," he says, nodding. "They're already like welfare recipients. Anyway, when they realize that, they'll look to government." He pauses a moment before adding, "Until we change their opinions, tell them that government isn't the answer, not the place to look for help."

"Right." She nods but thinks, *Why push public opinion in favor of the Democrats only to push it back in favor of the Republicans?*

Inhaling deeply, he runs his hands along his receding hairline and fixes his eyes on her.

What?

It's almost as if he is looking *through* her.

What? Why the look? What did I say?

"What's going on?" he asks, in a calm, steady voice. His agitated, animated voice is gone.

Guessing that he is asking about the *Cox* case, she stops her pen and answers. "I talked to Lisa Martin. She's on message, and I'm starting the defense." Alex goes on to explain her defense strategy.

He leans back into his huge, lavish leather chair before fixing his eyes on Alex. He stares at her intently, content, as if he does not mind her rambling when on other occasions he would have cut her off or urged her to quicken her speech. He appears distracted.

"Mr. Hanes, what do you think?"

"Mr. Hanes," she asks again, having not gotten a response from him even though he is staring at her.

"Mr. Hanes?" She begins to feel awkward.

"Yes, sure, do you have lunch plans?" he finally asks, almost as if he is awakening from a trance.

You change like the wind! Did you hear anything I said? She excuses him, though. *Is he thinking about other cases, more important cases?*

"No lunch plans," she says, shaking her head.

"We'll talk strategy at lunch—12:30—don't be late." He moves his chair close to the desk again and picks up the telephone.

I guess that's my cue to leave. Are you really calling someone else?

— 9 —

THREE HOURS LATER, ALEX sits at her desk working, sporadically looking at her watch until suddenly, like a gust of wind, Marshall rushes past her door. "You're late," he says. "Let's go." He speaks but keeps walking.

Alex scrambles for her belongings, hurrying to catch up. When she finally does, she asks, "Were you working on another big case?"

He smirks and mumbles, "That's an accurate characterization since I got tied up with Rachel McCay."

Three hours later, Alex and Marshall return to the office from lunch.

Yes, it was a long lunch.

No, they didn't talk about any cases.

Chapter Seven
Get Away

*T*AYLOR SEETHES, HEARING her assistant, Joseph, ask her the same question again!

"Are you sure you're okay?"

"Yes, for the tenth time, now go!" She grits her teeth.

Joseph does not budge. He searches her face for the truth.

Exhaling loudly, she stomps her foot and says, "No more questions! Leave!"

"Okay, I hear you." Joseph turns and walks toward the door. Just as he begins to exit, he looks back and adds, "I'm here if you need me."

Holding her position still, she nods.

He leaves.

Seeing him exit, Taylor immediately scans her calendar. *Clear, no appointments!* She grabs her oversized designer purse and her keys and bolts out of her office door.

Racing past Joseph's desk too fast for inquiries, Taylor tells him, "I've got to go. Doctor's appointment!"

"Your calendar's clear, I didn't see—"

"Call for emergencies only!" She is certain he's about to ask questions, so she darts ahead.

Passing a few co-workers, she coaches herself. *Put on your flawless executive façade!*

Exchanging cordial niceties while trying to shield her agony, she feels like a total sham. She manages to wear a convincing, "all things under control poker-face" when really she feels like she is falling off a cliff and there is no one there to catch her as she falls.

"Way to go, Ms. Ray!" Luther Smiley, the President of Miles Bridgestone, says to her from behind.

"Mr. Smiley, good afternoon." *Way to go what?*

"Your VIA-MAN commercial sales are spectacular; fireworks even! Fireworks, get it, fireworks? You're selling male enhancement products very well. Was it hard? Get it? *Hard.*"

She is silent.

"Sorry, MAN-joke, but your advertising skills are top notch!" He flashes her a million dollar smile.

"Oh yes, on the sales, right. I used my best skills, savvy negotiating! You know me!" Taylor responds. She recalls the advice of her executive coach. *Taylor, don't brush off compliments with comments like, oh it was nothing.*

Striding onto a full elevator, Taylor cringes. *Yikes. The sham must go on!* Seeing the jovial faces of colleagues and co-workers, she fake-smiles. Inside, her world is falling apart.

"How was your weekend?" a voice asks from the back of the elevator.

Taylor's anxiety mounts. *I don't want to talk about the Suns; I don't want to talk about the Arizona Fine Arts Show; the ballet; the symphony; I don't want to talk about the Rodeo; I don't want to talk unless you can tell me how to get out of debt pronto!*

"Taylor, you're the world traveler and events socialite, so how was the Fine Arts Show last weekend?" another voice asks.

Like long fingernails scratching on a chalkboard, the chatter fills the elevator, everyone talking about art, expecting Taylor Ray to be the most knowledgeable connoisseur. *If that woman is right about my finances, how will I afford the art I just bought?*

Wanting to cut the conversation short, Taylor says, "Why, the show was exquisite. You weren't there? You didn't make the show?"

"No, that's why we're asking you! Share your finds!"

"Yeah, and who was featured?"

"Did you get any pieces?"

Taylor arranges her face so that it looks like she's pondering their questions. Really what she's thinking is, *Yes, I got a lot of stuff, even originals, but I don't want to talk about art when I may be broke!*

"Keeping secrets? Do tell," Katie Lee says. She's the woman Taylor beat out for the vice president's position.

CHIME...

Saved by the bell...

"I'd love to chat about my art finds—they *are* fabulous—but I must go. Doctor's appointment. Got to run."

She bolts off the elevator and charges to her car. *Okay, look like you're in a hurry. Act busy, rushed...oh fiddlesticks, why does this always happen to me?*

Finally entering her jet-black convertible, she breathes a little easier. Exhaling deeply, she exits the parking garage and sunrays peak inside through the tinted windows.

Feeling closed in, she stops at a red light and peels back her convertible top. At once, all her pretenses of flawless perfection fly out as the sunlight rushes in. In clear daylight, she knows she is a woman with problems even though the rest of the world doesn't know.

With sun warming her soft, lightly-tanned face, Taylor deliberates about her life. *Where's my balance? I'm perfect professionally and a disaster personally.*

— ※ —

REMINISCING BACK TO HER sales award, last year, the paradox stands out in her mind. Her thoughts turn back to the Miles Bridgestone Achievement Awards' Night, a black tie affair. On that day, she wins an Exceptional Sales Associate award. The firm's major client, Dr. Rick Peck, praises her for boosting sales for his new penis enlargement product when he stands at the podium and speaks.

"Since Ms. Ray has been on board, our size has enlarged tremendously! And when I say big, I mean we get very big!"

The crowd breaks out in laughter.

Taylor thinks, *Silly*, but appreciates the accolades.

He continues. "All kidding aside, Ms. Ray is an extremely successful corporate executive. We stay with Miles Bridgestone mainly because she's on board. She's that good. No one can beat her. And we know her job is to sell airtime and advertising space for news, talk shows, and other forms of television media, but because she's so good picking the shows that will sell the most products, her efforts selling news in turn sells countless penis enlargement products for our company. Ms. Ray, step on stage and accept this small token of our appreciation." Rick Peck brandishes a golden envelope with a large, velvety chocolate bow.

Everyone claps.

Taylor stands and approaches the stage in a beautiful white orzo dress and four-inch designer heels. She accepts the award with a confident smile. This smile widens as she sees her perfect husband, Whitfield Ray, standing and clapping, cheering her on from afar. Stepping to the podium, she delivers an acceptance speak in the style of the Oscars or Academy Awards.

"Thank you, Dr. Peck. We appreciate your acknowledgment. We've had many successes and our clients, like you, have succeeded with us. We're always glad to grow your businesses with our advertising savvy and media expertise. As we all say, as you grow, we grow."

Everyone claps.

When the applause dies down, Taylor continues, praising Miles Bridgestone as the best advertising firm in the industry before adding, "What can I say; I'm a natural advertiser!" *Competition stinks, but that's job security.*

Before ending, she throws out the humility line. "Joseph, Lidia, Rochelle, can you please stand? I couldn't do what I do without you." She acknowledges only those who she perceives as non-competitors.

And then, just as everyone gives a standing ovation to her team, she adds the firm's president mainly to be political. Of course, she knows he shouldn't need to compete with her. He already has a succession plan, and she's his successor.

Later that night, while in bed with her husband, he asks her a question.

"How much money did Dr. Peck give you this year?"

"What money?"

"How much? Twenty thousand?" he asks, as if he is certain she has received a bonus.

"What bonus?" she asks her husband, deciding to hide the thirty thousand dollar check she received in the golden envelope. She plans to spend the bonus, in full, the next day at the shopping mall without thrifty suggestions from her husband. She does not want a fight.

"Awe babe, you increased his sales 75% and no bonus?"

"No, but I'm all right. I don't do what I do for the money." This is another lie.

"I'm your husband. You're not talking to strangers. I know you! You don't move unless you're making money!"

Whitfield knows she is singularly motivated by compensation, but she lies again. "Honestly, I did expect a bonus, but I also know the company is funneling their money into a new invention, some vaginal enhancement product, so they're cash poor this year, I understand. I'll get mine."

"Does Dr. Peck do everything below the belt?"

"Yes. Speaking of which, I need no enhancements." She slides up his bare chest wearing only a black teddy.

Chapter Eight
Calendar Warfare

ALEX EXHALES LOUDLY, checks off the final to-do item on her calendar for the day, and wonders, *Are there any good men?* Sitting in her office, staring at her calendar, she realizes that all of her tasks are complete except one: *Find a man.*

Hush! She tries to quiet the calendar. She feels as if it's always reminding her that she is twenty-eight, single, and has no man in sight.

Alex tries to ignore her desires and her calendar. She tells herself to forget about her age, the time flying by, and the ever-present ticking fertility time clock. *Exist! Live as if you are oblivious to time!* Yet, just when she begins to anchor herself in what she calls the *live and let live methodology*, she sees the calendar and thinks, *Here we go*, as the dates literally stand up and show themselves.

Alex also thinks about all the social gatherings that remind her of her single status. Usually peripheral acquaintances join in with the calendar and add fuel to the fire. The topic of conversation at any social or even business gathering usually turns to her marital status—or lack thereof. She cringes when people ask the standard questions.

"Are you engaged yet?"

"Any news? Any spring wedding plans?"

"Dear, a career alone isn't enough."

"Do you at least have a steady special someone?"

She has an answer, although not perfected. "Yes, me," she responds, with her nose scrunched, arms crossed, body swaying from left to right.

To this, the examiner might respond with a frown, perhaps an all-knowing sigh. "Well, yes dear, you have y-o-u, visibly, Praise the Lord." The questioner's eyebrows lift as the interrogation continues. "But you need a husband, too."

She always escapes, even if her exit is orchestrated. "Excuse me, I have a call," she says, waving her cell phone in the air.

"I didn't hear your telephone ring."

Swaying her cell phone in the air, she answers, "Silent, vibration!" She exits.

"I don't even hear that vibration sou—" a woman begins, but she is too late.

Alex is gone.

Alex has perfected swift exits.

Yet, while she escapes annoying intruders, there is one spectator she is always unable to avoid: THE CALENDAR!

Chapter Nine
Desert Sky Drive

Taylor passes her house on Desert Sky Drive. Consumed with thoughts, she drives, oblivious to her course, unaware of her destination. Allowing instinct to direct her route, she takes off towards the sky, to the mountains, where clouds tickle mountaintop peaks. Going upward, she realizes her life is spiraling downwards.

She has an odd relationship with money.

She lies to her husband about money.

And now a bill collector says that she is in trouble because the Ray's don't have enough money. *She's a liar. Whit and I make lots of money! She can't be right, can she?*

Turning the corner, she realizes that the bill collector's timing is off. Whitfield and Taylor have been trying to conceive for some time. Since they have been unsuccessful, despite using every method in the book, even the upside down method, she is planning to move forward with fertility treatment. *That is, until the bill collector called.* Now, with financial woes, she is unsure. *Should we change our plans?*

Taylor passes rock canyon-mountains and drives on, unsure of what to do. The bill collector who called her today has her all knotted up inside, taking her life off course. On the one hand, she senses she should wait to have a baby; on the other hand, she believes she can't wait. She must keep trying, *right?*

— ⁹ —

Hours pass as she mulls over her conflicting dilemmas, both seeming diametrically opposed. Her mind is so heavy in thought that she doesn't even realize where she is until she notices that the landscape has changed from red-brown desert to plush green vegetation.

She is near Prescott, Arizona, more than 100 miles away from her home.

Deciding to bask in something different from the desert she often enjoys, the other spectrum of nature, she exits the freeway. She drives through the town, whisking by trees and serene lakes. She tries to clear her mind.

Should we wait?
We can't.
How will I tell Whit?
I can't.

She can't escape her thoughts, even miles away from home.

One hour later, as the sun glistens against the sparkling lake waters she passes, she decides to return home. She makes a sharp U-Turn, still undecided.

As the sun sets, she pulls into her driveway with an empty tank of gas and a full dose of anxiety. Getting out of her car, she walks into her ornate yet empty house.

She sinks into her sofa. Her mind churns.

Should we start a family?
Should I tell Whitfield about our financial situation?
Is there a way to make more money?
I want a baby. I can't wait any longer; besides, if we get pregnant we're lucky because we haven't had any luck so far. . . .
Should—

The sound of the telephone ringing cuts her off.

Touching the Bluetooth piece affixed to her ear, she activates her phone and answers, "Taylor Ray."

"Ms. Ray, Katie Baxter with Dr. Boone's office."

"Hi—Hello, yes." Taylor gets to her feet.

"We had a cancellation, March 14. Interested?"

Just lay it on me heavy! Taylor has been trying to get into this fertility specialist for months to no avail and *now,* on the day she toils with the decision of whether she should put the baby on hold, she gets a call.

"Yes, I see," she responds, trying to stall while weighing the cost of the procedure against her means.

"Does March 14 work?"

"Well, what's the cost again?"

"Fifteen thousand dollars, but cost isn't an issue, is it?"

"No, babies are priceless, wouldn't you say?" She gnaws on her lower lip.

"Ms. Ray, making babies, theoretically no, but we're in the fertility business, so yes, yes babies do have a price. Have you had a change in financial circumstances?"

"No, no, of course not, no," she lies, feeling anxious again.

Obviously cuing in on her anxiety, Ms. Baxter says, "Do you want to talk to your husband?" Lowering her voice, she adds, "I understand, the procedure is costly. Do you require time?"

"Yes, but no. Well, I mean, actually, aren't these appointments hard to get? I mean, shouldn't I take the first available slot?"

"If you're unsure, I can do you a favor. I'll keep you at the top of the list, even though you're supposed to go to the end if you pass on an appointment. I'll keep you on top. Something else will come up. Does that work?"

That's a reasonable alternative? BUT—Taylor's desires prevail over reasoning and so she says, "No, no—sign me up today. We'll be there with bells and whistles!"

"Are you sure?"

"Yes, certainly, of course. We're there!"

"Okay, Ms. Ray. To reserve your space, we need advance payment. I can take your payment over the phone."

Gulp! "We'll pay cash!"

"Cash payment?" Ms. Baxter pauses before adding, "I'll hold your space, but I'll need your cash payment mid-day tomorrow."

I don't have the cash. I've spent all our cash and credit, too, for that matter, if that debt collector is right. But I do have that one card. Yes, I do, so I do have credit, I guess . . . .

"Ms. Ray? Do you need more time?"

Whit will kill me! "No, I'm getting my credit card."

Taylor pays on credit and instantly spends beyond her means.

Chapter Ten
Party Politics

REAGAN ENDS HER school day and meets her husband on an impromptu date at POETRY WINE & DINE. Walking into the restaurant, Reagan feels excited and tense at once. She is excited because she's going out with her husband tonight. She is tense because she feels like a failure professionally. *Hope tonight's the gold lining!* she tells herself, quickening her pace.

Stepping into the restaurant foyer, soft scents tickle her nose. Calming sights relax her mind. Captured by the ambience, she inhales deeply and smells a sweet and spicy aroma.

Observing the surroundings, she sees over one hundred dimly lit candles; red velvet booths; classic, tasteful chandeliers; and lush, black lounge chairs perfectly placed throughout the restaurant lounge.

Inhaling deeply, she smells lavender, thyme, nutmeg, cinnamon, and cayenne pepper. *Mom says change can be good; hope this is my joy coming in the night.*

The atmosphere, aroma, and the anticipation of Jackson combine to wrestle up a smile on her face for the second time that day. The first smile popped onto her face when he called and asked her out on a date.

"Hello. Hello!?"

Reagan jumps, startled by the hostess who has approached her from behind. Gaining her composure within seconds, Reagan says, "Actually, I'm meeting Jackson. Have you seated him already?"

"Name doesn't ring a bell, but there's hardly a wait," the hostess says.

"He's tall, curly hair, deep rich skin, green eyes."

"Oh, *him*," the hostess coos, puckering her lips. Her expression changes from blank to knowing. "Yes, can't forget him; he's delightful!"

What did she say? "He's my husband!"

"Since you're late, I've been caring for him. He's my priority." The hostess turns and walks away, not bothering to ask Reagan to follow her.

Please don't make me lose my religion. Following the hostess, her brow wrinkled, Reagan marks her territory. "Did you hear me? He's my husband!" *So keep your distance, Ms. Hostess-seductive.*

"Congratulations," *Ms. Hostess-seductive* responds sarcastically, holding out her chest and batting her eyelashes. Finally, Jackson ends the charade.

"Reagan." Jackson stands, grabs his wife, and warmly embraces her. "It's been too long. Missed you today," he whispers in her ear.

Reagan loses thoughts of *Ms. Hostess-seductive* in her husband's arms. Reagan smiles, feeling at ease as he gently kisses her neck, her cheeks, and then the curl in her beaming lips.

"How was your day?" He guides her to sit beside him in a large, red, velvety booth nestled in front of the table.

Inhaling deeply, Reagan tightens her shoulders. She exhales, and her shoulders fall before she speaks. "Where do I begin?" The tension rolls off her shoulders.

"Tell all."

She does.

Jackson listens intently as she rehashes her full day. Her test-taking teaching lesson plan, her disorderly class, her inability to complete the bare minimum lesson, and she ends with, "Jackson, I also almost ran out of gas! Did you know gas costs $3.11 a gallon? I almost paid more in gas than what I made today at work!"

"May I take your drink order?" a waitress says, interrupting.

Good she's appropriately dressed! Reagan sees the waitress is wearing a loosely fitting black turtleneck sweater, baggy black slacks, no make-up, and black face shielding glasses. *Much better!*

Reagan smiles and says, "I'll have unsweetened tea, curried shrimp, and steamed white rice."

"Water, pad thai shrimp, brown rice, steamed," Jackson adds.

As Jackson orders, Reagan turns her attention to a plasma television set. Reagan sees a panel of political analysts and commentators opining about the 2008 Iowa caucus.

— 𝄢 —

SPOUTING OFF OPINIONS, ONE after another, having to fight to get a word in, the commentators pontificate on the Democratic candidates.

"This election comes down to experience versus change," says one commentator.

"And change may win," says an overly-excited commentator. He drum rolls on the news commentator desk. He suggestively welcomes his co-commentators to join in his glee with his eyes, energy, and smile.

None do. Instead, another anchor changes the discussion to the Republican candidates.

— 𝄢 —

REAGAN TURNS HER ATTENTION back to Jackson and announces, "Politics—a lot of hoop-la about nothing!"

"You're exaggerating." He smiles.

"Don't patronize me. I'm not naïve!"

"I'm only questioning why—"

Seeing his smile, and knowing what he's going to say, she cuts him off. "Speech with no walk, that's why!"

"Or talk without the walk," Jackson says, still smiling.

"Whatever. Speech or talk, you get my point!"

"You're right, I was—"

Crossing her arms, Reagan adds, "Politicians only make nice speeches."

Jackson nods in agreement but says, "Reagan, you're frustrated, but you can't give up. Our democracy needs you."

Jackson please, don't start on your soap box.

He begins describing every method she might use to participate in the democracy.

Hearing his words, Reagan thinks, *Who has time to write letters, attend town hall meetings, lobby lawmakers, facilitate groups, host political fundraisers? I'm too busy trying to figure out how to make money to buy food and pay bills.*

"You've also got to vote in every election, even off-year elections."

"I do! But please, stop the get out the vote speech!" Reagan says, hearing enough.

Jackson smiles as if he likes to see her passion show, even if she is frustrated. Gently caressing her hand, he says, "Shape policy."

"Who, me?"

"Yes! I know this suggestion may sound cliché and inappropriate coming from me, because who am I?"

"No offense, babe, but you're what we call a pundit."

"Yes, I write theory, whereas you're in the trenches every day trying to get results."

"Yes, and government gets in the way."

"I understand, but Reagan, make your voice heard."

"Won't matter," she says, shaking her head. "Policymakers are too far removed to make policy that works."

"I understand. There's unworkable policy in your way," Jackson says, nodding.

"In my way?"

"Yes, creating a few roadblocks—but government matters."

"Please, Jackson, don't give me the policy is important mantra. Take no child left behind. It does not work!"

"I know you're not a fan, but NCLB does put accountability into the system."

"Yeah, but accountability without funding is a trap! NCLB requires testing without the means to pass the test!"

"Not to alarm you, but there are some benefits to testing; I'll acknowledge, the policy probably needs some tweaking—"

"What, tweaking?" she asks, mimicking a person holding a wrench, as if she is adjusting a fake bolt in the air. She laughs and then adds, "You're putting the situation lightly."

"I'll agree that the policy may need some modification in practice, but there are good aspects to NCLB, don't you think?"

"No, I don't! NCLB is an under-funded government policy that only causes mottos like the one at my school."

"What motto?" Jackson asks.

Reagan simulates pom-pom cheering and says, "You know, Mr. Lee's formula for success. That stupid, 'TEST REGULARLY, TEST OFTEN, TEST ALWAYS, TO PREVAIL' motto!"

"Right, that, yeah. I'll admit, that's a problem," Jackson says, raising his eyebrows. "And I can't agree with testing when there's no funding to prepare for the test," Reagan says, raising her voice. "See, rallying and cheering to boost scores without the funds to lift scores is senseless. You can rally and cheer all day, but a policy that makes teachers limit their curricula to test-taking only is detrimental; but I bet Bush II, the inventor of that policy, would disagree with me."

"While the policy was a Bush II brainchild, the bill passed Congress with bipartisan support," Jackson says, motioning for her to keep her voice down.

"Jackson, between you and me," she says, lowering her voice, "that law passed Congress only because the Bush administration lied." Reagan leans forward. "Democrats did not support the way the Bush education policies were implemented."

"No, President Bush pushed for NCLB because children were being shuffled through the system without any accountability. He wanted to fix the problem, offer a solution. So I wouldn't say President Bush *lied*," he admonishes, shaking his head.

Reagan knows he is an independent who doesn't see himself as "Democrat" or "Republican" because he doesn't fit within either category squarely. And so when he hears Reagan say "lied," she knows he's thinking that Reagan, who is a staunch Democrat like her parents, has chosen the party line and is riding along.

Seeing Jackson's clear annoyance with her position, Reagan defends herself. "Bush II never funded no child left behind, only the testing part, and every Republican President since Nixon has pushed standardized testing in lieu of school funding. So yes, *a LIAR!* What else would you call it?"

"A liar, no; pushing an ideology Bush II was elected to further, that of limited government and expanded private enterprise, yes."

Leave it to Jackson to break through all the drama. He won't listen to name-calling, party lines, or derogatory talking points. He does not believe in the party politics of choose a side and now let's paint the other side as evil liars, whore mongers, racists, tax evaders, or some other bad person. He likes his politics simple and to the point. What do you stand for? What is your plan? What are the pros and cons of your plan?

Reagan sighs when *Ms. Hostess-seductive* returns, replacing the Amish style waitress. *No way, she's got that gleeful smile, too!*

"Hi, big boy!" *Ms. Hostess-seductive* leans over Jackson.

Incredible! She's standing over my husband, butt raised in the air, chest angled straight at my husband—and I see she's unbuttoned six of the twelve buttons on her shirt. Tacky!

"Excuse me, but do you have my order, too?" Reagan asks, trying to interrupt.

"I'm taking care of him first, comprende?" *Ms. Hostess-seductive* responds, before turning back to Jackson, licking her lips.

Reagan holds her jaw until she's calmed down. *Jackson isn't even looking at this sl—.* Her husband began thumbing through his blackberry as soon as the hostess-turned-waitress approached the table. His eyes are locked on the phone even though he never uses it at the dinner table, believing the use of mobile devices during meals is inappropriate, particularly at a public restaurant. *Good for you, Jackson! Yield not to temptation in any way you can.*

Chapter Eleven
Let Go!

*A*LEX CLOSES HER calendar and walks out of her forty-second floor high-rise office to go home, leaving the calendar behind. *So what if I don't have a date tonight,* Alex decides, as she exits her building and strides through congested downtown Phoenix streets on her short walk home.

People are everywhere—some walking quickly, others simply strolling, and others standing around watching the action on this Thursday night. The Phoenix Suns are playing the Los Angeles Lakers at the US Airways Arena, and as a result, the restaurants and bars are packed.

Lots of girls are dateless tonight! Alex observes, visually comparing the number of single women to the number of couples. She gladly determines she's in good company.

Alex also decides to put her professional self-worth against her search for a man, and this time business prevails. She has a trial next week. She feels she does not have time for a man.

Unless? Alex's eyes meet the eyes of a well-groomed, handsome man who Alex can see in the distance. *Is he looking at me?* She unconsciously licks her lips, adjusts her hair, lifts her chest, adds a sway to her step, and readies herself to change her war's outcome. She is willing to make an exception for this man. *He's easy on the eyes! Work can wait!*

He walks toward her.
She walks toward him.
She is ready, available, and willing to mate.

Come to me! Yes, I can see more of him! He's fine! She delights in him as he makes his way closer to her.

People in the crowd start peeling off to either side, making way for him. Some are going into restaurants, others are darting into bars, and some are jetting into the US Airways arena. *Please, be the one,* she thinks. *You're amazing!* His chest is muscular. His tie is as handsome as his face. He is perfect! She smiles.

Until suddenly —POP—she sees his hand! He's holding another woman's hand!

Her dismay must show because *Mr. Handsome* cuts a flirtatious eye towards her, as if to say, "Why the long face? I'm game if you are."

I am! Alex nods and then quickly jots down her phone number as she walks toward him.

Five steps later, they're side by side, his body touching hers and hers his, conveniently so, given the crowds. Taking advantage of the opportunity, Alex gracefully slips her digits into his pocket, and as she does, he firmly rubs her hand, acknowledging his receipt of her message. He walks on, not breaking a stride in his step, all while his date continues to hold his hand, obviously oblivious to his wayward ways.

Catching a rear-view glimpse of this man, her insides fire up. *Nice tight end, you!* Suddenly, the grand entrance door to her downtown condominium swings open. Mr. Beatty, the bellman, opens the door.

"Good evening, Ms. Giroud," Mr. Beatty says. His eyes are suspicious-looking, suggesting he witnessed the entire ordeal.

"Ugh, Mr. Beatty, hi," Alex says, quickening her step. She is slightly embarrassed by his observation, wanting to keep her personal life private, particularly from the bellman of her condominium building.

Living in a luxury condominium with a twenty-four-hour-a-day, seven-days-a-week bellman is like a double-edged sword. She really likes the prestige and security a bellman brings, but she dislikes how her comings and goings—and more particularly the comings and goings of the men in and out of her life—are known by the bellman just because he's there.

She harbors feelings of guilt about her promiscuous relationships even though she isn't religious or overly moral even. She shields her dealings because her upbringing taught her that sexual promiscuity should be avoided, and if she engages in a highly active sex life, she should hide her relations, particularly if on some weeks her dealings involve various men—albeit one at a time, including some one-night stands.

So she really doesn't want Mr. Beatty to know that if *Mr. Handsome*, or whatever his name will be, wasn't walking hand-in-hand with another woman, she would have at least let her eyes lead him to lead her to wherever the night could have gone, and so she adds, "Mr. Beatty, that man, he's my cousin; I was marveling at how in love he is with his fiancé."

Mr. Beatty respectfully challenges her lie. "Mr. Dudley's your cousin? Get out of here!"

"Yep, he is."

"And he's marrying Ms. Carter? She seems like a nice gal, but marriage? He didn't tell me."

"Not that man, but another man—sorry, you misunderstood. Oops, I must go, my elevator, goodnight!" Alex hops onto the elevator. She doesn't look back.

Whew! Guess I'll take the fire escape for the next two weeks! Then shakes her head. *Nah, he's the help. Why am I thinking twice about what he thinks?*

Oh, that's right, because my mom became a renewed virgin after the divorce. She treated sex like something grotesque. She told me she wouldn't have sex again ever unless she remarried. Who has time for that! Besides, I'm a lawyer and my world is all about the law. Chastity is not a character trait necessary to pass the bar exam or excel in the practice of law! And tonight, I would have loved to push purity right out the door for a chance with—what was his name?—Mr. Dudley. Glad to know things aren't serious with Ms. Carter. I'll make a note to self to look out for him because chances are, he's a building resident.

But should I date a condo occupant? It could get tricky. She turns the thought around in her mind until she decides, with a smile, *Some tricks are worth turning!*

She daydreams about him. She smiles until—POP—the elevator chimes and bursts her bubble. Her fantasy turns into reality. She faces another night alone. *Won't be the first time alone, won't be the last. At least my aloneness is in grandeur*, she decides, gliding onto marble floors that lead to her condo.

Alex is right, at least as far as the splendor of her dwelling is concerned. She resides in Condo New Wave, Penthouse Suite Number 6303. Her condo was once an old office warehouse in the heart of downtown Phoenix. Some thirty years ago, the building was laced throughout with workers. Now, with urban revitalization, this once vibrant, then vacant, then dilapidated building has been changed into a luxury condominium building. Her condo building combines historic charm with opulence balanced against urban classic modern design, sporting marble floors, warm color pallets, grand chandeliers, ornate sculptures, striking furniture, and ostentatious artwork tastefully placed throughout the entrance and common areas.

Her heels click against the marble floor as she walks to her door. In the short distance, she decides that she will abandon her internal war. *I need rest and relaxation. I've been working hard, and I have a trial in Chicago next week. I need a little ME time, quiet time . . . read a few books, watch Lifetime, light a few candles, relax!*

Entering her condo, she walks onto her mahogany wood floors through her grand entrance, past her kitchen, into her master bedroom, and then on to her master bathroom.

Lighting the scented candles that surround her Jacuzzi bathtub, she begins to unwind.

She runs her bath water.

She adds bubbles.

She inhales deeply.

She breathes the environment.

She undresses and descends into the tub.

Just as she steadies into her surroundings, serenity gaining control, everything changes.

Ring, Ring, Ring. . . . . .

The phone!

Sinking into a warm bubble bath, Alex wants to bask in the moment and ignore the call because the telephone alters the air. She rarely arrives home early, especially with a trial nearing, and she has finally arrived at a point where she can completely embrace silence with time by herself. She inhales deeply. She ignores the call.

Until suddenly, in the quiet, a visual-image of the man she just met—*Mr. Handsome*— seeps into her mind.

She checks the CALLER ID just in case.

It's not Mr. Handsome. It's her ex. *The* ex. The one, or at least, the should have been the one. Duncan Anderson.

"Hi, there," she says, easing her back against the Jacuzzi tub.

"Glad I caught you."

Me too, she thinks, but she doesn't say it. She doesn't want to let on that she's alone, so she lies. "Barely, I'm on my way out."

"So, you're tied up tonight?"

"Yes." She lies again, because Alex does not consider her agenda of alone time with a book as being "tied up." She back peddles though. "But what's up? You called for a reason."

"I'm in town, but if you're busy . . . "

She peddles backwards more quickly now, but she must do so carefully. She must reverse the lie, but be careful how she does so. She'll make sure he won't suspect her charade. Her voice suddenly gets really cozy, almost southern. "You know w- -h - -a - -t . . . I can reschedule."

Then, she speaks quickly, not a hint of southern hospitality, direct, to the point, precise. "You're in town only a short while, right?"

He confirms that she's right. He's only available for one night. His chartered plane heads out in the morning.

She reverses her made up agenda and agrees to meet him at their favorite place at 8:00 p.m.

She hangs up the phone, blows out the candles, drains the Jacuzzi tub, and then steps into the shower.

Chapter Twelve
We're In

TAYLOR ANXIOUSLY CALLS her husband, who is away on business, whispering, "Whitfield pick up!" Hearing a beep and then background noise, she guesses that Whit has answered but is not talking because he's in a meeting. Her suspicions are confirmed a moment later.

"Reduce labor costs by twenty percent," she hears Whitfield saying.

He's working late, all night. Must be another corporate downsizing, she thinks, until he interrupts her thoughts and speaks directly to her.

"Tay, I'm busy. Are you okay?" he asks.

She can hear what sounds like a pen pressing down on a whiteboard.

Before she can answer his question, Whitfield speaks again, but the words are not directed to her. "Can't cut sales," he says.

I know you're cutting costs, but we've got to talk! She visualizes him sketching a business re-engineering flowchart. Wanting his attention, she jumps right in and says, "Whit, guess what?"

He does not respond.

Whit, hello? Are you ignoring me? You're in a meeting at 9 o'clock at night! Take a break!

Whitfield speaks in a non-debatable, authoritative tone. "Cut domestic customer service reps! We'll outsource to reps overseas."

"We can't, sir. Strong union contracts," someone says in response, perhaps wanting to debate despite Whitfield's tone.

"I'll deal with the union, cut the reps!" Whitfield stresses.

Interrupting, Taylor tries again. "Whit, we need to talk."

"One minute!"

Precisely one minute later, she hears a slamming door, and then Whitfield speaks.

"Late night. Are you all right?" His tone suggests that he is impatient to return to his meeting.

"Guess what, Whit?" she says, wanting to go through the whole deal, deliver her news in small doses rather than all at once.

He sighs. "Quickly!"

"Don't steal my thunder. Guess what?"

"Tay."

She knows he is a quick, to the point type of guy, so she says, "I'll keep it short."

"And to the point, Tay," he adds.

"Whitfield, we're in!"

"*I said* to the point!"

"We're in!"

"Got to run."

She hears chatter and then the phone hangs up.

He hung up! I know *he did not hang up!* She stares at the telephone for a few seconds and then dials him again.

He answers on the first ring, but he doesn't say a word. Taylor knows he's there only because she hears the meeting continue. "Cut all new hires. Rescind all outstanding offers!"

Apparently, he has already completed his analysis of the last issue and has reached a conclusion on the next issue: how to eliminate another job classification.

"Whitfield, I will be short, but I really have important news," she says, in a southern drawl.

The meeting continues. This time, Whitfield talks about how the company can eliminate more jobs.

"Come on, Whit. We need to talk!"

He continues, as if she hasn't said a word, until minutes later, she finally hears him say, "Review the technical support division next. I'll be back."

Good, he's leaving. She smiles, recognizing the exit line.

"Tay, what?"

"Whitfield, we're in!"

"Tay!"

"We're in the celebrity fertility clinic! We've been trying for months!"

"YOU'VE been trying! I'm done with clinics. We've tried two already!"

"But Whit, this is **the** clinic," she says.

"What clinic?"

"The famous celebrity clinic."

"What does celebrity have to do with having a baby?"

"CELEB FAB magazine rates this clinic number one!"

"Absurd. We don't get medical advice from paparazzi."

"I have other referrals, too," she says, although this is a lie.

"Who? A physician, or a reliable former patient?"

She lies again. "Most certainly, Whit!"

"We're done! We'll turn off the lights. That'll work!" Whitfield says, referring to Teddy Pendergrass' song, "Turn off the Lights."

"Whit, we can't get pregnant! That has nothing to do with turning off the lights. Be serious!"

"Tay, I *am* being serious. The docs say we can get pregnant, so you want a solution. I've got one: sex five times a day! Got to go!"

"Whitfield—be serious!"

"All right, you're right. I'll make that seven times a day. I'll mark my calendar."

"Whit!"

"Sorry, got to go."

"Can you hold March 14 on your calendar?"

"For sex? Yes. I told you: I'll calendar seven times a day. Got to go."

"Whit, plan to be in town. Save the date!"

"Tay, no. Got to run. See ya!" He hangs up.

She feels like shrieking. The fertility treatments are already paid for, only Whitfield is not on board.

Chapter Thirteen
So What's the Difference?

AFTER GETTING RID of *Ms. Hostess-seductive,* Reagan returns to politics. "How can you say I'm running with the party line?"

"Cuz you've picked up the party banner, and you're running!" Jackson answers, waving an imaginary banner.

"Jackson!" she yells, slamming her hand on the table.

"Lighten up. Channel your aggravation," he says, caressing her shoulders.

"Into what?"

"Grass-roots passion, not party bashing and rashing."

Rashing? What's rashing? Exhaling noisily, she says, "Won't matter."

"You can change policy; America's a democracy."

"Yeah, and?"

"And, Reagan, our democracy works best if you participate."

"Lawmakers don't care. They're too far removed."

"Look, Reagan, caring isn't the issue. What's important is your participation."

"How?"

"Speak up and rise above partisanship! Ask questions, demand solutions, and then when you vote, cast your vote for the candidate who offers real educational solutions." Jackson continues to caress her shoulders.

Feeling defeated, Reagan asks, "So that's why you're an independent?"

Clapping his hands, as if rallying up the team, he nods. "Yes, I sort through the hoopla and figure out who best represents my interests."

Smiling, she snaps back, "You're a Democrat."

He shakes his head. "Not true. When I lived in Texas, I voted for Bush II in the Texas Gubernatorial race because I supported his education policy."

"Which was obviously off."

"Well, I voted for Gore when Gore ran against Bush II in the Presidential race because the environmental policies were more important to me, and I didn't think the federal government should have a place in education anyway—local issue, in my view."

"You're right. That's what I'm saying."

She catches a playful twinkle in his eye, but then he keeps talking. "Reagan, you must vote your interests, not party lines."

Reagan sighs and turns her attention back to the plasma screen, where political analysts are announcing that the Republican candidate Mike Huckabee may actually win Iowa.

Reagan turns back to Jackson. "So, what's the difference between the Democrats and Republicans, Mr. Independent?" she asks.

"There's lots of talk about the differences, but the bottom line is the Democrats stand for a larger federal government—one that funds education, the roads, health care, and even business stimulus."

"Okay, and the Republicans?"

"Want a small federal government—except in the case of defense and business stimulus and business tax cuts."

"I see, how do the differences play out?"

"Most policies line up behind those two simple fundamental ideas," Jackson answers, and then gulps his tea.

"Since Republicans don't believe in funding education, will Republicans cut vouchers?" Reagan asks.

"No, that's where both Democrats and Republicans support the same thing for different reasons." Jackson smirks.

"Again, neither one represent my views!" Reagan declares, frustrated.

"I hear you, but vouchers are temporary Band-aids."

"Shouldn't use Band-aids to educate!"

"No, but if you fund education tomorrow, change won't happen instantly. Change is hard and takes time. While we wait, what are parents to do with a child caught in between?"

"Work with teachers to improve schools."

"Obviously, that's a solution, too, but some parents want an already put together, well run alternative."

"But vouchers take public school funds! We need more public school funding. Which candidate supports that?"

"The Democrats support more education funding—and early education programs, too!" Jackson answers, as if excited.

"Early education is a good starting place." Reagan chuckles nervously and adds, "While children don't start school until age five or so, the brain's capacity for learning is established best between infancy and age five."

"So you'll teach our kid to read at age one."

"You bet!"

He laughs.

She doesn't. "I will, really," she says.

"Cool, but baby, that's way down the road for us."

"True," she admits, shaking her head from left to right. *No! Sooner!*

"What?"

"Okay, fine! Babies can wait." She catches herself, nodding yes before changing the subject. "Back to vouchers."

"Yeah, vouchers. Vouchers help some kids," Jackson explains, and then pauses as if he is thinking, before continuing. "Kids whose parents can afford the private school tuition and can take the voucher tax deduction."

"Vouchers are a Republican scam to undermine public education; they only want to eliminate public education anyway," Reagan proclaims, exhaling noisily.

"The elimination of public education—I haven't heard that before, but I'll tell you, the elimination of public schools is not inconsistent with GOP ideas. I'm sure the Republicans are for shifting public education to the private sector. That's where the GOP thinks everything should be—private enterprise instead of government bureaucracy."

"Jackson, that's not the solution. If we shift education to the private sector, then the schools won't have any accountability to the people."

"Do you think the public schools are accountable?" Jackson asks.

Chapter Fourteen
The One or Should Have Been One

ADMIRING THE PHOENIX sunset before entering the dimly lit sports bar, Alex walks in and observes her surroundings. Easing through the crowd, flickers from the more than thirty large plasma screen televisions light a pathway. She searches for *the one* or *should have been one*, Duncan Anderson.

Where is he? Her eyes dart to the right and left.

Wonder if he still looks the same? In her memory, he is tall, dark, stealthy, and muscular. His eyes are a dark ocean blue. Those eyes are so magnificently stunning, and his physique and face are so uniquely handsome, that he can capture and hold any woman, particularly her. Seeing him from afar, her eyes landing on his behind, she confirms that he looks the same—at least from the rear. *I know that derriere anywhere—even in a crowd full of men! Hope the night ends with my hands on that!*

She glides closer and closer to him. Approaching him, Alex feels both anxious and elated. Anxious because she knows her relationship with Duncan is unpredictable and quick. She is also elated because she really cares about him. She believes he is the closest she has ever come to being in a relationship with the person who was made for her—*the one*. Getting closer, she prepares herself, understanding she should not get her hopes up too high. *He's probably only in town for a quickie! So what if he always pops in and out of my life from unknown places to be with me for just one night? I always enjoy every minute, and tonight I'll make the most of our time together. Anyway, our relationship hasn't always been like this. Who knows—things could change.* She thinks back to when her link with Duncan was serious, full of excitement, love, and adventure.

— 𝄢 —

IN COLLEGE, ALEX'S RELATIONSHIP with Duncan Anderson was different. There were days when he would call her to say, "Alex, let's get away this weekend." She would agree, and within hours, depending on the location and the distance, Alex would find herself bungee-jumping, hang gliding, water skiing, camping, or even skiing with Duncan all weekend!

Or like their dates after his Mergers & Acquisitions class. Duncan would show up on Wednesdays, right after class, and say, "Let's walk." He would grab her hand and lead her on a stroll through their college town, until finally they ended up somewhere like an ice-cream shop or local bakery, or even a lakefront, where they swam if weather permitted.

Or like Saturdays when he appeared right after sunrise and said, "Let's ride," and from there they would venture out on a thirty-mile weekend bike trip.

Fast-forwarding to the present, Alex acknowledges that, that was then, and this is now. Now, Duncan spontaneously pops into her life for late night hook-ups only.

Moving in behind him, Alex places her hands on his behind and squeezes, feeling his tight, firm buttocks. She coos in his ears.

He turns and looks her directly in the eyes. She knows he can see through her. *There was a time I could see through you, too—until . . . the brick wall.*

Suddenly, a 1980s song, written by Kenny "Babyface" Edmonds, and sung by the musical group, The Deele, begins to play—"Sweet November." Hearing the lyrics, butterflies flutter in Alex's stomach. She knows Duncan always requests this song when he is with her. He uses the song to get to her. The song is about two people in love who find their love changing like seasons. The lyrics say the words that she feels Duncan wants to say to her but can't—"But maybe Sweet November will tell us a story, that will bring us back the love that we once knew."

Alex winces and asks, "Duncan, did you request—"

Cutting her off, he whisks her onto the dance floor without answering the question. Dancing in his arms feels surreal. Hearing the music, she thinks, *Art imitating my life.*

Resting her head on his chest, she wishes that they could always be together.

He kisses her forehead.

She lifts her head from his chest.

He looks into her eyes. "How've you been?" he asks.

"Missing you," she answers, because she loses her defenses in his arms, against that song, while looking into those eyes. "Why aren't we together?"

Looking away before speaking, not looking into her eyes, he says what she knows he will say. "Alex, don't you grasp that the situation isn't debatable?"

"Duncan, say no to him!" *Stand up to your all-powerful, controlling, family-dominating uncle.*

Ending the discussion, he pulls her close to him again and dances.

I know you let the song say the words you won't say. I know you still love me, Duncan. But you won't tell me. Why? Because of your uncle and what he wants?

His familial duty has built an impassable wedge between them. Yet, while they both know that they can't be together like they used to be, in a real relationship, he always shows up, coldly, differently, but there—almost as if she is a magnet, pulling him to her, compelling him to come to her against his will. He always emerges, and then disappears.

Dancing in his arms, Alex wishes.

— ※ —

HOURS LATER, DUNCAN ENDS up in Alex's bed.

Why can't you stay? Alex looks into his deep blue eyes and snuggles close to him.

She feels safe in his arms, in her bed. Her skin rubs against his dark chocolate skin. *He feels like silk.*

But he gets up. Just like he always does. "It was a pleasure, Alex," he says, beginning to dress. "I'll see you next time."

He shatters her perfect world with his words, with his actions. *You've only been in my bed for thirty minutes and you're gone?*

Her heart sinks as she watches him dress, wishing she could only have more time with him. *Where are you going at 11:59 at night?*

Catching herself, realizing she must look distraught, she pretends she doesn't care when she says, "Glad you're leaving. I have a trial in Chicago next week anyway. Big case, have to prepare. You know how trials are."

"Glad we're aligned on time. I hate that I don't have more time to spend with you, but you understand the magnitude of the family business. Don't worry about seeing me out. Get your business done." He kisses her on the forehead and walks out.

"Best of luck next week!" he adds, right before the front door slams.

He's gone again!

Hot and bothered, and unable to sleep, Alex sits up in her bed and turns to work. *Gone again, who cares?*

I do.

Whatever, I've got trial in Chicago.

Alex begins coaching herself. *Work! I'll work! I'll prepare for the Chicago trial!* She changes the direction of her mind……*Yep, they're saying my client refused to pay health benefits insured under the State's Health Care Plan. I'll make sure they'll never prove their case.*

Chapter Fifteen
Orderly Chaos

TAYLOR SITS IN bed feeling tired but unable to sleep. She's tried every method known to the Salinas family—including a scented bath, chamomile tea, and two Melatonin tablets—but still she can't rest. Now, she sits in bed, eyes wide, like a deer caught in headlights. Why?

Because you're guilty! she hears her mother answer. Startled, she opens her eyes wider. Looking at the foot of her bed, she sees her mother standing there, like a sprite.

Mama? No, not now! She knows her mother usually appears to her as a little, feisty sprite to counsel her when she is intoxicated or extremely tired. Tonight, Taylor may be drunk from herbs rather than alcohol, and she is certainly restless, so the sprite's cameo appearance is timely.

"Yes, Tay, you're guilty, but don't be." The sprite points her finger as she speaks.

"Mom, please."

"Listen to your mother, and understand, don't wait."

"I know, Mom, but our finances?"

"Who cares about finances? You and Whit make plenty of money, too much money. You'll find a way; have the baby."

"But Mama, this isn't the perfect time."

"Baby, there'll never be a perfect time. Anyway, babies don't come in a little perfect package like your shoes and purses."

"I k-n-o-w," Taylor answers, thinking, *You may be right. We have tried twenty-four times. We only have twelve times a year to try. I'd be crazy to put a baby on hold even in the midst of a crisis.*

"BINGO!" the sprite says, shaking her hips. "So get busy!"

— 9 —

SHOOING AWAY HER ALL-KNOWING imaginary counselor, Taylor thinks back over all the arguments she has had with her mother about the perfect time. She remembers one spring day, eight years ago, she was walking with her mother at a Cinco de Mayo festival when her mother said, "Tay, see all these families?"

"Yes, and?"

"Put away your books and work goals."

"Why?"

"So you can marry Whitfield and have some babies."

Stepping around a giant piñata, Taylor says, "Not a good time!"

"You think you know, but Mama always knows best, Niña," her mother says, with an all-knowing smile.

"Yes, well we're different," Taylor snaps back. She doesn't say it, but she thinks, *Mom, you never really found a career. I'm not you!*

"No senorita, you're my child."

"Maybe, but I'm getting my MBA."

"Get your MAB, but get your MB first."

"Mom, MBA, but what's MB?"

"That's everything. 'M' marriage, and 'B' babies. That's what matters."

Taylor laughs. "No, Mama," she says, shaking her head. "I want a stable future. I also want to experience life. I'll be an independent professional first."

"Sounds good, but your clock is ticking."

"I'm only twenty-four."

"Which is ancient. I had you at twenty-one."

"Mama, you're talking about a different time, different era, and different circumstances." *Weren't you pregnant when you married Dad?*

"I'll admit, we had a shotgun wedding, but I wouldn't change my life."

"Awe nice, but that's not what I'm looking for."

"I'm not encouraging shotgun weddings, but you should open your eyes! Whitfield won't wait forever, and you won't always be able to have children."

"Whitfield has proposed three times," Taylor mumbles.

"Stop planning, Tay; start living. And understand that when you're ready to have a baby, you won't be able to speed dial a baby. Sometimes babies take time."

— ※ —

Returning to the present, she knows that her Mother was right back then, and she may be right now.

She appreciates that the perfect time has come and gone. *I can't wait on the perfect time.*

"Tay, also," the sprite cuts back in, "let's talk sex."

"No, no!" Tay pouts, not wanting to talk sex with her mother.

"Have you tried to stand on your head? Headstand sex works every time!" Her mom places her hands in the air, almost as if she is beginning to do a cartwheel.

"Mom, no, please!"

"Yes, Tay, look," the sprite shouts, in between heavy breaths. "Start off like a cartwheel to get into position."

"Stop! Stop!" Taylor yells. *She is standing on her head!* Taylor holds up her hand to shield her face.

"When you get into position, Tay, hold steady," her mom says. "Do you see how to do the headstand?"

"Stop!"

"Hold steady, and Whit will come in from beh—"

"Enough already! Stop!" Tay hollers, covering her ears.

Chapter Sixteen
Anger

*R*IDING AS A passenger in her vintage convertible sports car, with the top down, Reagan has a clear view to the sky. She watches the stars shine.

"Stay inspired, remember your purpose," Jackson says, trying to sound encouraging.

"We all have a purpose, but I worry I'm not in mine."

"Don't let policy take your destiny."

"Easier said than done."

"Reagan, life's hard, but you'll find a way."

"But I feel squeezed."

"Understandable."

"I'm a teacher because I'm gifted. I'm able to take concepts and turn them into magic. I can paint pictures so vivid children choose education first, above anything else."

"Nothing's changed. Teach how you want."

"I can't creatively teach standardized tests."

"Sure you can. Invent a way. The sky's the limit."

"I'm trying, but I'm lost. I don't see how because I'm locked in. I'm trapped in a bureaucratic box."

"Don't give up. You can be the change," Jackson says, pulling into the garage.

Reagan sighs.

— 𝄢 —

WALKING INSIDE THEIR PRISTINELY kept, modest but tastefully decorated home, Reagan passes the kitchen bar and lights two scented candles. Continuing to the great room, she plops down on the couch situated in front of a wall-mounted plasma television and picks up the remote control.

Jackson joins her, so Reagan hands the remote to him.

He flips channels, back and forth, between CSPAN, CNN, Fox News, and MSNBC.

News junkie! "Whoa—no politics!" she says.

"Reagan, you'll want to see this!"

"Barack Obama has won the state of Iowa," the CNN commentator announces.

Reagan leans forward on the couch.

Her jaw drops.

"He won the Iowa caucus!" Reagan screams, full of surprise and excitement.

Jackson smiles and nestles in beside her. "Anything's possible," he says.

"How? Obama's spent a lifetime working for ordinary, working class people. How can he win? Is that even possible?"

"Grassroots, baby," Jackson declares, and begins caressing her neck.

— 𝄢 —

JACKSON TRIES TO REDIRECT the night to romance during commercial breaks. He's kissing her neck and unbuttoning her dress when suddenly the cereal commercial ends and the news commentary picks up....

"Barack Obama is approaching the podium. He's delivering an Iowa victory speech."

Reagan giggles and pushes Jackson away. "Look, Barack Obama's on stage!"

"Don't you hate politics?" Jackson fumbles around with her last button.

"But this is history!"

Smiling, he states, "Then I'll place our relations on hold to watch history unfold."

She smiles.

"Hold only, I said," he emphasizes.

She smiles and nods.

Meanwhile, the broadcast continues with Barack Obama declaring a victory on television.

> "THEY SAID THIS DAY WOULD NEVER COME. THEY SAID OUR SIGHTS WERE SET TOO HIGH. THEY SAID THIS COUNTRY WAS TOO DIVIDED, TOO DISILLUSIONED, TO COME TOGETHER OVER A COMMON PURPOSE. YOU HAVE DONE WHAT THE CYNICS SAID YOU COULDN'T DO. YOU HAVE DONE WHAT THE STATE OF NEW HAMPSHIRE CAN DO IN FIVE DAYS. YOU HAVE DONE WHAT AMERICA CAN DO IN 2008. WE ARE ONE NATION, WE ARE ONE PEOPLE, AND THE TIME FOR CHANGE HAS COME."

After the acceptance speech, Michelle Obama proudly, yet humbly walks to the podium and speaks. *"For the first time in my adult life, I am really proud of my country."*

Reagan and Jackson smile.

"I'm so excited!" Reagan exclaims.

The spirit of HOPE walks in and joins them on the couch.

Chapter Seventeen
Tipping the Scales of Justice

*A*LEX SITS, SECOND chair, as defense counsel in the case styled: *State of Illinois v. Health Solutions, Inc.,* in Chicago, Illinois. Staring squarely at the scales of justice sketched into dark, mahogany wood above Judge Clyde's bench, she smiles. *We'll tip justice in our favor!* Feeling confident, she rethinks her case strategy, when suddenly her thoughts are interrupted by State Attorney Kevin Burke, who approaches the jury to begin his opening arguments.

"Ladies and Gentlemen of the Jury, we're here today because Health Solutions committed fraud. Health Solutions defrauded the taxpayers, the federal government, and the State of Illinois. How, you may ask? I'll tell you. Health Solutions got paid to market and sell health insurance services to fine citizens of the State of Illinois."

How's a subsidy fraud?

"Health Solutions got a huge subsidy so that they could then provide health insurance to certain Illinois citizens," Kevin Burke continues.

Why not say what you mean—poor Illinois citizens?

"The subsidy even had a premium, an extra treat. Why, you may ask? Well, I'll tell you. Illinois and Illinois taxpayers, as well as federal taxpayers, paid Health Solutions a large premium, an extra treat, because we understood that the cost to cover patients with pre-existing conditions and pregnant women would be high."

An extra treat—is the judge allowing this treat crap?

"And what does Health Solutions do? Health Solutions took the treat, ate the cake, got full on the cake, but didn't deliver the services."

Stop with the treats and cake!

"Ladies and Gentlemen of the Jury, we, the State, will prove that Health Solutions violated the law by taking our money and then refusing to insure pregnant women and patients with pre-existing conditions. The Defendant can't have its corporate cake and eat it, too!"

Wrong. My client cut the number of third-trimester women who could be covered to ensure continuity of care! My client publicly announced the cuts and all agreed, even government officials. That's how you provide care to more people. Everyone agreed to the cuts until it got politically convenient to sue. Plaintiff whiners!

Chapter Eighteen
Strategic Deception

TAYLOR SITS IN her office, eyeing a few commercial spots, when an idea strikes her. *I'll market to Whit.* Smiling, she sketches out a marketing strategy.

Marketing subject: *Whitfield Ray.*

Marketing strategy: *agony/joy. Make Whit think there is something missing in his life and then make him believe the product—fertility treatment—will fill the gap, provide the solution, fix his life!*

The Art of Distraction: *Since Whit has a strong constitution—he's a leader not a follower—roll out the commercials when he is distracted. When is Whit distracted? When he is doing what he likes most. What does he like most: sex, sports, and music.*

Key to Successful Implementation: *Always promote the product—fertility treatment—when he is having sex, watching or talking about sports, or listening to his favorite music.*

Completing her strategic blueprint, she turns next to execution. Just as she begins to write down the first item in her methodology, her telephone rings.

"Taylor Ray," she answers, still scribbling on her pad.

"Hi, Tay. Do you have a minute?"

Whitfield.

"Tay, are you there?"

"Uh, yes. Hi," she says, caught off guard by her husband.

"What's wrong?" Whitfield asks, sensing her anxiety.

"Wrong, what do you mean wrong? Nothing's wrong." Taylor tries to act normal. She wants to conceal that she is in the midst of developing a strategy to deceive and manipulate him.

"Good, glad you're all right. Sorry I've been busy; I'm swamped, downsizing firms."

"No problem. Busy is good business."

"Yeah, but speaking of busy, I missed the game. Did the Suns get that three-point throw?"

Did he say game? Is this a gift from the sky?

"Did you see the game? I heard the Suns shot three pointers all night, but what I want to know is did Nash make the shot at the end of the game?"

Yes, this is it! Act and act now. Mission Advertise to Whit take one!

"Tay, are you there? Did you see the game?"

"I did!" she answers, managing to sound enthusiastic, reeling him in.

"Great, cuz I made a bet with Lorenzo."

"Really? You don't say. What kind?"

"I bet the Suns would make a distant shot at the end. Did I win?" he says, excited.

"Whit, I have to tell you something. This is HUGE!"

"I'll hear you out, but what about the shot?"

"I have news! This is S-O-O-O-O, so important."

"Tay, the shot?"

"Wait wait, before—"

"I can't! Who won!"

"I will, but hear me out first."

"Tay."

- 75 -

"Whit, listen, please," she coos.
"Okay, whatever. What?"
"Madison and Abe are pregnant."
"Great, they've been praying!"
"With twins!"
"Like I said, 'turn off the lights' works!"
Now tie his excitement to the result, like a commercial. Connect pleasure—getting pregnant—to my product, fertility treatment.
"No Whit," she says. "They didn't turn off the lights. They turned on the fertility treatment."
"Whatever. Turn off the lights still works."
"No, Whit, Madison went to the celebrity clinic!" This is a slight stretch in the truth. While Madison *did* tell her about the fertility clinic, Madison did not conceive there. Taylor lies about the clinic because she knows Whitfield rarely talks to Madison and Abe, her cousins and his cousin-in-laws, so she gladly and easily lies about the source of conception and hopes she's planted a seed.
"Good, Tay. I'm glad fertility treatment worked for them. Back to the game. Did he get the three-point throw?"
"Whit, fertility can work for us!"
"Dang Tay, the game! And no, Tay. I've told you, we're done. Listen to my instincts. I have a feeling we can use the turn off the lights method—trust me."
"I'm sorry, but turn off the lights is a song, not a method."
"Trust me, there's a method in the song. I'll show you."
"I want a baby, and if we do what Madison and Abe did, we'll be pregnant in no time."
"All kidding aside, I've been meditating. We'll get pregnant; have faith!" Whitfield says, and then adds, "So the game. Did he make the shot?"
Yikes! The pain-pleasure distraction method isn't working. I'll up the ante.
"Yes, he made the shot, but I have to go. I'll talk to you later."
Before she can hang up the telephone, she is already at work re-designing her fertility treatment campaign. . . .

Chapter Nineteen
Here Comes the Bentley

Yep, you may have tricks, but we're eating your cake! Alex smiles as Marshall Hanes shreds the State of Illinois' witnesses one by one.

It's the third day of trial, and the State of Illinois can't prove their case. The State has been unable to establish that Health Solutions fraudulently refused to insure pregnant women and patients with pre-existing conditions.

Great work, Alex! she tells herself, feeling she has done her job well. *I've shredded, destroyed, and concealed all the evidence. Nice!*

"Any more witnesses?" Judge Clyde asks.

Want some truffle cake, Burkey?

"Yes, Thomas Bentley!" District Attorney Kevin Burke says on cue, answering the judge's question. He identifies Thomas Bentley, a *former* Health Solutions executive, as his next witness.

"Objection!" Marshall Hanes nearly screams.

No! Not Thomas Bentley!

Marshall explains his objection. "Your honor, Mr. Bentley is not a witness. He's not on the witness list."

"Mr. Hanes is mistaken. We've identified Thomas Bentley on the list," Kevin Burke says.

As Attorney Hanes and District Attorney Burke argue, Alex picks up the witness list.

Examining the names, Alex sinks. She sees that the witness list identifies Mr. Mitchell Wright as the witness, or to the extent Mr. Wright is unavailable, any other person from the Health Solutions' insurance coverage department. *No! Thomas Bentley is from the insur-*

ance coverage department—at least formerly from. How did I miss the ambiguous witness list before trial?

Lifting her eyes, she knows why sweat beads are forming on Marshall's face. *Thomas Bentley is a surprise witness who can prove the State of Illinois' case!*

Alex hears District Attorney Burke explain why Thomas Bentley is a properly identified witness.

"Your honor, I'm simply perplexed. Why's Mr. Hanes so worked up over a witness?"

"Counsel knows my concern. He's failed to comply with the rules. In fact, Mr. Bentley isn't a Health Solutions employee."

"The sweeter the cake, wouldn't you admit? And truly, he is from the department, as the witness list indicates," Kevin Burke says.

"Schematics!" Marshall demands.

"Perhaps, but he is a corporate witness who can testify regarding Health Solutions' corporate policy. He is from the department. What's the difference who testifies? Won't they all say the same thing?" Kevin Burke shrugs his shoulders, looking innocent.

All eyes are fastened on Marshall Hanes, waiting for an explanation.

Obviously wanting to preserve his appeal without sending any more signals to the jurors, Marshall concedes, "Your honor, let the record note my objection."

"Noted, but overruled, please proceed with your witness," the judge instructs District Attorney Burke from on high.

Alex sinks in her seat while she watches Thomas Bentley approach the witness stand. She knows that the difference between Mitchell Wright testifying and Thomas Bentley testifying is huge.

Wright wrote the policy that is at issue in this lawsuit: a policy that encourages Health Solutions' employees to deny insurance coverage to pregnant women and individuals with pre-existing conditions. He would do everything in his power to protect the policy.

Thomas Bentley critically opposes the policy.

In fact, years ago, after a heated Wright v. Bentley feud over the company policy, Bentley quit the company.

Alex knows his testimony will be scathing. Her insides curl. *We're screwed!*

Chapter Twenty
Sub-Prime Teaching

REAGAN TEACHES HER class with *change we can believe in* on her mind. Inspired by the chance of new leadership, even if change is a mere possibility, she faces her chalkboard with a smile and sets up her math equations with a twist. Just as she begins, raucous laughter erupts.

Turning and seeing the usual suspects—Dixon, Peter, and Jose, school-wide trouble makers—laughing at Marvin Walker, she grabs the reigns.

"Dixon, Peter, and Luke, STOP!" she demands, but then she is taken aback when she looks at Marvin Walker, a good student, and sees that he is snorting and making a deep, raspy sound. *Is he sleeping in class?*

Alarmed, Reagan rushes over to his desk and whispers into his ears, "Marvin, wake-up. Are you sick?"

Marvin raises his head and blankly stares at her. Locking eye-to-eye with her, he smiles, as if he is dreaming, and then frowns, as if he remembers he must slumber. He drops his head and returns to sleep.

Deciding to take Marvin into the hallway to address his behavior, Reagan awakens him again. "Marvin, in the hallway, *now*," she commands. She nudges his shoulder, but her prod is ineffective. He does not stir.

The children roar with laughter. Dixon, a usual classroom disruption, leads the class.

"Marvin is sleeping!" Peter giggles.

"I want to take a nap, too." José claps his hands once and then laughs. Her classroom dissolves into chaos.

Slamming her foot on the floor, Reagan barks out orders. "Quiet, or you're marching to the principal's office!"

"So what?" Luke shouts.

Knowing she must follow through on her threat, and at any rate, believing some children require administrative intervention, Reagan counts to ten, sucks air into her lungs, exhales deeply, and texts a message to Mr. Simon, the campus monitor. Arriving swiftly, Mr. Simon whisks Luke down to the principal's office.

Meanwhile, Marvin sleeps.

Reagan could have sent Marvin to the principal also, but she gives him a chance because his behavior is unusual.

Lifting Marvin's left arm, which is anchoring his head on the desk, and guiding him to a standing position, she helps him walk to the hallway. Seeing him sway and stumble towards the door, she stays beside him as they walk in case he needs someone to lean on.

His movement is so erratic, she wonders if he is drunk.

— 𝄢 —

STANDING IN THE HALLWAY staring into her fifth grade student's weary eyes, Reagan realizes that Marvin is not drunk; he is exhausted.

"Marvin, why are you sleeping in class?"

"Because," he answers, sounding nonchalant.

"Please explain."

"I'm sleepy."

No duh. "I can see that you're tired, but my question is more to why are you sleeping *here?* You shouldn't sleep in class."

"Where then?" he asks. Lines crease his youthful face.

Reagan crosses her arms and two-steps, left foot then right, not sure exactly what to say because she suspects her answer will not suffice. Rather than stating the obvious, she inquires further. "Why do you think school is the best place to sleep?"

"School is warm."

Leaning in closer, looking into his eyes, she asks, "Why class?"

"Safe."

Jumping backwards, overcome by shock, she catches her expression, realizing she must conceal her surprise. She asks in a compassionate, soft voice, "Do you want to tell me something?"

"I did."

Seeing her inquisition is going nowhere, she asks her questions differently. "Why do you think school is a safe, warm, and good place to sleep?"

Dropping his head, he answers, "You can't get heat in the streets."

His words yank off her blinders. She sees into his reality. *Marvin is homeless.*

Reagan is amazed to learn that a 5 foot 3 inches tall, ten-year-old boy in her class is living on the streets.

Reagan talks with Marvin. She wants to understand how one of her best students is homeless. *He's usually always attentive. He comes from a great home with dedicated, hard-working parents. How is Marvin homeless? His parents purchased that home years ago, in 2006, after his father received a promotion. How is he homeless?* Reagan wonders.

On days like this one, Reagan stands in disbelief. His homelessness tugs at her heart. She feels she should teach not only ABC's and 1-2-3's. She wishes she could do more. As she often tells her friends, "I'm a social worker! I'm a teacher! I'm a motivator and pastor, all in one."

When her attorney-friend, Alex, reminds her, "You can't preach in the classroom," Reagan adds a caveat. "Well, I can teach biblical principles in the name of values, but not religion. Separation of church and state, our Constitution says."

With Marvin, she must wear all these hats at once. She instinctively shifts to overdrive, including referring him to counseling.

— ♪ —

HOURS LATER, AFTER A parent-teacher conference with the school counselor attending, Reagan learns why and how Marvin Walker is homeless. His parents purchased a house with a sub-prime mortgage. Their monthly mortgage payment went from $875 dollars a month to $3,645 a month. The thought of this terrifies Reagan. She knows that if something like that had happened to her, she'd be homeless, too.

Chapter Twenty-one
The Bentley

"Your testimony is that Health Solutions got paid to insure pregnant women and individuals with pre-existing conditions, but then when it was time to insure those fine individuals, Health Solutions refused to insure them?" Kevin Burke says to Thomas Bentley. "In other words, your testimony is that Health Solutions had their cake and ate it, too?"

Hearing the question, Alex shoots Marshall a quick smirk.

Marshall stands and objects. "Objection—motion to strike."

"Overruled," Judge Clyde says, and directs the witness to continue by nodding his head.

"Yes, we got full on cake!" Thomas Bentley says.

"Judge is biased!" Alex scribbles on a notepad in front of her. She pushes it toward Marshall.

"You think?" Marshall scribbles back, and then adds, *"Cooke County—liberal country."*

Meanwhile, Kevin Burke continues, questioning the witness. "Your testimony today is that Health Solutions refused to insure fine folks with pre-existing conditions?"

"Yes, Health Solutions wouldn't insure patients with pre-existing conditions."

"What about pregnant women? Would Health Solutions cover nice, nurturing pregnant women?"

"No!" Thomas Bentley looks almost repulsed, as if he is the company and he is actually responding to a request by a pregnant woman for insurance.

Jeez, that Burkey even has Bentley acting melodramatic. And nurturing? His questions are so improper, so loaded!

"Why did Health Solutions deny coverage to pregnant women and fine folks with pre-existing conditions?"

Alex scribbles another note to Marshall. *"Aren't you going to object?"*

"Why bother? The Judge will overrule the objection, and objecting too much will only make me look bad to the jury. That's what Burkeman wants. Won't fall for that trick. We've—or better yet you've—already fallen for enough of his pranks," Marshall writes back.

"Sorry!" Alex writes, but wonders, *Whose team are you on?*

Kevin Burke is now in the middle of asking, "So you're telling me Health Solutions strictly excluded pregnant women and patients with pre-existing conditions?"

"Yes, of course," Thomas Bentley answers.

"How did the policy work?" Kevin Burke asks.

"Simple, not rocket science. We denied insurance to pregnant women and patients with pre-existing conditions!"

Alex cringes.

Thomas Bentley literally drives the nail in his former employer's coffin.

Alex sits at the defense table trying to take each one of Thomas Bentley's admissions without showing her angst because each one of his whistle-blowing words feels like a punch to her jaw. He literally lays out the plot, one statement after another. She sinks. *How can we beat this evidence?*

Almost on cue, Thomas Bentley asks a question that lifts Alex.

"Don't other insurance companies exclude pregnant women and people with pre-existing conditions?"

Yes, we can confuse the jury with Burkey's question. She begins to slip a note to Marshall—object to the question—but Marshall is already standing and speaking…

"Objection, Your Honor. Mr. Bentley is not an expert on what other insurance companies might or might not do."

Hearing the objection, which she knows is based on Rule 701, Opinion Testimony by Lay Witnesses, Alex feels confident that even this biased judge will sustain. If the judge sustains the objection, the defense can later confuse the jury. *We can make the jury think Health Solutions is like every other insurance company that excludes patients with pre-existing conditions and pregnant women. The jury will think we did nothing wrong. We can suggest, through our questions, that even Kevin Burke agrees that everybody does it. Why else would he have asked the question?*

"Overruled," Judge Clyde says, and instructs the witness to continue.

"Yes, most insurance companies exclude pregnant women or people with pre-existing conditions if they can, but this was a state plan, and the state plan prohibited Health Solutions from excluding pregnant women and people with pre-existing conditions."

"Why is the State of Illinois' plan different from other insurance plans?" Kevin Burke asks.

"Obviously, the state paid Health Solutions to cover poor people, even pregnant women, and people with pre-existing conditions. We couldn't exclude them under our contract with the State of Illinois."

"Did Health Solutions exclude them?"

"Yes," he says, nodding, "that's our policy. We only insure patients who won't have insurance claims. We insure healthy people, not sick people or pregnant women."

"Did you cover any sick people?"

"Not if we knew about the condition. We had internal policies, things we'd say to ourselves."

"What were the policies?"

"We'd say, 'fight the plague, fight the plague,' which meant avoid sick folks and pregnant women to keep profits up!"

"Objection, motion to strike," Marshall stands and exclaims.

"Overruled." The judge signals for the District Attorney to continue.

"Why did Health Solutions exclude pregnant women and people with pre-existing conditions?" Kevin Burke asks.

"Cash money, plain and simple," Thomas Bentley quickly responds.

Come on, Burke. Insurance isn't that simple! We exclude some costly people so we can insure other, less costly people. We're just balancing the risks, providing a service!

"Did excluding pregnant women and people with pre-existing conditions violate Health Solutions' agreement with the State of Illinois, the client that hired you to provide health care benefits to the State's poor?" the District Attorney asks, walking confidently over to the jury.

"Objection, form, legal conclusion, expert," Marshall stands and says.

"I will allow the question. Answer please," the judge says. "Disregard the outbursts from defense counsel, please."

No he didn't!

Alex's stomach knots as Thomas Bentley begins to answer the question.

"Yes, of course Health Solutions violated the contract. The State paid Health Solutions to cover people we refused to insure. The State paid us a huge subsidy to cover these people, but we denied coverage and pocketed the funds. Denying benefits increased our profits."

Liar!

"So basically, Health Solutions took the subsidy but then didn't cover the people the company was paid to cover?"

"Yes."

"Health Solutions had their cake and ate it, too?"

"Objection!" Marshall stands and says, but the judge quickly overrules the objection and the witness answers.

"Yes, we had lots of cake."

Sitting at the defense table, her stomach tightens. *Can this case get any worse?*

Yes, Alex thinks, as she sees Kevin Burke begin to introduce email evidence. *Yep, the case turned from bad to worse!* She sees Thomas Bentley identify and testify about email evidence that is blown up on the courtroom overhead projector....

⊠**To: Southeast Medical Directors & Staff**
  From: Thomas Bentley
  Cc: Legal Team
  Re: No Pregnant(s) & No Pre-Existing(s) Policy

Keep up the good work. Keep all pregnant women out. We also need all sick ones out, too! Remember our motto: No Pregnant(s) and No Pre-Existing(s).

We're toast! This evidence is so against my motto: destroy evidence! Hide evidence! Do not let the plaintiff find this kind of evidence! Unfortunately, the motto didn't work. This email must have fallen through the cracks somehow. Guess that Bentley jerk kept a copy! Jerk! My shredding didn't work. We're screwed!

Chapter Twenty-two
Gifted Education

*R*EAGAN JUGGLES CHALLENGE after challenge during her day until she finally takes a break. Approaching her principal's office to discuss a student, she knocks and enters.

"Mr. Lee, pardon me, but do you have a minute?"

Lifting his head and taking off his reading glasses, revealing heavy, baggy eyes, Mr. Lee answers in a slow monotone. "I see, yes, Ms. Hamilton, yes."

Observing impatience on his face, she clears her throat and adds, "Sorry to interrupt. I know you're busy. I'd like to bring Casey Johnson to your attention."

"Casey Johnson." He repeats the name in a slow, methodical tone. "Her scores are down, are they?"

Reagan holds up her hands to stop him, pull him back, so he can appreciate what she has to say. "No, her scores are perfect. She's gifted!"

Looking relieved, he says, "Gifted, is she? Why good—great. She'll bring up the others." He lowers his head and returns to his paperwork.

That's not what I had in mind, Reagan thinks, before saying, "Yes, she'll increase our averages, but Casey needs something, too."

"Awe, I see, there's always a catch," he replies.

I don't understand? What catch?

"We know her motivation, her inspiration. Why don't we consider what she requires? Why yes, does she require brownies, cookies, toys for great scores? Awe, yes certainly, great good; I'll make a note."

Education isn't about cheers, cookies, pies, and toys. "No, Mr. Lee," Reagan says. "She doesn't want a prize. She wants a challenge, a gifted program."

"Gifted program? Well I—but why? Why no, please." He returns his eyes to his paperwork as if the conversation has ended.

"Please, hear me out," Reagan says, feeling anxious.

Lifting his head and focusing his eyes on her again, he frowns. "What are you suggesting?"

"A gifted education program."

"We can't. We must test focus," he explains, tugging at his collar and then mumbling the test focus cheer: "Recall please, TEST OFTEN, TEST ALWAYS, RA-RA-RA!"

"I know the cheer." *I hate the cheer.* "But she's gifted! We must educate her, too! We have a duty."

"Duty, well yes, right, great grand, duty."

"Mr. Lee, not only do we have a duty, it's the law. We are required to identify and properly educate gifted kids." Reagan remembers what she learned at a teacher education law seminar.

"Awe yes, I see yes, the law," he begins, and then pauses. He massages his chin before continuing. "You're correctly stating facts, but—well, Ms. Hamilton, visualize, comprehend, between you and me, the budget."

"Yes, there's a gifted education budget."

"Well see, comprehend, we've had cuts."

"I know, but there's gifted funds, too," she says.

"Watch this," he says, throwing his hands up in the air and staring at an imaginary object. He points and says, "See that piece of paper floating in the air?"

"No, I don't."

"Use your imagination. There's an imaginary budget floating in the air."

"Right, of course."

"All right, and see my fingers?" he asks now, holding up his hands, simulating scissors.

She nods.

He aggressively cuts the imaginary budget in the air. Once done, he adds, "The budget has been cut! All funds left in this budget go to testing. TEST OFTEN, TEST ALWAYS, RA, RA, RA!"

Watching him cheer, Reagan thinks, *Please stop! No more cheers!* "Gifted education is a different budget line item." Her frustration level begins to rise.

"Awe well, see, line items." He looks in the air before adding, "How do I explain our very delicate situation? Awe yes, difficult, let's see, how, I ponder?"

Say it! Reagan leans forward; her eyes are bulging.

"Understand the line items, the funds, the dough, the cash—"

Mr. Lee, could you please make your point!

"We, well *they*, the powers that be, out of my purview, not in my control, they cut the budget. Because the powers made cuts, we, the little people, we don't have enough money to meet the testing requirements—not that I'm complaining. And gifted education, well we certainly have no gifted education money. Sorry, no funds, understand, do you?"

Her frustration boils and uncharacteristically, she speaks her mind, spouting off her thoughts without a break. Raising her voice, she blurts out, "I do, I understand. No child left behind was passed into law without funding, but we're still required to meet the demands the law requires without the funding necessary to meet the demands even though we need funding to meet the demands, and you're creating cheers and rigid test focus standards to fill the funding gap. I understand, but we have to educate gifted children. It's Arizona state law!" Her heart pounds, she is almost out of breath.

"I-I-I-I'm sorry, Ms. Hamilton, but I'm only doing what I'm told, out of my purview, out of my control," he admits. His tone is defensive. He raises his left eyebrow, as if he has been struck by her comments.

Reagan sighs. "I know you're stuck in a tough place, but can't we work together, bend the rules, find a way?"

"No, why, no," he answers, shaking his head fervently.

"But we must."

"Yet, we can't see, because I'm like a shopper at a grocery store who wants to purchase ten apples but only has enough money to purchase two. Like the shopper who is caught without enough money to purchase what he needs, I, too, don't have enough money to educate beyond the minimum."

"Can't we be creative? Can't we shift somehow?"

"Awe, well, see, if you only have enough for two apples when you need ten apples to meet the No Child Left Behind Standards, there's no way to shift to add two more apples for gifted education, correct?" He pauses as if he has asked a legitimate, thought provoking question.

"Can we talk numbers, real numbers, instead of hypothetical apples, with all due respect?"

Looking puzzled, he asks, "Awe, well, see, Reagan, apples are best. If you think apples, you'll understand. You can't purchase twelve apples when you only have enough money for two apples, particularly when the testing standards even require you to meet requirements as if you had enough money to purchase ten, but you only have enough money to purchase two, understand?"

"Why don't I create a curriculum on my own for gifted kids?" she suggests, sensing that she is getting nowhere, and deciding that she will need to take matters into her own hands to get results.

He pauses for a moment, as if considering her question. "Your own gifted curriculum? Why let's see, yes, well but understand, I'm not telling you to deviate from no child left behind; but of course, if you take your own initiative to do both that's on you, and of course I can't pay you more to do more, but if you can make a program within the testing guidelines and teach Casey, too, that's fine, go for it. Not that I'm telling you how to run your classroom beyond ensuring your students pass the tests, but if you can create two curricula, one for the majority of your students and another for your one gifted pupil, great grand."

Reagan smiles and then frowns. It's nice to hear that he is open to some form of curriculum flexibility, but then almost immediately she does not see how to make things work—not without additional materials, testing measures for gifted students, a teacher's aide, or something to assist in educating a dual student body.

"I can donate my time," Reagan says, "but to do this right, I'll need additional materials and maybe an aide. I'll require some help." She blows out frustrated air, causing her curly bangs to lift.

"Well, no, I see, but no," he says, shaking his head. "There's no funds here. You'll have to bake cookies or have some sort of fundraiser to come up with additional funds, and well see, an aide, that's not available. There's no availability—all our aides must test focus."

"Then I'm stuck."

"No, I'm not telling you how to do things other than ensuring your children do well on NCLB. If you want to do more, on your own initiative, not that I'm telling you how to teach beyond test focusing, but like I said this would be your own initiative, you can't forget about the test preparation, and I'm not telling you to shift from test preparation focusing, but if you can pull off a dual curriculum, go for it. But the budget, I have no funds available, so I'm telling you to test focus—that's our motto!"

"I'm sorry, I'm not following you," Reagan says, lost in all his babbling words, a habit she knows he has whenever he is nervous or faces an uncomfortable question.

"Awe yes, what are we talking about?" He ponders while caressing his chin. "TEST REGULARLY, TEST OFTEN, TEST ALWAYS. That's our motto, that's your charge."

Chapter Twenty-three
Waiting on the Jury

"IDIOT JURORS!" MARSHALL yells. Alex watches him curse and pace in a luxury hotel that almost seems to dangle over Lake Michigan in Chicago, Illinois.

Please, let us win somehow. She knows the trial went downhill the moment Thomas Bentley took the stand. Now, with the jury off deliberating, all they can do is anxiously await the verdict. Alex bites her nails while watching Marshall nearly burn the thread out of the carpet he is pacing.

"Liberal juries!" Marshall screams, fuming and pacing.

Alex knows a luxury hotel is not the best place to await a jury verdict, but she tells herself, *This is business. Besides, look at him. His face is red, his eyes are frantic, and his hands are shaking. He's mad.*

"The idiot jurors believed Bentley!"

"We have a solid defense."

"You're delusional."

"No, I'm not," Alex says. "We defended our client well. Remember, the plaintiff has the burden of proof, not us. I don't think they've met the burden of proof. The preponderance of the evidence."

"Were you in the same courtroom?"

"Yes, Marshall. Health Solutions did nothing wrong. Even the government knew we were excluding high-risk claimants. We had no choice. That's how you insure the masses. Don't you think the jury understands?"

"Hell no!"

"Well Marshall, they should because our client does the impossible. Don't you think they'll cut through all the sympathy and word trickery and get what we're in the business of trying to do? Won't they get that our client is charged with doing the impossible—insuring people who can't afford to pay for their own medical care?"

"Hell no!" Sweat beads form on his face.

I know....the evidence against us was bad—that jerk Thomas Bentley.

Rage mounts with each word he speaks. "Not only was the evidence bad—Alex, how did you let that Bentley take the stand? How did you miss that *from* crap! If you would have objected before trial, we could have kept that slimy opportunistic snake out of court. We could have fought—I swear hell would have frozen over before I would have shown up in court knowing that whistleblowing weasel was testifying."

"Marshall, I know I missed the WITNESS ID, but the judge shouldn't have let him testify."

"You're right, but he did! You can't wait until court to object! Hell Alex, we're in Cooke County, you can't expect fairness," Marshall nearly shouts.

I must calm him down. If he is not controlled, who knows if he'll make out okay without a heart attack. She tries to encourage him despite the bleak state of affairs. "You've won tough cases before, you'll win this one!" This is a lie. Rehashing the distinction in her mind, she knows that the difference between this case and the other cases is that in this case, they had obviously failed to destroy all the evidence.

"Thomas Bentley—he's a weak snake! I want to crush him!" Marshall slams his foot on the ground in emphasis.

Alex tries to divert Marshall's attention, so she changes the subject. "How about dinner, room service? What do you want?"

"Bourbon, and order merlot for you!" he barks.

"Lobster and filet mignon, too," Alex adds, picking up the telephone and placing an order.

– ♪ –

AN HOUR LATER, ALEX observes Marshall. She realizes his anger subsides by the moment, particularly with each sip of bourbon.

Staring into his eyes, she thinks, *He's so different. He's actually smiling.*

Placing a perfectly cut piece of meat in her mouth while fixating on her lips, Marshall says, "Do try, filet mignon!"

Eyes widening in shock, she accepts his offering. She tastes the meat and says, "Scrumptious."

"More wine?" he asks, lifting the bottle.

She nods yes.

He pours.

She drinks. . . .

– ♪ –

"ALEX, WAKE UP!" ALEX hears someone say. She opens her eyes, not really aware of the day or the hour. *Where am I?*

"We have a verdict!"

Marshall—what the—

"Get dressed! We're due in court in thirty-five minutes!" he demands, walking towards the bathroom. He is completely naked, showing his physique, which she does not find to be particularly appealing—especially nude.

Rubbing her eyes, Alex tries to un-fog her previously drunken brain. Realizing she is in her boss' bed, also nude, she nearly pukes.

– ♪ –

SCURRYING TO THE COURTHOUSE, Alex is disillusioned. *What happened last night and how? I don't even like Marshall!*

She tries to feign control while walking with Marshall, who is now hailing a cab on this cold, snowy day in the windy city.

He looks so together, like nothing happened.

She feels she must look a total mess. She is even wearing a nice blue suit—only the temperature is well below zero—and she is not wearing a coat. *I am so unprepared.*

His old mean self is back.

He treats her as the help who must jump at his every command. He even answers a call from his wife on the way to court on his cell phone, in front of Alex.

She hears every word.

"Hi love. I was busy working on the trial last night. I apologize."

Liar.

"The jury's in, so I'll catch the first flight out." There's a pause, and then he coos, "Miss you, honey."

Alex sinks, realizing the full extent of her recent relations and what her indiscretions might mean.

Alex, pull yourself together.

— ♪ —

STANDING TO HEAR THE jury verdict and the judgment, Alex is anxious.

"The jury finds in favor of the plaintiff and awards the State of Illinois $192 million dollars."

No!

Hours later, Marshall and Alex sit side by side in a chartered airplane traveling back to Phoenix, Arizona.

Sitting in silence, Alex feels stupid.

He hasn't spoken a word to her since he abruptly woke her up this morning to go to court.

He has been distant, tense, and different.

What did we do? I hope I didn't do that smack down trick on him. . . .

— ♪ —

AT HOME, ALONE, LATE that night, Alex can't sleep. *I had sex with my boss! Yuck! How? And my career, I mean I've dated many men, but this is tricky, too tricky. This one I probably can't turn!* She mulls thoughts around in her head for hours until she decides, *I'll go to work and act like nothing happened. I can't tell anyone. This one night stand will be our little secret. I will not say a word—not even to my closest friends, especially Reagan, Ms. Holier Than Thou.*

She practices the routine in her mind all weekend. She prepares to return to work and act so well she could win an Academy Award for her performance in *Business As Usual*.

Chapter Twenty-four
Persuasion

Fill up the ante and convince Whit, but how? Taylor thinks. Suddenly, it comes to her.

"SPAM!"

I'll send unsolicited commercial email to Whit, better known as SPAM!

I'm an expert advertiser! I'll entice him into agreeing to my way advertising style.

Opening her computer, she begins.

Searching the Internet, she looks for websites she knows will send SPAM to Whit if she inputs his information.

She tries to identify websites that will inundate Whit with fertility treatment infomercials.

Reviewing her search results, she smiles.

She signs Whitfield up to receive fertility treatment SPAM from at least 200 service providers by inserting his email address in the box entitled, PLEASE SEND MORE INFORMATION.

Chapter Twenty-five
The Office Rumor Mill

*A*LEX WALKS INTO work knowing she lost more than just the case in Cooke County, Illinois. She feels she also lost her professional edge. *I slept with my boss. How?*

Gliding onto the elevator, Alex replays her version of the story in her mind. *We didn't have sex. Business trip only! So, act normal.* Her insides curl, she is so nervous.

Stepping into her office now, she begins acting like she is working. She masters business as usual. She looks extremely professional, like a woman with nothing but business on her mind, when actually she is worried. Her mind focuses on her affair.

She is sure her charade is perfect until, out of her peripheral vision, she sees her assistant approaching. Seeing Heidi briskly walking towards her office, Alex feels her face. She is afraid her cheeks are turning tomato red the way they always do when she is really upset, embarrassed, or scared. Currently, she feels all three sensations at once.

Pulling out her mirror, she confirms her fears. She quickly covers her face with make-up that is darker than her skin. Looking into the mirror, she sheepishly grins, appreciating the camouflage. *Thanks Reagan for giving me this darker hue, works every time!* She quickly tucks the powder into her drawer and prepares. *Poker face on, let's go!*

Alex acts busy. She rustles papers and pretends to check email as her assistant, Heidi, darts into her office and speaks.

"I *heard!*" Heidi says, focusing on Alex with a mistrustful eye.

Alex reflexively flinches before responding. "Heard what?" She leans forward in her chair, salivating at the mouth, trying to maintain her composure, certain that Heidi knows the truth.

"Don't be fake with me, chica!" Heidi smiles.

Am I obvious? Do you know? "What?" Alex inquires, gripping the edge of her desk.

"You didn't have a chance," Heidi says.

Yes I did! Her stomach begins to knot. Her heartbeat hastens. *Does she know? Does the office rumor mill know? I must protect my reputation! Can't say I slept my way to the top!* Sitting up straight, squaring off her shoulders, she decides to lie and lie well. She puts the poker face back on because she lost her mask when Heidi said, "I heard." Acting busy again, pretending to check emails she says, "Heidi, you're wrong, so explain yourself."

"Alex, marriages aren't easily broken."

Marriage! Alex stops playing make believe. Fidgeting in her chair, losing her composure, she asks, "What marriage?"

"You're awesome, but you can't end a strong bond."

WHHHOOOSH, suddenly a gust of wind passes. Someone quickly walks past her office. Seeing his tailored suit jacket, Alex realizes the swift walker is her co-adulterer boss. *Marshall!* Alex gets up, adjusts her layered bob, and begins to tuck in her shirt. She fidgets.

"He's not taking the game well either," Heidi adds, looking outside Alex's door.

With her back to Alex, Heidi is completely missing Alex's fidget-dance, which is good for Alex because she knows she is losing her composure now that she is convinced Heidi knows about the affair. Wanting to find out how much and how Heidi knows, Alex asks, "I'm confused. Explain please?"

"He doesn't like to lose," Heidi answers, her eyes still on Marshall as he scurries down the hall.

"Heidi, make your point. Explain yourself. Lose what?" Alex demands.

Heidi turns and looks away from the door and back inside at her boss, obviously hearing Alex's tone. As her eyes hit Alex, she steps back, taken aback by Alex's appearance.

Do I look flustered?

"Alex, you look horrible. What's wrong? Your face is apple-red. Where's your make-up?" Heidi asks, quickly pulling out a mirror from Alex's cabinet and handing it to her. "Here. Let me grab your comb, too. What's wrong, chica?"

I adjusted and fidgeted too much when you turned your back to me. Poker face, I need you back on. "I'm fine, Heidi, absolutely flawless!" Alex exclaims, almost shouting now. "I'm busy, so get to the point and then get out!'

Heidi stares at her for a moment, then snaps her fingers in understanding. "You're like him, senorita! You don't like losses either!"

"Heidi!"

"Don't be upset. Illinois has too many liberal judges and jurors."

"True, but, what's your point about marriages breaking up?"

"The liberal judges and juries are virtually married in Illinois. You can't break up the liberal bond. You were doomed to lose as soon as you walked into the courtroom. You couldn't win!" Heidi finishes, shrugging her shoulders.

Alex breathes a sigh of relief, exhaling for what feels like the first time since Heidi walked into the room. The knot in her stomach begins to unwind. *She doesn't know.* Alex's bulldozer lifts, so she speaks again. "Of course! Cooke County isn't a fair place for any defense team!" She crosses her arms and nods her head furiously.

Alex continues to chat with Heidi longer, just enough to confirm that she knows nothing about the one night stand. Once done, she says, "Okay, you can leave!" Alex watches Heidi walk out. She decides her next course of action. *Back to work!*

Hours later, after spending the late morning *really working*, Alex suddenly feels a cool, deceiving breeze. Looking at the thermostat behind her desk, she pulls the sweater from off her seat back and wraps it around her shoulders. The temperature is seventy-eight degrees, which isn't cold to Alex, but she feels chilly. She shivers, and her mind begins to drift. She begins to think about Marshall and her intoxication-induced fling with him. She tries to retrace her encounter with him, but she was so drunk, she does not remember the night.

Before, she had always kept sex and business separate.

And now, this? A one-night stand with her boss has her anxious. She wonders whether her career is in jeopardy. She is concerned her professional reputation could be ruined if the word got out that she had sex with her boss. Her heartbeat begins to hasten until suddenly she decides she must construct a plan. Three words come to her mind—LEVERAGE, POWER, CONTROL! She decides to turn the fling to her advantage. But how? She ponders.

How do you have sex with your boss—when you're drunk—and gain LEVERAGE, POWER, AND CONTROL?

You don't—a voice whispers in her ear.

She feels caught in a conundrum, a jigsaw puzzle, where he holds the master plan.

Her chest pounds. She feels a lump in her throat.

She inhales deeply and decides to think strategically. She knows other professional women have come before her and successfully navigated a tricky extramarital affair with their boss and emerged un-scorned. She can too she is sure. But how?

How does having sex with your boss change your work? What will he expect? How can a woman protect herself? And his wife—Alex hears screeching brakes in her mind with the thought of his wife. What about his wife? What would happen if she found out? Would she sabotage Alex? Would she label her a slut? Would she declare Alex professionally incompetent? Would she say Alex slept her way to the top? Would she launch a campaign to destroy Alex in any and every professional and social circle in town? What happens?

She digresses, momentarily, before refocusing on her plan. She tells herself to use sex to gain power.

Wrong—she hears a voice whisper in her ear.

She quiets the voice and decides she will use her fling to force Marshall to fast-track her partnership with the firm. That way, as a part-owner and partner, she will have some power and be less vulnerable to the whims of this man and others too, *right?*

No! A whisper speaks into her ear—sleeping your way to the top does not work. And what about his wife, his children—.

Alex quiets the voice again, thinking, *too late*, but she also feels caught. She knows she must follow-through on her decision to use her leverage—sex with him and eventual control of him—to her advantage. But she feels awkward. She does not want to follow-through on the plan. She wants to end the relationship. She wants to play like nothing happened. But she feels she can't. POWER, CONTROL, LEVERAGE—that's how you win this battle.

Except feelings, she knows she can't let feelings seep into her leverage-gaining relationship with Marshall. When feelings get involved Alex knows that POWER, CONTROL, LEVERAGE subside. Many women, and men for that matter, have lost all three virtues when feelings stepped into the dual. The only question in her mind is can she get into the lion's den with Marshall, sexually too, and keep her feelings in check?

Absolutely, she is sure. She sees herself as a strong woman. She has unattached sexual relations with men all the time. She is the unattached sexual partner—except in the case of Duncan Anderson, of course.

Her mind drifts to Duncan…. She sighs.

A moment later, Alex looks up at the door to find Marshall, her co-adulterer boss, leaning against her doorframe, one leg crossed on top of the other. He's staring at her.

"Grab your things. Let's go!" he demands.

Alex weighs her options, trying to decide whether she should go or leave, end the relationship, or allow the escapade to continue.

Marshall smirks, as if he senses her internal deliberation. He is silent, gazing at her, as if he is looking through her, deep into her soul, before he speaks. "We'll work out our appeal strategy."

She grabs her belongings.

Alex and Marshall go to lunch.

Alex and Marshall have a long lunch.

Alex and Marshall do not discuss the appeal strategy.

Alex and Marshall have sex and nothing else.

Chapter Twenty-six
Ice Rink

Alex sits in her office, daydreaming about her boss. She smiles as thoughts of their lunch spree dance through her mind. Going out on a discreet date with him, mid-day makes Alex reconsider. She likes him, at least sexually. Good sex will make getting closer to him to achieve her goal—LEVERAGE, POWER, CONTROL—easier.

Alex turns from her desk and faces her glass office window. She catches a glimpse of the sun. The sight strikes her. *Arizona sunsets are beautiful.* Alex is in awe.

Moments later, she decides to get back to work. She turns back around and faces her desk. In the midst of spinning around in her chair, she catches a glimpse of the hallway outside her office—and gasps.

She sees her boss' wife, Liza Hanes, standing near her doorway with Marshall. Alex sinks with the sun, seeing Mr. & Mrs. Hanes holding hands. Her insides flip. *I had sex with him two hours ago! What a jerk!* Alex can't believe her eyes. *I thought he was unhappily married. I thought his wife was drab, boring, uninteresting. She looks better in person than in the photos he has of her in his office. I thought she was no rival for me. Wrong!*

Ms. Liza Hanes debunks each and every stereotypical image Alex had painted of her in her own mind in an instant. She is a shapely, petite, blonde, and beautiful woman who exudes sophistication and intelligence. Her hair flows in precisely cut layers, framing her face and then tailoring off past her shoulders in a lengthening wave. Her style is designer, but classic: high heels, business casual suit, tastefully fitting teal blouse and matching shoes. Her make-up shimmers, light and easy, so the coverage barely shows. Her beauty is so radiant that heavier make-up would take away from her natural glow.

Why are they standing in front of my door? Alex quickly understands. *The children....*

Drake Hanes, a two-year-old toddler, exclaims, "Da, Da, Da, Da, Da," while extending his arms to Marshall to be held.

Close beside him, six-year-old Kate Lynn jockeys for her father's attention, too.

Alex plays like she is reading email while she watches and listens to fragments of the Hanes' familial gathering in her doorway.

"Dad, guess what?" Kate Lynn shouts, skipping in place.

"Do tell me!" Marshall answers, bending over to face his daughter eye-to-eye.

Who knew he could be so kind and attentive? I guess they do, Alex quickly realizes, as she sees the Hanes family relationship, which appears to be as solid as a rock.

"Show him, Mommy!" Kate Lynn responds.

"We're going to the sold-out play!" Liza Hanes explains.

"Absolutely amazing, you are!" Marshall sounds sincere as he speaks to his wife. He then rustles his son's hair and hugs Kate Lynn before adding, "You, too! Good job helping Mom!"

Okay, okay, you're letting them down easy. You tell them you can't make it! We have a date tonight! Alex remembers that her lunch sex date with Marshall had been cut short. He promised to continue after work. *Surely he'll tell her he has to take a rain check,* Alex thinks.

"Wait here. I'll grab my things." Marshall turns back around and walks to his office.

You're choosing them over me? Absorbing the reality of his choice while remembering the sex she'd had with him only hours ago, her competitive nature ignites.

Obviously oblivious to Alex's relationship with her husband, Liza Hanes waves a friendly hello to Alex, most likely as a courtesy since she stands in front of Alex's doorway waiting for her husband.

Alex waves back. Her anger roars up inside.

A moment later, Marshall returns. "Okay, I'm ready, honey," Marshall says, grabbing his wife's waist and guiding her steps. Drake wobbles after, and Kate Lynn skips.

Alex sees the Hanes family walk away and scribbles on her notepad, Alex v. Liza Hanes and his kids, and he chose the kids. She fumes.

She grabs her belongings and decides to cool her rage at a local sports lounge.

— 9: —

ALEX STEPS INTO A Downtown Sports Lounge with a strategy. She wants to find a man! *Oh boy, there's the answer!* She hears her holier than though friend, Reagan Hamilton, say in her head. *Shut up!* Alex says, quieting the voice. She wants to focus on the night.

Poker face on. Alex tells herself to act like her life is perfect, not as if she is a mistress who just faced her co-adulterer's wife, and having done so feels like she has been smacked in the face with a hurtful taste of reality.

Alex feels like Marshall is using her. She also knows that she is upset, which is a bad sign, because it will be difficult to control him when he is clearly controlling her. She tells herself to refocus her mind.

Alex walks through the dark, cozy bar, then finds a lounge chair and sits down.

Eyeing the men who fill the club, Alex thinks, *There's so many men here tonight! Wow! Wow!* Observing a potential suitor, Alex lifts her chest and runs her fingers through her hair. The man is absolutely gorgeous and sexy. She names him, *Mr. Sexy*, and thinks, *Come on, baby, come on my way. You're looking at me, aren't you? Come to me, I'm ready!*

Suddenly, Alex's view is blocked by a waitress. She can't see *Mr. Sexy* anymore.

"May I take your order?"

"Cosmopolitan," Alex curtly responds, upset that the waitress is blocking her view. *Now move.* Alex adjusts her neck to the left and then the right, trying to see around the waitress.

"Anything else," the waitress inquires. "Appetizer, nuts, cheese, mini-burgers?"

Yes move! Alex thinks, but rudely answers, "No!"

"Gosh, I'm out." The waitress turns and walks away.

Alex looks to her left and to her right. She does not see *Mr. Sexy* anymore. *Where is he?* She searches. Finding him, she sinks. *No! He's talking to the girl directly behind me. He was batting those sexy eyes at her, not me?*

"Here you go." The waitress returns and places the martini down in front of Alex.

Alex gulps the martini in an instant and then orders another cosmopolitan.

And another one....

And another one....

And another one....

And another one...except just as Alex begins to gulp the fifth martini, she notices an easy-on-the-eyes guy inspecting her from across the room. *Hot! And he's looking at me!* Alex lifts her chest and puckers her lips.

He stares her down, as if he's undressing her with his eyes.

Come on! Come on, Mr. Hot Man! Alex thinks, licking her lips.

He walks towards her.

She smiles.

She wants to establish a future with this stranger based on her visual observation.

Wrong! This is what her holier-than-thou friend Reagan would say.

I agree, wrong move! Taylor chimes in, too, agreeing even though she's not holier-than-thou.

Shut up, you two! This is my night! Mr. Hot Man is only a few steps away.

Alex swallows martini number five just as *Mr. Hot Man* stands in front of her and speaks.

"Well, hello. Where have you been all my life?" He sits close to her.

Waiting on you? "Hello, you," Alex responds, making room for *Mr. Hot Man* to nestle with her in the petite lounge chair.

Mr. Hot Man must be at least 6'4, 230 pounds, but he snuggles in close to her, near her, squeezing his body on a lounge chair made for one.

Nice! Alex feels his muscles and frame. She does not mind his proximity. Her body is encased inside his, nestled in his chest. Her backside is in his lap. *Wow! His quads are so muscular, so fit!* She marvels at him in her inebriated state. Sitting close to *Mr. Hot Man*, Alex talks to him. About what, she will not recall. She will remember his eyes, his body, and his face. His perfect image was etched into her mind with her first sighting.

"My love, do you want to dance?" *Mr. Hot Man* inquires, caressing Alex's arms, making his way down her arms until he is holding her hands.

He's made up a name for me, too. Alex likes the name, *My love*.

Mr. Hot Man helps Alex up to the dance floor. The music swirls into a soft, silky, seductive soiree.

Alex dances with the stranger. She feels every muscle of his body pressing against hers as they dance. *Nice-night, please never end!*

— 𝛾 —

Hours later, after the lights set, ending the night at the lounge, the night ends with *Mr. Hot Man* in Alex's bed. She feels transformed and healed as she makes love with the handsome stranger. She thinks not about Marshall, his family, or her job. She basks completely in the stranger, without even knowing his name!

Chapter Twenty-seven
Strategic Business

Taylor is just completing her fertility treatment marketing campaign, directed at her husband, and turning to legitimate business when her telephone rings.

"Taylor Ray," she answers. The caller, Lewis Zimmerman, President of Teaser Shoes, is contacting her to tell her that he is canceling Teaser Shoes' advertising contract with Miles Bridgestone, Inc., her advertising firm. Immediately shifting into business high gear, she responds.

"Reconsider!" Taylor sits still in her swivel chair. Her feet are rooted. Her voice is made stern by the news. *Teaser Shoes is one of my top accounts! You can't cancel your advertising spots!*

Recognizing the significance of this account, Taylor adds, "I understand the economy isn't looking great, but women will buy shoes, even if the economy's got the blues!"

Chuckling, Lewis Zimmerman says, "You've a way with words, but projections don't lie. The economy's tanking."

"Lewis, projections are mere hypothetical theories. Consider reality. Your advertising hasn't failed you yet, right?"

"I'll admit, we've had awesome years; and frankly, we haven't seen a bad economy in decades."

"Absolutely, therefore, you should keep advertising and tweak your business model."

"Agreed, starting with advertising."

"With all due respect, Lewis, you're only talking about theoretical projections," she coos, trying to woo him back in and keep him advertising in high volumes despite his fears. She knows he's right—

the economy is slowing down—but if he cancels his advertising, that affects her bottom line, and she cannot let her sales volume go without a fight. She tries to convince him her way: *Kindness first.*

"We like doing business with you," he says, laughing nervously, "but the economy's out of my hands."

Kindness does not work, so I'll use coercion next! "We have a contract!"

"We'll terminate. There's a termination clause in the contract." He pauses and mumbles, "At least there'd better be one, given how much we paid that lawyer!"

Pulling out the contract from her files in her desk drawer, Taylor studies the terms, line by line, in silence, while Lewis waits, as if he expects she will have to think his termination threat over. She is doing more than thinking. She is reading the contract. There is no termination clause. *Great! He signed on the dotted line. I can fight!*

Relieved to be holding leverage in her hands, she says, "Lewis, there's no termination clause."

"I don't care about clauses. We're out!"

"I understand, but a deal's a deal. Our forecasts depend on your payment in full." Now she uses projections to make her case.

Lewis is not impressed. "Cute, but your projections are superfluous. We're getting hammered. Business is bad. We'll file bankruptcy. Anyhow, aren't projections theoretical? Isn't that what you expressed minutes ago?"

Taylor leans back in her chair. She knows he is telling the truth. Besides, when the economy turns around, she wants this relationship intact so she can sell more advertising. She negotiates.

"Look, Lewis, I don't want to add to your stress level."

"You have a funny way of showing concern for my stress."

"Well, but we have a business here, too."

"Yeah, but—" he begins.

She cuts him off, wanting to get her hook out there before she delivers the softened blow.

"A deal's a deal."

"Deals can be broken." He blows his nose.

Yuck! "Okay, listen, we can't roll over on our contracts because of a mere threat. If you file bankruptcy, we'll be there with your other creditors to take our share of what is left. But I'd hate to see you bankrupt. If we can work out a deal that makes sense for everyone, why don't we try? Here's my proposal."

"I'm all ears," Lewis says. He suddenly sounds enthusiastic.

"I know you want to sell shoes."

"Yes."

"I know your business isn't good now, so it's hard to sell shoes or even *try* to sell shoes because your client base is out of cash and maybe even credit."

"Yes."

"But you like the MBI advertising spots, right?"

"Yes."

"We do a great job selling your shoes, right?"

"Yes, but that's not the point."

"Okay, so how about we expand the contract term out…Let's make the repayment period ten years instead of five, but keep the contract rate at $5,000,000."

Lewis is silent.

"If we spread out your spots," Taylor adds, "that'll cut your advertising costs in half. Does that work?"

He is silent.

With no response, Taylor says, "Look, I meant what I said earlier. Women will still buy shoes, somehow, even in bad economic times. In fact, some may buy more shoes! You don't want to stop advertising. You should fight for a piece of the shoe pie."

There is still no response. "My deal gives you the best of both worlds; you can still advertise, you won't have to break the contract, and you can spread the volume out over time. Does that help?"

Finally, Lewis speaks. "Your option is creative. Maybe it could help."

Great! He's on the line—now reel that big boy in! "I'm glad to help, but I do want an exclusive. That's all I'll ask."

"What?"

"An exclusive on any future advertising. You see, I believe in you and your business."

"I do, too, but I don't get your point."

Taylor explains. "*When*, not if, but *when* your sales go up and your advertising volume increases with sales, I want you to buy that inventory exclusively from me."

"Again, MBI isn't the problem. You guys are great."

"Okay, then it sounds like we have a deal."

"Yes. Thank you!"

Hanging up the telephone, Taylor realizes that at the end, Lewis sounded elated. Why shouldn't he be? His costs were cut in half, his advertising would continue, and there would be no bankruptcy or prolonged litigation, which might cost a small fortune to sort out in court.

Swiveling in her chair, Taylor decides to call the Vice President of Levitran Peaks. She buzzes her assistant, Joseph. "Get Lucas Myers on the telephone."

Jumping up, Joseph quickly shuffles into her office. "What's up?" he asks.

"Sales call."

"Don't they already have an exclusive with another firm?"

"I don't know. That's why I'm calling. I'm recession-proofing my business."

"With erectile dysfunction medication?"

"I understand the medication is recession-proof—never goes down when used," she says, one eyebrow raised.

Joseph uncrosses his arms and ponders this before laughing.

Just before he walks out of her door, Taylor shouts out, "Connie, too. I'll talk to her next."

"Connie, your investment advisor? You're buying the stock, too?" he asks, turning around to look at Taylor.

"Yes, like I said, that business never goes down." *And of course, a girl's gotta do what a girl's gotta do!*

Chapter Twenty-eight
Small Distraction

ALEX GETS OUT of bed and begins her routine: jog, coffee, shower, office. By 6:48 a.m., she sits at her desk wearing a grey dress suit, a popping teal blouse, grey patent leather high heels, and skin-toned hose. Her long bob hair cut is pulled back into a tight bun. She looks stunning.

Alex is a high-end dresser with an unbelievable commitment to win. She can and will develop an iron clad lobbying and public relations strategy for her client, starting with her brainstorming ideas.

Stance stern, defense posture aggressive, Alex jots down thoughts about how to prevent health care reform.

Contact Public Relations firm in Washington. Have firm develop a mass campaign to get our message out: Health care reform will destroy the face of health care in America and lead to rationing of health care; reduction in Medicare and Medicaid; elderly death beds, socialized medicine, death panels, vouchers. We need commercials, town hall meetings, Internet grass roots efforts, press releases, non-industry public representatives to deliver our message. Hire a think tank to back our theories with scientific research. Make sure no laws are passed to create competition in the health care industry. Prevent competition at any cost—insurance company business model depends upon an "as is" approach or an alternative developed under our business model, which we need some MBAs to—

Just as Alex begins to complete her sentence, she hears someone speak.

"Well, hello."

Alex gasps. *Mr. Hot Man* is standing in her doorway, stalker like, looking completely unprofessional, like a person who only comes out at night. The problem is, he is out in the daytime. *Why's he wearing a too-tight shirt! Where are his buttons?*

"Alexandria Giroud!" *Mr. Hot Man* continues in a seductive voice. "You're a big-time lawyer!" he says, moving into her office and walking over to her desk.

She's in shock, and her blood boils. Understanding that perception is everything in business, she knows she must get rid of him—fast! She knows that her relationship with the likes of someone like him can only harm her professional reputation. He doesn't fit into the conservative White Anglo Saxon Protestant (WASP) environment where she works.

Alex immediately stands. She scans the hallway through her glass-walled office and sees no one in close proximity. *Good, he got in here unseen.*

Now, turning back to him, she flinches. "How did you get in this building?"

"I walked in behind a nerd dude in a suit," he answers.

"Okay, listen—you. . ." She still doesn't know his name. "Why are you here? And better yet, how did you find me?" The questions shoot off her tongue like bullets.

Either he dodges bullets well or he is ignorant because *Mr. Hot Man* responds to her razor-sharp words with a smile.

"Alex, boy oh boy. Alex, I had to find you! You gave me your business card at the club cuz you wanted me to find you. Glad I did!" He looks captivated.

Walking to him now, she gets in his face and answers, "No! I didn't!" She cringes, thinking back to the night when she met him, at a sports lounge, stone cold drunk.

"Wasn't hard, sexy. You're everywhere on the Internet." He speaks in a seductive tone. He touches her blouse top, as if he is oblivious to her frustration.

Alex jerks away. She struggles to maintain her poker face before saying, "Listen, you, don't touch me and don't call me sexy!"

Crossing her arms and planting her left foot at an angle, she adds, "Why are you here? I told you I don't want to see you again!"

Either *Mr. Hot Man* doesn't hear her, or her words go over his head because he continues speaking. "Big time lawyer! Boy, big time—jackpot! Mama told me my looks would come in handy! Can you say payday?" He looks around, marveling at her profession or office or both—or maybe just her leather chairs.

Adrenaline flashes up her spine.

Her face is tomato red, she is sure.

He continues, unaware that she's about to lash into him with full force. "Nice office. Do you get paid every two weeks? How much do you bring home?" he asks.

Disbelief overcomes Alex. His presence here like this makes her feel like she is being pricked by a million stick pins at once. *You lazy, gold digging, womanizing jerk!*

She wonders what she should do next. She wants to call security but that would create a scene. She does not want her relationship with him floating through the office rumor mill.

Think! How do I get rid of this idiot but also keep him hidden?

Eyeing the clock, she sees that it is 7:25 a.m. With heavy steps, she walks over to her light switch and closes her interior office electronic blinds with one simple touch. *Can't let my colleagues see this fool.* She watches the blinds close with her back to *Mr. Hot Man*.

Staring into the hallway while the electronic blinds are closing, Alex flexes her muscles to let *Mr. Hot Man* know she can take him if necessary. She replays her self-defense techniques, including the one hand body slam or single motion knock out, in her mind.

Obviously unaware of his impending take down, *Mr. Hot Man* continues to speak.

"You are sexy," he slurs. His eyes are locked on her figure. He is clearly taking advantage of his sudden rear view of her person.

Instinctively, Alex adjusts her posture so that her straight arm is in front of her backside. She feels violated.

Exhaling noisily, she tells herself to focus on her task at hand: defending her reputation, shielding this man's existence and her drunken relations with him from her colleagues, and getting him out of her office unseen. Walking back to her desk, knowing this idiot will stand and wait, she sends her assistant a text message.

Heidi, URGENT. Hold everything! AG

Having barricaded her territory, knowing Heidi will make sure no one will come into her office when she receives the text message, Alex gets right in *Mr. Hot Man's* face and says, "Listen, you!"

Looking into his eyes, Alex stops. She realizes she needs to know his name because she plans to file a restraining order as soon as he leaves her office. "What is your name? And your address, too?"

"I like you when you talk dirty and rough," he says, as if he takes her stance as an introduction to pleasure.

Idiot! She decides to use his ignorance or arrogance to her information-seeking advantage.

Licking his lips, he says, "Buke Dude Drake's the name." He pauses, smiles obnoxiously, and then adds in a seductive voice, "2874 Beauty Drive."

Is he real? Alex immediately walks to her desk, pulls up her browser, and checks to see if she can find Mr. Buke Dude Drake online.

She types but watches him out of the corner of her eye, not sure of what to make of this man, but certain that if he comes close to her, she'll use the steel scales of justice sitting on the corner of her desk as a weapon.

Reading the computer-screen, seeing the answers to her question, her jaw drops. *He's a male stripper for hire?*

Alex plans to end Mr. Drake's delusions. She surmises he is unable to pick up the vibes she's been giving off because he is so handsome. *He is a sight to see.* But that's the end of the measure of this man. He has no depth. Understanding this reality, she knows she must deliver a message to him in a very elementary, kindergarten teacher style. The problem is, he is not grade school age. He is at least twenty-three years old.

She gets in his face, staring him eye to eye, all while holding on to her self-defense techniques, having them at the ready.

"Get out of my office!" she says. "Do not come back to my office! Do not think about me! Do not look for me! And if you step within ten feet of me again, I'll have you arrested!"

Mr. Hot Man jumps. He clearly understands this lingo. "Got ya, baby, hold up!" *Mr. Hot Man* raises his hands to the sky. "I thought we were cool. I thought we made a connection in more ways than sex," he adds, now simulating bumping and grinding. "Hey, if you want me out, I'm gone, adios." He turns and leaps towards the door.

"Wait! One more thing," she shouts.

"I knew you couldn't resist this!" he says, simulating one big, large, hard bump and grind.

No, fool.....

"Carry out this box."

"You can hire me, love. I jump out of cages, boxes, you name it, even with baby oil, but I charge a premium. I can give you a discount, but I don't deliver mail—beneath my pay grade, unless you want me to jump out of the mail and strip!"

"Stop!" she demands, before softening her tone. She realizes he is so dumb, he will believe anything. She quickly makes up a lie. "I'm not hiring you. We're done."

"Yeah, right, but women can't resist!"

"Look Buke, take the box. If you don't, security will arrest you because you did break and enter into our building this morning when you followed that guy in. That's illegal."

Smiling widely, he says, "You're helping me. I get your game." *Mr. Hot Man* talks as if he completely believes everything she's saying.

"Don't get any wrong ideas. . ."

"No—I'll leave." He grabs the box and begins to dart out of her office.

"Wait!" Alex says again. She walks over to her blinds and peaks outside to make sure the coast is clear before he walks out her door. Seeing that the office hallway is full, she decides to hold him at the door until the coast is clear by making up stories, one after another. He stands there and listens. *Idiot!*

Being at a loss for more stories, she finally tells him that he must wait until her co-workers go into a meeting so that he can reduce his chances of getting arrested.

"You must really like me. I affect women like that—women like me like that. You can always call me if you get hot for me, or if you want me to jump out a cage nude."

She stares at him, thinking, *He is actually standing in my door with a box in his hand waiting, thinking I like him. Keep dreaming. Helps me hide, you idiot!*

Time passes awkwardly for her. Finally, Alex looks at the clock and sees that the time is 8:15 a.m. she peaks outside and sees that everyone is gone to a staff meeting. She'll miss the meeting, but her absence and the consequences are worth the risk because as soon as the coast is clear, she directs *Mr. Hot Man* out of her office and out of her life.

Walking out behind *Mr. Hot Man,* Alex goes straight to the courthouse to file a restraining order against him—just in case.

Hours later, Alex returns to her office and gets back to work. She is sharp, efficient, and her defense stance is stern. She continues her memo. *Make sure no laws are passed to create competition in the health care industry. Lobby to keep antitrust laws as is. Need to continue exemption for insurance companies. And prevent any public option plans!*

Chapter Twenty-nine
Public Relations

TAYLOR GETS BACK to business, scribbling notes about erectile dysfunction marketing, when suddenly her telephone rings. Seeing her husband's name on the CALLER ID, she smiles. *I miss him,* she thinks, *but... is my marketing working?*

Answering quickly, she chats with him about everything: her day, the election, his day, politics, and the economy. Talking about the economy, she sighs before saying, "I do think the economy's slowing down. I know there are press releases indicating the economy's strong, but that's PR. We're trying to keep consumer confidence up."

"Yeah, consumer perception drives the economy!"

"Exactly. So that's why starting today, we're officially heavy investors in the erectile dysfunctional industry. Stock won't drop."

"You changed our portfolio?" Whitfield asks.

"Sure did. Right after I got a dismal call from a client—a top seller of shoes. He didn't fall for the economy-may-have-the-blues-but-women-will-still-buy-shoes line. He's cutting his commercial inventory."

"Yeah, I've been downsizing and cutting costs; that's what clients want. Also, there's a lot of buzz in New York about Bear Stearns and credit default swaps."

Default what—but no, wait! She stops her thoughts in their tracks and listens closely to the background noise on the other end of the phone. She hears a loud ping, like an email pop-up, and then a successful conception testimonial coming through from Whitfield's end of the line. Taylor discerns that he's getting pop-ups and ads about fertility treatment and wonders whether the ads are working. Deciding to be direct, she asks straight out, "Whitfield, what's the background noise?"

"Don't know, don't care."

"Why?"

"Spam's irrelevant."

"Could be a client. You can't miss client email."

"Yeah, real email, but not spam."

"How do you know?"

"Easy, fertility infomercials. I've gotten thousands recently."

Thousands? Jeez, I'm better than I thought. "Wow, fertility treatment? Maybe that's fate?"

"Nah, more like a mistake—poor marketing." He pauses, chuckles, and then adds, "Hey, wait, speaking of marketing, are you responsible?"

"Ugh, no, why do you ask? No I wouldn't, not never."

"You sure? Cuz you're doing that weird talk like you always do when you're caught."

"Weird talk, no not me, I—well—someone walked into my office."

"I hear you, but the spam is awfully coincidental."

"I didn't send spam," she says, trying to sound firm. "Are you concerned someone hacked your computer?" Taylor feigns genuine concern.

"Nah, security will handle the madness! We'll find the culprit."

"Sigh."

"Tay, fess up. You're responsible?" he asks, in a deep but light-hearted voice.

"Whit, I can't believe you'd think that about me," she retorts.

"Hope you're telling the truth because while I'm not mad at you, I'd certainly be concerned about you if you're lying. I'll send you to counseling to work on your communication skills cuz you shouldn't have to play tricks to get what you want."

"I'm an excellent communicator, and I'm not playing tricks, so why am I defending myself?"

"I don't know. I'm only asking questions."

"I'm only saying you should focus on the enemy, the person who hacked your computer!"

"I have, don't worry, the tech guy will find the culprit."

Chapter Thirty
Experimental Treatment

ALEX FILES HER "Prevent Health Care Reform At Any Cost" memo and picks up the *Livingston v. Health Solutions, Inc.* file. Recalling the case history while scanning for a motion to dismiss template on her computer database, Alex thinks about the case history. *All right, Livingston—here we go—another whiner case. This time the mom says her baby died, in utero, because we did not pay for an experimental treatment that could have saved the fetus' life. Maybe, but she'll lose this case because we do not cover experimental treatments and the law basically says we don't have to. ERISA preempts and protects us from state laws. So we win…let's go…let's defend!*

She waits. She taps her fingers. Within seconds, the template pops onto her computer screen. She types and defends. Alex quickly scrolls past the introductory paragraph, which tells the court who she is and what she's requesting.

Josephine Livingston
(a resident of the State of California)
v.
Health Solutions, Inc.
(an Arizona corporation)

MOTION TO DISMISS

Defendant, Health Solutions, Inc. hereby files this Motion to Dismiss the lawsuit filed by Josephine

Livingston against Health Solutions, Inc. for the reasons stated herein.

She makes her way to the Statement of Facts and begins to type in the facts, slanted in her client's favor. She knows the plaintiff's response will do the same; the court will be left to sort out the truth.

STATEMENT OF FACTS

Plaintiff, Josephine Livingston wrongfully filed this lawsuit in federal court seeking damages for the death of her thirty-two-week-old fetus. The Plaintiff erroneously seeks medical malpractice damages from Health Solutions, Inc., a health care administrator. The law does not permit this type of recovery. Health Solutions, Inc. is *immune* from liability under the Employee Retirement Insurance Security Act ("ERISA") because it has simply been acting as an administrator of an ERISA-governed plan, not a medical provider.

Just as she completes typing in her first paragraph, her intercom buzzes and then a voice comes through on her speakerphone.
"Come. Bring the *Livingston* file," Marshall orders.
Stopping mid-motion, she springs to her feet.
Arriving in his office in less than a minute, she enters and sees he is on the telephone yelling.
What is up? she wonders.
Studying him, she tries to discern the discourse.
He has deep frown lines.
He is screaming curse words.
He stops and listens intently to the caller, pressing the telephone close to his ear.
He's holding the telephone to his ear! He always uses speakerphone.
Looking up over his rimmed glasses and obviously seeing Alex for the first time since she entered his office, his frown lines deepen before he shouts, "Get out! Close the door!"
Here we go again! She scurries out the door and waits.

Standing on the other side of the door, she suddenly hears one word, a curse word. *What?*

"Damn!" Marshall shouts again. She can hear him yelling and shouting loud words, but words beyond damn she cannot make out.

Standing motionless, she strains to hear what is being said until his secretary interrupts.

"Make a way, make a way!" Judy Carpenter marches towards Alex, her shoulders stiff, as if she is wearing a straitjacket.

Instantly, Alex steps away from the door.

Judy Carpenter, who is tightly clasping a manila folder in her arms, knocks twice on Marshall's door and enters.

Seeing the door slam behind Judy, Alex leans her body closer to the door. She listens.

Before she can discern what is being said in Judy's presence, the door opens again, Judy tries to exit, but Alex is blocking the way. Seeing Judy, Alex quickly thinks, *Pantyhose!*

Leaning down, feigning an adjustment with her hose, Alex says, "Gosh, you've got to hate those snags!"

"Do what you must," Judy suggests, looking suspicious. She disappears as quickly as she appeared.

Does she know about the affair? I mean, would he tell?

She wonders whether this commotion is about her relationship with Marshall. *Did his wife find out? Is Judy helping us cover up? I mean...*

Stopping her thoughts in their tracks, Marshall exits his office like a bolt of lightning and says, "Come!"

Speeding past Alex as he puts on his jacket, Marshall charges to the stairs.

"Where are we going? Should I grab my jacket?" she asks, as they enter the stairwell.

"No," he snaps, without slowing his steps.

She dashes behind him, trying to keep up, rushing down the stairs.

"Come on, don't you exercise?" Marshall yells in the stairwell, now at least one flight of stairs ahead of her.

Yes, jerk! I'm wearing six-inch heels and you're not! Pulling off her shoes, she navigates her downward descent in her stocking feet. If she didn't have snags before, she would now.

Chapter Thirty-one
Infidelity

*T*AYLOR SITS IN her office, holding the telephone to her ear, listening to her husband speak.

"Tay, we're vying, trying to get Bear Stearns' business, a reorganization, merger, something's up at that investment banking firm."

Hearing him talk business, she tunes him out. She starts thinking about her fertility appointment next week.

"Tay, hello, are you there?" Whitfield asks.

"Yes, sure, sorry," she answers, reconnecting with the conversation.

"So what time?" Whit asks.

"What time what?" Taylor inquires, having missed the preamble to his question.

"When are you coming home?"

Why? Aren't you in New York? "Whit, where are you?"

"Home. Didn't you hear anything I said?"

You're home? I've got fertility stuff everywhere, even on the calendar!

"Uh, well, you're home! Hallelujah! Uh, great, I'm so glad." She tries to sound excited. "Let's go out! Leave now!" *He's got to get out of that house before he sees.*

"Tay, what's wrong? What are you hiding?"

"What? Who me? Hiding? Nothing, I'm well, work, so I have to go. Can you meet me, Jazz Light & Easy—but if you want to go, you must leave right now!"

"Why rush? Come home first. I've got something—"

"Work, I'll explain later!"

"Are you sure you're okay?"

"Yes, Whit, as long as you leave."

"Okay, I'm on my way, but you've got to explain this madness."

Grabbing her purse, she rushes to meet her husband on an impromptu date.

— ♪ —

TAYLOR WALKS INTO JAZZ Light & Easy. She searches for her husband. She wants to get a look at him first so she can get a sense of his mood. She wants to determine whether he is livid or calm. If he looks livid, she can be certain that he has discovered her scam—found some evidence that she has sent emails to his in-box to coerce him into agreeing to fertility treatment. She will also believe he found evidence in their home that shows that she paid in advance for fertility treatment against his wishes.

If he looks calm, she will know that he is unaware.

Making her way through the crowd, she hears the music change.

Scanning the place, she sees all kinds of people—the tall, short, narrow, and wide—but she does not see her husband anywhere.

Believing perhaps he hasn't arrived yet, worry seeps into her mind. *Should I go home and intervene? Explain? Say something?* Finally, she sees her husband, and her heart leaps out of her chest. Her mind instantly changes from her fertility treatment farce to the young, gorgeous, blonde woman standing close to her husband chatting. Taylor marches over to end the chat-fest.

— ♪ —

"HI HUSBAND!" TAYLOR BREAKS in between her husband and the lady he's speaking with. *Did I say husband? Girl's got to mark her territory.*

Laying his eyes on her and then smiling, Whitfield grabs his wife and hugs her tightly, encasing her body within his.

Okay, good. He's excited to see me, so he doesn't know about my sham. Nice. But who's Ms. Blondie? I've got to find out what's up with her and deal with fertility later. So Whit, are you going to introduce your friend?

Nope! The introduction does not happen.

Kissing Taylor's neck, Whitfield whispers in between kisses, words that are inaudible to anyone except Taylor. "Being away feels like eternity. Come here. I've missed you."

Who's Ms. Blondie? Taylor thinks, as the physical exchange continues. He touches her back and leads her towards a cozy booth.

Walking with her husband, Taylor looks back at *Ms. Blondie*.

Ms. Blondie looks flustered, and Taylor gives the woman a mischievous look. *That's why he's with me not with you.* She flashes her 4-carat, flawless, FFL color and clarity grade princess cut diamond ring and 2 carat eternity princess cut diamond laced wedding band directly at Ms. Blondie before she walks away.

Whitfield misses this non-verbal communication, looking straight ahead at their reserved seats directly in front of the live band.

Walking with her husband, Taylor asks, "Who is she, Whit?"

"Who?"

"The blonde woman at the bar."

"What woman?"

"You know, tall, beautiful, blonde, brown eyes—that lady."

Looking at Taylor with a puzzled expression, he pauses, thinking. Seconds later, he opens his eyes wide, as if he is overcome with realization. He chuckles and asks, "The girl standing next to me when you walked up?"

"Yes."

"Tay, I don't know her," he answers.

"Really?" She crosses her arms and frowns.

"Yes, really."

"But you were chatting. Why, about what?"

"The time," he responds, his right hand on his forehead. "Tay, sit, listen to the music."

The jazz changes. Now, a saxophone player belts out a solicitous—questioning—agitated melody.

"What?" he asks, seeing her suspicious eyes locked on him.

"What am I supposed to think? She's beautiful."

"Didn't notice."

"Come on! How could you miss her breasts? Her triple D cup implanted twins practically smacked me in the face!"

Expelling a quick laugh, Whit shakes his head and says, "Didn't notice."

"Did you see her breasts? Her cleavage was tacky, but her breasts are a nice size. Her breasts look so round and perky." Taylor forms her hands in a circular, cup-sized shape.

"And her waist—her waist is pint sized. Oh and Whit, her eyes! Her eyes are a beautiful brown, and her hair."

"Really? Tay, really, are you seriously doing this? I haven't seen you in weeks and you're ranting about some woman who asked me the time?" Whitfield clearly looks frustrated.

"Yes, because her hair is voluminous and blonde—may be fake, dyed or something, but her hair looks good, Whit. Weren't you tempted?"

"No, are you serious?"

"Did I tell you about her body? She has a perfect Coca-Cola bottle shape. Shall I go on?"

"Hey, tell me when my wife gets here. I haven't seen her in a while."

"Whit!" she exclaims, convinced she is not crazy.

"All right, seriously, all kidding aside," he says, speaking to her in a sincere tone. "Tay, I don't know that woman, I'm not interested in that woman, but if I'm judging things correctly, sounds like I should be questioning you. Do women really check each other out that much?"

"When the woman is cozying up to your man, yes!" *Well and sometimes even if she's not. We do admire each other's outfits and hairstyles and purses. We notice!*

Grabbing and caressing her hand, Whitfield says, "Enough about her. You're the only woman for me. I don't care if there are hundreds of women around, I'm yours, only!"

"I hear you, but trust is hard for me. She was close."

"Relax, enjoy the night, and trust me. I'm your husband," he says emphatically.

"I know, but—"

The music changes and now a soft, sultry jazz song begins.

Guiding her to the dance floor, he grabs hold of her eyes with his and smiles. Pulling her close to him with his arm and pressing his body against her, he flinches, as if he is surprised by the tension he can feel.

Immediately, he begins to caress her ear lobes with his lips, whispering calming words into her ear.

"Tay, trust me."

"How?" she asks.

"Know me."

"I do."

"I can't tell."

She lays her head on his shoulder and grins faintly, sheepishly, as if she knows she is wrong.

Lifting her head, looking directly into her eyes, he stands still. "Your past is your past," he says. "Don't make your past your present!"

"I know, I know, but my dad."

"Is not me."

"That's true, but—" Taylor says, uncertain.

"Trust me."

She sighs, looking into his dark brown eyes. *I trust you. What am I thinking?* She inhales a breath of relief.

Chapter Thirty-two
The Marathon Race

ALEX HURRIES, TRYING to keep up with Marshall. Watching him walk through downtown Phoenix streets so quickly that his behind actually switches, Alex tries to discern their destination, but she can't. He whisks past all the places they usually frequent—the Phoenix courthouse, local restaurants, other law firms, Health Solutions' corporate headquarters, and The Grand Hotel—without slowing his stride. Just as she breaks into a full sweat, even though the temperature is 53 degrees, Alex looks up and sees The Spot, a local, quaint jazz eatery located on the outskirts of downtown Phoenix. She smiles.

Walking behind him, preparing to enjoy quality time with him, she wonders how she looks. Deciding to make a B-line to the restroom to pull off her pantyhose because she has many snags now, she smiles and says, "I'll be right back, Marshall."

"Hurry up. We'll be seated in the back. You'll find me there," he barks, still frowning.

— ?: —

ALEX FINDS MARSHALL AT the Back of the restaurant when she returns. She begins to sit, when Marshall shouts—"Sit down!"—as if she requires instruction on how to sit.

Just as she sits, his cell phone rings.

Examining the CALLER ID, he stands, walks away, and answers the telephone. Leaning on a wall a short distance away, he stares at Alex.

You're hiding something. What? You've talked to your wife in front of me before, why not now?

Sitting, waiting, trying to busy herself, she feigns like she is people watching when really she is watching Marshall. Finally, thirty minutes later, he returns to the table.

"Order what you want," he says, distracted.

She begins studying the menu, trying to decide what she wants, when he interrupts her deliberations.

"Where's your health care reform memo?" he asks.

You made me run to a jazz spot to ask me about a memo that's in the office?

"Hand it over!" He snaps his fingers, as if she is a genie and can produce on his command.

Pulling out her blackberry, searching her calendar and confirming that her health care reform strategy memo isn't due until next week, she answers, "I have a draft, in the office, but it isn't due until next week, so what's up?"

"No, the memo's due today. Next week isn't soon enough," he says, shaking his head.

"But you—"

"Alex, stay ahead," he nearly shouts. "If I said next week, which I didn't, but if I did, you should have a draft completed and ready!" The tension is thick.

"I do—in my office!"

"Not good enough. Your work should be on you!"

On me, how? Strapped to my butt? And besides, the memo isn't due! You told me next week. You can't change the due date like that, you jerk!

"What about winning? Do you know how? Do you know how to prevent real health care reform in America?" Marshall asks, and then grits his teeth.

"Yes. Why yes, I do. I have strategies in the office!" Alex explains, clasping her hands together and placing them in the middle of the table.

"If you've got answers, shoot!"

"Antitrust, anti-competition laws, that's important—"

Marshall slams his hand down on the table. "Cut the theory. I need guarantees! You're not even close to preventing meaningful reform."

"But—" she begins, starting to defend herself, but he cuts her off again.

"You're not in the ball park! Get in the game!" His face is red, and sweat beads form on his forehead.

Wait—whoa. You're over the top. We're not seeing eye-to-eye. There's clearly a disconnect somewhere. Your response does not match the rules of any game I know. Her anxiety grows, but she keeps her angst under control and responds. "I have a winning strategy."

Running his hand through his receding hairline, he says, "Honey, you won't get results. You can't stop the liberal machine with theory. You've got to focus on inside guarantees."

I'm not your honey! An image of his wife and kids pops into her head. Her angst mounts as he questions her effectiveness.

Interrupting, the waitress approaches and asks, "May I take your orders?"

"Burger and fries," he says.

Hurriedly scanning the menu, Alex tries to choose, but she is constantly interrupted by her boss' loud, impatient sighs. As her anger mounts, she quickly orders, "Vodka, straight up, no ice, seven limes, and a salad!"

Smirking, Marshall places his hand over hers. "Honey, focus, and you'll get ahead," he says in a patronizing tone of voice.

I'm not your honey, and I feel pretty focused, thank you very much, you jerk!

Chapter Thirty-three
Beaming Light

TAYLOR BELIEVES HER husband. *He's not interested in Ms. Blondie.* With her mind at ease, she turns her attention back to babies. *How will I convince Whit?*

"Tay, this beat is hot!" Whitfield proclaims, bobbing his head to the music. He is obviously enjoying the night and clearly oblivious to her scheming thoughts.

"What why yes, sure, hot," Taylor answers, feigning pleasure while her stomach knots. It feels like a rock has been dropped into the pit of her stomach.

Changing tunes, the music turns from smooth and easy to chaotic and choppy.

"Sounds different."

"What?" Taylor asks. Her mind is elsewhere.

"Unique even."

"Yes, sure." She nods her head in pace with the music but thinks, *I'm lost.*

"Smooth and easy," he says.

"But chaotic," she adds. *Like the story of my personal life.*

"Exactly, but rhythmic," he continues.

"Inconsistent." *Which is how I feel.*

"This sound—" he begins, but trails off.

"Captures the times?" she asks.

"Yes, exactly."

"Yeah, the music sounds like melodies sifting in sand; the musical notes are drifting, drowning in dust."

Be pop be du bop de be pop de du…

She says nothing more.

– 9 –

HOURS LATER, TAYLOR RUSHES into their home. She tries to find and hide the fertility treatment evidence before Whitfield enters. Sprinting, she picks up the marketing memo, the fertility treatment post-it notes, and the calendar with the appointment date listed. She shreds each item. Once done, she closes her eyes, rolls her neck, and inhales deeply.

Turning, preparing to walk downstairs and fake like everything is normal, she jumps, seeing Whitfield standing in the door, smiling.

"Why're you startled?" he calmly asks.

"Who me? What, me? I'm not startled." It might be hard to pull off this lie since she'd nearly jumped out of her skin when she saw him.

Chuckling, as if he doesn't believe her or thinks she is being hormonal, which is what he always thinks when he feels he does not understand her, he changes the subject. "Let's hop in the Jacuzzi."

His words peel away layers of anxiety. She knows he doesn't know, and so she is relieved. "Awe, the Jacuzzi, perfect—but outside?"

"Absolutely. Did you see the sky? Tay, the stars are aligned."

"Yes, but there's a slight chill," she says, moving closer to him so she can nestle against his broad chest.

"I'll keep you warm," he answers, pulling her close.

"I guess," she reluctantly agrees with a smile. She turns, grabs a towel, and turns back. Whitfield is gone. *Is he undressing outside?*

Walking outside with a towel around her body, she sees Whitfield get inside the Jacuzzi naked.

"Whit?"

"What, come." He extends his hand to her.

She slips into the outdoor Jacuzzi and slides close to him.

Remotely turning on the outdoor sound system with the press of a button, he watches her.

Looking into his dark brown—loving eyes—she is relieved. He knows nothing. She breathes easily.

He slips closer to her. He kisses her lips and then her neck, and then he slips underwater and physically adores her body. Rustling waters gyrate in motion with Whitfield as he caresses his wife. Meanwhile, heaven and earth move as the pair mate.

Hours later, as the sky opens and the sun peaks through, prayers are answered and blessings begin to take form.

Chapter Thirty-four
Snow In Phoenix

HEARING THE DOORBELL ring, Reagan rushes to her front door. She looks out her glass-stained window and smiles, but then frowns. She smiles because the Rays are on her front porch. She frowns because Taylor Ray looks terribly ill. Swiftly opening the door, Reagan says, "Come in you two, but Taylor, I have to ask, are you okay? You don't look well."

"I've, well, I'm dragging, feeling down," Taylor answers, entering the foyer.

"Are you sick?" Reagan asks, touching her forehead.

"Nah, she's been busy, enjoying—" Whitfield begins, but Alex cuts him off.

"Hello!" Alex enters, walking through the huddled crowd in the foyer entrance. She walks straight towards the kitchen toting gifts—Merlot, eight bottles.

Alex pops the wine cork and asks a question. "Who is he?"

"Who's who?" Reagan asks, looking innocent.

"I see everything's extra nice, and you have an extra plate setting, so that means you're match-making tonight. Who is he? Don't let him be a church-guy."

"No, she invited Calvin, my college roommate," Jackson answers, standing in the kitchen.

"How's his dough?" Alex asks, rubbing her fingers together.

"He's a doc," Jackson answers. He grabs a nut and pops it in his mouth. He tries to swallow the nut but stops. He pulls his fist to his mouth mid-stop. He tries again, slowly.

Seeing the trouble Jackson is having with the nut, Reagan asks, "Are you okay?" She walks over to him and rubs his back.

"Yeah, fine." He coughs a little and then swallows the nut.

"Your date guy, he's not a holy roller like you . . . " Alex begins, but trails off.

"He's great, but, I'm reluctant to make this match, you'll—"

"Stop the presses! Who's that?" Alex says, looking out the window at the man approaching. "If that's who you're talking about, I'm game. I'll even go to church with him!"

"Where've you been hiding him?" Alex whispers to Reagan as the man enters the house. He's tall, handsome, and his body—wow wow wow. Muscular and strong! I like, I like! What a man. What a man!" She raises her eyebrows and her chin.

"Good evening," Calvin says, as he walks towards the ladies. He smells like scents of chestnuts and cedar.

Reagan looks at Alex and sees that she is inhaling deeply. *Can I give you a biscuit? You're sopping him up with your eyes! Stop!*

— 9: —

ALEX ABRUPTLY STEPS OVER Reagan and introduces herself. "Alexandria Giroud." She points her cheek at him, welcoming a kiss.

"Calvin Reed." He rejects her cheek and instead, greets her with a handshake.

I'll have you kissing me soon enough, you scrumptious man.

"Slow down! He's old-school," Reagan whispers into Alex's ear, while Jackson rescues Calvin, placing his arm around his shoulder and whisking him away.

"Calm down. Go slowly. You'll have your chance."

"When?"

"Now," Reagan says softly, and then loudly announces, "Let's sit and eat. Your name cards are on the table."

"Reagan!" Jackson looks up in disbelief. "No name tags."

"I made special sparkly name tags tonight, come on," she replies. He obliges her.

Alex appreciates the fact that her name tag seats her next to Calvin. This gives her plenty of opportunity to marvel at Calvin's caramel skin and hazel eyes. *He's a delicious, eatable man!*

Wanting to break the silence, Alex thinks, *I'll go straight to common ground,* and so she asks, "Calvin, are you a Republican?"

"Rolls anyone?" Reagan says, frowning.

"No, thank you," Calvin responds, and then answers Alex. "Actually yes, I'm a registered Republican, but undecided this year."

"You're a doctor, aren't you? Don't you want tort reform?" Alex asks.

"Yes, but I want health care reform, too."

Shrieking inside, Alex says, "Reform? Are you a Republican socialist?"

"What's socialism got to do with reform?" Taylor chimes in.

"Health care reform is socialism," Alex answers.

Dropping his fork and placing both hands on the table, Calvin laughs. "You're hilarious," he says. "Are you a comedian?"

Is that a compliment, or should I be defending myself?

"I won't indulge you in an asinine debate about socialism," Calvin adds. "No plan I've heard lately is socialist. Sounds like you're against reform, so I'll ask you, why are you anti-reform?"

I'm defending myself. "America has the best health care system in the world."

"Do you have any scientific knowledge, meaning actual data, supporting your view?" Calvin asks.

Whitfield belts out a loud laugh, but then catches himself.

Why is he defining scientific data for me, as if I don't know? "Yes, I'm a lawyer. A health care HMO lawyer."

"Awe, there's the rub. You're conflicted. Well, I'm a physician, and HMOs are the problem."

Jackson pulls a tape recorder out of his pocket, presses play, and begins recording the conversation.

"Jackson!" Reagan slaps his hand.

"This is good material, continue, please." Jackson nods at Alex.

"Anyway, your friend, he's exaggerating. HMOs cut costs," Alex explains.

"No, HMOs cut *care*," Calvin responds.

"Yes, absolutely, unnecessary care," Alex says, confident.

"Who defines what's necessary?" Calvin asks.

"Health care professionals—" Alex begins, but Calvin cuts her off.

"Health care professionals my blue cheese!"

Taylor snorts.

Did he say blue cheese—my blue cheese instead of—

"Ms. Alex, unlicensed insurance clerks second-guess my medical decisions."

"Good, so HMOs use cheap labor."

"Not good, when the cheap, untrained labor is making medical decisions."

Jackson coughs and then fixes his eyes back on the repartee. His eyes dart between Calvin and Alex, watching the banter like a tennis match.

"HMOs keep costs down. Somebody has to second-guess doctors."

"Insurance clerks aren't qualified to second-guess my decisions."

"Well, they're second-guessing your decisions."

"And, that's the problem. Insurance clerks are opining about whether a patient needs brain surgery or cancer treatment or dialysis—so indulge me and explain to me, how?"

I'd love to indulge you all right, in other ways! "Actually, computers Calvin, that's how. We're in the information age."

Dropping his fork, either for emphasis or out of shock, he says, "You're suggesting computers can perform open heart surgery?"

"Yes, besides, why do you care? You can still make lots of money, that is, if you tweak your medical practice to get around HMO gatekeepers. You have changed your business model, haven't you? You do volume-practice?"

"No, and I'm not," he says, shaking his head.

"Don't you want to make money?"

"Not by playing word games and tweaking business models."

"Don't tell me you're one of those broke ethical doctors." *Cause if so, I'm going to work on your cash flow before we get together!*

"How about butter? Anyone want butter with your rolls?" Reagan asks.

"We don't have rolls," Alex shouts before continuing. "So, like I was saying, you know how to make money, don't you?"

"Again, I won't play games. I'll invent a product or medical device before I stoop to that level. I didn't become a physician to play games!"

You're frustrated. Can I replace some of your lost pleasure with sexual pleasure? "Look, Dr. Calvin, call my office, we'll consult your practice into order."

"I've already elucidated. I don't play games."

"How about dessert? Does anyone want dessert?" Reagan asks.

"No!" Alex nearly shouts.

"No, thank you," Calvin answers.

"Why do you say gamesmanship?" Alex asks.

"Isn't the truth obvious to you? HMOs are destroying medicine in America."

"You're exaggerating."

"No," he says. "Consider momentarily, last week, I billed an HMO $325.00 for a necessary routine procedure."

"Sounds reasonable—"

"The HMO paid me $12.00," Calvin says, slamming his hand on the table. "Quite frankly, I can't stay in business when I get paid $12.00 instead of $325.00."

"Wow, man, that's a problem!" Whitfield says.

"Yep, because he needs to tweak his practice, increase his volume," Alex explains.

"How about muffins, more steak?" Reagan asks, looking nervous.

"No, you guys keep eating, we're fine!" Alex says, seeing that everyone has almost completed their meals except for Jackson, who is barely eating his steak.

Continuing, Calvin says, "I won't volume practice because I'm a physician, not a fast food restaurant."

"Your point?"

"Your volume medical practice model turns medicine into a fast food assembly line; seeing ten to fifteen patients in thirty minutes to an hour, that's preposterous."

"Be efficient. That's the name of the game."

"I can't thoroughly see ten to fifteen patients in thirty minutes to an hour. Something or someone will slip through the cracks."

Get in the game! "Someone had to stop the spiraling health care costs."

"HMOs aren't the answer, and I agree that costs may be too high. I'll submit to you, however, that costs are high because we have layers of second-guessing and administrative bureaucracy!"

"No," Alex says, shaking her head. "Costs got out of hand. People were overusing insurance. Doctors were over-treating patients!"

"So what's your answer? Shift funds to administrative second-guessing rather than medical care?"

"Yep!"

"Rather than paying physicians, you'd rather pay a bureaucratic, second-layer, unqualified second-guesser to second-guess a physician's decisions?"

"Yes. We need accountability, and hiring low-level insurance clerks is less expensive. Besides, like I said, there are checks and balances to help the insurance clerk do their jobs, like computers."

"Unnecessary trickery. Speaking of which, aren't you against bureaucracy?"

"No, I'm not against HMO bureaucracies; someone has to stop the corruption." *And I make my money as part of the bureaucracy, so no, absolutely not!*

"Salad, milkshake, rolls?" Reagan asks, getting up. She shoots Alex a fierce look.

"I resent your comment. I don't over-treat patients! I'm a professional, and I worked hard to get where I am."

"I didn't say you didn't, but we need accountability."

"Administrative bureaucrats aren't the answer. HMOs increase costs. Consider a common scenario I see. My patients pay insurance premiums monthly, some as much as $750 per month."

"Good, they're carrying their weight."

"Yeah, but when they come to see me, the insurance company usually denies their claim."

"You're recommending unnecessary treatment or experimental treatment, that's why HMOs deny coverage," Alex explains.

"No, I'm using my medical expertise to recommend necessary, essential treatment to my patients, but the HMO steps in the way many times and prevents the treatment all while pocketing the premiums and leaving the bill with my patient!"

"Well, if what you're saying is true, then obviously you've violated some rule. Maybe your patient didn't call in advance to get the HMO's approval, or something happened, but you can't blame the HMO. Rules exist for a reason!"

"Absolutely, and so that's why I may change my vote this year. I'll vote for the person who'll change the rules."

"How about poker? Anyone want to play games?"

"No, I want to settle this health care thing first," Alex says.

"You guys can play," Calvin adds.

Taylor gets up and walks to the card table.

Whitfield and Jackson do the same.

Reagan leaves, too, but not before asking again, "Are you sure you don't want to do or talk about something, *anything* else?"

"We're fine," Calvin answers, and then immediately charges back in. "What do you think about uninsured Americans? Don't you think we should insure *all* Americans?"

"Nope—any uninsured person should go and get a job."

"What about employed people who don't have health insurance benefits at work?"

"Get a job with benefits! I shouldn't have to pay for the health coverage of others."

"You're already paying for uninsured Americans with your insurance premiums and health care costs. That's why we need reform," Calvin proclaims.

"I know, I understand, but we should limit that, too."

"How? Let people die in the streets?"

"If they're broke, why not?"

"Alex, America, we're a civilized country, we don't turn patients away, and when we treat patients who can't pay, we have to increase your next bill to cover the bill the other patient couldn't afford to pay."

"Well, that should be illegal."

"It's not. All businesses shift costs somehow. Don't you believe in the free market?"

"Yes, but health care costs shouldn't be shifted; people must work and get insurance."

"What if a person loses their job?"

"COBRA, that's the answer. A person can chose to take his coverage with him," Alex answers.

"What if the employer has fifteen or fewer employees? COBRA doesn't apply to small businesses," Calvin fires back.

"Not a good job. What should you expect?"

"Alex, many people work for small businesses—that's the backbone of our economy."

"Look Calvin, government can't solve problems."

"What's your solution?"

"We the people, everyday people."

"How?"

"Community organizations, churches, synagogues, and leaders can come together to help those less fortunate."

"That's your solution?" Calvin asks, laughing out loud.

"Yes, sure of course, and private enterprise works."

"Alex, profit maximization and a healthy populous do not necessarily mix."

"Okay, I've got to laugh at that one because profits aren't bad," Alex says. "You have many different options when buying coverage."

"You're fanatical," he says, sneering. "When's the last time you negotiated your medical insurance contract?"

"I—"

"Never!" he says.

"I wouldn't say never." *My employer does the negotiating for me, I think?*

"I'm almost certain the answer is never. That's the name of the game. Everyone thinks someone else is doing the negotiating for them, when really employers, physicians, business owners—we're out there asking questions. How can we maintain these benefits because the costs are spiraling out of control and the quality of care is falling?"

"If the quality of care is falling, that's on you, the physician."

"Again, I beg to differ. See Ms. Alex, Esq., the quality of care is falling because we're stuck in a box. Again, we must volume practice to make money. That's the HMO model, not ours. You can't volume practice and provide quality care."

"You don't have to do business with HMOs," Alex says.

"What's the alternative? Are you suggesting I should only accept patients who can pay cash in advance? When's the last time you did that?" he asks, again with a smirk.

"I have great insurance, but if—"

"You haven't. That's what I thought."

"If you'll allow me to complete my sentence, you'd know."

Cutting her off again, he says, "I'd know what? I'd know you have no leverage? I'd know you can't cross state lines to buy insurance? I'd know the market's locked up?"

No, not what I had in mind to say. Don't get so testy.

Pausing, he leans back in his seat before saying, "Sitting where I do, I know, HMOs and insurance companies have absolute monopolies. There's no competition—a mess which the government helped create with the antitrust exemption!"

Insurance companies lobbied for the exemption, speaking of lobbying, "Wasn't the American Medical Association at the table when the law was passed?"

"Obviously those American Medical Association representatives made mistakes. The HMO volume cost cutting method does not work. With the current model, there's no incentive to enter the medical profession. And to this, I say the future is bleak if physicians have no incentive either altruistic or financial to enter the profession."

"How can you say there's no incentive?"

"As I said earlier, the altruistic reasons fade when you must volume practice to make money; and the financial reasons are also waning because I have to play games to get paid."

I can't believe I'm saying this but— "Calvin, if you don't like the laws, contact your congressional representative, write letters, contact the AMA, lobby, make sure your voice is heard. Have you done anything?" Alex shrugs. She already knows the answer to this question.

"No, I'm too busy seeing patients every two minutes."

"Then you can't expect change," Alex says.

"I can *vote* change," he says firmly. "That's why this year, there may be a different party on the ballot."

— ♪ —

"I can see y'all are getting," Jackson pauses to cough, "temperamental. Who knew health care reform could stimulate such fiery debate? We'll need to add a segment to the website," he suggests, as he sits down again at the dining room table.

Taylor, Whitfield, and Reagan join in, too.

"Change the subject, please!" Reagan demands.

"No, I'm interested in your friend's misguided views," Calvin says, shaking his head.

Raising her voice, Taylor shouts, "Snowflakes!"

"What?"

"Snowflakes! It's snowing!"

"I realized that the temperature had fallen, but snow in Phoenix?" Calvin asks.

"Wasn't it seventy degrees this morning?" Whitfield asks.

"Yep, and now, what, it's snowing?" Alex asks.

"I can't believe the sudden change," Reagan says, smiling.

"And I'm supposed to go to D.C. next week. Hope the snow clears," Alex says.

Silence falls between them. All stare in awe. The soft, white snow changes the mood, creating tranquility and amazement at once.

— ♪ —

Snowflakes fall, sifting softly through cold night air, silently settling on dry desert sand, street-cars, cacti, trees, and the tiny window sill of the Hamilton home. In one day, nature changes.

Just this morning, the palm trees were swaying in a warm, 70-degree breeze. The cacti were safely sleeping in dry, desert conditions. The trees were thirsty, almost dead, in a coma-like condition.

Yet, now the sky has opened up and blanketed the dry-desert earth with snow. The palm trees shiver, the cacti seek cover, and the trees open their mouths wide to drink the fluffy snow.

A tiny snowflake twirls through the night air. It twinkles. It sparkles. It reflects bright shades of light until it finally rests on the Hamilton's window sill.

The snowflake peaks inside the Hamilton home and sighs.

He, the snowflake, an agent of nature and actor in her powerful variety, knows the friends inside do not realize that there is a parallel between the snowfall and the changes in their lives. The friends do not know that this beautiful, white, earth-covering sudden snowfall, in a place where it does not snow, is a prelude to the storm coming ahead.

The snowflake yells, "Prepare!" but the friends do not hear.

Chapter Thirty-five
Lobby It?

WEEKS AFTER HER, "If you focus, honey, you'll get it," meeting with Marshall, Alex rushes to her car and dashes off to the airport to catch a flight to Washington, D.C.

Just as she switches lanes to enter the freeway, her telephone rings.

Pressing the bluetooth already attached to her left ear, she answers, "Alex Giroud."

"Hold the plane!" Marshall yells.

Hold the plane? How do you hold a plane? They're both traveling on a commercial jet—not a chartered plane that comes and goes at the travelers' leisure.

"Okay . . . but how late are you?" she asks, as she moves from the far right lane to the left, adjusting her vehicle with the winding road.

She hears the dial tone.

Did he hang up the phone?

"Okay," she mumbles again. *He lives at least forty-five minutes away. How am I supposed to hold the plane?*

Accelerating, she charges ahead. *Guess I'll find out shortly. I'll improvise.*

Arriving in no time, Alex parks, leaps out of her car, and darts onto the elevator of the parking garage.

Going straight to the security line with her boarding pass in hand, she totes her rolling, carry-on suitcase, matching purse, and briefcase, all *Designer Couture*.

Standing at the end of the long security line waiting, her eyes are busy, searching, bouncing. *Where is he?*

As she approaches the security guard, he extends his hands out towards her and says, "ID and boarding pass."

Alex hands over her identification and boarding pass and then looks back behind her again. *Come on, Marshall, where are you?* She turns back to the security guard and wonders, *Why are you taking so long? Can't you read?*

Examining her documents thoroughly, he then meticulously examines her, back and forth, and back and forth. "Did you forget something?" he asks, with another suspicious look.

"No why?" she asks, confused.

"Did you lose something?"

"No, why?"

"Because you're fidgety."

Oh, I get it! She lifts her eyebrows and smiles. "No, no concerns, no problem. I'm waiting on someone!"

The security guard nods and then looks at her identification again, this time with a flashlight. He eyes her once more and then precisely instructs, "Proceed to LANE 3."

Grabbing her bags and strolling to LANE 3, Alex comes to an abrupt halt when she sees the lane. She stands still, shaking her head from left to right. She inhales deeply, comprehending that LANE 3 is the line for a full body security search. *Yikes!*

Deciding persuasion won't change things with airport security, she readies herself for the search.

"Bertha, female search!" Alex hears a male guard yell.

Within seconds, Bertha appears. She walks from behind a closed off vault-looking room. The woman approaches, glaring at her, all while placing white gloves on her hands.

Alex tenses. "Oh no. What is she going to do with those gloves, and why?"

Bertha grins, an evil grin. It's clear that she takes great pleasure in the power her job gives her, to search the ins and outs of people, going within their comfort zone.

"Walk ahead, this way!" Bertha demands, directing Alex to follow her back to the security search area.

Sighing, constitutional law dances through her head. *What are the triggers for body cavity searches? Surely I've set off none!*

Chapter Thirty-six
Daily Routine

"Gee, who needs fertility treatment?" Whitfield asks, rolling off his wife, on his way to fulfilling his promise to have sex seven times a day.

Cringing, knowing that her fertility treatment date is around the corner, Taylor decides she must tell her husband somehow.

Deciding to gently ease into the discussion with her husband, she turns on his favorite song and gets on top of him.

Whispering into his ear, she says, "We can try both ways."

"Nah, seven times a day is a-okay," he answers, running his fingers through her hair.

"Whit," she begins, but stops to whisper Johnnie Gill's *My – My – My* in his ear in between her pleas. "Shouldn't we try both?"

"Both what? More positions?"

"No, not positions."

"Then what?"

"Fertility treatments," she whispers, nibbling on his ears.

Obviously struggling to resist her, he turns off the lights, figuratively speaking, as soon as he hears the word fertility. He focuses on the discussion without distraction.

He gets up and puts on his robe, then moves to sit in the oversized lounge chair in their master bedroom. "Tay," he says, "I thought we agreed?"

"About what?" she asks, now playing dumb.

"No treatments."

"Well, but Whit, we got in."

"We don't need treatments."

"I think we do. Hear me out."

"I'll listen to your medical evidence only."

Taylor tries to convince Whitfield. She pulls up every website she knows about to show how their situation is similar to that of many other couples.

Whitfield considers her evidence, but returns to the tests from three fertility specialists and physicians who all opine that there is no medical reason why the Ray's haven't conceived.

— ♪ —

AFTER LISTENING TO HER reasons, Whitfield firmly and unequivocally ends the fertility discussion.

"Have you told me every possible reason?"

"Yes, sure, certainly," she answers, fiercely nodding her head. But she has not told him the one primary reason; she has not told Whitfield that she has already scheduled and paid for the fertility treatment.

"My position's the same."

Gulping sparkling champagne left over from the night before, Taylor is speechless.

"Tay, trust me; we don't need the procedure."

"So many couples like us have kids because of fertility treatments!"

"I know and I agree. Some people *do* need medical intervention, but we don't."

"But Whit, so many couples—"

"I understand. There are amazing options, but countless docs have told us we don't need treatment. I'm not letting you go through another procedure because you've given up. Relax."

I'm in trouble! She knows Whitfield has made up his mind. *What am I going to do? I've already paid, and besides, I really want the treatment.*

She sighs, pondering her next steps while he bobs his head to the music and walks towards her, taking off his robe.

Seeing his body, she realizes just like that, he is fully ready to begin his baby making method for the fifth time this morning—and the day is only beginning.

How?

Chapter Thirty-seven
Commercial Planes Don't Wait!

ALEX BREAKS AWAY from Bertha, the airport screener, feeling off-balance. Inhaling deeply, her lungs fill. She rants internally about how the screener treated her like a criminal until she looks at a reflection of herself in an airport window. She sighs because she looks untidy. Her shirt is un-tucked, her hair is frazzled, her make-up is smudged, and her clothes are hanging out of her designer luggage. Alex refocuses. She immediately begins to readjust her hair, clothes, make-up, and then her luggage.

Feeling put-together again, she dashes ahead but stops and grabs two cups of coffee first. She decides to order the coffee of the day instead of the usual latte. She knows she needs to rush ahead to hold the plane! She has no time to wait for her latte today.

Moments later, coffee in hand, she darts to her gate.

Scurrying to the gate, she balances two coffee cups, her *Designer Couture* purse, and her luggage. She tries to avoid spilling coffee on her grey designer pant suit.

Approaching her gate, she hears an announcement and hastens her steps.

"Final boarding call, Washington, D.C. Flight 286. If you are ticketed on this flight, please proceed to the gate entry."

"Wait, here's my boarding pass," Alex says, rushing ahead. Recalling that she must hold the plane, she searches the flight attendant's nametag and says, "Ms. Carmen, is the flight delayed?"

"No, we're closing the doors," Carmen answers.

No! Marshall. "You can't! There's another passenger. He's not here yet. Can you hold the plane a few minutes?"

"Let me check." Carmen scans the computer monitor.

Good, maybe she's halting the plane electronically.

After typing on her computer and scanning the monitor, Carmen says, "I'm not finding any delays. Can you help? Which red-eye did he take last night?"

"Red what?" Alex asks.

"Red-eye, also known as an overnight flight. I can check and find his flight. If the flight is here already, we can wait."

Alex exhales noisily and says, "Oh, no! You're misunderstanding. We're attorneys, not red-eye flyers!"

Instantly, Carmen stops typing. "What's your professional status have to do with delayed flights?"

"We're attorneys, officers of the court."

"Good, but help me out. I don't understand," Carmen says, appearing annoyed.

"You must hold the plane because we're lawyers. My partner, he's a lawyer, and he's a bit late," Alex explains.

"Again, I don't understand, we can't—"

"You must, see, Congress is expecting us."

Dropping her jaw for a second, stepping outside her professional stance before lifting her jaw back up, clearly remembering her customer service training, Carmen looks at Alex's boarding pass and says, "Ms. Giroud, you're flying a commercial plane. Next time, consider a private jet. Commercial planes don't wait."

"You were going to hold the plane for red-eye people, weren't you?" Alex asks.

"Yes, maybe, that's different," Carmen says.

"You hold the plane for weather, don't you?" Alex asks.

"Ms. Giroud, I'm not debating. We don't hold planes for late passengers."

"Can't you make an exception? We're talking Congress."

"Ms. Giroud, please board the plane or you'll miss the flight."

"But I can't."

"I'm closing the doors," Carmen says, walking towards the gate entry, releasing the hold on the door.

"Fine, but our country's future hangs on your shoulders," Alex adds, trying to find any way to appeal to Ms. Carmen. *Maybe she's patriotic!* Alex hopes she will fall for the flat out lie.

"I'll take my chances," Carmen says, smirking.

Responding in kind, Alex smirks, lowers her head, grabs her luggage, and boards the plane.

– 9: –

ON BOARD, ALEX FEELS anxious. Looking at her ticket, and seeing her seat is 4A, she thinks, *At least I got upgraded to first class, but now I don't know what to do about Marshall.*

Stepping on towards her seat, she considers what more she might be able to do to hold the plane. *Can I do something last minute without getting arrested? Maybe play like I'm having a heart attack?* She strategizes until she looks and sees Marshall, reclining in Seat 4B, relaxing! She drops her bags.

He sees her and sits up, coffee in hand. "Why are you late?" he asks.

I was trying to hold the plane for you!

"Alex, I'm telling you, focus, you can get ahead!"

Jerk! "Marshall, I wasn't late, I was—"

"We've been waiting, get organized!" he tells her, shaking his head.

She begins to put her bag in the overhead compartment above their row when he leaps out of his seat and shouts, "You can't use that overhead compartment!"

"But there's space," Alex exclaims, feeling frustrated, opening the overhead compartment and seeing that it's nearly empty. *You've only got one bag overhead—your briefcase.*

"Yeah, dude, what's your gripe? The overhead's empty!" a hippy artist type says, standing up for Alex.

"Mind your business and shut up," Marshall snaps back.

Other first class passengers begin to mumble while others break out into laughter.

Deciding to give in, she puts her luggage above another overhead and begins to sit when she realizes he is already sitting! As she climbs over him to get to her seat, he says, "I thought I was going to have to hold the plane for you."

You jerk! I can't—

"Here's your latte, but your foamed milk is flat, and your coffee is cold."

"Thanks," she answers with a smirk, until suddenly Carmen, the flight attendant, approaches. Seeing the flight attendant, Alex sinks into her seat.

"Ms. Giroud, everything okay?" Carmen asks.

She's not going to bring up the hold the plane incident, Alex surmises, assuming Carmen understands her blunder. *She knows I was trying to hold a plane for a jerk who was already on the plane relaxing!*

Alex concludes that Carmen will keep the silly ordeal a secret because she doesn't want to embarrass her. She agrees to an unspoken sisterly bond even in a state of discord.

"I'm fine," Alex answers, appreciating the union between strangers but unable to avoid the *awkwardness* of the ordeal.

Handing the two unnecessary coffees of the day to Carmen, given his purchase of the preferred latte, Alex says, "*Thank you!*"

Alex rarely genuinely thanks those she perceives as help, but she does this time. "I really appreciate *everything!*"

"Not a problem," Carmen answers back, with a smile that says she understands.

Watching Carmen walk away, Alex stands, gets her memo out of her briefcase, and begins to sit, placing the memo in her seat pocket.

"Not there!" Marshall yells, closing the seat pocket in front of her seat.

Why? You don't own my seat pocket!

"I'm using both seat pockets!" he adds, pointing to two large manila folders, one in her seat pocket and the other one in his seat pocket.

"We can share, can't we? My paperwork can fit, too!"

"No!" he answers, frowning. "We don't need to talk about your work."

Why did you have me staying up late last night, all night, trying to finish this work?

Rather than speaking her mind, she asks, "What about the PowerPoint? Won't I present the slides and graphics?"

"Relax, Alex," he says. "There'll be time later."

Sighing and adjusting her hair, she places her memo under her seat and turns to her latte. Beginning to open a calorie-less sweetener, she pauses when she hears Marshall say, "I've already added sugar."

"What?"

"Your coffee is already sweet. I know what you like." He grins mischievously.

Feeling awkward and trapped, as if she is in a two-way dance where he controls all the moves, she sighs.

Leaning forward, he gazes directly into her eyes and adds, "What, that's what you like, correct?"

"Yes, but—" she awkwardly begins.

"Thought so," he says, and runs his hand across his receding hairline before sitting back and closing his eyes.

— ♪ —

ONE HOUR LATER, ALEX watches Marshall sleeping calmly. *What do I see in him?* she wonders.

Almost on cue, he opens his eyes and smiles at her.

"Are you tired?" she asks him, looking into his eyes.

"Who me? No. I was thinking, not sleeping. This is business."

Liar, you were snoring.

"Check into the hotel first, for both of us. I'm heading straight to Capitol Hill."

"Okay, and after I check in, where'll we meet?"

"We won't until 8:00 p.m."

At night? "Wait, I'm not presenting my findings?"

"I'm taking the lead. Don't worry about anything!"

"Okay, but what's my role?" *This is business; I must make my mark. We're in D.C. I can't be seen as his insignificant counterpart.*

"You have a role all right." He chuckles.

Hearing his words, she wants to crawl into a fetal position. Her heart sinks. "Shouldn't I present, too?"

"No, you'll take care of our hotel suite, manage the accommodations."

Crossing her legs, barely able to conceal her anger, she says, "We're sharing? That's presumptuous."

"What?" he asks, grinning. "I'm in if I want to be!" He winks at her.

— 9 —

MARSHALL WATCHES ALEX CLOSELY and senses doubt filling her mind. Knowing the game, he decides to say enough to put her relationship angst at bay.

"You're important to me, Alex, you understand?" He places his hand on her hand and rubs softly.

"I'm busy. Lots of pressure. You get that?" He tries to sound sincere.

"Give me time, that's all I need." He watches her closely, continuing to throw out one-liner hooks until he sees a slight smile tug at the right corner of her mouth.

Seeing she has taken the bait, he reels her in.

Chapter Thirty-eight
Red-Eyes

Taylor sits in bed watching Whitfield nap. She marvels at how he can fly on a red-eye, travel around the world, consult about lay-offs, mergers, reorganizations and poison pills, and then come home and make love so intently—seven times a day, in fact.

Staring at him, she catches a glimpse of her wall clock in her peripheral vision. Seeing the time, 9:15 a.m., she calls her assistant, Joseph, and says, "I'll be late—mid-day—hold my calls. Bye."

"I know what you're doing," Joseph teases.

"Bye Joseph."

"Hubby must be home. You always disappear when he—"

"Bye!" She hangs up the telephone, shaking her head. *He's so nosey! But he's right.*

Snuggling close to Whitfield, Taylor feels dwarfed next to his body.

She tries to relax, but she can't. *I want the fertility treatment, but he said no!*

My appointment is in one week. I've paid already. What am I going to do?

Cancel! She hears her good friend Reagan pop into her head and say.

I can't cancel; I've paid! she answers.

Cancel, or you'll destroy your marriage, Reagan says.

Stop with the judgment! Taylor shoos thoughts of her friend out of her head.

Thinking of her husband, she knows Reagan is correct. *What was I thinking?*

You weren't, she hears her friend say again.

– 9 –

SHE MULLS OVER WHAT to do for hours, unable to rest, unable to relax, until finally, after thinking, she decides to call the clinic and cancel. *Surely they'll accommodate and maybe even give me a refund if someone else takes my place.*

The sound of the telephone ringing interrupts her thoughts.

She answers, trying not to wake Whitfield. "Taylor Ray."

"Ms. Ray, this is Mike Right, Debt Collections. This call is monitored for quality assurance."

Taylor's shoulders drop. She is in shock. *A debt collector again? I thought I got rid of that menacing debt collector weeks ago! I left her a message, told her we've made our payments on time each month! So… who's calling now! And no, can't tell Whit.*

She fidgets as she listens to the debt collector, then notices that Whitfield is awake. He is sitting up in the bed staring at her.

Seeing the look on her face, he says, "Tay, what's wrong? Whose calling?"

Chapter Thirty-nine
Government as Usual

*A*LEX IS STRETCHED out on the hotel bed staring out of the windows into a dark, gray sky. Rain pours down, thunder roars, lightning illuminates continuously—each exchanging sound with one another, creating music. Even though she is inside, she feels drenched, saturated, and caught in a thick and slimy web. She knows her POWER, LEVERAGE, CONTROL strategy is not working. Marshall is lobbying on Capitol Hill, and she is in the presidential hotel suite *waiting*!

What's wrong with this picture? She sinks until suddenly fearful thoughts pop into her head. She is sharing a hotel suite with her boss. Judy Carpenter will undoubtedly see the bill. She realizes her secret could get out into the office rumor mill if Judy Carpenter sees the bill. *What can I do? I've got to stay out of the office rumor mill, which starts with this hotel bill.*

Picking up the telephone—*Can't let the bill tell the story*—Alex dials Guest Services and waits.

"Good afternoon, Mrs. Hanes. How may we be of service?"

Mrs. Hanes? I'm not Mrs. Hanes, but I can play like I am so... "Yes, we require separate bills? Can you split the charges in half?"

"Mrs. Hanes, I apologize, but I don't understand. Do you want us to check you and your husband out each night and give you daily bills?"

"No, see, I'm, we're, well, we require split bills. Cut the bill in half—two bills. That's what we need."

"I'm not following you."

"You know how people go out and split the check in restaurants? We need to split the check for this suite."

Gasping, as if this is something unheard of, the attendant says, "Mrs. Hanes, I apologize, but we're a five star hotel."

Okay, I'll be blunt! I'm not Mrs. freaking Hanes, and I need my own bill! "My name is Ms. Giroud, and I need my own bill!" *So handle it. This is D.C. I'm sure you're used to scandal!*

"Oh," the attendant blurts out before adding, "BYM situation. Why didn't you identify your issue from the beginning? Sure, I'll separate the bills. No one will know. You're safe."

"Thank you, but so I know, what's BYM?"

"Code, in D.C., between you and me, or you can also use CYA. You know what CYA means? We handle secret situations frequently. Next time request a BYM or CYA bill."

Hours after receiving and approving the bill—a bill which indicated that they were on separate floors even—Alex faces the storm in her life. She knows her fling with Marshall is wrong. She wants to end the affair. She knows to successfully end things with him, she must regain control of her mind.

Hours pass….she tries to cease thoughts about him, but she can't. He continues to slither into her mind. Deciding to clear her head, she goes to the hotel restaurant. *Vodka will work. It'll block him out!*

Drinking, alone, she begins to relax. Downing one shot after another, vodka on the rocks, she feels almost-numb at first until finally she feels nothing.

"Alex, there you are."

"Ugh," she lifts her head and sees Marshall standing there, smiling.

"I've been looking all over for you. Have you been drinking?"

"Just a bit, a tad, not much, but what?"

"You're sober?"

"Sure, absolutely, why, what?" she slurs.

Smirking, he examines her closely before speaking. "Good, I've got a project. Ready?"

"Yep, what do you need?"

"You're meeting Justin Walker, Congressional Aide to the Health Care Committee Chair, Congresswoman Jodi Baker."

"Awesome! So, what, do I deliver." She fights to control her slurring.

"Give him your best points, talking points, reasons to block health care reform."

"All right, I'm ready, should we go-go-go-over my speech?"

"You're ready. Give him your best five-minute elevator speech."

All right! That's what I'm talking about. Real action—ma-ma-making an impact—ch-ch-changing the world—making a di-di-difference. I'll be on Fox News, CNN, CSPAN, MSNBC!

She leaps to her feet. She begins to make a bee-line to the suite to tidy up. Marshall stops her in her tracks with his hands first and then his words.

"Wait, sit," Marshall says, motioning to the seat behind her.

"What, why, where?"

"You're meeting him here. He'll be here in five minutes, so sit. I'm going up, another meeting," he says, turning and walking away.

"Okay, but wait. Can you wait for him here so I can go up, powder my nose, you know, look presentable?"

"You look fine enough—you're ready," he says, smirking.

Is he lying?

"Alex, relax. Trust me," he adds, beginning to walk away. He stops and then turns back, adding, "Knock 'em out of the park." He mimics a ballplayer swinging a bat.

You're so un-athletic looking, but thanks for your support!

"Alex, also," he says, almost as if he suddenly has a thought, "since you're meeting him tonight, give him this briefcase. He'll know what to do."

"Sure," she says, accepting the briefcase, still thinking through her talking points. *Health care reform will destroy health care in this country. Health care will be rationed, there will be death beds. Okay, that's an exaggeration, but someone will believe us. The quality of care will fall....*

A tall, twenty-something man appears and speaks to her. "Alexandria Giroud?"

He's so handsome! Well-polished, manicured. His teeth, they're gorgeous and white . . . and his suit, absolutely stunning, Italian custom I'm sure. What a man, what a man. . . .

"Yes, sure, absolutely, I'm Alexandria Giroud!" She drops her notes as she stands.

Bending over to pick up her notes, Alex catches a glimpse of his buttocks. *What a butt!*

Straightening, facing her eye to eye, he extends his hand and introduces himself. "Justin Walker."

Here he is, this man, like a ray of light.

— 9 —

"Justin!" Alex screams, climaxing in Justin Walker's bed as the sun rises.

Sliding off of her, he shakes his head, trying to compose himself. "Alexandria Giroud," he says, "splendid you are."

"The pleasure's all mine," she says, smiling. She admires his naked body as he gets out of bed.

"Are you always so forward?" he asks, walking, naked, in his Georgetown loft, looking gorgeous. He steps toward his bathroom.

With you, I'd be any day, she thinks, but she says, "No, Mr. Walker, not always. Only when someone is special. When a man sweeps me off my feet." She wants to make him feel as if she has made a special exception for him, and perhaps the comment is appropriate given that he *did* wine and dine her before bringing her back to his Georgetown loft condo and seducing her.

"Always dandy to be special, Ms. Giroud," he answers, stepping into his shower. "I do have to run," he calls out. "Senate Committee meeting, but when can I see you again?" He sounds sincere, as if he eagerly wants to see her again.

She gets out of bed. She puts his button-down shirt from the night before over her naked body, and walks into the bathroom. She watches him lather and wash his muscular body. She wants to join him, but she decides to wait . . . play hard to get, if that is possible.

"We're leaving today. But actually, Justin, I'm only a short flight away," she says, allowing her comment to hint at a long-distance relationship with Congressional Aide, Mr. Justin Walker.

"Phoenix, Arizona? Frankly, I wouldn't mind frequenting the city. Especially if time with you is involved," he says, stepping out of the shower. He dries off and winks at her, then walks toward his closet, smiling.

"Yes, well come, whenever you'd like, I'm there," she responds, following him to his closet. Standing close to him now as he dresses, she stares at his gorgeous body.

Slipping a shirt on and then buttoning his buttons, he says, "I'll check my calendar and plan to journey regularly to court you. Is that acceptable?" he asks.

"Absolutely!" she agrees, actually wanting to commit, even if the commitment seems strange to her. *Aren't one night stands just that—one night?*

Admiring her surroundings while he puts on his tie, she sees that his closet is neatly organized with tasteful, custom suits throughout. Not seeing any casual clothes or off the rack clothes in his closet, she wonders, *Does he ever slum it?*

Watching him tie his pink tie, unable to help herself, she asks, "Do you always dress so . . . dapper?"

"Depends on the day. Depends on the audience. Today, there's a women's group testifying before Congress, hence the pink," he answers, as if her question is directed to the color of his tie rather than the quality of his clothing. As if his million dollar plus wardrobe is normal. *I can tell the cost of things. Who's funding your lifestyle, Mr. Walker? You're not living and dressing like this working on Capitol Hill as a Congressional Aide.*

— ૪ —

RETURNING TO HER LUXURY hotel suite, Alex tries to enter unnoticed.

"Alex, where've you been?" Marshall asks, standing in the suite grand entrance, waiting.

"Working, long night." She pauses and thinks, *How do I explain? He looks so mad.* "I've completed the assignment," she adds, trying to keep the subject off her scandalous rendezvous with Justin Walker.

"Good." He walks towards her, undressing her first with his eyes. "Come," he adds, extending his hand, "we have a few hours before our flight back to Phoenix. I've ordered breakfast in bed." He undresses her next with his hands.

Engaging physically with him, she thinks, *I've got to end this fling somehow!*

Chapter Forty
On to the Next Dilemma

TAYLOR LIES TO Whitfield, telling him the debt collector was a psychic trying to drum up business.

He leaves to go to work.

She turns to her work, albeit at home, so that she can guard the Ray home telephone just in case a bill collector tries to call Whitfield and warn him.

Did you know your wife can't manage money?
Did you know she constantly spends?

She works.
She guards.
She blocks calls.
She avoids.

Now, at day's end, she watches television and sees a talk show host rant and rave about debt free living.

Who lives debt free—and why?

Sitting at her desk listening to the messenger, she accesses the Internet. She begins a search.

Living debt free. Only misers live debt free, right?

Seeing a text message box pop open on her computer screen, she types in a query. *I've got to know, what's the deal with debt free living? Is this a fad or for real?*

> **Living Debt Free**

Why live debt free, we're rich, right? She questions her search. *We make lots of money. Why should I need a debt-free living model?* Suddenly, her friend, Reagan, pops into her head to warn her. "Taylor, I'm not judging you, I'm only suggesting that you try living within your means. I'll admit I haven't mastered debt-free living quite yet, but I'm close. Jackson and I work hard…"

"Shut up!"

Silencing her friend, she is surprised by what she sees on the Internet: website after website, caution, suggest, and recommend that people find a way to live debt free. Reading the websites while half-listening to the talk show host, Taylor thinks, *Sounds familiar.* She begins to reminisce about her husband's cautions throughout the years.

— ♪ —

TAYLOR SITS AND THINKS back in time. She can hear her husband's words clearly in her mind, as if they are being spoken to her today.

"Tay, budget and manage our money."

I thought I was?

"Pay all bills on time."

I did…automatic electronic payments. Don't you love computers!

"Tay, double-check the automatic payments you set up—compare payments to the bills." *Okay, I will, next month.*

"Tay, go easy on the extra niceties. You can buy fancy, but save, too!"

She cringes, thinking of her response. *Did you see those jeans, those shoes, that dress, that purse? I've got to have it. What's a girl to do?*

— ♪ —

IS WHIT RIGHT? SHE wonders.

Yes, Tay, Reagan says again in her head.

Reagan, get lost!

Now Taylor thinks about the house. *Whit didn't want the house,* she recalls, remembering the day she told him, "I found the perfect house."

"Yeah?" Whitfield answers.

"Yes, you won't believe the house."

"I bet I can imagine."

"No, you can't, Whit. This house has an outdoor heated swimming pool and an indoor/outdoor Jacuzzi."

"Nice, but so does our country club."

"I know, but we have to share there. This would be ours alone."

"I guess, but I'm okay sharing."

"But Whit, there's also Brazilian cherry hardwood floors throughout, except the grand entrance, and that's marble. It's more than 7,500 square feet."

"We have hardwood floors here, and we don't need a house that big. I'm fine with the house we have already. We barely use the space here."

"We don't have a grand, double wrought-iron staircase, top of the line appliances, modern light fixtures, and crystal chandeliers. I can hang off those chandeliers and do—"

Cutting her off, he asks, "How much?"

She cringes but answers. "We can afford the house. I have the approval letter here. The builder arranged the financing."

"Well said, but how much, Tay?"

"We're approved."

"And the price?"

"Only a few million—but, Whit."

"Tay, we can't."

"We *can*, Whit. The payments, look at the payments."

Looking at the loan documents, Whit frowns. "Tay, I know numbers. There's number games in these docs. Besides, is the house worth this much?"

"Whit, we're approved, relax," she says, walking away. Within minutes, she returns with champagne, wearing a slinky negligee.

Seeing her, Whitfield chuckles. "You're hot, but this house, we're not!"

"Whit, the house, isn't the house a savings account?"

"Hell no, Tay—and that's why we're not buying the house."

"I'll hang off the chandeliers, can't you imagine?" She glides closer.

Undressing her with his eyes, he says, "You're all right, right here. Hang off this lamp!" He points to a small, crystal embroidered table lamp. He grins.

"Whit!"

"What, try this lamp. Hang here."

"No, but listen, Whit, there's a grand loft, with columns. We can partay there!"

"We can partay here!"

"No, not like there, Whit. The loft is huge. Why there are roman columns throughout the grand loft! I can even put a pole in that loft!" she says, mimicking pole dancing while lifting her butt in the air, striking a pose.

Obviously aroused, he pulls her close to him. He turns the conversation from house-hunting to sexual relations.

Feeling Whit inside of her, she can't let go of her dream home. She continues the discussion even in the midst of relations.

"Whit, I deserve the house. I work hard, you work hard; we make lots of money."

"Whit, I'll rub your back every night. We can do this every night in the Jacuzzi tub."

"Whit, the countertops are perfect. There's so many tricks we can do on those marble, snow white, cotton looking countertops—wait and see."

He begins to smile, looking euphoric.

She continues to tell him all the things she plans to do to him sexually, in this new house.

"Whit, the house and sex this."

"Whit, sex and the house that.

"Whit, sex…sex…sex….house….house…house."

Climaxing, he yells, "Yes!"

Slipping off from on top of him, she shouts, "Great, yes! We can get the house!"

Breathing heavily, he says, "Not what I said. You're good, Tay, but you're not sexing me into buying a house."

"But you said yes."

"Yes, to sex . . . " he begins, but trails off.

"What, Whit, what about the house?"

He is silent, still breathing heavily.

"Whit?"

"What?" he asks, looking dazed.

"The house, can we get the house?"

"Tay, look, dude's got to fix the interest rate. Did you see that rate? That's an adjustable rate. I glanced at the docs for seconds and saw there's tricks in that loan."

"Okay, I can, I will. He said he had other loan products, so will you say yes?"

"Tay, also, curb your spending."

"What?" she asks, trying to slap on her innocent look.

"You know what I'm saying."

"What?"

"Shop less, Tay. Save—two years' worth of living expenses—and we'll easily pay that mortgage."

Returning to the present, she realizes, *Whit was right?*

Chapter Forty-one
Rag Doll

JERK! IDIOT! ALEX watches her boss stalk around her office playing games with her. It's been weeks since their trip to Washington, D.C., and she still feels deflated. Even though she vowed to end her relations with her boss, she hasn't. In fact, she has had sex with Marshall every day since returning to the D.C. hotel suite the morning after her one night stand with Justin Walker.

Why? I don't even like him, she tells herself again.

Almost on cue, he looks at her as if he controls her. He swings her emotions around like a rag doll, twisting her, playing with her, toying with her.

"What do you want, Marshall?" she asks him, as he zips up his pants.

"Nothing, I'm done," he answers. He walks towards her office door, opens her closed blinds with one touch, then turns back and smirks.

Wanting to talk, since he doesn't really talk to her anymore, she asks, "How about lunch—sushi?"

"No, other plans," he answers, and then he quickly exits her office.

Her stomach churns. She feels anxious. She knows her POWER, LEVERAGE, CONTROL strategy has backfired. She has feelings, strong feelings for her boss—or alternatively, maybe she is just competitive. Either way, she knows their relationship has changed since returning from Washington, D.C.—in a twisted, toxic, way.

He has sex with her, but it is as if he is using sex against her. He is even more domineering, distant, and detached than he ever was before. He acts as if he wants to toy with her. She has lost control in this dual. He controls her. He controls her mind.

Exhaling noisily, wanting to clear her mind, she calls Taylor Ray on the telephone. "Sushi, lunch?" She knows Taylor's always game.

"Ugh, well . . . " Taylor says.

"Come on! Today's perfect. We can sit outside."

"I know but, well . . . "

"Biltmore sushi bar?" Alex asks.

"Well, but I . . . well, the weather *is* perfect."

"Yep, I know. Days in March are the best. Seventy degrees today."

"Well, why not. But Alex, don't be late."

"I won't. I'm walking out, bye," Alex tells Taylor, checking her email.

Seeing she has twenty new emails, Alex decides to read each one.

— ♪ —

FORTY MINUTES LATER, ALEX stands up. She begins to exit her office when suddenly she hears Marshall's voice in the distance. *Did he just ask someone else out to lunch?* Alex's heart speeds up. She leans around the threshold of her door, peaks, and sees her boss chatting with Rachael McCay, another associate.

She eavesdrops and overhears Marshall's invitation. "Rachel, grab your things!"

Hearing his plans and observing his demeanor, Alex wonders, *Is he doing Rachael, too?*

Answering her own question, she decides, *Yep, probably! Jerk!*

Chapter Forty-two
We the People

TAYLOR WALKS ON the red brick walkway leading to the outdoor seating area at the Biltmore Sushi bar. She searches and does not see Alex. *Knew she'd be late!* she thinks, sitting down at her favorite table next to a row of sun-shading pigmy palm trees. Settling herself into the plush chair, Taylor relaxes. *I can't afford lunch, but I'm glad to be out! Get my mind off of debt, babies, Whit—*

The desert breeze interrupts her thoughts. She inhales deeply and smells jasmine and sage. Relaxing even further, rolling her shoulders, she feels the breeze tickle her cheeks. Eyes, closed, she sits in silence. Her mind is even silent. She does not hear or think about anything for what seems like hours—until she feels a nudge. Turning and seeing Alex, Taylor tenses up and immediately asks, "Why are you late?"

"Work. You understand."

"Alex, can't you manage your time?"

"Get over yourself. Anyhow, the table's nice," Alex says, looking impressed.

Did she say get over yourself? Why—why . . . "Alex, *you* called *me*, invited *me*, and your office is closer to this place than mine! And the table, you had to get here early to get this table. Now there's a long line!" Taylor says, ranting.

"Glad you were early, thanks!" Alex responds, clearly oblivious to Taylor's rage. Staring at Taylor for a moment, Alex changes the subject. "You're not watching the fanfare?"

"What's up?"

"Today's a worship fest. Your candidate." Alex points to the plasma screen television affixed on the wall a short distance from the table.

"Guess you didn't see the Barack Obama pep rally. I thought you'd be all over the TV, watching the news."

"What?" Taylor turns and looks at the plasma screen behind her and sees "Breaking News" flash across the television screen. The news commentator announces, "Barack Obama will begin his Race in America speech in minutes."

Taylor gets up and moves her chair to the other side of the table so she can get a clear view of the television screen. Anticipating the speech, Taylor smiles and says, "Maybe he'll put this Wright controversy to rest."

Alex is silent. *Thought you'd jump all over that one!*

"Alex, I know you're a Republican, but you can't believe the rhetoric. Obama's not racist."

Alex is still silent.

"We need to talk about real issues, like the economy, health care, national security, education—don't you agree?"

Alex is silent.

"Alex? Alex?" Taylor turns her attention to Alex and realizes she is not responding to her because she is fixating upon a man and woman who are standing directly below the wall-mounted plasma screen, waiting in line to be seated.

"What's up with the couple?" Taylor asks, curious. If Taylor is reading the situation right, Alex is eyeing the couple with a bit of jealous concern.

"What?" Alex asks, as if awakening from a trance. She tries to look surprised, and innocent. "What?"

"Your eyeballs are glued on that couple!" Taylor replies.

Flickering her eyes, nervously so, Alex answers, "Who me? I'm not staring. You're imagining things."

"Yes, you are!"

"No, silly. I'm looking at the television screen and the fanfare, the flags," Alex says.

Focusing her attention on the television screen again, Taylor is unable to discern whether Alex is telling the truth. *Yes, there are American flags lining the stage, along with a podium and microphone because Barack Obama is about to speak on race. But that couple, well they're standing underneath the television waiting. Is Alex lying?*

"You girls ready?" Ishi, the waitress, asks.

Alex orders, still staring at either the television screen or the woman and man standing beneath. Taylor can't tell.

Taylor orders but then abruptly, the man Alex is eyeing approaches the table and interrupts—

"Alexandria Giroud! Surprising seeing you here," he says.

Taylor sees that he is middle-aged, and wearing an arrogant grin. His date or wife or friend or whoever she is has disappeared.

She lied! I knew it! Now it's obvious that Alex knows the man. Taylor leans in closer to watch the exchange between them.

Shock and disbelief flicker across Alex's face before she speaks. "Marshall, I didn't see you."

You liar! Frowning, Taylor watches Alex's eyes dart back and forth, wildly, as if she is nervous or uncomfortable or both, Taylor can't tell. And her thumb, Alex is fidgeting her thumb up and down, all while biting her lip in between her words.

"I'll put your orders in!" Ishi says. Taylor has almost forgotten she was standing there.

Has Ishi seen Alex here with him before? Taylor wonders, but her thoughts are again cut short by the man.

"Seat us, inside! We got here when they did, but they're seated, we're not. I don't know why we're in line," Marshall demands, and follows Ishi, as if he expects her to oblige him, irrespective of the fact that he is lying.

The nerve! Taylor thinks, before asking, "So who is he?"

"Who?"

"What's his name—that man, the Marshall man?"

"Him?" Alex responds, waving her hand as if to say, *He's nobody.*

"Yes, him, and the woman," Taylor snaps back. *Don't give me that who are you talking about look!*

"He's my boss. And the girl, that's Rachael McCay. Anyhow, I'm watching the television screen. Something's going on, caught my attention, not him."

Your boss, wow! Who looks at her boss like that? Taylor thinks, but says, "Are you sure because I could have sworn—"

Suddenly, she hears Barack Obama speak. His words come through on the plasma screen television, loudly, clearly. . . .

Hearing his words, Taylor shushes her friend so that she can listen to the candidate, Barack Obama, speak.

> "*We the People In Order To Form a More Perfect Union.* . . .
>
> "*Two hundred and twenty-one years ago, in a hall that still stands across the street, a group of men gathered and, with these simple words, launched America's improbable experiment in democracy. Farmers and scholars; statesmen and patriots who had traveled across an ocean to escape tyranny and persecution finally made real their declaration of independence at a Philadelphia convention that lasted through the spring of 1787.*"

Eyes fixed on the screen, Taylor smiles and mumbles, "Maybe he'll stop the spin!"

"Don't be so naïve," Alex snaps back, and then adds, "His association with the Wright-man won't go away with a speech."

Taking her eyes off the screen for the first time since Barack Obama took the stage, Taylor says, "Reverend Wright isn't Obama!"

"Guilt by association—" Alex begins, but Ishi returns with their food and interrupts, placing a Philadelphia Roll before Taylor and a California Roll before Alex.

"Mmm—nice combination," Alex says, immediately digging in. She chews slowly before fixing her eyes back on the television. Seeing the oratory action on screen, Alex quickly swallows her food, frowns, and says, "Here we go. Meaningless excuses!"

"Listen to his speech," Taylor says, cutting Alex off.

"He's distracting, won't work," Alex declares, wielding her fork.

"His opponents are distracting, not him. So listen," Taylor demands.

> "*I am the son of a black man from Kenya and a white woman from Kansas. I was raised with the help of a white grandfather who survived a Depression*

> *to serve in Patton's Army during World War II and a white grandmother who worked on a bomber assembly line at Fort Leavenworth while he was overseas. I've gone to some of the best schools in America and lived in one of the world's poorest nations. I am married to a black American who carries within her the blood of slaves and slave owners—an inheritance we pass on to our two precious daughters. I have brothers, sisters, nieces, nephews, uncles and cousins, of every race and every hue, scattered across three continents, and for as long as I live, I will never forget that in no other country on Earth is my story even possible."*

Cutting back in, Alex says, "So what, vote Obama because his family's diverse?"

"Alex, he can't be racist. Isn't that obvious?"

"His family may look like the United Nations, but that doesn't clean his militant slate," Alex quickly snaps back.

"He's not militant! He'll explain," Taylor says, trying to get Alex to focus on the speech.

> *"In my first book,* Dreams From My Father, *I described the experience of my first service at Trinity: People began to shout. . . .a forceful wind carrying the reverend's voice up into the rafters....And in that single note—hope!—I heard something else; at the foot of that cross, inside the thousands of churches across the city, I imagined the stories of ordinary black people merging with the stories of David and Goliath, Moses and Pharaoh, the Christians in the lion's den, Ezekiel's field of dry bones. Those stories—of survival, and freedom, and hope—became our story, my story."*

"Alex, you know the black church is the one place some blacks feel comfortable expressing unrest, even if the speech is politically incorrect at times."

"Yep, and that's why he's in this political mess. Wright's wrong."

"I agree. Wright's views may be extreme, but Wright's not Obama, now listen."

"Nope, your guy even coined phrases after that Wright man in his dream book. He admits Hope comes from Wright, who furthers hate!" Alex finishes with a laugh.

"Obama's books encourage inclusiveness, not hate, right?"

"Haven't read his books, but I'm sure the text shows, if anything, that Obama isn't American. He's African or Indonesian. We don't know where he'll go as some immigrant."

"He's not an immigrant."

"He's traveled everywhere, so he might as well be. Anyway, he's not core American. He has no true American roots."

Speechless, stunned by the comment, Taylor wonders, *What is core American?* before she turns her attention back to the candidate, who is discussing the history of discrimination in America and the vestiges that flow there from.

Obviously hearing Barack Obama talk about discrimination, Alex interrupts again and says, "Here we go, pity-party! Race is superfluous! In fact, color of skin is the least distinguishing characteristic between humans."

Shocked, Taylor drops her jaw before responding. "I know race is a divisive tool, but that doesn't change the sting of discrimination. Government must help people who have been disadvantaged by discrimination. Some people are stuck."

"I agree, people are stuck," Alex proudly proclaims.

"Good, so you acknowledge—" Taylor begins.

"Yep, they're stuck all right. Government gets them stuck in a rut, makes 'em lazy."

Appalled, Taylor asks, "So if government can't assist, where should people go to demand equality in America?"

"There are many alternatives. Like my firm. We raise money for disadvantaged youth. We sent twelve disadvantaged kids to an ivy-league summer camp."

"I understand," she says, nodding, "my PR firm helps, too. But to your example: you send kids to camps, but once the summer camp is over, the kids go back to the same disadvantaged environment. It takes an entity as powerful as the government to fix the root causes. These are policy issues, not humanitarian issues."

"How can sending money to D.C. help people in Phoenix?"

"Easily. Take what Obama said a minute ago."

"About what?"

"Obama said 'segregated schools are inferior schools and the problem with the inferior schools has not been fixed yet.' Shouldn't government fix education?"

"No, but the private sector can."

"How? Excellent education isn't profitable, right?"

Alex swallows a bite of sushi quickly and gulps her iced tea before she continues, leaning forward for emphasis. "If you put education in the private sector, we can make education profitable and effective."

"Please, we can't put education in the hand of profit-seekers, and nothing against making a profit, I'm for making profits, but there's a place for profits, and education isn't the place."

"Why not? Profit seekers have a direct interest in being effective, whereas bureaucracies don't."

"Yeah, but people cut corners to make profits. That's a way to be effective, too. Or greed steps in—that's why the government must oversee and regulate."

"Ha!"

"No, seriously," Taylor says. "Like the child labor market in the 1920s and the S & L crisis in the 1980s, or obesity today."

Chuckling, Alex says, "Obesity, please. People are obese because they eat too much!"

"No, people are obese because farmers and corporations started to use corn syrup as a filler without understanding the scientific effects."

"And that's where you Democrats go wrong: the government's not your daddy!"

"I'm not talking about who's your daddy. I'm saying government must work for the good of the people. Who'll ensure that America has solid domestic policies?"

"We the people, non-profits, religious organizations, the United Way, Red Cross, Friends & Families, Meals on Wheels—these organizations act for the public good, too. And my firm, we also raised money and donated school supplies to children in Africa. We can make a difference. We don't need the government to act."

"Alex, again, I believe in philanthropy, too, but how do we ensure the roads are monitored and maintained or that our borders are secure? How can we make sure the public good is taken care of if we don't have a large federal government?"

Shrugging her shoulders, Alex answers, "Simple. With roads, the government can have a limited role, and that is inducing private enterprise through tax incentives or government contracts. And with the borders, well, that's national security. Government should be powerful, large, and strong when it comes to national security—then and only then!"

"I disagree. Private enterprise working for the public good doesn't always work."

"Of course private enterprise works! You'll see. We Republicans will reverse the FDR and LBJ federal bureaucracy that's interwoven into the fabric of America with time. All this social security, Medicare, socialism must go."

"The policies aren't socialist. I mean, didn't LBJ and FDR policies spur middle class expansion, while the Republican policies shrank the middle class?"

"Nope. The socialist policies make people dependent on government."

"Did you hear what Obama just said about legalized discrimination?"

"What did he say?" Alex asks.

"He's pointing out that legalized discrimination limited economic opportunities for minorities to own property, buy homes, secure jobs, and ultimately amass wealth. What do you think about that? Shouldn't the federal government establish uniform anti-discrimination laws? Don't you believe in the Civil Rights Act of 1966?" Taylor asks.

Pausing to consider, Alex finally answers, "Actually, I'm glad the civil rights laws were passed, but, I'll admit, locals could have solved race problems."

"In Alabama? I mean, seriously, Alabama?"

"Maybe, with time, but anyway, slavery's ancient history!"

Chuckling, Taylor says, "The vestiges exist to this day, just like your trust fund from your great-grandfather still bears fruit for you today." Taylor puts in play some of Alex's own personal history to make her point.

"No, my inheritance is chump change, but it also proves my point." Alex defends herself, perhaps believing that since her great-grandfather had one fifth of one drop of African American blood in his veins, he was arguably African American, thus establishing African Americans were able to get ahead under discriminatory laws.

Taylor debunks the theory. "Alex, your great-grandfather lived as a white man!" Taylor says, knowing that while technically, legally, Alex's great-grandfather was African American by the one drop rule, since his hair was straight and his skin was creamy-colored, no one was the wiser. Legalized discrimination did not apply to him when he amassed his wealth.

"Oh, listen to the speech." Alex obviously wants to change the subject.

Listening again, Taylor hears Barack Obama say that Sunday is the most segregated hour in American life. He continues and acknowledges that while frustrations are expressed in churches on Sunday mornings in ways, at times, that are distracting, that reality alone does not dismiss the adage that there is work to be done between the races. He suggests we should take time to understand the roots so solutions can be made.

Interrupting again, clearly unable to listen, Alex says, "See, he's harping on race."

"His speech is *about* race! Look, we've got to come together because although we live in a democracy, people can't come together and truly participate because we're stuck on race."

"I'm lost. That's circular nonsense. What're you talking about?"

"Okay, let me see . . . I've got it! Let's say Tyrone, Bob, and Jose are trying to decide whether they're for health care reform."

"All right, and so what? Tyrone is black, Bob is white, and Jose is Hispanic?"

"Yes, and Tyrone is Harvard educated and a small business owner, Bob is an assembly line manager at a major corporation, and Jose owns a local ice cream parlor."

"Okay, so what?"

"So at a town hall meeting, health care reform comes up. Tyrone wants reform, Bob isn't sure what he wants, but he likes his plan at work, and Jose wants reform."

"So what?"

"So, Tyrone stands up and says he wants reform. Bob hears Tyrone say he is pro-reform, and unconsciously, he sees Tyrone is black and immediately thinks, if the black guy wants reform, I'm against reform, because black guys are usually unemployed, poor, and I can't support a person who's taking advantage of other hard working Americans."

"Okay, but sometimes, that's true."

"Rarely, but sometimes, not always, like here. Tyrone isn't a stereotypical, overplayed, and often untrue statistic. Again, remember, he is Harvard educated. He owns his own business. He wants reform because he has been paying his own health insurance as a small business owner. He thinks health care costs are climbing at an unsustainable rate. He wants to expand his practice, hire additional employees, but he is not sure if he can provide health benefits because of the high costs."

"Okay, so, he should hire additional workers as part-time workers or independent contractors and axe the insurance benefits for everyone but himself and his family."

"You would throw everyone under the bus? What about the poor and middle class?"

"He should do what he can afford. Accept reality. He'll go broke if he keeps trying to carry the poor and middle classes."

"Alex, there's an alternative, like the government. See, take Jose. He agrees with Tyrone. He's a small business owner who constantly reduces employee wages to offset rising health care costs, but he doesn't know how much longer the offsetting will work."

"Okay, so, again, axe the health care plan."

"Right, but he can ask government to create a solution."

"He could, but I don't think he should."

"Of course he should. But he won't. He'll be drowned out because Tyrone and Bob will hear Jose, who is Hispanic, stand up and say he wants government intervention, and they'll unconsciously think, no, not you, you must be an illegal immigrant. You're trying to ride off the system, and you shouldn't be in America anyway."

"Okay, and?"

"But Jose was born in America."

"So..."

"So, we started the town hall meeting talking about health care reform, but before we were done, we were making health care choices and decisions based on race."

"So, race is a great distraction. Great, because you already heard me say government isn't the answer, as far as I'm concerned."

"Right, but Alex, the point is, Bob, his employer, is just like Jose, even as a large corporation. Bob doesn't know this yet, but his employer is about to ship his job overseas to avoid paying the high health care costs."

"Good, that makes sense."

"Yeah, but my point is, Bob, Tyrone, and Jose all need the same thing—health care reform, but they never got to discuss the issue, blinded by race."

"Like I said, race is an awesome distraction. I'm against reform for Bob, Jose, and Tyrone, and so if they want to get distracted because of race, that's all the better for me because I'm against reform."

"Yeah, but what if you're like Bob?"

"I'm not. I'm independent and resourceful. I don't depend on others to make my way, not even my employer," Alex proudly proclaims.

Exhaling noisily, Taylor turns her attention back to the speech, where Barack Obama is talking about how many of the issues that were once potentially viewed as African American problems only are now simply American problems, irrespective of race. He uses health care and the economy as examples. He opines that health care is an American issue; all Americans must face the challenge of a health care system that is in need of reform. Likewise, all Americans are dealing with an economy that is seeing jobs shipped overseas.

Obviously listening, too, Alex picks up on the shipping jobs overseas comment and says, "Corporations ship jobs overseas to be competitive. The game has changed. American businesses aren't charities, they're businesses."

"Yes, I understand competition," Taylor says, "but don't you know the Republican policies relaxed conditions to make it easy to ship jobs overseas?"

"No, you can't tag that only on the Republicans. I'll admit, Nixon opened up trade with China, but Clinton opened up trade with NAFTA."

"Yeah, but trade deficits have increased under Bush, which has caused manufacturing to disappear in America."

"And—that's progress. Look, we can't be stagnant. We've got to expand and grow."

"Yeah, but our expansion is weakening our domestic economy. In fact, we can't even educate a working class. Didn't you hear what Bill Gates said about education?"

"No, what?"

"He wants Congress to allow more green cards because there aren't enough qualified workers in America."

"Okay, and—he should have access to the global free market."

"Yeah, but we should educate Americans so that we can compete for those jobs."

"We will, as soon as we get rid of public education."

"Alex, but what's the answer in the meantime? Our public schools are collapsing."

"Good, then the private sector, the place where all ingenuity takes place, will step in."

"And in the meantime?"

"Survival of the fittest. At least we Republicans are doing something, unlike you Democrats."

"We're too busy trying to fix your mess. Alex, your free market, que sera, sera—whatever will be, will be—approach is devastating."

"What?"

"You know, que sera, sera, whatever will be, will be?" Taylor sings the lyrics. "That's your free market model."

"Oh, please. Free market isn't like your kay sara song!"

"*Que* q-u-e, Alex, and sera, s-e-r-a," Taylor explains.

"Yeah, right, whatever." Alex shrugs her shoulder.

Meanwhile, the speech continues, with the candidate turning the discussion to health care and specifically honing in on a story told by a twenty-three-year-old white woman who organized for his campaign in an African American community in South Carolina. Taylor hears Barack Obama retell the story told by Ashley during the campaign. He explains that Ashley's mother became ill with cancer. She had to file bankruptcy because of her illness. Ashley, who was nine at the time, chose to eat mustard and relish sandwiches because she knew that was cheap.

Hearing the story, Taylor turns to Alex and says, "I don't get your indifference."

"I don't get your victim liberal mentality."

"I'm not really that liberal. I'm only saying we have to invest in our country. If we don't, we'll be uneducated, sick, and insecure." Taylor raises her eyebrows and shakes her forefinger at Alex before adding, "But sufficiently local." She pauses and shakes her head.

"So what's your alternative? I know, I've got it—let me get my violin." She pretends to play an imaginary violin until she looks at her watch and says abruptly, "Taylor, I've got to go, deadline—see ya!"

Taylor sits and watches Alex throw her part of the bill down on the table, plus a large tip, before leaving.

Sitting alone, she turns her attention back to the television screen where Barack Obama concludes his story about his campaign worker. He says Ashley could have been harsh towards African Americans and Hispanics, blaming these people for her problems because countless people throughout her childhood had told her that her mother was in the situation she was in because blacks were on welfare and too lazy to work, or Hispanics were coming into the country illegally, but Ashley chose a different path. She refused to accept the views and instead chose to roll up her sleeves and develop coalitions with others in her fight against injustice. And sure enough, at the campaign, Ashley found an African American man who joined with her in the fight for justice because when she asked him why he was present at the campaign drive, he said he was there because of her.

Barack Obama brings his speech to a close.

> *"By itself, that single moment of recognition between that young white girl and that old black man is not enough. It is not enough to give health care to the sick, or jobs to the jobless, or education to our children. But it is where we start. It is where our union grows stronger. And as so many generations have come to realize over the course of the two hundred and twenty-one years since a band of patriots signed that document in Philadelphia, that is where the perfection begins."*

Chapter Forty-two
Running to the Truth

ALEX RETURNS TO work and finds Marshall in her office. He has closed her office blinds. *He's playing games,* she thinks.

"You're looking good today." He walks towards her. He undresses her with his eyes.

Backing away from him, walking towards her desk, she says, "Marshall, what was that about, telling me you couldn't do sushi but then going with Rachael?"

"You're not jealous, are you?" he asks, with a snide grin.

"No, I'm only asking." She leans back against her desk, trying to distance herself from him.

"Are you sure, because I like you when you're jealous. That's a turn on. That's why I do what I do." He steps closer to her until they are face to face, then leans his body against hers, kisses her earlobes, and rubs his groin against her hips.

Feeling his arousal, she tries to stop him. "Marshall no, I'm serious, you're—"

Cutting her off, he lifts her on top of her desk, pulls up her dress, tears off her pantyhose, and slips inside of her.

He moans.

Feeling him inside, she stares at his face. His eyes are closed. She senses she has him.

She wants him.

She wants him to want her, really, so she enjoys him until she begins to kiss his neck and smells floral scents. He smells like another woman.

She knows he's not loyal. He's married, and maybe seeing someone else. *Will we ever have a real relationship?* she wonders. He grinds inside her body, his eyes still closed, almost as if he is engaged in a solitary act.

Watching him climax and exit her person, and then her office, she decides, *I've got to talk to a friend.* Alex calls Taylor Ray first. There is no answer.

She calls Reagan Hamilton second, and gets an answer.

"Can you meet me, the walking trail, fast?"

Reagan agrees.

— 9 —

As the sun and dusk change hands at the horizon, Alex walks up to the red rock-laden desert trail and wonders, *Where's Reagan?* Beginning to stretch while waiting, and wondering how to talk to Reagan about Marshall, Alex sees Reagan quickly approaching.

"Done two miles already," Reagan says, in between heavy breaths.

"Wait!" Alex says, completing her stretch.

"Can't—runner's high," Reagan answers. "Put your foot to the metal." She begins to run.

Pedal to the metal! Alex stands up and races to catch up to her friend. Approaching Reagan, Alex says, "Another busy day—"

"At the office, yeah, yeah, yeah, I know," Reagan says, nodding her head with each "yeah."

Alex remains silent for a while, trying to figure out how to say what she needs to say. Finally, she starts with, "I'm in a situation."

"What've you done?" Reagan asks.

"Well, a guy."

Looking over at Alex, Reagan manages a heavy sigh. "Okay..." She pauses, then says, "And?"

"I don't think he's right for me. I don't really like him, but I keep seeing him. I can't stop being with him, I don't—"

"Don't like him, but you see him?" Reagan asks, sighing again.

"Yes, because, our—well—situation . . . happened."

"Situation? Does he respect you?" Reagan asks.

Well, I think ...

"Is he loyal, honest?"

He's—

"Does he go to church?"

Nah, but I don't either; is that all you care about?

"Is he in touch with your feelings? Does he care?"

"Reagan, stop!" Alex shouts, hearing Reagan list the characteristics like there is no end. "Look, listen, Reagan, I, I want to talk. I have to ask you a question."

"Okay, shoot," Reagan says.

Struggling to keep up, wanting to find the words to tell her friend, Alex decides to cut to the chase. "Reagan, we got together. I didn't plan on it, but I can't end our relationship."

"So you're going steady? Seeing him exclusively?"

"Yes, sort-a."

"What do you mean, sort-a? Alex, monogamous relationships are good. I know that's not your custom, but trust me. Exclusive relationships are good."

Why do you always sound like a nun, and why am I asking you? "Reagan, he's, well, he's seeing a woman."

"Okay, but you're exclusive with him. Why?"

"Well sort-a, not really, but Reagan—he's married—well, unhappily married. Really unhappily married." Alex says unhappily married at least three more times before she adds, "Really, very unhappily married."

Bracing herself, preparing for the wrath of Reagan, she is surprised to be greeted by silence instead. *Why isn't she saying anything?*

Looking beside her, she sees that Reagan is no longer running with her. Reagan has stopped in her tracks. Her body is fixed on the track.

Reagan looks firmly rooted in her conservative Christian values. Alex turns and runs to her.

"Reagan, listen, I didn't plan—" Alex begins, trying to explain herself.

"Stop!" Reagan holds her hands to her ears.

"You don't understand. I didn't know."

"You didn't know what?"

"Well, we were together, and well I had a few—"

"Drinks? You're blaming your sins on your drinking habit?"

"Well—I woke up with him in bed," Alex says, shrugging her shoulders.

"Alexandria Giroud," Reagan says her full name like a parent might to a child. "You've got to get your life together."

"But how?"

"Stop! You're playing a vicious game! You're running in circles! Get out of the chorus you're stuck in. Rewrite the song of your life. Find yourself and leave him and the others alone!"

"How? I can't."

"Alex, I don't get you. Don't you remember your dad?"

"Yes, but—"

"You were so upset because your dad cheated on your mom."

"Yes," Alex screams, before adding, "Don't remind me." She holds back tears.

"Alex, you must quit. I'm sorry. I can't help you beyond that. I can't participate. I want no part." Reagan walks away, leaving Alex standing alone, trying to figure out where to run next.

Chapter Forty-three
Gross Domestic Product

TAYLOR SITS AND thinks, *How and why am I broke? Lying to my husband, and—*

The telephone rings.

Taylor smiles, answering after seeing the caller ID flash up her mother's name.

"Hi, Mom!"

Hearing what her mom wants, Taylor's smile disappears.

"I don't have any money." Lines of frustration fill her face.

"Taylor, I need a short loan."

"Not a good time."

"I'm in a bind, Tay."

"Me, too, Mom. In fact, can you help out?"

After that, Taylor is forced to tune out all further conversation. Cash and Jearlean Salinas have always had odd relations.

In her hands, money seems to glide away.

Her spending habits are compulsive, Taylor is sure—a habit that is curbed only when Mr. Salinas steps in and cuts her means.

Then and only then does her mom show any restraint, at which time Taylor is convinced the Gross Domestic Product (GDP) significantly descends.

— ⁀ —

HOLDING THE TELEPHONE TO her ear, Taylor recalls the last time her dad brokered a deal with the bank. Taylor replays the scene, as told by her dad, in her mind.

Mr. Salinas returns home from work and finds twenty-four credit card bills in the Salinas mailbox. He opens each bill and sees that his wife has charged each credit card to the $100.00 credit card limit. Shaking his head, he thinks, *I told her no more credit cards, and what does she do? She goes and gets twenty-four credit cards with one hundred dollar limits?*

He walks past his wife, who is Internet shopping, and returns to his car. He drives a few miles to the local bank and demands that the bank close each and every credit card account immediately. Waiting on the account closures, he thinks, *I've tried everything . . . counseling, discussions, divorce threats, even weekly confessions. Nothing works! The woman thinks she has a constitutional right to shop! I'll stop the spending today!*

Returning home, feeling that his house is in order, Mr. Salinas sees that Mrs. Salinas is still Internet shopping. He smiles when DENIED flashes across the screen. When he sees his wife's distraught looks, he actually laughs.

Mrs. Salinas asks her husband, "What's so funny?"

When he answers, the onslaught sets in. Mr. and Mrs. Salinas bicker and argue all night without really dealing with any of the root causes of their money management disconnect.

Taylor cringes, remembering her dad's recollection. She realizes that her parents' money-fights affected her as a child. She recalls one fight in particular. She swore then, *I'll never have such fights. I'll never let a man dictate how I spend money.*

"It's my money, too!" her mom exclaims.

"Do you need one hundred pairs of shoes?" her dad answers.

"Yes, one hundred pairs—that's reasonable. There are 365 days in the year, you comprehende?"

Remembering the arguments, Taylor understands that her parents' relationship with money affects her perceptions and shapes her thinking about finances.

She knows she harbors conflicting emotions about money. She likes to make lots of money, but deep inside, she feels like money is bad. She works hard for her money but spends money freely, too, while feeling guilty each time she spends a dime. She suppresses her anxiety about money by adopting a cavalier attitude: *I make lots of money; I spend my money freely!* All while recalling the vow she made to herself as a child. *When I grow up, I'll buy one hundred cabbage patch dolls if I want to. No one can tell me I can't!*

And so, when she wed Whitfield Ray, she brought all these feelings to the marriage, countering each of his philosophies with her own opinions. As for his insistence on budgets, she says, *Too restrictive; too difficult to plan and follow.* And as for his two-year emergency savings plan philosophy, she says, *There's time for saving later. I grew up with scarce money in my childhood. You won't take me back there with your saving philosophy. Jeez! Two years! That'll take us saving more than one-third of our earnings.*

Money seemed scarce in her childhood, but now she feels she has abundance—even though her monthly cash and debt rarely line up; she almost always owes more than she makes. And so when the bills come due in her household, and some months, she can't make everything line up where the Ray's aren't in the negative, she tells herself, *I deserve it!* She then goes on justifying her spending with some professional accomplishment as she thinks back to childhood, vowing not to go back there where luxuries were rare.

When the other girls wore Guess jeans, she wore no-name brand jeans instead. When others wore Roper boots, she wore the Five & Dime label's latest pair. When others shouldered Dooney & Bourke bags, she carried her mom's hand-me-down, man-made, faux-leather bag. Now, with better options available, she makes up for those days with designer this and designer that; thousands of dollars spent on luxury that fills the void she felt as a child.

Whitfield does not object to her purchases, as long as she stays within their budget; problem is, while she is responsible for managing the budget, she only pretends everything is in order: she doesn't believe in budgets, and so she doesn't budget!

Until she received the call at home—the call that changed everything. With a debt-collector threatening to take her house, she realized that her financial house of cards might be tumbling down around her.

Accepting that she must curtail her spending, she knows she can't help her mom, even if she really wants to. Instead, she has to pull out all of her own debts—credit cards, student loans, mortgages, second mortgages, and equity lines of credit—and try to sort things out. *I've got to get the Ray family on a budget!*

In fact, she even plans to stop using her credit card, even for reimbursable business expenses. Sure, she gets paid back for these expenses, but sometimes she does not receive her reimbursements until months later. Meanwhile, interest compounds on her costs month after month.

As for her mom, Taylor just can't help her out financially; she'll have to find another way. *Maybe I should tell her about budgets, too?* she thinks, as she listens to her mom declare, "Tay, I need boots!"

Chapter Forty-four
The Waltz

*S*ITTING IN SOLACE in a bar alone, Alex wonders, *Will I ever find the one?*

Drinking Vodka on ice with eight orange slices, she relaxes while searching, looking for Mr. Right. She sits. She waits, listening to music for hours until suddenly she feels someone brush up against her neck.

Inhaling deeply she thinks, *Smells nice,* before she hears the stranger speak.

"Hello," a man whispers in her ear.

Turning, seeing him, she smiles. *He's gorgeous. Rich looking, too! Who are you?*

"Alexandria Giroud," she says with an exaggerated smile. She admires his confident stance. Knowing she is smiling from ear to ear, she tries to rein in her excitement. *Look like you don't care,* she tells herself.

He takes her hand and asks, "Shall we dance?"

When she nods, he leads her to the dance floor.

He's so formal, authoritative but gentle. I like, gosh I like! Stanley leads her in a waltz, a close waltz, while tastefully maintaining a one-inch distance between their bodies. *Is he waltzing to this music, R & B? That's different. I haven't waltzed since my days in The Beaus & Belles.*

Interrupting her thoughts, he whispers into her ear. "What's your story? Why are you alone?" He guides her body across an empty dance floor.

Did he drop from heaven? "I'm a professional, independent woman! I know how to have a good time." She lies. She tells only the clean and impressive version of her history. She doesn't tell her closet secrets. *I'm having an affair, and I'm here drinking too much.*

"How about you?" she asks.

"I frequent this place. I appreciate classical music, so here I am."

She wonders, *Is his story as edited as mine?*

Chapter Forty-five
Nice Guy?

Alex approaches Taylor Ray, who is waiting at the bottom of the Piestewa Peak hiking trail. "Have you talked to Reagan?" she immediately asks.

"No, why? I've been out of the loop, barely made the hike today."

Not answering Taylor's question, Alex continues. "Glad you're here. Been too long. I'm ready to hike this big boy!" *Or should I say hike this girl, since the mountain is named after a woman!*

Knowing Reagan did not tell Taylor, Alex decides not to share the news of her affair just in case Taylor has a similar type of response.

Alex and Taylor begin climbing, enjoying the crisp, morning air, when Alex says, "Taylor, guess what?"

"Who is he?" Taylor asks, as if she knows what Alex is going to say.

"He's a lawyer, and he knows how to waltz!"

Huffing, as if she is out of breath, Taylor asks, "Does he represent people with bad loans because—I, well, nothing?"

"No, he represents banks, not losers." The ground beneath her feet crunches, the rocks and dirt grinding together as she continues to climb. "He gets rid of dead beats!" Alex adds, gesturing with her right thumb.

"Wait!" Taylor yells, almost slipping on the rocky path.

"Taylor, are you all right?"

Bending over to catch her breath, Taylor holds up her hand. "Wait, give me a second. I, well, this headache is throbbing."

"We can turn back?" Alex leans in closely, noticing Taylor's weary eyes.

"No, no, let's keep going." Taylor lifts herself up and begins climbing again. "Your—" she pauses to take another breath before adding, "—guy. Tell me more."

"Him. Right. He's gorgeous, and he's also smart—rich, too. At least I think. I can't tell, but he knows how to waltz, and I'm thinking he may come from financial means, wealth."

"No, not about *him*. I mean about that kicking people out of their homes. How can he do that in good conscious?"

"You want to know about his profession?"

"Yes, and the houses."

"Well, he's a chameleon!" Alex chuckles.

"What do you mean? He's a lizard? Sounds more like a snake!" Taylor mumbles.

"No, he's not a snake, and actually he's not a lizard; he's a chameleon. He'll survive any economy! See, he can change to meet market demands. He can be whatever to whomever whenever needed."

"Odd."

"Nope, he's flexible, enterprising, and perfect!"

"I don't get how changing who you are is perfect. I'm lost."

"He's a partner, Riley & Bailey. He's been representing banks throughout the mid-to-late nineties to the present."

"I hear you, and?"

"He lobbied Congress to relax the lending rules."

"In what way?"

"You know," she says, throwing her hands up in the air, "he spearheaded the anything goes loans legislation!"

Inhaling deeply, Taylor slows down, almost slipping.

"Are you okay? You seem slow today? How's your headache?"

"I'm fine, but dragging. Not feeling well, but I'm here, right? That's what's important." Taylor struggles to pick up the pace.

"Yep, I guess, as long as you don't slip off this mountain."

"I won't." She pauses again, breathing heavily, before adding, "Go on, tell me more about your Mr. Banker guy."

Slowing down, Alex says, "Right, chameleon, yeah. So he represents the banks and mortgage companies and even the mortgage brokers who made loans to any and everyone, even no good dead beats."

"Why's that great, Alex?" Taylor almost slips again.

"Taylor, don't you see, the guy knows how to make a buck. He rode the housing market bubble straight to the top, right along with bankers, mortgage brokers, Wall Street investors, real estate agents, real estate brokers—you must admit, the market has been hot!"

"I'm not against people making money—*legitimate* money—but anything goes loans and kicking dead beats out, that doesn't sound right."

"Lending is legitimate," Alex says, feeling defensive. "In fact, lending to unworthy borrowers gives disadvantaged people a chance, private enterprise style."

"What do you mean?"

"Taylor, you know there has been an effort, since the Carter Administration, to give everyone, even people who can't afford a home, a chance to buy a home. And then Clinton and Bush only furthered these policies, trying to help people who can't help themselves out."

"I'm not following you."

"Well, policies encouraged creative loans, and the private sector stepped in and responded to the loans with genius! I think his firm and others like him helped pave the way for huge sums of money, from around the world, to be flushed into our market. With all that money for housing, anyone, and Taylor I mean *anyone*, could get a loan, even if they couldn't afford the loan, or didn't deserve the loan. It's crazy!"

"That makes no sense. Why lend money to a person who won't make their mortgage payments and ultimately default?"

"Cash money, baby. The market players made their money on the front end."

"What market players?"

"The players like real estate agents, brokers, Wall Street bankers, lawyers—the players all made their money on the front end, either as a commission or fee, but basically, the players aren't sticking around to see if the risky debtors will fold on their loans."

"Okay, I'm sorry, Alex, but I'm lost. How's that good?"

"He's made money hand over fist, and he'll keep making money if things change. I don't see why things would, but he senses something is on the horizon, and he's gearing up to lead the way on foreclosures." Alex kicks pebbles with her right foot, as if to say, "kick 'em out."

"Whoa—wait!" Taylor balances herself. "Has the mountain changed?"

"Nope, same Piestewa Peak we always climb," Alex declares, looking at her surroundings and then at her friend. *Why can't she climb the mountain today?*

"Jeez, usually I'm climbing straight up this rocky terrain, not minding that there are no guardrails, but today, I need to hold onto something."

"Do you need a break?"

"No, let's keep climbing!" Taylor answers, and then asks, "Does your Mr. Right have a conscious?"

"Why do you ask?"

"Sounds like he created the housing market mess he expects will collapse, and now he's benefiting from the mess he made while people are losing their homes."

"Awe, greed." Alex smiles.

"So you get the problem?"

"What problem?" Alex asks, confused.

"This mess was made by greed—bank greed, industry greed, and Wall Street greed!"

"No, sorry," Alex says, shaking her head. "*Individual* greed. Folks were greedy, getting what they couldn't afford!"

"Alex, the banks and Wall Street, there's the greed," Taylor barks back, huffing again in between breaths.

"I didn't see banks forcing people to take loans."

"No, but—"

"I didn't see any handcuffs."

"No, but—"

"Personal choices, personal greed, plain and simple!"

"But the terms were not necessarily fair, I—I mean."

"Yep, but people weren't reading the documents, too excited about buying a house they couldn't afford."

Taylor comes to a stop, resting on a cliff where there is a full view of Phoenix. "Alex, most people thought their mortgages would stay the same. We, I mean people, did not expect to be upside down on their mortgages with the principal debt exceeding the homes' worth."

"I disagree. This is business, not charity. The terms were there."

"Corrupt or fraudulent business," Taylor says, throwing her hands up in the air.

"Nope," Alex says, shaking her head. "Lending isn't fraudulent. Lending's good for people."

"You sound like lending's altruistic."

"Actually, no. I'm not saying lending's good like Goodwill."

"Alex!"

"Look, a deal's a deal, and the Bush administration pushed lending standards to give people more, a slice of the pie, a piece of the American dream. If people overreached, that's on them, not Wall Street, the banks, the brokers, the agents, or anyone else."

"Yeah, yeah, right. Look, are you seeing anyone other than Stanley?" Taylor asks, obviously trying to change the subject.

Why do you ask? "No, only Stanley. I'll make this one work. He's a keeper."

"Humph," Taylor mutters, slipping again as they resume climbing. "Jeez, the climb's so hard today. I feel so unstable, like I'm climbing on an unstable foundation."

"You are. This is a rocky mountain."

"Yeah, I know. I climb this mountain all the time, but today, well my life, I don't know, I haven't been feeling like myself."

"In what way?"

"I'm sleepy all the time, and I'm craving meat—lots of meat."

"You don't eat meat."

"I know. I'm going to the doctor."

Chapter Forty-six
The Game

WEEKS LATER, TAYLOR sits on the couch in the Hamilton home and feels like she wants to puke. She smells a noxious odor and shouts, "Yuck, what's that smell!"

Jackson coughs.

"It's coffee. You like coffee, don't you?" Reagan asks.

"Yes, usually, but today, I have a throbbing headache, and the smell, the smell makes me want to puke. What kind of coffee are you brewing?" Taylor asks.

"The usual, Kona, your favorite."

"I'll admit, yes, that's usually my favorite, but not today." Taylor sinks into the sofa.

Reagan stops brewing the coffee. She lights a ginger-scented candle.

Whitfield rubs Taylor's shoulder and asks, "Are you okay, babe?"

"I don't know. I think I have pneumonia!"

Reagan rushes to her side and touches her forehead. "You don't have a fever."

"No, but I feel like I'm terribly ill, but I don't know, PMS maybe."

"Do you want ginger tea?"

"No, I'll be okay, especially if we can get the game started—and I can take a nap while you guys play—so speaking of getting the game started, where's Alex?" Taylor asks.

"Chasing some guy, I'm sure," Reagan responds.

"Why are you surprised?" Taylor asks.

"What?"

"You act like Alex being late or chasing men is new."

"Who me?" *You don't know about her affair?* "No, she knows where I live, and game night's always at the same place, at the same time." Reagan tries to change the subject.

"You can't change the subject, Reagan. What's up?"

"Nothing," Reagan says, shrugging.

"I've been out of the loop, so what's up? No secrets."

"Nothing. Here, look, try my new tea," Reagan suggests.

"Something's up because Alex has been acting strange."

"I'm sure she has," Reagan mumbles under her breath.

Obviously not hearing Reagan's whispers, Taylor continues. "Actually, we went hiking weeks ago, and first thing she wants to know is if we've talked. She looked relieved when I said no. Why?"

"I—well, nothing—yes something, but *she* has to tell you."

"She's not here, so talk! She's dating some guy. His name is Stanley," Taylor says.

Reagan begins to speak, but seeing the television screen, she shouts, "Wait, guys, wait!" Lifting the remote control and turning off the mute button, she shouts, "Look!"

"Wow, Will I Am," Whitfield mumbles.

"And other artists, they're—" Jackson pauses to cough, "—singing a song…"

"Yes we can, that's what the song sounds like," Reagan says.

"Genius!" Jackson proclaims in awe, watching Barack Obama on a background screen deliver a speech while Will I Am and countless other artists stand on stage delivering the Obama campaign speech as a song.

"Dude put a speech to lyrics, made a speech a song." Whitfield is shocked.

All stare at the screen while the song plays.

> *"It was a creed written into the founding documents declaring the destiny of a new nation. It was whispered by slaves and abolitionists blazing a trail toward freedom. Yes we can! It was sung by immigrants as they struck out from distant shores. And pioneers*

who pushed westward against an unforgiving wilderness. Yes We Can!

"It was the call of workers who organized and women who reached for ballots. A President who chose the moon as our new frontier. And A King who took us to a mountain top and pointed the way to the promised land. Yes We Can to justice and equality. Yes we can to opportunity and prosperity. Yes we can heal this nation. Yes We Can! We will remember there is something happening in America. That we are not as divided as our politics suggests. That we are one people. That we are one nation. And together we will begin the next chapter in America's story with three words that ring from coast to coast. Yes. We. Can."

Alex charges into the Hamilton home. She claps her hands and shouts, "Hello, hello? Snap out of your trance! Let's play Spades!"

"How about hello? What are you watching? What's the game?" Whitfield says.

Walking into the kitchen, Alex says, "You're caught up in the fanfare, as usual."

"What fanfare?" Whitfield asks.

"Obama, and the Will I AM worship fest. You're caught up. Snap to! I'm here for games, not politics. Let's play Spades!" Alex pours a glass of wine.

"Actually, we're watching the video while waiting on *you!*" Reagan exclaims.

"Great! So I'm here. Turn the television off. Let's play!"

Ignoring Alex, Reagan turns to the others and asks, "What's the game? Chess, Scrabble, Yahtzee, Taboo?"

"How about tricks?" Alex suggests.

"No! No! No! We're not turning tricks!" Reagan says. *No sin here!*

"Reagan, do we need to talk?" Alex asks.

"No, I'm not talking about your guy, la—la—la!" Reagan covers her ears. Noticing that Alex has stopped moving her mouth, Reagan takes her hands off her ears and adds, "And no turning tricks!"

"I'm not talking about turning tricks, I said a *game* of tricks, which means, Hearts, Spades, Whist, so please, calm down."

Relieved, Reagan smiles and says, "Good," but she thinks, *Never know with you. And these men are married, and you, well you—you're tricky!*

Rubbing her eyes, Taylor lies down on the couch and says, "I'm not playing, okay?"

Whitfield walks over to Taylor and whispers into her ear before clapping his hands and saying, "All right, Jackson, you're my partner. Let's go!" He heads to the table, like a coach rallying a team.

— 9: —

WHITFIELD SHUFFLES THE CARDS and thinks, *Good old Ray shuffling trick works every time!*

"Don't play games, Whit!" Taylor mumbles from the couch.

"Nah, I don't cheat, don't need to," Whitfield declares, although Taylor knows that *he* knows how to stack cards in his favor—a Ray male family tradition.

"Go easy," Taylor says.

"Nope, we'll take 'em, Tay!" Alex proclaims.

Sliding the cards towards Alex, Whitfield tells her to cut.

Smirking as she makes a clean, simple cut, Alex then slides the cards back to Whitfield, winks, and says, "Give me your best shot!"

"No winking, not at this table," Reagan says.

"We're playing Spades, Reag."

"Clean Spades," Reagan admonishes.

"You're not thinking what I think you're thinking, because I would never," Alex sincerely declares.

Whatever's going on between those two, we're using to our advantage, Whitfield thinks, dealing. He sporadically turns some of the cards face up as he deals.

"Don't turn my cards over!" Alex shouts.

"Can't take the heat, get out the kitchen," Whitfield suggests. He observes the cards closely that have turned face up. Seeing the cards, he surmises his hand is awful, and so is his partner's hand. He is certain Alex and Reagan have their cards. *How did the deck of cards get flipped?* Knowing the deal isn't going well for his team, he decides to balance the field by distracting the women.

"Alex, man yet?" Whitfield asks.

Ignoring Whitfield, Alex fixes her eyes on her cards.

Completing the deal and picking up his cards, he confirms that he has a bad hand. He tries to look like his hand doesn't faze him when he is actually terrified. Building himself up, deciding not to accept defeat, Whitfield organizes his cards. With all the cards lined up, he flinches. *Only one spade!*

Fake smiling while staring at his hand, he realizes he is toast. The game of Spades strategically rests with the number of spades a player has. Spades are the only trump cards, and he has next to none!

"Five tricks. I've got five tricks, how about you, partner?" Alex says.

How do you have five Spades? Whitfield wonders. *Cuz you have my hand!*

"Can you say books instead of tricks? I don't like that word," Reagan says, and then adds, "four, I have four books."

"Should we go board?" Jackson asks, which Whitfield knows is code. *Man, my hand is terrible. We've got to bid as low as we can go!*

"All right, they're going 9, we'll go 4!" Whitfield declares, and then immediately asks again, "So Alex, aren't you dating that guy, Stanley?"

"He's not the bad guy, is he?" Reagan asks.

"No Reagan, no, he's new. We've been dating, but not anymore," Alex answers, playing a spade.

"Come on, why not?" Whitfield asks, thinking, *No, she's not leading with spades! She's taking my only spade!*

Picking up the cards she won on this round, Alex says, "He's a jerk!"

"Is he single?" Reagan asks.

"Yes, but still, he's an idiot!"

"Reconsider, if he's single," Reagan chimes in.

"Yeah, Tay said dude was perfect for you!" Whitfield says, trying to engross Alex in a conversation.

"I did not!" Taylor says, getting up from the couch.

"Who cares, I'm done with him!" Alex answers, as Jackson plays an Ace of Diamonds and wins a round.

Whitfield high-fives Jackson, smiles, and then turns to Alex. "I bet he doesn't have a heart," he says. He winks at Jackson. He's trying to send him a code. He knows Jackson won this last round and will lead in the next round. He wants to tell Jackson he only has one heart. Hopefully Jackson will pick up on the code. The last thing he wants Jackson to do is play a heart, and more particularly a high valued heart like a King, Queen, or Jack, since Whitfield has only one heart, an Ace.

Jackson smiles and slams his card on the table.

"No, not the King of Hearts. I said he doesn't have a heart, doesn't have a heart!" Whitfield shouts.

"If he doesn't have a heart, what's the problem?" Jackson asks.

Resting his head against the back of his chair, Whitfield sighs. *We'll barely make four books I'm sure, and we just lost two books on this one hand.*

Reagan plays a 6 of Hearts.

Alex plays a 9 of Hearts.

Whitfield plays an Ace of Heart. He sighs.

"You said he doesn't have a heart, that's a huge heart!" Jackson yells out.

"Ha, talking your hand!" Alex smiles.

"You never win playing unfairly," Reagan says, scolding him.

"Your hand must be awful," Taylor adds.

"Nah, anyway, back to your guy. Who is he?" Whitfield asks.

"He's a bank lawyer," Alex answers, as if his profession and the clients he represents sum up the measure of the man, the full explanation of who and what kind of man he is.

"You don't say?" Whitfield says, eyeing his hand and then his partner, sighing again. He sends a non-verbal signal—*I hope you've got the rest of the books. I've got none.*

Jackson shrugs his shoulders. "Alex, you don't say," he pauses to cough, "a bank lawyer. Why break up?"

"Yeah, why?" Whitfield asks, like he really cares.

"While I thought we'd be the ultimate power couple, I was wrong."

Good. I think she's starting that female, too much information crap, feelings, keep going. "Ah yeah, you sound like the perfect match," Whitfield says, encouraging her.

"We had perfect dates—walks in the parks, front row seats to the Suns. He's a connoisseur of fine wines. He even has a wine cellar in his house!" Alex blushes.

"Sounds like a match made in heaven!" Whitfield holds back a laugh. *Can't believe we're talking this crap!*

Jackson asks an out of character question. "So, if he's everything, why didn't your relationship work?"

"Yeah," Whitfield says. "Shouldn't you try? You understand relationships take work."

"No, I know what he's about, seeing his true colors. We're done!"

"Really, wow! Why?" Jackson adds.

— 𝄢 —

ALEX PLAYS A JOKER and explains. "I went on a hike and brunch date with him, Camelback mountain."

"A what?" Whitfield asks.

Why does he care so much? Alex wonders before explaining. "Hike and brunch. You know, hike up Camelback and then go to the fresh market for brunch afterwards."

"Right, of course," Whitfield says, nodding his head.

"Okay, so we're hiking up the mountain. I'm really excited."

"Why end the relationship? Isn't a hike and brunch date enough for you to say I do?" Jackson asks, losing another round of the game.

"Yes, until he starts talking mid-hike."

"What, he's married?" Reagan snaps.

"No, Reagan, he's not married, he's single."

Looking relieved, Reagan says, "Just checking, again!"

She's so upset.

"Back to the new guy, what did he say, what's wrong?" Jackson says, then coughs.

"He tells me he's getting promoted."

"That's progress, a brother's moving up," Jackson says.

"Yeah, so what's wrong?" Whitfield asks.

"Nothing, I like progress. He's Managing Partner, I'm thinking great, more money."

"Right, so why didn't you marry him then and there?" Whitfield asks, his voice heavy with sarcasm.

"I would have. We were actually hiking and holding hands, until suddenly he tells me I was great the other night."

"So, what's wrong with that?" Whitfield asks.

"Sounds like a compliment!" Jackson adds, with a high-five to Whitfield.

Cutting her eyes at Jackson before turning and cutting her eyes at Alex, Reagan quietly asks, "You've slept with him already?"

Shrugging her shoulders, picking up yet another hand won, Alex continues, ignoring Reagan. "Frankly, I like compliments, and actually I'm standing there, looking into his eyes, thinking what you're probably thinking." *Surely he enjoyed the sex! Right?* "Yes, I'm certain he's giving me props when he continues and shocks my conscious."

"Your conscious?" Whitfield asks, surprised.

"You have a conscious?" Reagan asks.

"Yes! He tells me I completely satisfied all the men the other night."

Reagan drops her jaw.

Taylor sits up on the couch.

Jackson and Whitfield appear to suddenly connect with the conversation differently, like men fully engaged in a football game or some other activity that she's usually not privy to with them—porn or something. Their eyes are wide, as if the idea of Alex engaging in a threesome is of great interest to them, entertaining even.

"While you guys look creepy, I'll admit, I'm standing there on that mountaintop pretty pale. I'm thinking what I know you must be thinking. I know I was drunk that night, but did I have an orgy?"

"Alexandria Giroud!" Reagan looks like a nun who wants to punish Alex for her promiscuous ways. She inhales deeply, as if she is breathing in a full ball of fire along with the smoke, trying to hold back her wrath.

I know the idea of an orgy makes you want to go to the altar and pray for me all night. Alex thinks, before continuing. "So anyway, he says he'll close many deals with me by his side, pleasing his clients, stroking their happy spots!"

Wiping sweat off his brow, Jackson yells, "Wow!"

"Alex, I had no idea!" Whitfield says. He looks fascinated.

"Ice anyone?" Reagan asks, finishing off her lemonade and offering up her cup with ice chips to the men.

Ignoring the question, Alex continues. "He's standing there, telling me this, like he is experiencing uncontrollable excitement."

Biting on ice like popcorn, Jackson says, "I bet!"

"Hush!" Reagan says.

"He says Mr. Hiroshima admires my moves, appreciates my skills, and can't wait to touch me again! His words exactly, I swear!"

"Unbelievable, Alex!" Whitfield says, playing a Club.

"I know, and hearing the name Hiroshima, I'm immediately thinking, please—please—please, not his Japanese clients!"

Whitfield and Jackson burst out in laughter.

Reagan frowns, playing the King of Clubs.

Taylor shakes her head.

"He also says Hiroshima, Takarkta, and Toshiba like me on the pole."

"Alex, pole dancing?" Taylor asks, walking closer to the table.

"Exactly. That's what I'm surmising. Did I pole dance with four men?"

"You don't remember?" Reagan asks.

"I don't remember anything after my fifth Saki."

Reagan closes her eyes, as if she is praying.

Whitfield and Jackson lean in closer.

Taylor shakes her head.

Picking up another trick won, she adds, "He finally tells me what he's talking about, and once he does, I feel okay about my orgy."

"What, you got paid?" Whitfield asks.

"Whit!" Taylor shouts, before turning to Alex and asking, "How?" She places her hands on her hips.

"He clarifies and explains that I have a role," Alex says.

"I bet! I can only imagine what kind, too!" Whitfield grins.

"Yeah, boy I have a visual," Jackson says, smirking.

"Surely he's not prostituting you?" Taylor asks.

Reagan sits with her eyes closed.

"No, he wants to marry me. He wants to consider me as a suitor if and only if I understand my place. Again, his words exactly!"

"How does dude go from pole dancing and strip teasing to marriage? He wants," Jackson coughs, "a hooker wife?"

Whitfield jumps in. "I bet! I'll be honest. If Tay wants to jump on the pole, I have no objection, as long as she jumps on there for me only!"

"Jackson! Whitfield!" Reagan shouts.

"I agree. You guys are enjoying the whole debacle a bit too much!" Taylor adds.

Alex goes on, ignoring the men. "Well, actually, he wasn't talking about a pole but a poll, saying I'm on top of the poll of women he's considering as marriage material."

"Oh!" everyone says in unison. Taylor and Reagan look relieved. Jackson and Whitfield appear disappointed.

"I see," Reagan says. "Poll like a tally, ranking system, versus a pole like a strip pole or hooker table or whatever you call that stuff."

"Exactly, even though your terminology may be a bit off, you get my point," Alex says, nodding her head. "So see, this nut is talking marriage and tells me as long as I know how to be Ms. Stanley Robinson well, maybe I can pass the tests."

"Weird guy!" Whitfield says, before adding, "I thought he was talking real action."

"Come on, Whit, really!" Taylor says.

Alex nods. "Yes, this fool, he's talking about a poll, and then he says there are other tests, like having a stellar past or the ability to shrug off scandal and recreate myself."

"What?"

"He wants Ms. Perfect, or Ms. Crisis Manager as a wife."

"Interesting," Taylor says.

"Oh and don't forget, fertility! He's telling me his wife must produce two sons plus a daughter to boot!"

"He told you that?"

"Yep, that's what that self-centered, egotistical jerk said!"

"Why didn't you push him right off that cliff?" Taylor asks.

"Come on, Tay," Whitfield says.

"Well not literally of course," Taylor responds, not apologizing.

"So, what next?" Reagan asks, reengaging with the conversation, as if her time in prayer has ended seeing that the porn discussion has ceased.

"I tune him out while thinking, I should have known because this guy is only about business. He's an idiot!"

"What's wrong with business?" Whitfield asks.

"He structures deals like leveraged buy-outs, IPOs, and bankruptcies while having sex!"

"So you did have sex with him?" Reagan asks, playing the ten of diamonds.

"Yes, yes, yes, sex, sex, sex! Get over sex! You can say the word! I can have sex! I'm sure *you* have sex."

"I do, but I'm married."

"Yeah, yeah, blah, blah!"

"Wait—let me be clear. Since you say dude structures deals in bed, and I said I like business, let me say, for the record, I don't structure business deals in bed," Whitfield explains, defending his person, his honor. He plays a club.

"Did you renege?" Alex asks.

"No, actually I played what I meant to play."

"You have no diamonds?"

"No, I know what I'm doing, I didn't play off suit!" Whitfield says.

"I obviously have all the diamonds over here," Jackson says, playing his card.

"Don't talk your hand," Alex demands.

"Won't make a difference. Not this hand," Jackson mumbles.

Whitfield frowns at Jackson. "Hey, back to your story!"

Reagan rolls her eyes.

"Reagan, lighten up. She can keep the story clean, right?" Taylor asks.

"Yes, the rest is super G rated, Reagan, so relax," Alex says, chuckling. "Okay, so he tells me he's relocating, and he'll agree to date me long distance."

"As if he's doing you a favor?" Taylor says.

"Yes! And he asks me to sign a Letter of Intent!"

"What's that?"

"A binding agreement that includes the understanding between the parties in advance, before a formal contract is finished," Alex explains, playing the Joker because she wants to get it out of her hand. She does not want to clash later with her partner, who may be left with the Ace of Spades while she has another Joker.

Alex slams the card down on the table and says, "He lays out the deal while standing on the mountain."

"I know he's a lawyer, but that's too much," Reagan says, playing the Ace of Spades.

Smiling, Alex answers, "Yep, that's why all the way down the mountain, we're arguing. I keep a safe distance, too, so no one conveniently slips—which is good, because I really was close to pushing him off that mountain!"

Whitfield laughs.

Jackson coughs and laughs.

Reagan shakes her head in disbelief.

Interrupting the laughter, Alex plays another card and says, "I also canceled our brunch date. I asked him to take me home."

Reagan smiles and grabs their last book. "What did he say?"

"Nothing. He took me home!"

"Have you heard from him?" Reagan asks.

"Well, I call blocked his number!" Alex proclaims, raising her finger and pointing straight up to the ceiling.

"You call what?" Reagan asks.

"Call blocked. I call blocked him, which means when he calls, he gets a message that says, 'I'm sorry, but the caller does not accept calls from your line. If you feel you reached this message in error, please hang up and call again.'"

All laugh again, except Reagan, who looks perplexed.

"So I'm done with that chameleon!"

"Did he call?" Reagan asks.

"Yes, he was blocked though!"

"How do you know?" Taylor asks.

Pulling out her blackberry and scrolling through her email, Alex says, "Because that idiot sent me an email! Here, take a look!" She finds the email and passes her blackberry around for all to see.

✉**To: Alexandria Giroud**
From: Stanley Wiley
Re: The Demise of the American Family
Attachment:
The Good Wife's Guide, Housekeeping Monthly, 13 May 1955

As you may recall, we discussed roles and responsibilities during our climb on Camelback Mountain. From your response, it appears you are out of touch with a good woman's role. Please see the attached article. Gender roles were staples in my home growing up. My mother used the attached model to train my sisters, who, by the way, are both happily married, with two sons and one daughter each. Perhaps you should weave some of these values into your 21st century female power lifestyle.

In addition, your phone appears to be out of order. Give me a call if you think you can fall in line. Besides, I am flexible. You can work if you can balance.

By the way, read the attached article closely. What do you see? I know you watched "Black In America" on CNN recently. You saw the demise of the black family, which really spills over to all American families now if we're not careful. The article shows that everybody was happy. Perhaps if more American families followed this model we wouldn't have broken homes. Think about it, Alex—think!

Housekeeping Monthly 13 May 1955
The Good Wife's Guide

Plan ahead, even weeks in advance, to have a delicious meal ready for him when he comes home.

Prepare yourself. Take 30 minutes to rest so you'll be refreshed and ready for him.

Be happy and gay! Be interesting to him. His boring day may need a lift and one of your duties is to provide him joy.

Plan ahead and light a fire for him to unwind by. Your husband will feel he has reached a haven of rest and order. After all, catering to his every need will fill you with immense personal satisfaction.

Be happy to see him. Greet him and show him your desire to please him.

Put a ribbon in your hair. Powder your nose.

Listen to him. You may have many things to tell him, but the moment of his arrival is not the time.

Let him talk first—remember, his topics of conversation are more important than yours.

Always smile. Never fuss. Never complain, even if he comes home late or stays out all night. Count this as minor compared to what he might have dealt with during his day.

Your duty: Be ready when he comes home. Make your home a place of peace, joy, pleasure, and tranquility.

Don't ask him questions. Don't question his judgment.

Always remember a good wife knows and stays in her place.

"Ha, he's sick!" Jackson says, coughing.

"Dude's got tricks!" Whitfield pauses, then adds, "Like that line—ha—'be ready,' classic."

"Yep, he's sick, but I'm done with him. Besides, I'm going to L.A. next week. I've got a corporate deposition, but maybe I'll find something more than jewels and clothes and purses on Rodeo Drive?" Alex says, smiling.

Chapter Forty-seven
Everlasting Hope

Taylor calls her OB-GYN and asks the receptionist, "Can you slip me in today?"

"Ms. Ray, sorry to hear you're not feeling well. What are your symptoms?" The receptionist speaks with a soft, nurturing tone of voice.

"A throbbing, continuous headache, nausea, and fatigue." *I can fall asleep anywhere, even now, holding this phone.*

"All right dear. We can fit you in at 2:00, but I bet I know what's going on with ya."

"What? I'm pre-menopausal?" *Because I feel like I have PMS on wheels, triple amped, except this isn't my time of the month! I mean I get—*

Chuckling, the receptionist says, "No, Ms. Ray, I doubt you're pre-menopausal."

"Then what? Tell me what causes nausea, headaches, a strong sense of smell, odd cravings, and—"

"Ms. Ray, listen to yourself. Don't you hear what you're describing?"

"Yeah, PMS on wheels, right?"

"No, I think you're pregnant."

— ?: —

Hours later, Taylor sits in the OB-GYN's lounge. She bites her nails, feeling trepidations. She is certain she is pre-menopausal. *I know I'm reproductively dormant—that's why I can't get pregnant!* She feels anticipation, too, because she hopes the receptionist is correct. *Please let today be the day. Please—*

"Taylor Ray!" Nurse Wiley, a tall, twenty-something woman with milky chocolate skin and deep brown eyes calls her from the doorway, clipboard in hand.

Taylor gets up and walks towards Nurse Wiley, feeling at once both heavy and light. She smiles. *I feel so excited, and nervous—so conflicted.*

"Not feeling well?" the nurse asks.

"I'm not—I'm, well, something has taken over me," Taylor answers, following the nurse down the bright, narrow hallway leading to the examination room.

"We'll take care of you. Let's get your weight." Nurse Wiley stops at the hallway scale.

Taylor steps on.

Nurse Wiley announces, "One thirty-five. Good, and your height."

She pauses as Taylor steps up to the metric system.

"Your height is 5'7"."

"Ms. Ray, next I need you to step into the restroom. Please leave a sample in the ladies room and proceed to exam room three once you're done."

Entering the dark restroom, Taylor washes her hands. *Don't want to contaminate the test!* Then she squats and urinates in the cup provided.

Wanting good news, Taylor prays over the urine before placing the white cup in a small, two-way door affixed to the bathroom wall right above the sink.

Come on! Come on! She wants to confirm that the lab technician or nurse or whoever performs the pregnancy test gets the urine before she exits the bathroom, and so she waits. *Tick tock tick tock, come on already, the pee can get cold or contaminated or—wait, she's grabbing the cup! Awesome, and she's wearing gloves, too—good!*

Taylor felt like she could go now. It was no longer necessary to cover and protect her sample. *I know I don't pray much,* she thought, *but please, let the news be good!*

Chapter Forty-eight
On the Road Again

ALEX SITS ON an airport runway, waiting to exit a plane. She plans to meet her client's corporate representative, Dr. Seth Anu, as soon as she exits the plane in L.A.

She smiles, thinking about meeting Dr. Anu. She has heard about him, she has even seen pictures of him. She hasn't met him in person. She anticipates his arrival with glee—*a full view of this man and time alone with him would be nice!*

Walking off the plane and into the airport, she searches the crowd until she sees the man. He doesn't disappoint. He is Middle Eastern looking, with jet-black curly hair and hazel-eyes. He's standing outside her gate holding a briefcase with a HealthSolutions, Inc. logo.

"Dr. Anu?" Alex approaches him and extends her hand.

"Yes, Ms. Giroud?" He takes her hand and shakes it, firmly.

Nice, warm hands, she thinks.

"How was your flight?" Alex asks, turning and leading the way to the executive car that is waiting for them outside the airport. She chats with him about the usual cordial niceties. His flight, her flight, the weather, L.A., their agenda, and lunch plans.

– ♪ –

ONE HOUR LATER, ALEX sits with Dr. Seth Anu in a cozy, outdoor, beachfront, European-styled bistro, sipping on an iced coffee—Caffè freddo—while preparing for the deposition. Watching him sip on an iced Sangria, Alex says, "Dr. Anu, you've had your deposition taken before obviously?"

"Many times," he answers, nodding his head.

"You know the preliminary issues?"

"Yes, same challenge, different people," he says, sounding calm.

"Right. So going to the heart of the matter. The Estate of Rita Luiz is suing Health Solutions because she died."

"Like all the other cases."

"Right. So they're saying Health Solutions is responsible for her death because—"

"Health Solutions did not pay for an experimental treatment. What was the actual treatment this time?" He pauses to consider. "Breast cancer, experimental treatment."

"Yes, so, as I was saying, Dr. Anu, we know she died."

"Yes, clearly."

"And the cause was breast cancer."

"Yes, she had Stage IV breast cancer, which is usually always fatal. She had an aggressive cancer. We couldn't help her."

"Precisely. Except the Estate believes the experimental treatment could have saved her life."

"I understand. Akin to others, families always want to exhaust all measures, even if the measure won't work," Dr. Anu says.

"Which is understandable but irrelevant," Alex says.

"Yes, cleary," Dr. Anu agrees, as if she is merely stating the obvious.

Alex consults her notes and then says, "I've reviewed Ms. Luiz's Health Solutions policy and the facts are undisputable—"

"Yes, experimental treatments aren't covered. Why are we here?" he asks, as if he is agitated by the deposition preparation.

"I want to make sure you understand our strategy. Her physician told her a bone marrow transplant would save her life."

Dr. Anu nods.

"She wanted the bone marrow transplant."

Dr. Anu nods again, still looking uninterested.

"We didn't agree with her physician. We believe the treatment was experimental and unnecessary."

"Which the treatment was," Dr. Anu says. "There's only a 25 percent survivability rate with the treatment, which we believe is insufficient, and thus we classify the treatment as experimental."

"Exactly, Dr. Anu, but let's work on your delivery…" she says. "Those are the facts, but let's tweak the facts a bit, work on the delivery, so the facts don't seem so harsh."

Hours pass. Alex coaches and tweaks Dr. Anu's testimony. She tries to get his words to ring out as understandable statements; she tries to get him to sound likeable. He listens and nods continuously, almost as if he is bored, as if the deposition preparation is a mere formality rather than a necessity.

Alex persists. She parses and slices and dices his words until finally she feels he is ready. "I think we're done," she says.

Leaping up from his seat and heading towards the door, like a convict who is suddenly released from prison, Dr. Anu disappears.

Why are the good ones already married? Alex wonders, watching him exit. She recalls the wedding band sitting on his finger.

Chapter Forty-nine
Corporate Deposition

*A*LEX WALKS INTO a dimly lit, cold-feeling strip-mall office building, thinking, *We're choosing the deposition location next time. This place stinks!*

The floor is old linoleum, green and tan fake tile. It contrasts oddly with her designer shoes and clothes. The hallway is lit only with flickering fluorescent lights, which from the looks of things, could give off their last flicker any minute.

Stepping ahead on this unfamiliar, aesthetically different and financially distinguishable hallway, she tells herself, *Don't let the slum throw you off. You've got a job to do.*

She picks up her pace and steps towards her destination. She is crisp, tailored, and prepared.

Seeing her destination in front of her now, Alex stops to adjust her hair and attire. She tucks in her already neatly tucked-in shirt before opening the door and entering.

Jumping to her feet, a woman says, "Hi. Lula Smith. Smart Court Reporting Agency."

"Where's everyone?" Alex asks. She hands Lula Smith a white business card that boldly displays her firm name, her title, and contact information.

"We're early! I mean, I'm always early. I'm the court reporter. You can't start the depos without me. I please my clients. I always come early. What about you?"

"I understand." Alex keeps her sentences short. She hopes to serve as an example. She wants to silence the chatterbox.

"I'm glad we're early. We'll have some time to get to know each other. We'll talk girl talk, before the others come. And we may be here waiting and chatting awhile. Did you know the others may be late because something's brewing in town? There's a circus, I think, a mad house. I reckon someone's causing trouble."

Too much information, and no, we're not getting to know each other. Alex ignores the court reporter and focuses on where she will sit and where she'll have Dr. Anu sit.

Obviously unaware of Alex's thoughts, Lula Smith continues. "I think there's some protest. I saw some commotion, huge deal, on my way here.... The streets, they're lined with locals. Folks chanting and hollering, and protesting, waving signs, saying stuff like PEACE and THE REAL AXIS OF EVIL: POVERTY, RACISM, AND WAR, and Ms. Alex—can I call you Ms. Alex?—Ms. Alex, the folks, their eyes, they were wild-eyed. Like they were mad, but I can understand, but still...I mean, I'm thinking, I may be strapped for cash, but please people move. I've got to get to work. My deposition. I'm here, gladly employed, and looking forward to working with you."

Alex decides not to converse with Lula about politics. *Unpatriotic liberals don't get it,* she thinks. *Bush and Cheney have kept our country safe! I swear...* Alex sees the door opening and is glad she won't have to spend any more time listening to *Ms. Talks Too Much.*

Walking in, looking arrogant and debonair, Dr. Anu says, "Good morning." He introduces himself to the court reporter and then glances at Alex. "Are we ready?" he asks.

"Yes, absolutely, we're ready," Alex answers. She bolts over to Dr. Anu and pulls him aside. She engages in small talk outside Ms. Lula Smith's reach.

Alex is just beginning to wonder where the plaintiff's counsel is when suddenly, a confident woman enters, looking put together but understated.

"Good morning, I'm Renee Moss," the woman says, introducing herself. "I apologize. I'm usually timely, except there was traffic. I think protesters were out exercising their constitutional rights."

Glancing at Alex with a smirk, Renee asks, "Ms. Giroud, the accommodations, how do you find them? I hope you like the location."

"We're not here to address accommodations. Shall we get started?" Alex asks, wanting to get down to business. She surmises that the location was purposefully selected to throw her off, make her feel uncomfortable, and get her off track.

Alex has heard about Renee Moss, and she is familiar with her firm, Moss, Renard & James, a national firm that sues rich businesses with deep pockets. Alex knows corporate slip-ups are Renee's claim to fame.

Alex also knows that Renee uses tricks. She tries to distract, act like she's poor and feeble. She is known for throwing out lines like, "We're a small outfit, unlike the silk-stocking, corporate insiders on the other side of the courtroom. We help the little guy with limited resources." Alex does not fall for the "woe-is-me; we're poor," trick. She knows the slogans Renee touts are untrue. Renee and her firm are extremely rich.

Renee begins the deposition like a pro.

"State your name for the record," Renee begins.

"Seth, Adu, M.D.," Dr. Anu answers. He sounds professional, likeable even.

"What is your full name?" Renee asks, as if to suggest Dr. Anu is holding something back.

"Dr. Seth Anu," Dr. Anu answers again, with the same posture and tone. He is not flustered by her follow-up question. "Seth Anu is my name, and I am a medical doctor, so Dr. Seth Anu."

Renee asks him at least twenty follow-up questions about his name. Afterwards, she moves to his background. Hours later, she turns to the case.

"What is your title?" Renee asks.

"Medical Director, Health Solutions," Dr. Anu answers.

"What are your duties?"

"I'm the Medical Director. My duties are broad."

"Let's hone in on your denying legitimate insurance claims," Renee says.

"Objection, form," Alex says.

"Please answer, focusing in on your denial of legitimate health insurance claims," Renee says, ignoring Alex.

"Objection, again, and I'm instructing the witness not to answer."

"Why, I'm only asking a question?"

"When you ask a question, he will answer. You're making statements."

"I believe he asked *me* a question. I believe he stated his duties were broad. He asked me to narrow the scope of the question. I did," Renee explains.

"When you ask a question, he'll answer," Alex says, standing firm.

"Your job. Your job was to deny insurance claims, correct?" Renee asks, ignoring Alex.

"Yes, unnecessary claims, yes, correct," Dr. Anu answers.

Renee continues, asking Dr. Anu at least one hundred questions about his day-to-day duties before moving on to her next line of questioning, the medical necessity of treatment.

"How do you determine medical necessity?"

"We use the standard generally accepted in the medical community."

"Which is?"

"We compare the requested treatment against scientific and medical research to determine whether the treatment is necessary or experimental. We use scientific and medical evidence to determine whether the requested treatment will actually work. We only classify a treatment as medically necessary if the treatment is proven, which means the treatment is capable of curing the patient."

"By what percentage? Isn't a 5 percent chance proven to cure a patient 5 percent of the times?"

"Scientific evidence requires a cure rate higher than 5 percent," Dr. Anu answers.

"So if I'm dying, you won't save me even if there is a 5 percent chance I could live?"

"If the scientific evidence shows the method is only effective 5 percent of the time, and the cure is ineffective 95 percent of the time, we would deem the cure medically unnecessary."

Guess she thinks she won one, Alex thinks, watching Renee Moss fire off more questions about medical necessity.

Three hours later, Alex is able to determine that the plaintiffs clearly have a different view of medical necessity. As far as they're concerned, if there is a 00000.1 percent chance the treatment could work, they believe the insurance company should treat the cure as medically necessary.

After exhausting any and every question Alex has ever heard asked about whether a treatment is medically necessary, Renee Moss next turns to experimental treatments, which is Health Solutions' basis for excluding treatment in this case because an experimental treatment is not medically necessary.

"Isn't it true Mrs. Luiz had cancer?"

"Yes."

"Isn't it true a bone marrow transplant is a cure for the type of cancer Mrs. Luiz had and died from?"

"Remotely, yes, but not medically necessarily so."

"I'm not following you. Either bone marrow transplants cure breast cancer or not. That's a yes or no question."

"Objection!" Alex says.

"Your objection is noted, but your witness must answer."

Alex argues about the question for minutes until finally she agrees. She allows the witness to answer.

"Yes, remotely so—a 5 percent chance."

"Yes or no, and your answer is yes?" Renee Moss asks again.

Alex objects again.

Dr. Anu answers, "Yes. Remotely, unscientifically."

Renee Moss continues, asking questions about experimental treatment, necessary treatments, unnecessary treatments, whether the treatment could have saved Mrs. Luiz's life, whether Mrs. Luiz paid insurance payments but when it was time for her to receive insurance coverage Health Solutions denied her claim, asking questions over and over for many hours, questions, answers, re-questions, re-answers, objections, questions and on and on, until twelve hours later, the deposition ends.

Alex beams. She feels the deposition went well, even though Renee got Dr. Anu to make a few significant concessions.

Yes, Dr. Anu admitted that he received a bonus for denying medical benefits.

Yes, Dr. Anu admitted that he received a one million dollar bonus for saving Health Solutions 30 million dollars in insurance claims over a six-month period.

Yes, Dr. Anu admitted that he excluded benefits mainly by relying upon the "experimental treatment" or "medically unnecessary" labels.

Yes, Dr. Anu admitted that a bone marrow transplant could have saved Mrs. Luiz's life.

Yes, Alex understands that these concessions, along with a surviving widow and young children, could be compelling to a jury, but she walks out of the deposition wearing a confident smile. She knows she has a weapon—a weapon that insures the case will never be heard by a judge or a jury. She plans to stop this case, like so many other cases, with a Motion to Dismiss.

Chapter Fifty
Rodeo Drive, Los Angeles, CA

"YOU WERE GREAT!" Alex tells Dr. Anu, leading him towards the elevator. "Any plans?" *Perhaps we can do something?*

Her cell phone rings before he can answer.

Seeing Richardson, Davis & Hanes flash across her CALLER ID, she tells Dr. Anu, "Got to take the call. Can you wait?"

"No, I apologize. I'll barely make my flight," he answers, looking at his watch.

She wishes he would change his flight plans, but Dr. Anu gets onto the elevator and disappears.

The phones rings again, and this time, she picks up. "Hi, Heidi, sorry I didn't answer the first time. How's the office?"

"Alex, they're everywhere, like beeves in hives!" Heidi whispers.

"Beeves, hives? Speak English, Heidi. What are you saying?"

"Alex, they—they are swarming. Alex, they're raiding!"

"Like an immigration raid? You are legal, aren't you?"

"Si, I mean yes. I don't know, but Alex."

"What? Speak!"

"Alex, they're here searching and looking, but I don't think this is an immigration raid. Alex, I'm concerned because they're peaking and searching like it is. I think this is a raid."

"Who's searching?"

"IRS, Justice Department, and FBI agents, everywhere."

"What?" Alex glances at her watch. *Do I have time, Rodeo Drive?*

"Alex, that's why I'm calling you, senorita. What should I do?"

"About what? Didn't the firm fight the search?"

"I think Marshall tried, but the IRS and Justice Department had a warrant."

A warrant? How? Warrants are only issued if there is reasonable suspicion that a crime has been committed. "Okay Heidi, listen—" Alex begins, but Heidi interrupts.

"Alex, I've got to go."

"Why?"

"Alex, they're coming. They've been searching your office and Marshall's office—but, oh my, pray for you!" Heidi gasps.

"Heidi what?"

"Alex, an agent has your desktop computer in his hands. He's taking the computer out of your office. And Alex, wait, oh my, he's closing your blinds!"

In my office, my computer? I don't use the desktop, but closing blinds, why? "Heidi, what—?"

"Alex, I've got to go."

"Wait."

"Can't."

"Why?"

"The agents are heading my way." Heidi hangs up.

"Heidi wait!" Alex hears a dial tone. *Did she hang up? She did! What the—!*

Chapter Fifty-one
Get Here Now

ALEX, STILL STANDING in the barely lit hallway, stares into florescent flickering lights as if the dim illumination can shed light on her situation.

Her thoughts flash through her mind with each flicker until one flickering light brightly flashes and then burns out, making the hallway even darker.

Her telephone rings again. Seeing her firm name, Richardson, Davis & Hanes, flash across her CALLER ID, and particularly her boss, Marshall Hanes' extension, Alex answers. "Alexandria Giroud!"

"Come! Our hotel suite!" Marshall demands.

What? Her body actually leans forward as she asks the internal question. Going on a mental tirade, her thoughts continue. *You're seeing your wife of course, and I think Rachel McCay, too, but you want me to come to your hotel suite now? Nope! Sorry!*

"Alex, did you hear me? Get here!" Marshall commands.

"I can't, Marshall!" she answers. *I want to make you wait. How do you feel now that the shoe is on the other foot?*

"I'm not shitting around. Get here!"

Deciding to take up for herself, she says, "Marshall, you're not serious about me."

"Alex, I don't have time for your shit! Get your things and meet me at the hotel suite."

"Sorry—I can't," she declares. She knows the distance helps her deny him. She appreciates the distance because she hears the tension in his voice. She knows that if she were in Phoenix now, she would not be able to turn him down; but with the distance, she can. With distance on her side, she adds, "Marshall, we can't do this anymore. I can't." She wants him to have that gut-wrenching, stomach-turning feeling one gets when a person wants something really badly but can't have it. Alex wants to orchestrate chaos in his heart. "Sorry, other plans!"

"Alex, get here!" he demands again.

He really needs me, wow. "Marshall, I'm out of town, sorry—but—"

"I know you're in L.A. Why do you think you're in L.A.? I needed you gone, so you were gone. Do you really think Richardson needed you to take that deposition? No. You work for me! Anyway, understand Alex, I need you back!"

Her rage ignites. "I'm not your puppet!" she shouts, stomping her foot.

"I can't believe I'm having this conversation," he says, exhaling noisily. "Get your skinny butt here!"

Alex cringes.

Her blood boils.

"So get your shit!" he commands, "and understand, Alex, I own you! Go downstairs; get in the car that's waiting for you. The driver will get you to the chartered jet!"

"But—"

"Alex, I'm not shitting with you. If you don't get your shit and get here within the next three hours, don't show up at work on Monday!"

Chapter Fifty-two
Chartered Jets

*A*LEX SITS ON a chartered jet where luxury abounds, but her heart sinks. She feels like an empty vessel that is being used up and spit out by a malicious man.

I can't go to that hotel suite, not tonight. . . .
But I feel I must. If I don't go, what will he do?

She feels like he has her caught in a musical refrain; she is unable to escape the chorus.

Is he right? Does he own me?

Her cell phone rings.

Seeing the caller, she answers, "Hi, Mom."

"Alexandria," her mother says, in a soft, soothing voice. "I woke up with you on my mind. Are you well, dear?"

Alex pauses, wondering if she can tell her mom what's been going on. She needs someone to talk to, so she tells her mom the full story—starting with Marshall and what his demands are after a long, drawn out, empty affair. After telling her mom about Marshall, she finds herself talking about the other men in her life—Duncan Anderson, Stanley Robinson, Mr. Hot Man, except she makes up a name for him, Luke Wellington. She then turns back to Marshall Hanes and how he uses her. He has sex with her. He mistreats her. He does have a hold on her. He has been manipulating her. She asks her mother, "What should I do?"

Her mom is silent.

Hearing silence, Alex next talks about her life, which she feels is spiraling out of control. Finally, her mom interrupts.

"Alexandria, I'm sorry."

"Why?"

"I haven't always been an example."

"Mom, you're like Mother Teresa."

"I set rules, certainly, but I wasn't an example."

"You're practically a nun!" *You never once had sex or a date after Dad left! Come to think of it, you weren't really having sex even before Dad left.*

"Yes, but I did not guide you, and as a result, you've obviously rejected my rules, my guidance, and adopted some cavalier relationship about men and sex."

Okay, not what I was expecting.

"I know I was broken when your father left me."

Well yes—

"Understand, too, your father—we were in love when we first married, but our relationship wasn't healthy, and that's what you saw, until one day, he cheated."

Right.

"And I accepted his cheating. I did not believe in divorce and as a result, I let him cheat. I thought the young woman he dated could fill a void and bring his and our happy back."

Yep, I saw that helplessness…Mom, that was sick.

"And so I stayed. I kept up appearances while he cheated on me, mistreated me, until one day he couldn't stand to keep up the appearances any longer, and so he left. You saw that."

Yes, I did, but—

"You developed the wrong impressions about relationships. Alex, I think because of us, you don't know how to love."

"Mom, you're exaggerating, I think I know…"

"Alex, you can't, not from what you're telling me."

"Well, Mom, with all due respect, do you?"

"Yes, Alex, I do, and listen, love-joys are yours to share. You want someone who cares for you more than you care for you and vice versa—in love, you shouldn't have to defend your own honor because your love champions your honor, and vice versa."

Okay.…

"Alex, you want someone who thinks only of you. You want a love that stands the test of time and strengthens you. A person who you will share your youth and aged-times with, completely fulfilled. You must wait for the one—the great one—your soul mate, the love of your life."

Mom....how do you know? You've only been with Dad, and he cheated on you. He even left you. He surely didn't love you....

"Alex, if you waste your life with people who are ailments and only feed your sorrow, you will not experience life-pleasures, life-treasures."

Mom, have you been to therapy or something because you sound different....

"Understand? You can choose differently. You can choose life! Alex, life is love. If you choose love, you'll experience life's riches. But you must patiently wait and stop settling. Greatness takes time."

Sexual pleasure is greatness!

"Also, please understand that being alone is preferable to miserable company. Baby, learn to love *you*. Stay in love with yourself, and once you do, misery has no place in your space. You should release yourself only when greatness appears!"

"Mom, again, I'm young, single, and—"

"Professional, I know, but alone, miserable, and aching, and terribly unhappy." She pauses before adding, "Alex, wait on love."

"I don't have time."

"Do you remember the Bible?"

"Okay, I really have to go."

"Corinthians has the perfect definition of love."

"Oh brother," Alex says.

"'Love is patient, love is kind. It does not envy, it does not boast, it is not proud. It is not rude, it is not self-seeking, it is not easily angered, it keeps no records of wrongs. Love does not delight in evil but rejoices with the truth. It always protects, always trusts, always hopes, and always perseveres. Love never fails.'"

"Mom, be real, those are ancient times."

"I am, Alex. Learn to love. Your choice, but I hope you choose love."

"Mom, I love myself, can't you tell?"

"Do you really? If you did, you'd know that allowing yourself to affair with a married man while sleeping with countless unknown men isn't love."

Do you understand how many orgasms I've had? "Mom, you're upset because Dad cheated on you."

"No, let's be clear. I'm not bitter, and I'm not guilty; that affair was your father's failure, not mine; understand, life has good times and bad ones, but you control the compass of the road."

Okay?

"Consider a rock. A rock can be either a burden or a stabilizer. A tree can be either a nurturer or a road block. A mountain can be either an obstacle or a summit. In life, you have choices; you must decide what you'll make of the choices you have. You decide."

"Mom, I *am* deciding. I'm deciding to do whatever with whomever I want whenever I want. I'm free."

"Then why are you sitting on a chartered jet, flying back to Phoenix, deliberating over whether you have to go see this married man, in a hotel suite that he affairs in, when you don't want to go see him? Didn't you say he told you to get there or not bother showing up for work? How is that being free? Honey, to be frank, I swear, that's the same persecution our ancestors fought from, fled from, demanded to be free from. You're free but doing the same thing—difference is, they didn't have a choice; you do."

"Mom, you're exaggerating."

"Now, I understand why my great-grandmother often warned, freedom starts in the mind."

"Mom, please don't go back."

"Alex, I know I've shielded you, but actually, you must know your past to see your future; so you don't repeat mistakes."

"Mom, I'm not, so no history."

"Listen, okay, your history, our history, I'll wait, but choices, choose wisely."

"Mom, my life's complicated."

"Complicated or not, life is still about choices."

"I understand."

"Yes, and back to why I'm apologizing. I didn't make good choices always; I wasn't the best example."

"You were a good Mom."

"Yes, I did my best, but I can see why you're confused."

"I'm not confused."

"You are, and I'll acknowledge my part. I was unhealthy and you saw that."

"No, Mom, you're too hard on yourself."

"No, I'll acknowledge, I spent sixteen years where the rock was a burden not a stabilizer; the tree, a road block, not a nurturer; the mountain, an obstacle, not a summit."

"O-kay."

"Alex, woe is me was my theme. I was a victim."

"Yep, you were good at the woe is me."

"Yes, but for a season; I've awakened. Now, I spend each day climbing summits with stabilizing rocks and nurturing trees. I smell the flowers in the valleys, and I hear the symphony in rain."

Alex is silent. *Did she say she climbs summits with stabilizing rocks and nurturing trees? Did she say she smells the flowers in the valleys and hears the symphony in the rain? Wow! Is she in love?*

"Alex, I've enjoyed life's journey, each hike. I know life is beautiful if you give real love a chance."

"Mom, have you found love?"

"Yes, Alex."

"No way! Who is he?"

"Alex, me. I fell in love with me. I released the burdens. I want the same for you."

"So, what, you've been having a love fest with you?"

"Yes, Alex. I am in love with myself, and after I fell in love with myself and truly loved myself, I was ready for him."

"Mom, are you serious?"

"Yes, Alex, and I must say, this love is the greatest of my life." She pauses and adds, "Well, aside from my kids, of course. That love being different but a great love, too. Alex, dear, I want the same for you. But first you must rid yourself, get rid of the baggage. Don't go and see that man. Instead, you stand up! You tell him no, I'm not coming! And then you dare him to fire you!"

Chapter Fifty-three
Executive Cars

"Ms. Giroud, we've landed. Your driver, he's waiting," the pilot tells Alex, as she sits in her seat, on the airplane, staring out at the black executive car that she knows Marshall Hanes has waiting on her.

Sitting there, she reminisces. She hears Marshall's words and her mother's words again in her mind, each sentence bouncing off the other until the words actually blend together.... *Don't bother coming in on Monday! You dare him! Don't bother. Dare him. Don't bother. Dare! Bother! Dare!* —

"Ms. Giroud, again, may I help you?" the pilot asks, standing in the plane doorway now, obviously wanting to deplane but waiting on her to exit first.

"Ms. Giroud?"

"Yes, I'm fine," she says, awakening from her trance.

Getting up, she exits with her decision in hand. *I'm going home!*

Passing the executive car driver, Alex walks towards the airport entrance.

"Ms. Giroud," the driver yells, running towards her.

She ignores him.

Reaching her in no time, the driver says, "Ms. Giroud, you need a ride, don't you?"

"No, I'll pass, unless you're taking me home."

"I do have a hotel listed as your location, but I want the business. I'll take you anywhere you want. I don't have to follow the instructions."

Certain the driver will take her home now, she gets inside the executive car and rides.

On her way from the Scottsdale Airport to her home in downtown Phoenix, she tries to call Taylor Ray. There is no answer. She calls Taylor Ray again. Still no answer.

Since Taylor does not answer, Alex calls Duncan Anderson instead—*The one or should have been the one.*

He answers.

She tells Duncan Anderson the details, well, the *clean* details. She also lies. She describes her sexual relations with Marshall as unwelcomed sexual advances by him.

In an instant, Duncan Anderson has a solution.

"Sue him, Alex. Sue him if he tries anything, understand?"

Why aren't I with you? she wonders, as she listens to Duncan talk her through to a solution.

— ♪ —

PULLING INTO HER CONDO, she exits the car and hands the driver a sizeable tip. "I don't know if you heard anything, but, the details, keep quiet, do you understand?"

"Like I said, I'm only the driver with an executive car service. I'm no messenger," he concedes, smiling at his hand, which holds a one hundred dollar tip.

She turns and swiftly walks to her condo building.

"Ms. Giroud, welcome back," the doorman says, opening the door.

How did you know I was gone? You're so nosey. "Hi, Mr. Beatty." Alex briskly walks to the condo elevator and thereafter ascends upwards to the penthouse floor.

Entering her home, feeling alone, she sits on her sofa and picks up a book, trying to clear her mind. The telephone rings.

It's Marshall Hanes.

She does not answer.

He calls again.

She does not answer.

He calls again.

She does not answer.

She checks her voicemail.

She hears message after message, one after another….

"Alex, Marshall, I'm waiting," he says, in an agitated voice. He hangs up.

"Alex," he pauses. "The pilot told me you're in town. Where are you?" In the next message, he sounds irate; he's almost screaming. "Alex, shit, get your ass here!" He hangs up.

Next message: "Alex, shit, stop playing games! I'm waiting." He stops, then says, "Don't keep me waiting," He sounds calmer now.

He waits.

Her phone stops ringing, then he calls again and leaves another message.

"Alex, I'm sorry, but I need you." He says this in a soft, needy voice.

Hearing his messages, she thinks one thing: *I need a friend.*

Alex calls Taylor Ray again, but she does not answer. Next, she calls Reagan Hamilton. "Hello?"

"Reagan, I'm stuck…"

"Doing what? Wait, please don't tell me."

"No, not sexually, listen, I'm stuck. He wants me there, but I want to be here."

"Wait, slow down. Who, when, and what are you talking about?"

"Marshall. He wants me to meet him at our place."

"You have a place?"

"Yes, we have a hotel."

"He, you guys, you actually own a hotel?"

"No, not actually, he rents one specific room; that's our place, he's there."

"Alex, that's sick! I'm sure you're not the only one…that's not *your* place…"

"Okay, fine, whatever. I wasn't going to go, but he keeps calling. He was nice the last time at least. I want to go."

"Alex, do you hear yourself? He was nice the last time?"

"I know, I know, and I know. I see now. Marshall, the others, these guys, these men, they've been like band-aides, protection over other wounds…."

"Alex, you *do* see," Reagan says, as if in shock. "How?"

"I talked to Mom, I talked to Duncan. I've been thinking, I know, I see...."

"Duncan? Isn't he one of the guys?"

"Yep, well sort-a, but, well, we're—look anyway, listen. I know, I understand the wounds. They're open...I'm hurting...all the band-aides, they're off."

"Alex, I'll come over. I'm on my way," Reagan says.

Alex smiles and thinks, *Guess that's why they say that's what friends are for.*

– 9 –

REAGAN KNOCKS ON ALEX'S condo door.

Alex does not answer, so Reagan knocks again. Still no answer. Holding her key chain in hand, Reagan remembers that she has a key. She has one from when she takes care of the plants when Alex is out of town.

Reagan locates the key and uses it to open the door. Once inside, she sees complete darkness. She searches the bedroom. No Alex.

"Alex!" she shouts. No answer.

Alex, I hope, please tell me you haven't done anything . . . Finally, she sees a flickering light from Alex's guest room/home office.

Quickly walking towards the flickering light, Reagan steps inside the guest room and sees Alex, asleep, at her desk, with her head down next to the computer. The television is on, casting shadows across the room.

Seeing Alex, Reagan thinks, *Poor thing.*

Reagan walks closer to Alex and says a quick prayer. "God, please give my friend peace..."

Reagan grabs the remote off the desk, meaning to turn off the television, when she hears a news announcer say, "Local firm, Richardson, Hanes is under investigation for Congressional Bribery. The firm's offices were raided on Friday. The allegations are that firm lawyers bribed Congressional Health Care Legislatures to block Health Care Reform in America."

"Lawyers and politicians, can't trust 'em," Reagan mumbles, as she turns off the television and walks over to the office/guest room couch.

Sitting down, Reagan looks at Alex, who is still sleeping, and thinks, momentarily, about her comment and the news story. "Oh, except you, Alex. You're a lawyer, but we can trust you—sort-a." She smiles.

Eventually nodding off, Reagan awakens as the sun begins to set. She gets up and decides to help Alex get into bed.

Before helping Alex move to her bedroom, Reagan glances down and sees Alex's notes. It appears that Alex is plotting a strategy, a way to challenge Marshall. *She fell asleep while researching sexual harassment laws!*

She's written a memo entitled sexual harassment!

She's slaying this dragon head on!

Chapter Fifty-four
I'm Talking Sexual Harassment!

*A*LEX STEPS INTO a quiet, empty office building. She coaches herself. *Stay focused! Defend yourself like you've defended others! Take Marshall down!*

Glancing at her watch, she sees the time and is in shock. The office is vacant at 8:00 a.m. Shrugging her shoulders, she walks onward. She focuses on her task—*Marshall Hanes!*

Gliding across the marble floors, Alex quickly steps to a fourbeat cadence. Her steps are quick and deliberate. She is wearing a designer white pant suit with a neatly tucked in pale pink silk button down top and designer pink pumps. Her pumps make a clicking sound.

Entering her office, she sits. She notices her desktop computer is missing, but decides to focus on her task. She pulls out and turns on her laptop computer from her briefcase. She reviews her notice to the firm.

**NOTICE OF SEXUAL
HARASSMENT CHARGE**

Dear Messrs. Davis, Hanes, and Richardson:

This letter serves as formal NOTICE of my intent to file a sexual harassment complaint against Marshall Hanes. Mr. Hanes used his position of authority, as my direct supervisor, to cause me to engage in unwanted physical advances. Pursuant to this NOTICE, I hereby request that this law firm conduct a formal investigation.

Please be advised that if you choose to retaliate against me, I will have no choice but to file a formal charge with the EEOC. Notwithstanding the foregoing, I hereby reserve the right to file any and all applicable claims under federal and states laws. Nothing in this notice waives that right.

Very truly yours,

Alexandria Giroud, Esq.

Pressing print, she smiles, marveling at her tactics, until she hears footsteps, quick footsteps, approaching her office.

She sees them through her glass-walled office before they get to her door—*the named partners.* Quickly, she gets to her feet, retrieves the letter from her printer, and prepares to talk to them in the hallway.

They enter first. "Alexandria, we must talk." Blake Richardson and Michael Davis close the door behind them.

What? You need to talk to me? I need to talk to you... Okay, be calm, they can't push me out. State my case. She stares at the men, eye to eye, and answers, "Interesting. I was heading to your office."

Looking at each other first, as if in shock, Blake Richardson says, "Good."

"Yes, that's what we're desiring—for you to be candid, honest," Michael Davis adds.

Exhaling noisily before speaking, looking anxious, Blake Richardson says, "Alexandria, I'll admit, we're . . . " He pauses.

"Awkward, the situation is awkward," Michael picks back up.

What are you guys, a tag-team?

"Yes, awkward, that's what I meant to articulate," Blake says.

Why are they acting so differently? Maybe they know I have a sexual harassment claim, but jeez, they're lawyers, they should know how to handle—

"Alex, we'll be blunt." Michael rubs his nose.

"Not blunt, but what we want to tell you is we want you to admit the facts. We require you to state what happened, slowly and clearly. We want to know if you and Marshall—" David Richardson stops mid-sentence, crossing his legs and fidgeting.

Does he have ants in his pants?

"Did you and Marshall do it?" David Richardson finally says.

"Gosh, don't be so brash," Alex says.

"Alex, we're sorry, we only want the facts."

Standing up, remembering Duncan Anderson's words—*Sue him, Alex!*—and her mother's advice—*Dare him!*—Alex admits the truth. "Yes, we did it. Yes, we did, but he took the lead. He used his position of power. He made me do it!"

David does a double take, as if in shock. "Oh . . . so."

"Yes, I paid the price, but he's responsible. He's the partner. He's the leader."

"Why, I—I," David Richardson begins, but then he says nothing, lost for words.

"You do understand, people do serious time," Michael Davis says.

"We're talking jail time," David Richardson picks up, adjusting his tie.

Wow. They're supporting me, but isn't that taking the situation too far? "He should do jail time, but obviously we can settle the case early. I'm open to compensation for the ordeal."

Holding up his hand, as if he wants to separate himself from the events they are discussing, David says, "Oh no, we can't."

"We—our firm—we're upstanding. We have a history, a reputation," Michael says.

"I understand," Alex says, nodding, "and if you want to keep your stellar reputation, you'll need to compensate me. I've been wronged."

"Why Alex," Michael Davis says, fidgeting.

David Richardson looks suspicious. "We can't."

Alex sees blue-jacketed men walking briskly towards her office. *Why the stampede? Are they coming to my office? Yes. . . .*

The men step into her office. One of them says, "We've heard enough. Alexandria Giroud, you're under arrest."

"What? What! What's going on!" Alex exclaims.

No one responds to her questions. An officer begins reading her rights. "You have the right to remain silent, anything you say can and will be used against you in a court of law; you have the right to speak to an attorney; if you cannot afford an attorney, one will be appointed for you—"

Alex hears the officer spout off the Miranda warning while he places handcuffs tightly around her arms.

"Dave! Mike!" Alex stomps her foot. Her partners stand there sheepishly.

Yanking at the tight handcuffs, Alex says, "Do you really need handcuffs? I'm an officer of the court."

Pulling the handcuffs tighter, the officer answers her question without words. He continues reciting Miranda; the warning flows like water in a river until he reaches the end and says, "Do you understand your rights?"

"What is going on?" she asks.

"Do you understand your rights, yes or no?"

"Yes!" she answers. *I understand the law—the enforcement thereof in this instance I do not understand!*

Chapter Fifty-five
I'm Behind Bars, Why?

*A*LEX SITS, HANDCUFFED, in a dark, cold, grey and gloomy, damp-feeling interrogation room and waits. Sitting in a steel chair, in front of a grey table, she tries to get comfortable, but she can't. *Why am I here? What did I do? He harassed me, but I'm in jail?* Her thoughts ramble until an oversized man wearing too-tight slacks enters.

"How do you want things?" he asks, and jostles with his too-long mustache. The police officer walks towards the grey table, staring at Alex. He is toting a tape recorder, notepad, and pen.

He turns the chair directly across from Alex backwards, so that the chair-back faces her. "Did you hear me? How do you want things?" He plays with the curl in his long mustache again.

"Want what?" *Are you from Mars, Venus, or Pluto?*

He pulls the chair close to his body. It makes a loud, scratchy noise against the floor.

I think this is an intimidation method gone wrong! He sits. He leans his chest against the seat cushion. He faces her.

"Again, how do you want things?" he shouts, rocking forward and backwards in the chair now, going from four legs to two legs, and then back to four legs, then two legs.

"Sir, I apologize, but I have no idea what you're talking about," Alex answers, deciding to be deferential, verbally at least.

"Easy or hard. You decide. What do you want?" He manhandles the chair as he rocks, back and forth, back and forth. The seat squeals with his movements.

Feeling awkward but not intimated, Alex says, "Sir, I'm not sure why I'm here. What are you trying to ask me?"

"You're up on charges. I'm asking you about your crimes," he says.

"Charges, I've done nothing wrong; I've been harassed, that's it, nothing else."

"You've already confessed. We've got your confession on tape." He pulls out the tape recorder and pushes play.

She jumps as she hears her voice played back to her.

"Yes, we did it. Yes, we did, but he took the lead. He used his position of power. He made me do it!"

Hearing her words, she begins to connect the dots. *You were taping our conversation at the law firm? You thought my conversation with Dave and Mike was a confession?*

"Yes, I paid the price, but he's responsible. He's the partner. He's the leader."

"I understand, and if you want to keep your stellar reputation, you'll need to compensate me!"

Hearing these words, she realizes that they could be taken to mean anything!

Deciding to defend herself, she says, "I'm talking about sex, not bribery. Don't you understand?"

"So you're admitting you used sex, too, to bribe Congress?"

"No, not Congress!" She shakes her head. "My boss and I didn't bribe anyone!"

"Do you think I fell off a turnip truck?" he asks. He stops rocking but is still leaning in the chair.

"No, no, that's not the point, you're mistaken."

"Ms. Giroud, we have your confession. We've checked your office. We've your desktop computer; we've Marshall's computer. We know the facts. You and Marshall went to DC and bribed Congress."

Remembering her conversation with her assistant, she completes the puzzle in her mind. *Heidi! Investigators in the office, searching—but for what, and why!* "I'm innocent, I didn't admit anything!" she says.

"You want to make this investigation hard?" He stares at her and slowly massages the curl in his mustache. "I can do hard. You'll do the time, not me!" He quickly stands.

He's crazy! "I need one call and a lawyer!"

Chapter Fifty-six
Great News Interrupted...

Taylor stares at the television screen while sitting with Reagan in the Hamilton home. The TV's volume is off, but the close-caption is on, and so pictures and words flash across the screen. Seeing Sarah Palin, Taylor reads the news commentator's words: "Sarah Palin says America is a place where 'every woman can walk through every door of opportunity,' in her vice-presidential nomination acceptance speech."

Guess you are the perfect example? Let's see, Hillary Clinton v. Sarah Palin. What's the difference?

Interrupting Taylor's thoughts, Reagan says, "I support Barack Obama, but I am proud of her."

"Who, Sarah Palin? Are you serious?"

"She's impressive. She was the mayor, now the governor and vice-presidential candidate."

"Yeah, right, of course, very impressive," Taylor says, smirking. "Look, she's a decoy. GOP cheerleader, and awesome eye-candy."

"Taylor, you're worse than the worst male-chauvinistic. We don't put other women down. We support them."

"Right, yeah, and guess what—a male chauvinist probably catapulted Sarah to her vice-presidential throne. Wonder why? And is that really progress for women?"

"Yes, who cares how she got the nomination. She's an awesome role model for young girls. She didn't sleep her way to the top! She worked her way to the top! And she is a Christian!"

"Right, of course. You like her Christian values!"

"Well, I like to see Christian women getting ahead."

"Right, of course, sure. Wait till she's really vetted, then you'll see."

"She was vetted by McCain, wasn't she?"

"Couldn't of been, but just wait, you'll see."

"No—"

"Enough about Sarah. Guess what?" Taylor decides to turn the conversation from the media story of the day to her personal life. She opens her eyes wide and shouts, "I have fabulous, great, huge, fantastic news!"

"Cat in your mouth? What? Do tell!"

You mean the cat's got your tongue. "I wanted to tell you both, but I can't get Alex."

"Alex, she's soul searching, but she's finally seeing the flame."

"You mean the light?"

"Light, flame, whatever. I'm creative, I like to change things up, that's all."

"Right, great, but I have to tell you, the news, this is great news!"

"Do tell then, what?"

"I'm ignoring doctor's orders. I can't wait."

"What, tell?"

"Well, usually the doctors say wait until the end of the first trimester."

Reagan gets up, her eyes beaming.

"But I couldn't. I had to tell, so—we're pregnant!" Taylor announces, excited.

Jumping up and down, like she is doing a holy dance, Reagan screams, "A baby!" Her knees literally touch her chest with each jump.

Taylor smiles. *You're in good shape, girlie!* Taylor sees Reagan jumping and shouting until out of the corner of her eye, she sees Alexandria Giroud flash across the plasma television screen in handcuffs.

"Reagan, turn up the volume!" Taylor demands.

"No, we can't! We've got no time for TV. We're having a baby!"

"Reagan, look!" Taylor says, pointing to the television.

Reagan reluctantly turns toward the TV. Seeing the screen, she is frozen for a moment before she leaps for the remote. Turning up the volume, sensational words flow with the image.

"We are the first to show you a photo of the criminal."

Criminal? Aren't you supposed to report rather than opine! Taylor thinks, staring at the polished, almost shiny news anchor delivering the news.

"Her name is Alexandria Giroud," the anchor continues. "She is an associate with Richardson, Davis & Hanes. She got caught, red-handed, bribing Congressman Mills and his aide."

"Yes, and you may ask, why? Why would she risk everything to bribe a Congressman?" a female anchor adds.

In unison, both anchors state, "She wanted to fix health care laws to work for her client, Health Solutions."

"A crooked crony, that's what Ms. Giroud is, but she got caught," the male anchor says.

"That's right. And we know she's guilty because Ms. Giroud confessed to the crime," the female anchor adds.

"And the police officers found five hundred thousand dollars cash in Congressman Mills' office, along with a PowerPoint Slide entitled '*Health Care Reform, Who Needs It*' by Alexandria Giroud. According to our sources, Ms. Giroud bribed the congressman because she wanted guaranteed results."

"Authorities have linked the law firm banking records with this bribery scheme. Officials also found plane tickets and hotel records that prove Ms. Giroud was in Washington, D.C. at the time of the crime."

Crossing her legs, Lisa Lewis adds additional commentary. "So here's the new spin on lobbying."

"I'd say so. She paid to fix health care," Steven Meyer says.

– 9: –

GETTING TO HER FEET, Taylor touches her belly.

"Alex, she's innocent. She wouldn't!" Reagan exclaims.

Taylor nods her head in agreement. "We've got to find Alex!" she shouts.

"Yes, but where?" Reagan asks, keys in hand.

The television screen answers the question. "Alexandria Giroud has been released on bail. We're live at the courthouse."

Reagan and Taylor stand motionless, watching the events unfold on television.

Chapter Fifty-seven
Media Fascination

Exiting the courthouse with her attorney, Shannon Klaxon, Alex tries to make her way through the media swarming around her. In unison, different questions ring in her ear. Each tumbles over the other, blending in to sound like rubble. She surmises that at least fifty questions are coming at her at once, but she can only make out a few. The rest sound like garbage…

"Ms. Giroud, why did you bribe the congresswoman?" "Ms. Giroud, how much did Health Solutions pay you to fix health care?" "Ms. Giroud, will you plead guilty?" "Ms. Giroud, you don't have a defense, do you? Isn't this case open and shut?" "Ms. Giroud, how much time do you expect to do behind bars?" "Ms. Giroud, your life, as you know it, is technically over." "Ms. Giroud, how will you deal with spending your child-bearing years in prison?"

What the he—what kind of question is that? That darn clock…tick tock tick tock—always shows up!

Ignoring the questions, she tries to see her way through blinding lights and oversized microphones being pushed into her face. She feels closed in, like she is imprisoned in a small box, even though she stands underneath a wide open blue sky.

Feeling like prey, she follows Shannon Klaxon, step by step, until both women reach the podium where a microphone sits.

Approaching the podium, standing closely to Shannon, seeing the cameras flash one after another, Alex wonders, for a brief second, *How do I look? Wasn't planning on being on television.* Adjusting her hair briefly, tucking her layered bob behind her ears, and glancing at her clothes momentarily, Alex decides, *Yep, I'm wearing the new designer pantsuit with the new shoes. I look good enough.* She knows her designer clothing starts from a place of elegance, so even if she is slightly disheveled, *Designer always holds up.* This is true even in the midst of a crisis, except, *Wait, why is there a grey smudge on my white designer pantsuit? The darn chairs in that holding cell I bet. Cheap chairs!*

"Ms. Giroud, are you requesting a special prison?" a reporter asks, jolting Alex from her thoughts about designers and appearances.

Refocusing on the matter at hand, Alex looks straight ahead, as the questions continue to roll in.

"Are you going to a white collar prison? Have you selected a cozy prison cell?"

"How about kid gloves? Do you want prison kid gloves?"

"Ms. Giroud, are you wearing a three thousand dollar suit?"

"Ms. Giroud, is it true that your shoes cost at least two thousand dollars? Will you hold up in prison?"

Shannon Klaxon, Esq. stands firmly in front of the podium, holds up her hands, and silences the crowd. She speaks into the microphone. "First and foremost, my client, Alexandria Giroud, is innocent. The prosecution cannot and will not prove their case against my client because she is innocent. Now, to your questions. My client deserves a fair trial. And so you know, a fair trial includes having her case tried in the court of law, not in the court of public opinion. We ask that you respect Ms. Giroud's privacy and understand that she deserves her day in court. No further comments."

Hearing her attorney's words, Alex sinks. Reality truly hits her for the first time today. *I was arrested today because people think I tried to conspire and bribe the government to fix health care. Did Marshall set me up?*

— 9 —

REAGAN TAKES HER EYES off the television screen for the first time since she saw Alex come out of the courthouse with her attorney.

Looking at Taylor, she asks, "What should we do?"

"I—I—what do you do? What *can* we do? Help?"

"Yes, but how?"

"I—that's—well—that's what I was trying to say."

"Okay, I, we, should think, think," Reagan begins, but the television interrupts her again.

"Breaking news…we have Alexandria Giroud's confession, on tape…. That's right…we are the first to break this story. Alexandria Giroud confessed to the bribery and conspiracy charges during her jail cell interrogation. We'll play the confession…listen carefully. . . . 'Yes, we did it!'"

Hearing the confession in full, Reagan and Taylor are both shocked.

Meanwhile, the media continues to opine. "Ms. Giroud is anti-health care reform. She believes capital markets can manage health care costs best, not the government. Her beliefs are so strong that she actually paid a congressional aide five hundred thousand dollars cash. She handed him the cash in a briefcase. She asked for guarantees. She wanted an absolute guarantee that any meaningful health care reform would be blocked in America."

"Alex wouldn't do that, would she?" Reagan asks Taylor.

"I—I—heard—I think I heard the words, but—"

"There's a mistake." Reagan shakes her head. "No, no, no way."

"Let's go!" Taylor shouts. The two friends charge out the door.

Chapter Fifty-eight
His Scapegoat

Driving home, Alex swerves to miss a pothole in the road. Barely missing the gaping abyss, Alex readjusts her car while retracing her relationship with Marshall in her mind. *I'm his scapegoat!*

She approaches her condo and instinctively slams on her brakes before accelerating again when she sees a large crowd standing outside her condo entrance. There are piles and piles of cars filled with paparazzi and reporters—*Or is there a difference nowadays?* she thinks. *Why are paparazzi hanging around my condo? And the better question is how am I going to get into my condo unnoticed?*

Feeling the walls around her closing in, she pulls off her jacket and places the jacket over her head while driving. She tries to hide and pass the media unseen.

Passing her condo, she drives more than fifteen blocks, until she realizes, *I can wear my Halloween costume! Got to love chic power!*

Parking her car at a nearby gas station, she reaches behind her driver's seat and pulls out her costume.

Alex puts on a brunette wig.

She pulls a Miss. Alaska sash over her white suit.

She begins to stick a Vote McCain/Palin button on her white designer suit but stops. *Wait, stickers and buttons on my designer suit? What about the sticker and pen marks?*

She deliberates.

She wonders…until she finally concludes, *What the hell. I need a cover! Can't pull this costume off without the pomp and circumstance!* She finishes getting changed.

Glancing at herself in her rear-view mirror, she smiles.

Yep, you bet ya. I look like Sarah Palin! I'll definitely avoid the media! Nowadays, the media's so biased; they won't cover a Sarah Palin look-alike fan! Nope. Not today! I'm safe.

While driving, Alex practices saying, "Yep, you bet ya!" and "A pig with lipstick!" with a twang a few times. She does not think the media will think she is Sarah Palin, but she believes the media will think she is a wacky, obsessed, Palin-want-to-be, and she is certain the media won't want to interview a person who is interested in or obsessed with Sarah Palin. Now, if she were wearing a Barack Obama costume, why, yes, certainly. They'd follow her and ask her why she supports Barack Obama; why she believes Barack Obama should be President—but Sarah Palin? *Nope.*

Entering her condo parking lot, and parking, she gets out and heads towards the condo freight elevator.

Approaching the elevator, she sees men and women with cameras, hiding out, waiting. She walks past the reporters without them paying her any attention. *See, Sarah doesn't get a fair shake in the media! Jerks! I'll turn your male-chauvinist ways into my gains. Thanks, jerks!*

Heading up to the penthouse level, she prepares herself. *I'll use the pigs with lipstick line, if I have to.*

Alex gets off the elevator. She feels relieved. She passes more reporters, unnoticed.

She walks.

She walks.

She walks.

Almost to my condo. Walk, walk, walk, oh crap! She sees four feet poking out near her doorway. *I can't see on the other side of the wall, but I know, I'm sure someone is standing in my doorway.*

Seeing the dingy tennis shoes the women or men or whoever they are, are wearing, she is sure the culprits are undercover or desperate paparazzi. *I need a plan! Act!* she tells herself, surmising that she can act like a crazed-Sarah Palin fan, distract the paparazzi who are standing near her door, hiding, and then when they start flashing pictures, distracted, she can sneak into her condo and slam the door.

She jumps into action, believing not that Sarah Palin fans are delusional, but thinking the idea is not so far-fetched to the paparazzi, since they're so biased, and she can create the impression with her actions.

Opening her eyes wide and fixing them into a firm gaze, so much so that she tries not to blink, she starts talking like a robot or computerized doll.

"Yep, you bet ya!" she says.
"Pigs with lipstick!
"Yep, you bet ya!
"Pigs with lipstick!
"Yep, you bet ya!
"Pigs with lipstick!
"Yep you bet ya!
"Pigs with lipstick!
"Yep!
"Pigs!
"Yep!
"Pigs!"

She speaks the words, while walking closer and closer to her condo, hoping the paparazzi are taken off guard.

She is so certain she looks so fanatical and fantastical that even Sarah Pain would call security if she saw Alex approaching her at a fundraiser or election rally with this get up.

"Pigs!
"Yep!
"Pigs!"

Just as Alex is almost facing the back of the people standing in her doorway, "Pigs! Yep, you bet ya! Lipstick! Pigs! Yep, you bet ya!

Pig with lipsticks! Pigs! Pigs! Yep! Pigs!" She is cut off because she can't see the faces but she recognizes the voices.

"Alex?"

"Are you all right?"

"Reagan, Taylor?"

"Yes, what are you doing?" Reagan asks.

"Hiding," she responds, while unlocking her door and pushing her friends inside. Alex locks her front door, bolts it, and then places a chair against the door, *Just in case.*

Staring at the closed door for a few minutes, her heart finally begins to slow down.

"Why are you dressed in torn jeans and skateboarder sneakers?" Alex asks, breathing heavily.

"We're undercover," Taylor answers.

"We didn't want to be seen. Good thing we had these outfits with the hoodies because we've been here awhile. Your key, the one that I had, it doesn't work," Reagan explains.

"Enough about us," Taylor asks. "What about you? Why do you look like Sarah Palin? Why are you chanting?"

"I'm hiding, too. Didn't you see those paparazzi?"

"With a Sarah Palin costume?" Taylor asks.

"Yes, perfect cover. We're talking about the media. They're not interested in following a Sarah Plain fan," Alex answers.

Reagan and Taylor simply look at each other for a few moments before Reagan says, "I guess your cover worked."

"Yep! You bet ya!" Alex responds.

"Okay, so enough about Palin. What about you? Did you do it?" Taylor asks.

"No!" Alex shouts. "How can you ask—"

"We're here to listen," Reagan says, trying to be comforting. "To support."

Alex grabs a glass of Merlot and sits. She explains how her confession wasn't a confession. "I was talking about sexual harassment!"

She continues to tell the entire story until the sun rises the next morning. Finally, Reagan asks, "Alex, what will you do?"

"I have no idea."

"Can you prove he set you up?" Taylor asks, since she was dosing in and out of sleep most of the night.

"I don't have a choice! I can't go to jail."

"I'm sorry, Alex," Reagan says, reaching her hand out to comfort her friend.

"Do women wear weird panties in jail here? I heard men wear pink panties?" Taylor asks.

"Yep. Can't do that crap," Alex says, but then she pauses. "You know, tent city is probably nothing compared to real prison."

Taylor stands up, looking distracted when she says, "Sorry to change the subject, but do you have any bacon? I'm sorry. I'm hungry and craving bacon."

"You don't eat bacon," Alex declares.

"I know, but today—well, it's a long story."

"Yes, really Alex, you have no idea." Reagan chuckles.

"What?" Alex asks, frowning.

"Nothing, let's talk about you—as long as you cook bacon. We'll talk about me later," Taylor says.

Pulling out bacon and eggs from her refrigerator while still sipping Merlot, Alex says, "You know, that Marshall, that jerk idiot, he played me."

"Like a fiddle," Taylor says, nodding.

"Taylor, be supportive, please!" Reagan says, opening her eyes wide.

"It's okay. She's right!" Alex says, scrambling eggs. "I should have known he was up to no good. Everything about our relationship was odd. And yes, he played me like a fiddle! He always had me on edge. He also had me off guard. I was thinking about sex and relationships when he's talking about guarantees—health care guarantees. He even handed me a briefcase, full of cash, and I didn't question his actions. I didn't even look in the briefcase. I just did what he asked me to do." *Well, and I slept with the aide, too.* "But there were signs, clues I missed. Like the aide. He was way too rich looking to be an aide. I was going to question him, but I didn't. I wondered when I saw him the next morning getting dressed in custom suits, where do you get your money?"

"What do you mean the next morning, getting dressed?" Reagan asks.

"Yeah, he got dressed in a meeting?"

"Ugh, well, that's—look, listen. I've got to figure out this thing… what I'm going to do."

"Do you have a good lawyer?"

"Yep, Duncan helped. He found her. He's well connected."

"He's connected with Arizona lawyers even though he lives in Texas?" Reagan asks.

"Honey, money runs deep," Alex says. "Money knows no borders. Besides, I'm sure his Texas law firm made some calls to Arizona. I'm sure his connections found Shannon. Because frankly, there's no way I could have hired Shannon without him first initiating the connection."

Reagan looks surprised.

"How are you paying?" Taylor asks.

"I'll be broke, that's how."

"But how?" Taylor asks. "Your trust fund?"

"No, my trust fund is locked up until I'm almost fifty. So for now, I'm using the equity in my home. I'm surely upside down on my mortgage."

"How can you be inside out on your mortgage?" Reagan questions.

"No, upside down."

"Yes, that's what I meant. How?"

"Easy. I drew on my line of credit to pay the retainer."

"From jail?"

"Yes, actually jails do have Internet, can you believe that? I'm sure liberals made that happen, but this time liberal-machinery worked out for me. I made a huge withdrawal!"

"How much is your line?" Taylor asks.

"A lot!" Alex answers.

"What's a lot? Fifty thousand?" Reagan asks.

"Nope! How about five hundred thousand dollars," Alex answers.

"Alex, that's ridiculous. Your condo can't be worth that much, is it?" Reagan asks.

"Well, when I got the line of credit it was. The condo was actually worth $700,000, you know, during the market hey day."

"How much did you pay for the condo?"

"No more than $200,000, cash."

"You paid cash?" Taylor asks.

"Yep, why not?"

"Well, I'm just wondering, why pay cash?" Taylor says.

"I'm glad you paid cash, but what does that have to do with your defense?" Reagan asks.

"Well, a few years after I paid for the condo, I saw the market was going crazy. So I got a line of credit, thinking I could tap into the equity in my home if necessary. And sure enough, sitting in jail, I remembered the line. I drew on it. I got $500,000 dollars from the bank as a home equity line of credit. That's how I'll defend this case."

"That's awesome, but is that enough?" Taylor asks.

"It's a start."

"And how will you finish?" Reagan asks, looking genuinely concerned.

"I also have an emergency fund—$200,000—so hopefully that'll be enough to defend the case and to get me through this rough time."

"Can you afford your new mortgage? Haven't the payments tripled?" Taylor asks.

"Yep, absolutely," she says, nodding. "Not only tripled, but probably quadrupled. Remember, I paid cash; I had no payments. But, I'll deal with my upside down mortgage later. I've got to use that cash to stay out of jail."

Taylor changes the subject. "Look, how about the bacon?"

— 9 —

ALEX SITS, CHATTING WITH her friends, trying to take her mind off her ordeal. She turns on the television, momentarily, simply to see what lies they are telling about her now, when suddenly Jackson

Hamilton appears on the screen, standing in crowds with the paparazzi, at the courthouse.

Obviously seeing the same thing, all women say, "Jackson?"

"He's a reporter, but I didn't know he was covering your case," Reagan says, defending her husband.

"Maybe he can put a good spin on the story. Speaking of spin, can you influence him? Ask him to get my side out? Can't he write a blog article and set the record straight?"

"Hadn't thought about Jackson before," Reagan says, "but I'd think he'd want to help the media get the facts correct."

"He can sell this story, make tons," Taylor says, lost in thought.

Chapter Fifty-nine
Where've You Been?

TAYLOR WALKS INTO her house, feeling exhausted. Readying herself to slip into bed, she begins to climb her winding staircase when suddenly shocking words jolt her.

"Where've you been," Whitfield shouts. He stands behind the large wooden door, leaning on the wall, in the Ray grand foyer. *He looks angry!*

"I didn't know you were home. I thought you were out of town." Taylor smiles, walks over to him, and kisses his lips.

He pulls away.

"Tay, you didn't answer my question. I've been calling you all night!"

"I didn't know. Gosh, are you jealous?"

"Tay, what's the deal? Where've you been?"

"Don't be jealous. The girls, there was an emergency."

"That's an understatement. The situation is serious."

"Relax, there's no situation, Whit." Taylor tries to kiss her husband's lips again.

His lips are closed, tight, and tense. He jerks back.

"What, you're actually jealous?"

"No, Tay! I'm pissed!" He pushes her away.

"Whit! Wait! Why are you pushing me away?"

"Tay, you've been creeping, cheating, hiding, and lying."

"Whit, I'm not cheating on you. I wouldn't." She enjoys his jealously for a moment though, thinking, *He does care.* She knows that when he hears that she was with Alex and Reagan all night, he'll lift her into his arms and caress her, sex her, wine and dine her—without wine of course—like he always does. Perhaps they'll even relax in the Jacuzzi. *I could use an afternoon in the Jacuzzi tub. I've missed you, Whit...*

"Tay, I'm done. I'm tired of your mischief!"

"You're jealous! Don't be. What ya thinking?" she asks, rubbing her leg against his leg, trying to stir up passion. She wants to engage in foreplay before she tells him the full truth. *I'm no cheat, so calm down.*

He pushes her away again and walks over to the answering machine. He begins to play messages. Her heart sinks as she hears the recording.

"Ms. Ray . . . Jessica Bell again with DebtConsolidators.com. I have left messages and sent notices, but you have not responded. I don't have a choice. Your bank is beginning the foreclosure proceedings. Your account is out of my hands. Again, I'm sorry. I've tried to work with you, but there is nothing else we can do. Best of luck."

Whitfield stares at Taylor with upset, questioning eyes before he speaks.

"Tay, this message is one of twenty." Raising his voice, he adds, "Didn't you get the calls? Didn't you read the mail?"

"What mail?"

"Tay, there's been a notice on our door for ten days!" Whitfield walks over to the marble countertops. He picks up a piece of paper.

"What notice?"

Handing the notice to her, he says, "This one!"

Kneeling down to pick up the paper from the floor, Taylor reads and is stunned by what she sees. **NOTICE OF TRUSTEE'S SALE...**

"Not our house! We're not in foreclosure!"

"Yeah, Tay, they're foreclosing. That's what happens when you don't pay bills—bills that I gave you money to pay. Tay, what in the hell did you do with our money?"

"I paid the bills. There's a mistake, our mortgage—our mortgage, we paid the mortgage each month." *Even if we didn't pay everything else. . . .*

"Did you pay enough?"

"Yes, I think I did. I paid what we owed?"

"How did you know what we owed?" he asks, his eyebrows coming together.

"I looked at our mortgage papers."

"But you didn't read the mail?" he asks, gathering up the piles and piles of mail and throwing it at her.

Picking up the papers from the floor, she sees letter after letter, each letter she missed, but that he'd obviously found and pulled the pieces together. Reading the mail, she sees letters and notices dating back as much as a year.

NOTICE
INCREASE IN
MONTHLY PAYMENTS

Pursuant to the terms of your loan agreement, this letter serves as written **NOTICE** of an interest rate increase. Under this rate increase, your interest rate will adjust to **14.2% percent**. This means your new monthly payment will be: **$11,707 (Eleven Thousand Seven Hundred and Seven Dollars and No/Cents)**

Guess that's how the whole mess started…I missed the notice and failed to increase our payments…so even though we paid each month, we were getting behind with each and every payment…oh no.

Watching her read the notice with his arms crossed, he asks, "Did you pay the increased amount? And didn't I tell you not to get an adjustable rate mortgage?"

"Actually, I thought—"

"You thought nothing! Tay, why don't we have a fixed rate mortgage? You promised."

"I meant to . . . " *But they insisted I take this adjustable rate, said it was the best deal! I never checked with anyone else, and I never told you.* "But, I guess . . . "

"You didn't, and the acceleration notice, how did you miss that notice?" He throws another letter at her.

NOTICE
ACCELERATION

NOTICE YOUR ACCOUNT IS PAST DUE. YOUR LOAN HAS BEEN ACCELERATED PURSUANT TO THE LOAN AGREEMENT. Pursuant to this NOTICE, the BANK hereby demands payment in full: **$1,044,959. This includes penalties and interest as of the date of this** NOTICE. **Any and all additional amounts will be accrued and included in the final payment amount.**

Picking up another letter, she reads and says, "They want us to pay $1,044,959 to keep the house?"

"Yeah. We either pay in full or we're out."

"So what are we going to do?" She wants a solution.

"We're out!"

"But we can't. This is our home, and our baby."

"Tay, our mortgage payments went up more than a year ago, but we've been paying the old amount, so we're late."

"I know, but—"

"And the mortgage has been accelerated, so there's no more mortgage. We either pay them 1.1 million dollars, or we're out."

"I don't think it's that much, is it?"

"Tay, I'm not putting good money in a bad deal."

"Whit, we make tons of money. We can find a way, refinance."

"Nobody in their right mind is going to refinance our mortgage when we've been late every month for a year. Tay, the mortgage is being accelerated for non-payment! Do you get that? And even if we find a lender, the interest rate will be ridiculous because our credit is shot. We're out!"

"But Whit, haven't you heard, the fundamentals of the economy are strong. Isn't that what John McCain recently said?"

"Tay, I doubt John McCain has our situation in mind when he says the fundamentals of the economy are strong. Actually, I'm sure our situation and situations like ours may prove him wrong."

"Whit, we can figure out a way. This is our house. We're having a baby . . . "

"Tay, looking at you, listening to you, observing how you've been handling our marriage, our finances, our life, we have more to worry about than this house. I'm out!"

He grabs his keys and walks out.

Chapter Sixty
Sell Out

TAYLOR STANDS THERE and watches her husband exit. *How do I fix this?* she thinks, panicked. *We can't lose our house. I can't lose my husband over this house. If only—*

Her telephone rings. She hopes that it's Whit.

She checks the CALLER ID and sees that it's Bianca Sheridan. Taylor is surprised. She and Bianca go way back; they started in the media industry together, working side by side, except Bianca breaks the news and delivers stories while Taylor Ray sells her stories. *I haven't heard from Bianca in years. Why's she calling? What does she want?*

Answering the telephone, she disregards cordial niceties and simply asks, "Bianca?"

"Taylor Ray, bon jour, darling. I'm pleased you're in your abode. Listen closely!" Bianca sounds out of breath.

"What's up?"

"Darling, I've a proposition—a deal you can't refuse…"

"What type?"

"A huge story, darling. I can come over and explain."

"Before you do, tell me what you're up to."

"I'm in a media frenzy, darling. I can be your way in a jiffy. Will you be in your abode?"

"I'm here, but I—I want to know, what's your story?" Taylor cuts to the chase, knowing Bianca Sheridan does both legitimate news, and tabloid news, and given her last few days, she surmises this may be a tabloid deal she is working up.

"Your friend. That's all I can say over the phone."

"What about her?"

"I'll tell you this much, darling, if you have details, I have a deal that's worth more than one million argent."

"What's argent? Speak English?"

"Yes, darling—bucks, dollars, one million dollars!"

Chapter Sixty-one
Chasing Reform

ALEX WATCHES THE **Giroud-Hanes Health Care Prevention Scandal** unfold on national television. Seeing Jackson Hamilton running behind Marshall Hanes with a microphone in hand, Alex asks Reagan, "Why's Jackson chasing Marshall?"

"He's blogging, he's writing, he's producing news, I'm sure."

"Why there and not here?"

"I don't know. We haven't talked today."

"Can you call him?"

"I've tried. I think his cell battery is dead."

"Gosh, this is killing me. He's taking Marshall's side?"

"I don't think so, no! I know my husband."

"Why's he chasing Marshall then?"

"I'm sure he'll come. He's probably trying to make sure he gets the latest, breaking news. He wants to be front and center."

"If he's with the other outfits, how can you expect to break real news given what we've seen today?"

"Don't worry. Again, he'll probably get what they have and then add a twist."

"When you say twist, do you mean the truth?"

"Yes, Alex," Reagan says. "You didn't do what they're accusing you of, I know."

Smiling, Alex says, "Thanks for the vote of confidence," but then trails off when she sees Calvin dash across the television screen, briskly walking behind Jackson. She quickly asks, "Isn't that Calvin, the doc I met at your house?"

"Yeah, sure is."

"Why's Calvin with Jackson?"

"Actually..." Reagan trails off. "I'm not sure..." She trails off again before she adds, "I know Jackson and Calvin talk a lot. They want to work together."

"So, Calvin, a physician, is doing a blog with Jackson?"

"Yes, I think so. Jackson and Calvin are working with a few other college classmates. Jackson has huge plans. He has a vision. He thinks TheKnowSite.com can take off like other major information websites."

"What, like the Huffington Post?"

"Yes. He wants to be the place where people turn to get their news and info like the TalkingPointsMemo.com, NewsMax.com, Politico.com, MichelleObamaWatch.com, TheGrio.com, and TheRoot.com."

"I see, I understand that, but Calvin?"

"I'm not sure. I think Calvin may do medical stories."

"A medical correspondent?"

"Yes."

"Like that Dr. Sanja Gupta?"

"Exactly," Reagan says. "Calvin wants to be the Sanja Gupta, M.D., on the Internet. That's the plan, I think. Maybe this is his first story..."

"So TheKnowSite.com will have a medical correspondent sensation?" Alex says, thinking about his eyes, his legs, his body. "He is easy on the eyes."

"Alex!"

"What? He is. That Calvin, he's fun to watch. So tell Jackson I'd watch TheKnowSite.com even if the website is full of liberal mumbo jumbo, at least when Calvin is on." Alex smiles.

"Jackson's fair and balanced."

"Then why's he chasing Marshall rather than calling me trying to get the truth? Why's he doing what all the other reporters are doing? Look, they are actually chasing him down in front of his house."

"I don't know. He probably does not want to miss a chance to get Marshall's side. He'll get your side and accurately report."

"Will he bring Calvin when he gets my side?" *If I'm in hiding, it would be nice to have a special easy on the eyes someone....*

"I don't know, but I've got to go. Will you be all right?" Reagan gets up and walks towards the door.

"Sure, but I'll be even better if you send that Calvin over."

"All right, take care of yourself. I'll swing by tomorrow and bring you a sample of the dinner I'm cooking tonight for Jackson—salmon, asparagus, and a loaded baked potato, okay?"

"Sure, thanks, but bring that Calvin over, too, okay?"

"I'll see what I can do," Reagan says. She comes back and hugs Alex quickly before exiting and heading home.

Chapter Sixty-two
Dinner Anyone

REAGAN EATS AND reads *As I Lay Dying*.

Just as she begins to take her last bite of salmon, her telephone rings.

Anticipating a call from her husband, she quickly answers the telephone and begins talking about the meal and the book. Suddenly, the caller interrupts.

Hearing the voice, she thinks, *This isn't Jackson*. And then the caller's words: *There's an emergency*. She drops her fork on the plate.

Hearing her husband isn't coming home, she is in shock.

She is in a trance.

She repeats the words she hears in her head. *Jackson's in the hospital*. All she can think to do is call her friends.

She calls Taylor Ray.

No answer.

She calls Alex Giroud.

She answers and says, "I'm on my way!"

— ※ —

HOLDING ALEX'S HAND, REAGAN charges into the hospital lobby. Seeing not Jackson but Calvin approaching, she hastens her pace. Her blood boils, her adrenaline flows.

Racing towards Calvin, Reagan studies his face. His frown lines are deep. His eyes are glassy.

Firmly gripping Alex's hand, Reagan drags her along, even though Alex is already running to keep up.

Reaching Calvin, she asks, "He's okay, right? Was he, did he get hot, heat stroke?" Reagan stands face to face with Calvin. She looks directly into his eyes.

Hugging Reagan before speaking, Calvin says, "Why don't we go to an office?" Calvin takes Reagan's other hand and starts to lead her through the hallways, towards offices, when Reagan stops, in the hospital waiting area, and says, "No, here. Tell me! He's okay?"

Stopping, looking at Reagan, Calvin says, "Jackson . . . he is in . . . a . . . coma, a medically induced coma." Calvin glances off into the distance, as if he can't make continuous direct eye contact with Reagan.

"He's in a what? He's asleep? Did he faint?" She asks questions because while she hears what he is saying, she can't process what he is saying. His words aren't understandable to her. His words are frozen to her. All she knows to say or ask is what she wants. "He is okay?"

Inhaling deeply, looking off in the distance again briefly, Calvin takes his hands and places them on her shoulders, as if he is trying to get her attention. He focuses her on his words. "Reagan, I know this is difficult, but Jackson had a seizure. He is in a medically induced coma."

Gasping, hearing the words, Reagan thinks, *Seizure? Coma? How? He's healthy! How?* She asks this out loud. "Jackson's in perfect health, so how?"

"I understand. Jackson, he does exhibit signs of good physical health—well, except he has been presenting a persistent cough."

"What? He's got allergies! That's what his specialist, his allergy specialist, said."

"I believe she's mistaken, Reagan. I don't know how to tell you this."

"Just tell me!" Reagan pleads.

"Jackson—he's been coughing, coughing uncontrollably lately."

"Yes, but like I said, allergies."

"Can you tell her please already?" Alex says, interrupting.

Cutting his eyes at Alex, as if annoyed, he gently caresses Reagan's hand. He looks her directly in her eyes and says, "Reagan, Jackson, he has a mass in his throat."

"What are you saying, Calvin?" Reagan tilts her head and frowns.

"He has a large tumor."

"Is that why he's been coughing nonstop? Having a hard time swallowing, complaining about an irritated throat…." She rattles off the once subtle but now obvious signs. The only words that come to mind, the words that shield her from what Calvin is articulating.

"And Reagan," Calvin begins, but Reagan continues.

"I know, I saw the signs. He *has* been coughing, and he couldn't swallow walnuts, peanuts, and he stopped eating steaks. He was always hoarse. He said his throat itched and ached."

"Reagan, I understand," Calvin starts again, but Reagan cuts him off.

"How did we miss the signs? I—" She laughs, a nervous, overpowering reflex because as she chuckles, her eyes also begin to water. Instinctively, she continues speaking. **She talks about the past to avoid the present.** Her statements buffer her, so she talks.

"Reagan, calm yourself. Breathe." Calvin lifts her up in his arms and hugs her. She cries in his arms. Whispering in her ear, he says, "Reagan, I'm here. We're here. We'll walk this walk with you. We must walk the walk. We must accept Jackson's condition."

Pulling away, Reagan looks Calvin up and down before saying, "But his grandfather and his uncle, I mean, they died—Calvin!" She begins to cry hysterically.

Alex takes Reagan into her arms and tries to encourage her to sit.

— 9: —

SEEING REAGAN WEEP IN Alex's arms, Calvin steps away. He tries to determine how to tell the facts to his best friend's wife, who is also obviously in shock.

Calvin knows his bedside manners aren't the best, but he tries to find a way to deliver scientific evidence in a sympathetic, compassionate way. He does not know how. Science is factual, and the scientific facts are grim. He believes science and hope usually don't mix. Yet, he knows, Reagan requires hope.

But I can't deliver, he thinks, reconciling the facts in his mind. The reality is that while Jackson's physicians aren't certain, because a biopsy has not yet been performed, the scientific evidence available so far indicates that Jackson Hamilton has cancer. Calvin has seen the images, and the size and shape of the tumor suggest that the cancer has spread to other organs and lymph nodes, and the cancer may be incurable. Looking at Reagan, he decides, *I can't tell her my hypothesis. I can't tell her the whole deal—not until we have definitive scientific proof.*

He walks back over to Reagan and explains the facts, except he tells her half-truths.

"Will Jackson be okay?"

Looking off before speaking, he answers, "Yes, he'll be fine." He can't look into her eyes.

Chapter Sixty-three
What's a Friend?

Hours pass. Calvin, Alex, and Reagan wait.

Glancing at his watch, then at Alex, then at Reagan, then back at his watch, and then thinking through the scientific facts, Calvin fidgets. His insides curl. He is anxious because he knows his friend may die.

He justifies concealing the facts from Reagan, at least momentarily, because he wants actual scientific evidence, like a biopsy, rather than his hypothesis, a mere educated guess....

He also knows Reagan is in shock. He wonders if she will be able to pull through this ordeal when suddenly, Dr. Codi Wiseman, Jackson's physician, approaches.

Reagan races towards her.

— ღ —

"How's Jackson?" Reagan asks.

"Ms. Hamilton, please, why not walk with me and let's sit?" Dr. Wiseman talks in a soft, compassionate voice. Her huge grey eyes look concerned and sympathetic at once.

"No, I'll stand," Reagan says. "What?"

"All right, we'll do what makes you feel comfortable," Dr. Wiseman says. She glances at Calvin, almost as if she is sending a code to a fellow colleague, before speaking. "Ms. Hamilton, I'm sorry to tell you—"

Reagan cuts her off, hearing the word sorry. She wants to wait. She does not want to know just yet. She unconsciously believes that if she does not hear the news, the news won't be true. "He's in a coma, right? Why?" Reagan asks, trying to control the flow of the conversation.

"Understand, your husband, when he arrived, he was losing blood. Customary practice is to stop the bleeding. A medically induced coma helps slow down the bleeding. We've contained his blood loss. He is stable. His bleeding has ceased, but—"

"Couldn't you add pressure to stop the bleeding? Did he really need to be put in a coma?"

"Ms. Hamilton, a medically induced coma is the best method, but the bleeding is contained, and he is resting, albeit in a comatic state; but that's not the only issue or concern, Ms. Hamilton. Your husband has Stage IV cancer, which I believe we can treat, or at least make him comfortable, or help him fight."

"Cancer? Stage, what, cancer...how?" she asks out loud.

"I'll be honest. Stage IV cancer is a high stage, but there are aggressive treatments available today."

"So you'll cure him?" Reagan asks, looking back and forth between Dr. Wiseman and Calvin. "Right, Calvin?" She looks at them, wondering, *Why do they look like they know more than me?*

Lowering his head, Calvin says, "Yes, Jackson, why—" He stops, mid-sentence, and looks directly into Dr. Wiseman's eyes. He looks even more anxious now.

"Ms. Hamilton, come, walk with me. We have an office," Dr. Wiseman says.

"No, tell me without codes, and you two," Reagan points at Dr. Wiseman and Calvin, "stop the eye contact. What's wrong with my husband?"

Dr. Wiseman glances at Calvin again.

Calvin nods once, as if to give Dr. Wiseman the okay.

Dr. Wiseman nods back. "Ms. Hamilton, Stage IV cancer is very difficult to treat. We do have treatments, and I recommend surgery followed by aggressive chemotherapy and radiation. While a cure isn't guaranteed, there is a marginal chance."

Alex walks away.

"Alex?"

Calvin puts his head in his hands.

Reagan stands alone, looking at Dr. Wiseman eye to eye, and asks, "So marginal is a chance. So let's fight."

"I will, I would but—your insurance company won't cover the costs. His chances are too remote, and the costs are too high."

"Wait, stop, hold it. What are you saying? We're covered."

"Yes, you are, you are insured."

"I'm a school teacher, a public servant. I've been on that Health Solutions policy for years. I've paid on the policy for years. Jackson is covered on my policy, so what's—why wouldn't the insurance cover him?"

"Your insurance company, well, because the survivability rate is remote, the insurance company classifies the treatment as experimental, unnecessary."

"Stop. Wait. Who?"

"Your insurer, Health Solutions. The Health Solutions insurance clerk has reviewed your husband's file and determined that the treatment is unnecessary."

– 9 –

STANDING AT A DISTANCE, Alex thinks, *I know what she's saying… Health Solutions does not insure Stage IV cancer treatments. We classify the treatments as experimental and deny insurance coverage.*

Looking back at her friend, seeing her standing there with popping veins and protruding eyes, Alex knows why her eyes are bulging, her tears are flowing. Alex is certain the physician has told her, *We have the medical means to fix **your husband**, but you lack the financial means.*

Alex knows the gap between medical science developments and patient resources is widening by the day. She also knows that she works daily to ensure that her client, Health Solutions, isn't caught filling the gap. She helps them deny claims like this one everyday….

The countless cases in the past rise up and show themselves as she stares at her friend from a distance.

Chapter Sixty-four
Saved By the Bell?

REAGAN STARES INTO Dr. Wiseman's steely grey eyes. She sees the empathy there. She hears the words she speaks, but Reagan does not respond. *Jackson needs surgery and treatment to save his life, but the insurance company won't insure him for the medical care he needs?*

Reagan sinks. She feels duped, like she has been tricked and then kicked in the stomach.

She also feels lost; she does not know where to turn until suddenly, she thinks, *Wait, my friend, she's a lawyer!*

Reagan turns away from Dr. Wiseman and turns to her friend. Seeing Alex in the distance, talking on the telephone, Reagan briskly walks towards her.

Interrupting Alex, Reagan says, "I need your help!"

Holding up her finger, signaling for Reagan to wait, Alex continues to frantically talk on the telephone. "I've had a tragic emergency," Alex says.

Hearing her friend's words, Reagan mouths, "What's wrong?"

Hanging up the telephone, Alex says, "Reagan, sorry. I forgot. I'm due in court. I've got to go!"

I forgot about your scandal! But—I need you!

Hugging Reagan, Alex adds, "I'll assist in any way I can, but I've got to run now. Calvin's here."

"Go, get to court. Good luck, but hurry back. You've got to help me fight my insurance company!"

Reagan feels torn. Her world is falling apart, and the one person who can help her is in her own crisis. She wishes her friend could abandon court to fight her insurer. Watching Alex run away, Reagan wonders, *What am I going to do? How do I fight a giant? How do I slay this dragon?*

Almost on cue, Calvin approaches her from behind. "You must appeal the decision," he says. "You can't let them deny your claim without a fight."

"But how and why? I'm lost. How do we have insurance but don't have insurance?"

"I can spend weeks, if not months, trying to explain the answer to that question to you."

"Can you try? That's the only way I can fight, right? I have to understand."

"You're right, so in a nutshell, your insurance policy is a contract."

"Right, a contract that insures us against health care costs when necessary, right?"

"Not exactly," he says, shaking his head. "Insurance contracts usually always have limits, loopholes, exceptions, and exclusions."

"I don't understand."

"Reagan, insurance isn't a guarantee. Most people think they have insurance until they need the insurance for a life-threatening procedure that is usually also very costly. Usually, only then, do people find out the limits of their insurance coverage."

"What limits? What loopholes? What's a loophole?"

"An escape clause, if you will, for the insurance company. Reagan, that's how they balance their risks and limit their costs."

"Calvin, we need the insurance company to insure us."

"Yes, but they won't because they're saying you don't have insurance for the procedure Jackson requires, hence the loophole."

"I'm lost," Reagan says, feeling confused.

"I understand. I'll call the insurance company with you. We must call and demand that they cover the treatment."

"Should I wait for Alex? She's a lawyer."

"Actually, a lawyer would be helpful, but we don't have time. Isn't Alex going to court?"

"Yes, but—"

"We can't wait." He looks as if he is thinking. "Cayla Anthony," he finally says, snapping his fingers.

"Is what?"

"She's the hospital's Associate General Counsel. Let's walk over to her office. She can help."

Chapter Sixty-five
In Justice We Trust

ALEX SCURRIES INTO the court house, late. She rushes to the defense table and whispers to Shannon Klaxon, "Sorry, my friend—"

"Save your excuses!" Shannon whispers fiercely into Alex's ear. "Be timely next time because this judge will hold you in contempt, throw you in jail, and throw away the key! She doesn't play!"

"I know, but—"

"No buts! I called in favors to keep you out of jail. Unacceptable, Alex! I save favors for strategies like pleas and deals, not nonsense like tardiness, understand?"

She pulls away from Alex's ear and smiles, maintaining the pretense that they're having a girly, cordial, kind conversation.

Alex tries to smile and nod, thinking, *Dang, my friend's husband is in the hospital.*

"Here ye, here ye, the Court of the Honorable Judge Lucille Mann is now in session…."

Judge Lucille Mann swiftly approaches her bench.

"You may be seated," she commands, and sits. "Glad you've obliged us with your presence, Ms. Giroud," Judge Mann declares. She looks at Alex sternly over the rim of her fire-red plastic glasses.

Jeez, she looks like she would throw me under the bus!

Moving on to the case, Judd Mann asks, "What's the matter before the court today?"

Shannon Klaxon stands. "Your honor, Shannon Klaxon on behalf of the defendant, Alexandria Giroud. We are here to ask the court to dismiss the criminal complaint against my client because the prosecution has no case."

The prosecutor stands. In a loud, overpowering voice, he says, "Your Honor, Richard Pierce, prosecution. We can prove our case. Ms. Klaxon is show boating…"

Pulling off her red glasses and giving Richard Pierce a sharp glance, Judge Mann retorts, "I'll judge the validity of her motion." Looking back at Shannon Klaxon, Judge Mann gestures with her glasses. "Continue, Ms. Klaxon."

"Thank you, Your Honor. As I was saying, the prosecution has not set forth any essential facts to prove that my client bribed anyone. Moreover, not only is the complaint deficient, but I submit that even the prosecution's warrant was insufficient. Simply put, there was no probable cause to search and seize her office."

Interrupting again, Richard Pierce stands up and says, "The defendant's law firm consented. We didn't need a warrant."

"So you're conceding that you did not have a warrant?" Judge Mann asks.

"Respectfully no, Your Honor. We had a valid warrant, but we did not need the warrant because her firm consented."

"Your Honor, Mr. Pierce knows a law firm can't waive my client's constitutional rights. Ms. Giroud had a reasonable expectation of privacy in her office."

"There's no reasonable expectation of privacy in the workplace," Richard Pierce says, shaking his head.

"Actually, employees do have a reasonable expectation of privacy… *United States v. Ziegler.*"

"Yes, but *Ziegler* also says the employer can consent to searches and seizures that would otherwise be illegal; so again, the firm consented to the search. This discussion is superfluous."

Knowing *Ziegler* does grant the employer the authority to consent, Shannon Klaxon moves on. "Defense counsel and I agree on one thing: this case is superfluous."

"I said discussion."

"Yes, well superfluous still because you don't have a case. You don't have sufficient evidence, and there is no probable cause to proceed with this trial."

Judge Mann gazes at Richard Pierce; she gives him a stern, powerful look.

"Your Honor, the defendant bribed a member of Congress. She tried to use influence to fix health care for her client."

Interrupting, Shannon asks, "So you're dragging her into court because she is a lobbyist? Slanting the laws in your favor's no crime. If that's all you have—"

"You can lobby to influence policy, but she did more. She had sex. She paid money. She bribed the Congresswoman."

Judge Mann lifts her eyebrows.

Seeing that the judge is interested, Shannon Klaxon interjects. "Your Honor, the prosecution proves my point. He's babbling off scandal like he's reading a tantalizing romance novel, but he has no evidence! He only gives us scant, general assertions, which are not sufficient. He did not attach an affidavit to his criminal complaint. He has no witnesses. His case is meritless."

"We'll amend our complaint," Pierce interjects.

"And bind my client over until you find evidence? That's unconstitutional. My client has rights, and the constitution and the laws protect my client from the prosecution's overreaching."

"We have a case. We'll prove our case at trial!"

"Your Honor, the prosecution has no case. This is a witch-hunt, and my client is the hunted witch. While witch-hunts may have been widespread and acceptable in the Middle Ages, we're in the twenty-first century. We don't classify powerful, smart women as witches and then persecute them; but that's what the prosecution is doing here. He's attacking an otherwise powerful, smart, and innocent woman because she had sex!"

"Cease the dramatics! We'll prove your client is guilty! We'll show our evidence at trial. You should save your arguments for the jury!" Richard Pierce says.

Chapter Sixty-six
Wait...

Alex stares at the scales of justice above Judge Mann's bench. She feels anxious. She hopes the Judge will dismiss the criminal lawsuit against her on the spot!

"I'll take the case under advisement," Judge Mann says.

Alex knows this means she will have to wait. *Wait? He has no evidence, a deficient complaint, and I've got to wait? How? He's on a witch-hunt. Judge Mann has to think about it!*

The knot in Alex's stomach drags her and pulls her into sand.

She sinks.

Judge Mann rises and exits.

"Not what I wanted, but at least you're out on bail still after that showing up late to court trick you pulled!" Shannon Klaxon whispers into Alex's ear as the women stand to exit the courthouse.

Briskly walking out with her counsel, Alex steps on white marble floors and makes her way through the halls of justice.

Heels clicking, not missing a beat, Shannon discreetly talks through her teeth, not wanting anyone to make out her statements from afar. "Don't worry, we'll prepare and beat him at trial, if necessary!"

Shrinking at the word trial, Alex lifts her shoulders and tries to hold herself together. "Shannon, we can't go to trial."

"I'm confident that I'll get the case dismissed, but you understand, the scales of justice—"

Yep, those scales...

"Justice can tip either way. We'll be ready in case the scales tip the prosecution's way."

"How's that justice if I'm innocent and the scales tip in their favor?"

"Alex, you don't think justice is literal, do you?" Shannon looks appalled by Alex's naiveté.

"No, actually, but in my case—"

"You want the scales to work differently for you?"

"It'd be nice…"

"We'll work hard, but justice sometimes goes to the one with the most tricks, skills, will, power, money—you know how trials work."

Yep, I do! I'm innocent but I could be found guilty! Her insides curl up. Agony and fear weigh down her heart and spirit. She is afraid. Sand covers her. She feels like she can't breathe.

Chapter Sixty-seven
Now Choose: Your Client or Your Friend...

ALEX STEPS OUTSIDE the courthouse and is immediately struck by flashing camera lights and fierce words. Feeling terrified, she tries to put on a confident front while making her way through the crowd. Shielding her face with her hands and ignoring the reporters' shouts, Alex stays close to Shannon, who scurries through the media cluster so fast that Alex can barely hear the beginnings of the questions flying at her. Shannon and Alex are many feet ahead of the questions....

Suddenly, Alex sees the black sports utility vehicle Shannon's firm uses to transport high profile clients in the short-distance.

STEP, STEP, STEP.... *We're closer, we're closer...we're here, yes!* Alex leaps into the SUV but hears a question lash out at her before the door closes.

"Ms. Giroud, you had sex with the congresswoman's son?"

He's her son?

The driver closes the door. *Perfect timing...*SLAM!

Silence is golden.

Alex deeply inhales.

She feels like this is the first breath she has taken since she stepped outside the court house.

Alexandria Giroud looks out the tinted mirrors in awe. She feels she is in a pretend, make believe story.

Shannon talks defense strategy as the driver takes off, whisking through the crowds. Alex hears her words, but she does not hear any guarantees. *I've given this advice before. I know the scales of justice may tip unfairly for me if we don't find a way, some way, to prove that even though I gave that Congressional Aide a briefcase full of cash, I didn't intend to do so. I was duped—set up—I had no idea. And yes, I slept with the aide, but that's because he was hot, not because I was trying to bribe his boss…or mother, or whatever or whoever he is!*

"Alex, I know you say you didn't know cash was in the briefcase, but understand, Alex, no jury is going to believe that you, a lawyer, walked around with all that cash without asking the million dollar question: what's in the bag?"

"I know, dumb right? Why did I take that briefcase?" *'Cause I was caught up in Marshall's web, not thinking. . . .*

"I wouldn't start that dumb, stupid, beat myself up game. We'll need your smarts, girlfriend, so think. I'll work my end, look for angles, legal loopholes and such, but you do your end."

"I will," Alex says, nodding her head.

"Go inside your condo and think. I'm your lawyer and I like to win, so call at any time, understand?" Shannon says with a smile.

First time I've seen her smile since I met her. Alex gets out of the SUV, sneaks up the freight elevator, and slips into her condo. . . .

Once inside, her shoulders fall. Her façade is gone. She flops onto the couch and thinks.

She tries to retrace her steps. *How can I prove that Marshall Hanes is the guilty party?*

He asked me to do the memo, which I did.

He had a lot of odd phone calls. Who was he talking to, and about what? He demanded—

The telephone rings. She answers immediately, knowing that it's Reagan.

"Alex, I need your help."

Weights lodge and anchor around Alex's neck. *How can my world fall apart two-fold at once? How can I assist Reagan now . . . I need assistance. . . .*

"Alex, did you hear me?" Reagan says. She is clearly weeping.

"Yes, sorry. Just got back from court. How's Jackson?"

"Not well. He needs surgery, chemotherapy, and radiation treatment, but Health Solutions won't pay."

Feeling like she is choking, Alex stares blankly out of her window at the sun setting over the horizon. . . .

"Alex, did you hear me? Health Solutions, we have to fight!"

Alex is still silent.

"What should I do?" Reagan asks.

Alex knows exactly how to handle a claim denial, but she is not sure whether she can get involved. Health Solutions is her client. She helps Health Solutions *deny* claims. In fact, if Reagan challenges the claim, the lawsuit would probably end up on Alex's desk—*Except, do I still work there? I mean, I've been arrested . . . I'm out on bail!*

"Alex, what do you think?"

You can't win. Health Solutions can deny your insurance claim. I know. **I wrote the exclusion clause in your insurance contract!** *You have no case, no recourse!* Alex thinks.

"Alex?"

Alex continues to stare out of her window at a vibrant, blue, cloudless sky. She sees ahead of her. She faces an ocean of blueness in the sky; yet, while she sees what is in front of her, she has no idea what to do next.

"Are you there? Are you okay?" Reagan asks. Finally, she screams, "Alex! Alex!"

"I'm here, yes. Look, I don't know what to say."

"Do you need to research the issue? Do you need to come up with a strategy? We'll pay you," Reagan says, pleading now.

"No, it's complicated." Alex feels like she is choking. She barely has enough air.

"You're smart. I'm confident, with you, we'll win."

"No, well, yes, but no. Look, I know what to do, but I can't. I have a relationship."

"Alex, let's not talk about your sex life."

"I'm not talking about sex! I'm talking *professional* relationship."

"And?"

"I don't know how to tell you."

"Just tell me."

Inhaling deeply, she says, "Reagan, I represent Health Solutions. That's my client."

"I appreciate your honesty, but you'll stop representing them now, right? Now that you know how unethical they are, you'll drop them, right?" Reagan says, as if the answer is simple.

Almost everyone in the industry does what we do. Where've you been? "Reagan, the answer isn't simple. I am bound by ethical rules."

"Good, so ethics says you must help a friend?"

Okay, how do I explain this to her? "Reagan, lawyers, when we represent a client, we can't take a client or interest contrary to our client's interest without the client's consent."

"Why? That's strange."

"No, not really, if you think about the rule. A client has to know he can trust his lawyer; otherwise, the client can't tell the lawyer information that can be used against him. Do you understand?"

"No, not when you're a friend. That's different. You can break rules, especially weird rules, for a friend, can't you?"

Inhaling deeply again, she says, "I can't. I'm sorry."

"You're choosing them over me?" Reagan screams.

Feeling as if the air has left her condo, Alex opens her window.

"Reagan no, again, understand, I am Health Solutions' lawyer. I owe Health Solutions certain protections, including confidentiality and attorney-client privilege."

"I don't care about your confidences and your privileges with Health Solutions. I'm standing here, alone, needing a friend. Jackson has a tumor lodged in his throat, and Health Solutions won't pay the claim to remove the tumor and save his life even though we've paid that insurance company money for years to insure against this type of risk and that's wrong. *They're* wrong, and so since they're wrong, they shouldn't have any confidences or privileges with you! You're my friend!"

"You are my friend, Reagan, nothing changes."

"His physician says the surgery and treatment can save his life! Did you hear me? Jackson can live with treatment, but he will die, Alex, *die,* if we don't have the surgery and treatment."

No!

"And you, you're a so-called friend if you'll let my husband die because you owe a backstabbing no good company some duty! Alex, they owe me a duty but don't care! And you're taking their side? You're helping them kill my husband!"

No, I'm not. I didn't know. If I had known, I would have told you to get an extra policy, too. "Reagan, I'm sorry. I don't have a choice. I didn't know."

"You know now, so choose," Reagan snaps.

"I don't know what to say. I can't put my career in jeopardy. Don't you understand that ethics rules prevent—"

"What ethics? You're relying on ethics? Ethics should have prevented you from ever helping Health Solutions trick consumers."

You're taking this too far. There's nothing unethical about writing contracts to favor your client . . . Besides, you can't expect me to write the contract for consumers. I represent the insurance company! "Reagan, that's low."

"Accept the truth, Alex. *You're* low."

"Reagan, please—" Alex says.

"Again, so choose. What's your choice? A friend or a client? A client that's probably set you up anyway. What's your choice?"

"I'm sorry—"

"Your choice is predictable, Alex. You no good betrayer. That's what I thought, you so-called friend. Don't ever call my house or look for me again!" Reagan hangs up the telephone.

Chapter Sixty-eight
Friendship: The Cost...

Taylor watches Bianca Sheridan approach her front door. Opening the door to greet her, she begins to say hi, but Bianca Sheridan takes charge and says, "Good afternoon, Taylor. Smooches! You're glowing!" She walks past Taylor and enters.

Hastily stepping ahead, through the foyer, Bianca surveys the room before declaring, "Your home's gorgeous, darling. You've outdone yourself. How?"

If only you knew. "We're hard workers," Taylor answers.

"When's hard work paid so well, darling? I'm looking for your kind of work because that chandelier, Taylor, I'm telling you, darling, hard work alone usually doesn't buy top of the line twenty-four layer chandeliers." Bianca stares at the crystal chandelier with starry-eyes.

Changing the subject, Taylor asks, "What's your great proposition?" In other words, *Do you have a deal that can save my home?*

"Wi, I do, darling." Bianca speaks with an odd French accent.

You aren't French. Taylor wonders why Bianca suddenly has a French air. Taylor is suspicious. Surveying Bianca, she asks, "What's the deal?"

"See, darling, I understand you associate with Ms. Alexandria Giroud," Bianca says. Her eyes are glazed. She looks hungry for details.

"Yes, we—"

Bianca cuts her off. "So, darling, I want the story. I must break the news, *premier à rompre les nouvelles.*"

"Bianca, I don't speak French. What are you saying?"

"Certainly, darling, if you require a translation. I'm communicating to you in French that your story is worth the most if you're the first to break the news…"

Bianca, you're acting odd . . . why are you acting French? You're not.

"So, darling, if you'll give me an exclusive, I'll give you a lush deal—one you can't refuse."

"What's the deal?" Taylor asks, thinking, *How much?*

As if on cue, as if she hears the unspoken question, Bianca answers, "One million dollars, darling."

One million! "What's the catch?" Taylor asks.

"Darling, I haven't a catch. I only require an exclusive."

"You mean you'll pay one million dollars, and I get to tell Alex's side, explain her innocence?" *Alex wants to tell her side anyway . . . yes, I'll snag the story from Jackson, but Alex is my friend. . . .*

"Yes, darling, you'll tell the story, in your voice."

Reagan, she'll get over that. Besides, I need the money, really badly.

"Bianca, what's the downside?" Taylor tightly closes one eye, focusing her attention on Bianca. She knows Bianca well; in fact, Bianca and Taylor split ways years ago because they couldn't see eye to eye on a story. Watching Bianca run her fingers through her dyed, fire-red hair, Taylor surmises that Bianca is up to something.

Bianca sees Taylor staring her down. "What?"

"I know you, Bianca. What's the catch?"

"We'll want editorial control."

"Okay, typical. That's all?"

Nodding quickly, as if she has gotten away with something, Bianca says, "Most certainly!"

Not convinced, cuing in on Bianca's demeanor, Taylor asks, "What else?" *Bianca plays dirty.*

"Look, do you want the million or not? If not, se la vie! I can get my story either way," Bianca says, biting her lip.

"I'm game, I me—I mean, I want to do business with you, but I've got to know, when you say editorial control, you're not talking about splicing and dicing my sentences are you?"

"Taylor Ray, of course not," Bianca answers, in a tone that suggests she is surprised by Taylor's suggestion. "As long as you say what we require," she adds.

"Wait, what do you mean?"

"We have a script. If you follow the script, you'll be paid. . . ."

Handing her the script, Taylor reads the words and is in complete disbelief.

Lifting her eyes from the paper, she stares at Bianca, who is now fidgeting... *You should be fidgeting,* she thinks. *Why do you think I'll tell these lies?*

Smiling a little defensively, Bianca proclaims, "Again, we're paying one million dollars, darling. We don't pay such sums for simple news."

"I can't lie!" Taylor says.

Laughing, Bianca says, "Taylor Ray, reclassify what you're doing. Why not call what you're doing reality television or alternatively giving the people what they desire. You're in the news business. You understand, scandal sales."

"Isn't the truth scandalous enough?" Taylor asks. She wants to make a fair and reasonable deal—not a dishonest, sell-your-friend-out deal.

Before Bianca can respond, her telephone rings.

Her eyes widen, and Bianca says, "Pardon me, darling. I must take the call outside."

Watching Bianca step outside, Taylor Ray thinks, *The way you do business, you would have to take calls outside.*

Watching Bianca in the distance, Taylor Ray takes another look at the script. *Bianca wants me to say Alex is basically a slut who slept her way to the top, had an affair with her boss, and had sex with a congressional aide to fix health care for her client—and when that wasn't enough, she bribed him to fix the law to work in her client's favor. How can I say that? I mean, even if Alex slept with the congressional aide, and even if she bribed him, I can't throw her under the bus, can I?*

Yes, Tay! You're about to lose this house. Are you crazy? Whit says we've got to move and one million bucks could save our house . . . and the baby . . . the baby? Where will we go? What will we do? We're talking one million. Taylor touches her stomach because she feels something there. *What's that? Was that the baby . . . I feel like I have tiny butterflies in my stomach. . . .*

Reconnecting with her own life, her husband, her pregnancy, her baby, she feels… *one million dollars sure could make our life easier.*

"Taylor, darling, 'Au revoir, ta ta. I've other affairs!" Bianca says, returning.

"What?"

"Wi bon, I must go, but have you decided?" Bianca fixes her gaze on Taylor Ray.

Taylor looks into Bianca's blue eyes and decides.

"I can't!" she says, nodding yes.

"Wi bon, so are you communicating yes? Did I hear you correctly?" Bianca asks, practically salivating.

"Yes, I mean no. I can't because Alex, she's a friend," Taylor answers, feeling her stomach turn. *I'm giving up one million dollars to be true to a friend?*

"Wi bon, friendship! I've heard about friendship, but I'd sell out my Madam for one million dollars. Did I use the correct vernacular? Sell out?"

"Bianca, stop!"

"What? I'm expanding my horizons."

"Gotcha, but stop, really Bianca!"

"Wi bon, sure, back to Ms. Alexandria Giroud."

"Yes, she's a friend. I can't sell out a friend."

"I'd sell out my spouse for one million."

"You're single! You don't have a spouse!"

"I know, hypothetically speaking!"

"I can't, but we can give you a story." Taylor smiles.

"What kind?" Bianca asks, managing to look curious and uninterested at once.

"How about the truth—if Alex agrees?"

"Ce qui est trop mauvaise!"

"Stop speaking French, Bianca! You're not French!"

"Wi, wi, but I'm immersing myself. I'm trying to become French, learn French!"

"But you're not, so speak English, at least with me! So in English, what are you saying?"

"About what?"

"Your ce qui whatever you said when I said I could tell you the truth if Alex agrees."

"Wi wi, ah that, yes. I said too bad."

"Aren't you interested? The story's a seller."

"Yes, but we have a great story line. Darling, the truth can't beat our story."

"What storyline?"

"Understand, darling, our writer, he's French, and he's written a tantalizing plot and storyline. Darling, once you read our script, you'll desire wine and cheese, and a French baguette, imported from France, to watch our news story. Speaking of the French, don't you think the language and culture and the men are so absolutely sexy?"

"Bianca, are you on something?"

"No Madam, well actually, yes. I'm dating the French writer. Taylor Ray, he's gorgeous…but I'm professional, too. He hasn't impaired my judgment, if that's what you're asking, but he is lighting my fire. Is that the correct vernacular? How you people say things?"

"Bianca!" Taylor Ray shouts because she feels Bianca always expects her to be the authority on pop culture and ethnic speech. *Why does she always ask me questions about what she perceives as slang?*

"Stop asking me about vernacular in that tone!"

"What I'm learning, I'm expanding—"

"Yeah, whatever, anyway you think the deal is good and the story is great?" Taylor frowns. *I believe you. Even if he's knocking it out of the park with you each night, that's not what has you here acting like this right now. You've always wanted the easy, scandalous story, that's your style. You also make lots of money doing that crap, you no good—*

Cutting off her thoughts, Bianca asks, "So, darling, again. I want an actor to tell our story, preferably a friend. Do you want to sell?"

"Yes!"

"Merveilleux! Merveilleuse!" Her eyes are wide. Her smile is, too.

"Stop speaking French!" Taylor Ray yells.

"Oh why yes, wi bon, great, I'm only saying, 'Marvelous! I knew you'd come around!'" Bianca raises her voice in excitement.

"Yes, Bianca, I'll sell, but not to you! Alex is my friend! I can't sell her out, not even for one million dollars!"

Chapter Sixty-nine
Sorry, but that's Experimental

REAGAN PLEADS WITH Tyra Lake, the Health Solutions insurance clerk. "Please reconsider your denial. Jackson is my husband."

"We have, and Ms. Hamilton, I sincerely apologize."

"But Dr. Wiseman says Jackson needs medical intervention."

"I'm sorry, Ms. Hamilton, but your policy excludes Dr. Wiseman's prescribed treatment method. We can't approve surgery, radiation, or chemotherapy because in the case of the insured, the treatment is deemed experimental under Health Solutions' policy Section L IVB. Do you have a copy there? I can go over the provision with you if you'd like?"

"No, I'm not carrying the policy in my pocket! But that's not important! I do know the prescribed treatment is standard."

"Yes, but Ms. Hamilton, the insured's survivability rate is remote, which makes the treatment experimental."

"His name is Jackson, and his doctors say he can survive with the proper care."

"Yes, perhaps, and I suggest you proceed with treatment, but Health Solutions won't cover the costs."

"Then how can we proceed with treatment if you won't pay? You're our means; you're our insurance; you're our way to pay."

"No, Ms. Hamilton, you haven't been advised? You do have rights, but don't look to us."

"If not you, then who?"

"Ask your physician. You can demand that she proceed with treatment and then you pay her back over time. If you can't afford to pay, you can file bankruptcy, too. You do have other options."

"*You're* supposed to pay, not us! We can't file bankruptcy! We pay our bills! Why must we file bankruptcy because you won't do the same? Besides, Jackson is sick! Don't you get it?"

"I know this may be surprising to you, but doctors, they're in the business of making money. We deny doctors' request all the time; that's how we save you money, that's how we keep your premiums at affordable levels."

"I'm not trying to save money. I'm trying to save my husband's life," she says.

"Ms. Hamilton, as I said, the insured is not covered, but you can demand treatment."

"His name is Jackson Hamilton! Stop calling him 'the insured' because that's so informal, so tacky. He has a name! Also, you're not insuring him, so why are you calling him the insured!"

"Please review your policy. We can send you a courtesy copy in the mail."

"I don't want a courtesy copy. I want you to pay his claim!"

Tyra Lake tunes Reagan Hamilton out as she rants and raves on the other end of the telephone.

She merely waits for a pause and says boilerplate words when there is space to interject. "I understand," or "I'm sorry, but this is standard practice," "You have rights, but we're not responsible."

As Reagan screams and yells, Tyra Lake types.

✉ **To: Nancy Prago, Medical Director**
  From: Tyra Lake
  Re: Utilization Review

This email confirms that I have denied coverage to Mr. Jackson Hamilton. I discussed the denial with his wife. I explained the policy. I advised there's nothing we can do. We probably won't hear anything further on this one, so I will mark it closed. We've probably saved anywhere from $150,000 to $200,000 on this one. :)

This is another great case of policy claims DENIED, DENIED, DENIED.

Tyra presses send and then smiles. *I should get a huge Christmas bonus with this one!*

Chapter Seventy
HMO Not Liable

ALEX SITS AND watches the moon change hands with the sun. Darkness sets in. Staring outside into the cloudless, night sky, her heart sinks. Her new reality—*A friend is dying AND I'm on trial for bribery*—disturbs her, drowns her, suffocates her. She feels like she can't breathe.

Her new reality feels like an anchor hoisted around her neck. The anchor of unfortunate circumstance is tightly wound and pulling her out into a deep blue ocean. She sinks.

What can I do to save myself and my friend?

She is not sure until a powerful word comes to mind.........*Think!*

Okay, so what? Assist Reagan in navigating the insurance denial process? She knows the process well, but she also understands that there is no legal way around the cards Jackson Hamilton has been dealt. She created the cards. She knows Health Solutions, Inc. has a valid basis to deny Jackson Hamilton's insurance claim. First, Health Solutions can deny the claim as a pre-existing condition because the stage and nature of his cancer means that this cancer has been in his body for at least three years. Jackson only changed over to his wife's policy last year, when he left his corporate job to work at the start-up political blog he now runs. He has no options there. Second, Health Solutions can also deny Jackson's claim because the treatment his doctor recommends is experimental in his case. Jackson has only a remote chance of surviving, even with treatment, and the Health Solutions insurance contract gives Health Solutions the right to deny an insurance claim if the insured only has a remote chance of surviving with treatment.

Alex considers her past work. She knows she has spent years assisting Health Solutions deny health care to insured claimants. Before, she bolstered each success like a badge, like proud victories at her feet. She made coverage denials without fault. She appreciates that her representations prompted emails like the one she knows exists and sets the stage for Jackson's situation. Recalling the emails in her head, she thinks, *I used to fight like hell to keep these emails out of court!*

✉ **To: Regional Medical Review Directors**
From: Nancy Prago, Medical Director
Re: NOTICE

DENY expensive cancer treatments! Deny whenever there is a low chance of recovery. ERISA will protect your decision and save money lots of $$$$$$$$$$$$$$$$$$$$$$.
:)

Now the email seems cruel! Now Health Solutions is denying care to a friend. He will die!
She rests out in the deep ocean, on her back.
She sees a dark blue ocean.
She can't breathe.
He will die!
Until suddenly, wanting air, she thinks forward rather than backwards and decides she can change the outcome. She can act!

Lifting herself up, she grabs onto an anchor. She acknowledges and accepts her new reality. She hoists the anchor. *Yes, I made the deck, but I can fix this situation. I can if I think!*

Taking the anchor from around her neck, she charges towards the shore, fighting to stay alive....

Alex charges to her home office and gets to work. Staring at her laptop computer screen, which flickers with a blue neon light, she knows that today, her law books cannot serve as a life jacket. She knows the law won't work. It would take an act of Congress to change Jackson's situation if she goes the legal route. If she waits on Congress to act, Jackson will be dead. She must take matters into her own hands.

Seeing her cursor flashing, she changes course.

Chapter Seventy-one
Search & Seizure

AFTER THINKING FOR HOURS, Alex has an idea. She takes her mouse and puts it on the program icon, SpyonHim. Opening the program and waiting on her computer to connect with the data, she thinks back to the night she put the SpyonHim spyware on Marshall's computer.

Late one night, three months ago, she is working with Marshall Hanes in his office.

On that dark, muggy night, he suddenly turns the conversation from work to sex when he says, "Come here, you." He lifts her up and places her body on his desk.

She smiles.

He lifts her skirt.

She squirms and whispers, "Isn't Judy here?"

He shakes his head no.

"But Marshall—"

He enters her and that ends the discussion.

He groans.

She wails.

She climaxes.

He climaxes.

He exits her.

His telephone vibrates.

He charges toward it.

"Why the rush?" she asks, wanting more than his usual abrupt endings, her body still on fire.

Looking at the CALLER ID, he says, "I've got to take this. You've got to go."

She shakes her head no, demanding more from him.

He zips his pants, opens her office door, and takes the call outside his office.

Seeing him walk and talk on the telephone while heading into another partner's office, Alex decides to take matters into her own hands. *I've got to know. Is he seeing only me?* She adjusts her clothing and walks over to his computer. Pulling out software she's downloaded from SpyonHim.com, she inserts her key swab and downloads the program onto his computer.

What is SpyonHim software? Ingenious software invented by a woman to help other women spy on their men.

With SpyonHim software on Marshall Hanes' computer, Alex receives blind copies of any and every email or text message Marshall Hanes sends or receives.

With SpyonHim, Alex will know if Marshall is sending text messages or emails to another woman other than Alex and his wife.

Sitting in her condo alone, searching, Alex opens the fake email she set up to connect with her SpyonHim account.

Opening her SpyonHim email account, SheIsWatchingYou@SpyonHim.com, she smiles. *Jackpot!*

She sees email after email pop up.

She searches.

She reads.

Hours later, she sees something promising. She sees emails from Richard Livingston to Marshall Hanes.

Richard Livingston is HealthSolutions' cost containment risk manager. He is also the CEO's right hand man. Alex knows Livingston is unethical. She calls him *slimy!*

She begins reading an email trail between Richard Livingston and Marshall Hanes. Richard Hanes writes an email to Marshall.

"WE NEED GUARANTEES. *The old way doesn't work.*"

Seeing guarantees, and remembering how Marshall told her he wanted her to deliver health care reform guarantees, she surmises that this is a great starting place. She follows the email trail, reading on. Marshall responds to the email with a question.

"What do you have in mind?"

Harmless, she thinks, but reads on, knowing that Richard Livingston always makes deals around the law, pushing the law to the edge, trying to get his lawyers to sign-off on illegal transactions. Richard answers Marshall's email with a question.

"You're kidding, right? YOU'RE THE LAWYER. VTY, Richard Livingston, Vice President, Risk Loss Prevention."

We're getting warmer.

"Richard, what do you want?"

She nearly flips when she reads his answer.

"I have a guy. He has our favorite senator's ear. Word is if we pay $3,000,000, we'll own the Health Care Committee. We just have to pay $500,000 up front. VTY, Richard Livingston, Vice President, Risk Loss Prevention."

What? She leaps up from her chair. She has email evidence in her hands. Her heart hastens as she continues. Marshall and Richard exchange email after email.

"I understand, but how?" Marshall writes.

"Cash only, no paper trail," Richard writes.

"I understand because cash is fast, easy, and untraceable, but who's got the cash?"

"Same guy as always…Blakely…he always has the cash. Just keep his name out of this."

"Should have known, but how do I get the cash?"

"I'll set up the meeting with our favorite Senator's Congressional Aide. You'll fly out to D.C. We'll meet you before the flight, coffee shop near the airport," Richard answers.

Alex gasps and continues reading.

"Give me the dates and times and I'll be there."

"Stupid, can't be only you," Richard adds.

"Who else?"

Alex stomps her foot as she reads the next email. Her eyes open wide. Her blood boils. She bites her lower lip.

Red covers her face as she is overcome by rage.

"We need a woman," Richard writes.

"Women work here," Marshall answers.

"Yeah, but I want someone who you can control."

"I control many," Marshall responds.

"I want an order follower," Richard demands.

"I have plenty," Marshall answers.

"You fucking any young associates?" Richard asks.

"A few, but I do have one in mind. She's easy, and she won't question me. I'll butter her up a bit, but she's mine. Get ready to own the Committee," Marshall answers.

"Grand! I'll deliver the briefcase to you at the airport coffee shop. Give the briefcase to your dumb chick and have her give the cash to the aide. They'll never know. This aide is a charmer, and the ladies like him. She'll be too caught up trying to fuck him, trust me, that is, if she is a slut. Is she?"

"Absolutely. She put the S in slut. We're good," Marshall answers.

— 9: —

ALEX PUSHES HER HAIR behind her ear. All the pieces fall into place. She looks at the time. 4:30 a.m. She pushes back from her desk to put on her best suit, but not before calling Rachel McCay.

Chapter Seventy-two
Grab Justice and Hold

Before the sun rises, Alex briskly walks into Health Solutions and marches straight to the CEO's office with one purpose: *Grab justice and hold!*

"Mr. Blakely, good morning!" She enters his office after merely one knock, holding a stack of papers in her hands.

Quickly rising, startled by her entrance, Mr. Blakely walks around his desk to meet her at the door. He extends his hand. "Ms. Giroud, why are you here, and so early?"

She firmly shakes his hand before walking past him, then sits in a chair facing his desk. "I'm here because I understand you like to do business over early morning coffee runs," she says.

He sits, but his right hand fidgets, as if he is nervous.

"I'm a coffee connoisseur, but there're many coffee shops—"

Cutting him off, she adds, "And business."

"Yes, business . . . " he begins, and trails off. He stands, walks over to his office kitchen, and begins to pour a cup of coffee.

Walking towards Alex with coffee in hand, he says, "I brewed a fine roast this morning, Africa—"

She cuts him off. "No thanks."

He looks like he is lost, standing there in a polished suit with a cup of piping hot coffee in hand.

Silent, Alex hands him the email trail she printed out, including the email that says that he provided the $500,000 cash to bribe Congress to fix health care.

He begins to read.

He turns pale white, even though his skin is brown.

She does not say anything, not a word, just in case his office is bugged. *We're under investigation, so this place probably is bugged, so I'll have to be discreet, watch what I say. Here goes . . .*

Picking out the one email that incriminates him in the bribery scheme, she points to the email and says, "Mr. Blakely, focusing on business, I'm here because I understand there's been a terrible mistake."

Sweat beads form on his face. He is silent. He looks ghostly.

She continues, sensing she has his attention. "So, Mr. Blakely, I know Health Solutions' policies well. I wrote them as your lawyer, understand?"

He nods. He does not say a word. He wipes sweat beads off his forehead.

"So as your lawyer, it has come to my attention that a friend, Jackson Hamilton, one of your insured claimants, has been denied cancer treatment."

His eyes open wide.

"Yes, see, and I'm sure your insurance clerk has the denial wrong. Jackson Hamilton is a good friend, and he is insured."

With his lower lip quivering, he says, "You'd know, you wrote the policies." He looks as if he is in shock, but he also looks as if he is beginning to feel less frightened. *Yeah, you're easing up cuz you sense I'm here to deal, and you're ready to do anything to save your butt!*

"Right, so see, I need your assistance."

He nods.

"We need your insurance clerks to understand the wide-breadth of Jackson Hamilton's insurance coverage."

He tilts his head and shrugs his shoulders, as if he is asking a question.

She holds up the incriminating email and explains, "Yes see, this will disappear when you print out a copy of Jackson Hamilton's policies—all three."

"Three?" he asks.

"Yes, his Health Solutions general policy, his Health Solutions supplemental policy, which kicks in when his general policy does not insure his medical needs, and then his Health Solutions cancer policy, which kicks in when the general policy and supplemental policies deny his claims."

"Ah yes, your friend is careful," he responds. He turns to his computer and types.

Alex watches him peck at the computer. He manufactures insurance policies on his computer screen—the price he agrees to pay to keep her quiet about his involvement in the Senate bribery scheme.

Seeing him work his magic, Alex also adds, "Since you're printing out policies, can you print out mine, too?" *Just in case.*

He nods.

She smiles.

Chapter Seventy-three
September Skies

ALEX CALLS REAGAN from her condo, to no avail. She thinks Reagan is avoiding her calls. Wanting to get through to her friend, Alex hops into her car and travels the short distance to Reagan's home, thinking, *I'll knock and call my way inside her house somehow!*

She leaps out of her car and marches onto Reagan's porch.

She knocks. Reagan does not answer.

She calls Reagan from her cell phone. *No answer.*

She knocks. She calls. She knocks. She calls. *No answer.*

Hours pass.

Reagan does not answer the door. She does not answer the telephone either.

Calling again, hearing Reagan's salutation again, Alex decides to try to break inside the house with her words as she hears the answering machine beep.

"Reagan, I've got great news. Answer the door!"

Reagan does not answer.

"I've chosen you, Reagan! I've fixed everything!"

Reagan does not answer.

"I know you think I'm self-centered, but Reagan, you're my friend. I had to find a way."

Reagan does not answer.

"Answer the door, the telephone, something, Reagan, please?"

Reagan does not answer.

"Reagan, I've even prayed."

Alex hears a loud noise come from inside the house, as if the word prayer caused something to jolt or fall down.

"Reagan, that's right. Did you hear me? I've *prayed*."

Reagan does not answer.

"Almost got her," Alex mumbles.

If I can't get her with prayer, I know what will make her answer.

Alex starts singing an odd rendition of Dionne Warwick's "That's What Friend's Are For," in a loud, off key voice.

Alex knows the words, but she can't carry a note.

She makes a sacrifice to reach her friend. She sings, "In good times and bad times, I'll be on your side forevermore, that's what friends are for—"

Pausing, Alex tries to see if Reagan is responding because she knows Dionne Warwick would probably tell her to cease if she could hear this rendition, her singing is so awful. *Anything to reach a friend,* she thinks. Hearing no response, she begins to sing again....

— 9: —

REAGAN STANDS AND LISTENS to the screeching bouncing off the walls of her tiny bungalow. Recognizing the sound, the song, and the singer, Reagan thinks, *Alex can't sing, but—*

"I'm usually not forward. I'm a lady and I tend to my own business! But sweetheart, you're acting like a mad woman. You've been marching and knocking and carrying on like a lunatic. I could take your shenanigans, but your singing, honey, that's got to stop!"

Mrs. Georgia! Reagan realizes her next door, elderly neighbor must be confronting Alex.

Reagan rushes to the front door and peaks out her peak-hole. She sees Mrs. Georgia standing on her front porch wearing a robe and hair rollers.

Mrs. Georgia is holding a leash with one hand, with her cat, Diamond on the other end. She has her other hand on her hip.

She is giving Alex the suspicious, *Are you nutty?* eye.

Reagan also sees that Mrs. Georgia has a cordless telephone in her robe pocket. *Mrs. Georgia will call the police!*

Reagan opens her front door and says, "Alex, Mrs. Georgia, hello."

Mrs. Georgia turns her suspicious gaze from Alex to Reagan and asks, "Wait, child, you've been here all this time and you had this child on the front porch knocking, then screaming, then yelling, and now crying?"

"I'm singing, not crying!"

"Call your cackling what you want, but you sound mad!"

"Mrs. Georgia—" Reagan begins, but Mrs. Georgia cuts her off.

"Do you know how long this child has been on the porch, disturbing the neighborhood? Diamond couldn't sleep, I couldn't rest, and my last evening's company left—"

Last evening's company? Mrs. Georgia, you're wearing your robe and Mr. Georgia, he just died... "Mrs. Georgia, I apologize, but—"

"Anyhow, child, watch the company you keep because this one over here," Mrs. Georgia gestures towards Alex with her head, "is coo-coo. Understand?"

Alex points to Mrs. Georgia's tube socks and fluffy house shoes and says, "Look who's talking! You're calling *me* coo-coo?"

"Shush, stop!" Reagan demands, cutting an evil eye towards Alex.

"Child, let me help ya get rid of this one. I'll call 911," Mrs. Georgia says.

— 9: —

THIRTY-FIVE MINUTES LATER, MRS. Georgia seems almost convinced that Reagan does not need her to call 911, and that Alex is her friend.

"All right, baby, but I'm a phone call away. See my cell," Mrs. Georgia says, brandishing her cordless phone.

"I know, Mrs. Georgia. I appreciate you, thank you," Reagan replies. She watches Mrs. Georgia nod and then switch back across the street with Diamond on a leash.

With Mrs. Georgia gone, Reagan speaks to Alex. "Yes, I've been avoiding you. You know why! Why are you here?"

"I'm your friend."

"You're no friend of mine. You showed your colors, Alex."

"No, I had a trial, a test, but I've passed."

"Can't tell, you wouldn't help; you made me fight those snakes alone!"

"Perhaps, but only for a short season. I was scared; but I didn't leave you. I never left you," Alex says, holding up the insurance policies and showing them to Reagan, one after another.

Seeing the insurance policies, Reagan gasps before asking, "What have you done?"

"I've solved your problem, Alexandria Giroud style. You're insured."

"How?"

"Reagan, you know I'm a Republican, and I believe in personal responsibility. I took matters into my own hands," she says, with a mischievous smile.

"Look, I believe in personal responsibility too. It's your client that doesn't. But anyway, I'm not talking politics, Alex! So explain yourself without the political antics."

"Look, you don't need to know what I did, just understand that your bills will be paid. Your insurance policies will cover any and all procedures he needs."

"How?" Reagan asks, biting her lower lip.

"You don't need to know," Alex says, shaking her head. "You don't *want* to know. Just know both you and Jackson have lifetime insurance coverage." She points to the policies.

"How?"

"You have an HMO policy through your employer."

"Yeah, but that wasn't enough."

"Right." She nods, an affirmative, singular, nod. She then adds, "You also have a personal cancer policy; and an incidental policy, too. With all of these policies, your medical needs are covered."

"Alex, but how? I don't understand. We didn't buy extra insurance."

Alex begins to butcher the chorus again. "**I'll be on your side forevermore....**"

Reagan smiles and joins her. "**That's what friends are for....**"

Chapter Seventy-four
New Means

REAGAN WATCHES HER husband. It's been sixteen days since his surgery, and he is still in a coma. Reagan knows the road ahead may be difficult, but at least they are fighting the cancer with new means. Watching his lifeless body rest, she wonders, *Why? Why do bad things happen to good people?* She hears an answer. *Trials are for but a season. Trouble does not last always. This may be a mere test.* Hearing the words in her mind, Reagan remembers her great-grandmother, Emma James. Her great-grandmother would always tell her encouraging stories and words. She feels her presence with her now in the midst of this storm.

Sitting in silence, Reagan holds Jackson's hand and prays.

Hours later, she opens her eyes, hearing someone clearing his throat, interrupting. She turns and sees Calvin standing in the hospital room. He looks a little nervous.

Startled, she rubs her eyes, catching the tear that fell despite her efforts to hold back tears. "Calvin, I didn't hear you, hi," she says.

Standing with his hands inside his front jean pockets, Calvin says, "No, I didn't want to disturb you. I'm here to support. How are you holding up, Reagan? Jackson?"

"We're doing our best," Reagan answers, but she feels her lower lip trembling.

Calvin walks closer to her and embraces her. He whispers, "Reagan, he'll be okay."

"How do you know? Do you know something I don't?" she asks, unconvinced but wanting to believe him.

"I've seen his EKGs; while he has an uphill battle, he's improving," Calvin says.

"Calvin, really, what do EKGs mean?"

"It will take time to know all things for sure medically, but his EKGs say he's making some progress. I've also seen his pathology report; I think they've gotten all the cancer."

"But how? What do you know? How can you tell?" She rambles off questions. She asks the same questions over and over again in different ways until finally she feels relieved.

She looks at Calvin and says, "Thank you, thanks so much." She hugs him, tears still flowing.

"You don't have to thank me, Reagan. I'm a friend."

Her cell phone interrupts.

Reagan pulls it out and sees the CALLER ID. "Can you stay with Jackson while I take this call outside?" she asks.

"Sure, go, you need a break, I'll be here," Calvin says.

She walks outside the hospital room and out onto the hospital lawn to take the call.

— 9: —

CALVIN APPRECIATES TIME ALONE with Jackson. Sitting with him, he does what he knows best. He prays. Opening his eyes, he looks at Jackson and begins to talk.

"Listen, dude, you must pull through. We have too much living to do. I'll be the top medical correspondent on the net, and you'll be the top political columnist."

No response.

Remembering the EKGs, Calvin says, "Jackson, also I know you've been busy, but I'm getting married. You'll be the best man when I tie the knot."

No response.

All right, I'll up the ante! Calvin adds, "Jackson, I'm marrying your girl, Alex!"

Calvin sees Jackson's right leg pop. Calvin smiles and says, "Yeah, I know you're here man. Welcome back!"

Chapter Seventy-five
Come Clean

ALEX BRISKLY WALKS into her condo building. She feels at peace, knowing that she fixed everything that has gone wrong in her life *lately*. Jackson is insured. She has established her innocence. She is certain the case against her will be dismissed. She holds her head up high, appreciating her hard work.

Exiting the elevator and now preparing herself to relax, she approaches her condo when suddenly she hears her name.

"Alex!"

"Taylor? Where've you been? Did—!" Alex stops when she notices Taylor's appearance. *She looks terrible!* "What's wrong?"

"We've got to talk!" Taylor answers.

"All right, come in, but why the long face?"

"I'm in a terrible situation," Taylor says, walking into the condo and sitting on Alex's couch.

"Stop picking your nails!" Alex says.

"I'm nervous, and I'm in trouble, and I need you."

"Okay, that's been the story of my life lately, but I'm in friend mode, so what?"

"Alex, we're in foreclosure—"

Jeez, that's a bummer! I know how much you love that house, but it is over the top. "I'm sorry, Taylor," she says. "Really I am. What I can do?"

"Let me sell?"

"Sell what?"

"Well, do you remember the chick I worked with, Bianca?"

"How could I forget her? She's a piece of work."

"Well, she wants me to sell your story."

"Taylor, you didn't?"

"I didn't, but I want to because she's offering one million dollars!"

Gasping, Alex asks, "Did I hear you?"

"You did." Taylor nods.

"Sell the story! I would have—business is business."

"Yeah, but there's a catch. She wants me to lie, read a script," Taylor says, handing the script to Alex.

Alex reads.

Alex paces.

Alex reads.

Her mouth opens wide. *Bianca's a no good lying tramp! Yes, I slept with him, and yes, perhaps I like to have sex, lots of sex, but that doesn't make me promiscuous.*

Alex almost chokes on her own saliva when she reads the next line. *She wants you to say I did bribe Congress. She's a witch!*

"Taylor, you can't!"

"I know! That's why I'm here. I can't, but I need the money, so what should I do?"

"Why are you asking me? You know what I'll say—"

"I do, that's why I'm here."

"No, you can't!"

"No, we're smart. We can find a way around the rules, but I can't do this without your okay, because I'm your friend. We should do this together."

Pausing, thinking, Alex says, "Let me see the contract." Alex reads over the Media Rights agreement with Taylor for hours. After carefully scrutinizing the contract, Alex rewrites the terms. She changes the words to make the terms benefit them!

Feeling confident the deal is now titled in their favor, the women look at each other in unison and say, "We've trapped her!"

"Yep, so you know what to do, right?"

"Yes, I'll read the script, but we've changed the contract terms to say she can only publish the footage if the facts are true."

"Which we know they're not," Alex says.

"And when I read the script, she'll be forced to pay one million dollars!"

"And since we included a liquidated damages clause to the tune of twenty million dollars for publishing untrue facts, if she is dumb enough to publish, who cares, we'll be multi-millionaires."

"But wait! Are you sure she won't read the contract?" Alex asks.

"Nope, not Bianca. She'll never know we changed the terms. She will sign and tape the footage ASAP," Taylor responds. "Now, on to the next challenge, the house!"

"I'm not a real estate lawyer," Alex says.

"Please, don't call that Stan—what was his name, Stan man?"

"I won't," Alex says, shaking her head. "Don't need to. If we work together, and read all this liberal mumbo jumbo, maybe we can figure out how to save your house."

"You mean legal mumbo jumbo?" Taylor asks.

"Well, yes, legal, but more specifically, the liberals recently passed some law, we'll find it. I think it helps people in foreclosure!"

— 𝄞 —

Hours later, the sun rises. Taylor slumbers on the couch after working with Alex most of the night. Alex prints a letter to halt the foreclosure. She finds and relies on the people's bailout, the Foreclosure Prevention Act of 2008.

Chapter Seventy-six
Ballot in New Shoes

Days later, Reagan walks barefooted on a beautiful sprawling hospital lawn with her friends, Taylor and Alex. Feeling anchored, she smiles and thinks, *A great gift is a friend who proves she will lift you when you're sinking. She'll hold you up when you can't stand alone.* Hearing a loud noise, Reagan instinctively looks upwards and sees a flock of birds changing direction, in unison, in the sky. She feels in sync with her friends, like the birds who harmoniously travel great distances as one. *We, too, are one, despite our differences.*

"I'm no saint, but come on, this year, I'm wondering, is my Karma that bad?" Alex says.

"We had a season of trials, but good people have trials, too," Reagan says.

"I don't know." Taylor is still not convinced.

"Yep, our world was rocked! Everything was turned upside down," Alex adds.

"I agree. I feel so unstable, like everything I knew before was a farce, an actual sham," Taylor adds.

"Yep, like nothing's real or as it seems."

"Right, and that's why I'm unlearning everything I thought I knew and starting over," Taylor explains.

"Why unlearn?" Reagan asks.

"I've got a shaky foundation. I'm responsible."

"Okay, but I'm lost."

"I've been busy living my life, expecting someone else to look after the things I couldn't tend to," Taylor explains.

"You don't take hand-outs? I don't get what you're saying?" Alex says.

"I thought—wrongly, I see—that someone was looking out for my consumer interests, like my 401(k) plan."

"Awe, I see. Yep, that tanked," Alex says.

"Right, and I thought someone was making sure no one was cheating on my mortgage and that the housing market was stable."

"Right, but that market has collapsed, too."

"And I remember my real estate agent said the market wouldn't go down, that it was impossible," Reagan adds.

"Right, see that's actually—"

"WRONG!" All women speak in unison.

"And health care, too. Don't forget about health care," Reagan chimes in.

"Yes, and what I see is that I've had blinders on because sure my employer insures me and gives me access to a 401(k) plan; and yes, I had a great mortgage broker and real estate agent; and yes, I even relied upon someone else to get and dissect all the information that exists in the world about the state of health care, my 401(k) plan, my house, my mortgage; I thought everything was in order, in a perfect box."

"So what, you're thinking you're savvy with everything under control?" Reagan asks.

"Exactly. But, nothing against these professionals, I have a role, too."

"Yes, I learned that the hard way. I hadn't looked at my insurance contract before the cancer," Reagan says.

"And now, with the baby, education, gosh, I will be in the education game soon!"

"Well and take it from me, that's tricky," Reagan says.

"Unless you understand public education is the problem."

"Please don't start, Alex!" Reagan shouts.

"I agree, no politics, please!" Taylor demands. She pauses before adding, "But Reagan, seriously, my baby's not going to public school, unless I find a good one, because many are failing."

"I'll acknowledge that we have challenges! We're stuck in a bureaucratic box! We have to teach children how to take tests. We're not teaching them how to think! But look, I don't want to talk about the education travesty!"

"Yep, that's what I know, and so again, we Republicans believe—"

"Please, stop!" Reagan covers her ears.

"Reagan, I won't, okay." Alex pulls Reagan's hands off her ears and adds, "I'm only trying to help you find a solution."

"Alex, we're under a Republican model now!" Reagan adds.

"Which is my point. You're both looking to others for solutions without having a participative role in the process," Taylor explains.

"What do you mean?"

"We rant and rave about party labels; but we don't talk accountability. You know why?"

"Why?"

"We want scandal."

"I don't want scandal."

"Yeah, you're off, I'm not talking scandal!"

"No I know, but the national discussion always turns to name calling and bickering, so we rarely talk about real policies. We rarely know what a candidate stands for, and therefore we can't hold anyone accountable."

"You're exaggerating. I know exactly what I want and expect, and I always stick to policy. I don't get into that name-calling crap," Alex says, a little defensively.

"Really, weren't you just talking about the Democrat versus Republican way and not really touching on root causes and real solutions?" Taylor asks.

"No," she says, shaking her head. "The elimination of public education is a real solution."

"Look, I know where you're going. We're distracted aren't we? That's what you're trying to say?" Reagan says.

"Exactly. We focus on dissecting a candidate's personal life when we should be dissecting his or her policies," Taylor says.

"So you're saying rather than asking Sarah Palin how much her wardrobe costs, we should be asking her to assess the current state of the American educational system and then ask her how she would fix the system?" Reagan asks.

"Right. What's your education fix?"

"Yep, or rather than asking Barack Obama about his affiliations with Reverend Wright, ask him to assess the current state of the economy and how he would stimulate the economy?" Alex asks.

"Yeah, because I know the election is in a few weeks, and I have yet to hear the answer to either question."

"I don't think the question has been asked. Not yet."

"Perhaps when the candidates debate?"

"Maybe, but candidates spend years on the campaign trail. Let's talk policy on the trail, not scandal."

"I can't believe I'm saying what I'm saying, but I think I agree because the government is the foundation," Alex says.

"And to work, we the people must participate."

"And be informed."

"So what, we're saying goodbye to questions about lipstick, race, gender, sex, age, and focusing on the issues?"

"Yes, we must make a pact because laws and policies do affect our everyday. And now, more than ever, we need policies that work!"

"I see, because our foundation is slipping."

"I know. Everything I thought I knew is different. I mean, didn't the government bail out AIG today?"

"Yes, and Lehmann Brothers—one of the most powerful investment banks in the world—just collapsed."

"Into rubble."

"Into sand."

"Lehmann Brothers no more."

"No one was minding the field," Reagan says.

"And the accountability starts with we the people."

"This year."

"This election."

"We must hold our leaders accountable."

"I'm ready! Let's make some calls. I want to know who, when, where, what, and how!"

"Yep, with the focus on policy and results, nothing else."

"I don't care what color, race, age, or gender you are."

"Issues only! That's what we need before you get my vote."

"This year, I'm voting my interests!" Alex adds.

Chapter Seventy
New Year

REAGAN WALKS HAND-IN-HAND with her friends on a sandy beach far away from home, where the Indian and Atlantic oceans unite, and illustrious waves crash in on the shoreline.

Inhaling deeply, she smells clean, salty-sea air. Listening closely, she hears cawing seagulls and howling coyotes until suddenly she feels a swift breeze on her skin, and she begins to breathe deeply again; the sea air tickles her nostrils.

Glancing first to her right and seeing Alexandria Giroud, and then to her left and seeing, Taylor Ray, Reagan feels in balance. Serenity, faith, and hope encase her being until suddenly, a loud sound jolts her.

Listening closely, over the sounds of the seagulls, ocean waves, and coyotes, she hears a song in the distance....

She stands still, but sinks in the sand. In the distance, the song, "Celebration" plays.

"Do you hear what I think I hear?" Alex asks.

"I think so," Reagan says, nodding.

"Kool & The Gang, here?" Taylor asks.

"Yep, sounds like a local band, singing 'Celebration' with an accent!" Alex says.

"I'm running!" Taylor says.

"I agree, here we go!" Reagan runs, hand-in-hand with her friends, along the beach.

Finding refuge in a hollow sea cave, the ladies stop and listen. "Are we far away enough?"

"Yep, we're safe."

"I love Kool & The Gang, but we've traveled far away."
"Can't bring in the New Year in the same way as last year."
"Yep, *déjà vu*," Alex proclaims.
"Can't do last year over again. I've learned enough lessons, and actually I'm still dissecting the year," Taylor admits.
"It was a doosie," Reagan concludes, shaking her head.
"Understatement—last year was hell!" Alex declares.
Meanwhile, the sound echoes out again. . . .

C-e-l-e-b-r-a-t-i-o-n!

Hearing the song, Reagan asks, "Is the band following us?"
"Yep!"
"Let's run, run faster!" Reagan takes off.
Three friends run, passing sand dunes, caves, and canyons along the African shoreline. Far away from home, the New Year comes in with each friend unequivocally deciding to take refuge from reality, miles away from home.
Each friend has a new reality.
Each life is different from when they first brought in the New Year. Yet each friend is committed to steadfastly enduring the journey with confidence and persistence.
Sitting now on a sand dune, Reagan looks up and sees the full moon in the clear sky.
Feeling serene, the friends sit in silence, until Alex speaks. . . .

— 𝄢 —

"I can't believe I let that man use me the way he did," Alex proclaims.
"He's not a good man," Reagan says, comforting her.
"He twisted and played with me, so I actually fell into his traps!"
"Glad you're saying what you're saying and not me," Taylor adds.
"I've been so busy with Jackson, I didn't realize. How did you prove your innocence?" Reagan asks.
"SpyonHim.com paved the way," Alex answers, and then explains how she installed SpyonHim.com software on Marshall's

computer months ago, and how the software gave her a blind copy of each and every one of his emails, including the ones that proved that Marshall Hanes framed her.

"Wow, Alex, you, why I—I wouldn't have ever thought about doing something like that," Reagan says.

"I would have," Taylor says. "Speaking of which, since Whit and I are technically separated, can I borrow your SpyonHim software? I'll put it on Whit's computer!"

"No, you can't manipulate him, you can't," Reagan counsels.

"I need to know if he's seeing someone else," Taylor explains.

"I can't believe I'm saying this, but if you're going to work on your relationship, be honest with him. Besides, my relationship with Marshall was corrupt. You don't want to bring that nastiness into your marriage," Alex says, and then suddenly lightning strikes.

"Did I hear you correctly?" Reagan asks, in shock.

"Yes, I know. Don't push your luck. That's how I feel today, out here, like this, thinking in the wide open clear universe. Who knows what I'll think when I get back to my day to day!" Alex smirks, knowing that what she is saying is right, but she can't completely change her ways without sarcasm.

"So, SpyonHim cleared you?"

"Yep, that's the start, but then the ultimate game card was my girl power."

"You used sex again?" Taylor asks.

"Yep, well actually, no, I used sisterly girl power, what I call women working together, that's a weapon," Alex says.

"I don't get what you're saying."

"Taylor, do you remember our Sushi lunch?"

"Yeah, you were acting weird."

"Exactly, because Marshall was with Rachel McCay after he had told me he couldn't go out to lunch with me."

"Oh, that's why you were squirming in your seat, and that's Marshall—yuck Alex, I'm lost!"

"Look, in any case, I had a suspicion he was having a relationship with her, too."

"An affair, not relationship," Reagan chimes in.

"Right, yeah, whatever, so look, after I found the incriminating emails about the bribery scheme, I started looking for emails between Rachel and Marshall."

"Okay, why?"

"So I could confirm my suspicion, which I did. I thought our relationship was bad, but boy some of those emails, I swear, he had her all twisted up, too, and I mean literally, bondage games."

"Yuck, Alex!"

"Again, affair, not relationship. He's cheating," Reagan counsels.

"So with the evidence in hand, I called Rachel, told her everything, and asked her to help."

"How could you trust her?" Taylor asks.

"I had to. I needed her help," Alex answers.

"What did she say?" Reagan asks.

"She was mad because Marshall was cheating on her."

"I'm lost. He's married—of course he's cheating on her, even if he's only in a relationship with his wife and no one else. I don't get this."

"Look, sometimes when women date married men, they want to believe that the wife, well, she's a mistake. We hope he'll leave."

"Alex, that's sick, of course he'll cheat! He's already cheating on his wife, so why not cheat on his mistress? What do you expect from a cheating, disloyal man other than disloyalty?" Taylor asks.

"And I'm curious, only asking, why do you think a disloyal man will leave his wife when he can have both his wife and his mistress?" Reagan inquires.

"Look, disloyalty, yes, got it, you're preaching to the choir now. Look, what matters is we turned our hurt into vengeance."

"How?"

"She met him at his hotel."

"Her, too?"

"Yep, so in the midst of sex…"

"I knew it!" Taylor laughs.

"She told him I was the mastermind behind the bribery plot."

"Okay, so?"

"He could not stand the idea of her believing that I was a mastermind instead of him."

"Why, he knew the scheme didn't work? Wouldn't he know not to say anything?"

"Yep, if he had good judgment, but this man, all good judgment goes out the window when his ego is in play. He could not stand the idea that his girlfriend thought I was the brilliant mastermind behind the scheme. So he admitted everything to her; the idiot was actually boasting, showing off!"

"Get out of here!"

"Yep, he did. He said I knew nothing. I was only carrying out his orders, and that he was the mastermind!"

"Really, wow!"

"Yep, and she was wearing a wire!"

"He didn't suspect anything?"

"No, he was too busy nursing his ego."

"What do you mean?"

"His ego causes him to think unclearly. His judgment flies out the window when he starts protecting his ego!"

"So did he get arrested on the spot?"

"Nope, better, in court. When Shannon Klaxon introduced the evidence in court, I turned and looked at him with a wink."

"Did he leave?"

"He tried to, but the District Attorney knew the deal, so the police were hovering over Marshall in court, waiting; that rat couldn't escape."

"So what, he just sat there?"

"Yep, but his bald spot turned red in fury."

"Red, Alex, stop?"

"Yep, he must have what I have on my cheeks on his head. His head sweats and then turns red when he gets mad. But anyway, look, after the evidence was played, I was released, and he was handcuffed. At that point, Rachel and I looked at Marshall in unison and mouthed Gotcha!"

"No, seriously?"

"Yep, we practiced that move."

Three friends laugh in unison, obviously enjoying triumphant victory under the glistening sky.

− 9 −

IN THE QUIET, TAYLOR begins thinking back.... *My house was foreclosed on despite our efforts!* She sinks, realizing that while she tried to stop the foreclosure with the help of her friend, Alex, their efforts were futile. The Foreclosure Prevention Act was useless in practice because the lender does not have to agree to participate. Alex invoked Taylor's rights under the Act when she forwarded the letter to the lender, but the lender did not agree to work out a modification to save the house from foreclosure.

Remembering the day the friends decided to take matters into their own hands after the Foreclosure Act failed, Taylor looks to her right and sees her friends, Reagan and Alex, and smiles. *We actually went to that court house, hand-in-hand, to STOP that foreclosure!*

She thinks back to that bright, sunny, Arizona day, weeks ago, and recalls meeting her friends at the auction block.

Taylor leads the pack, sitting in the first row, with her stash of cash from selling the news story to Bianca Sheridan in tow. Alex sits to her right. Reagan sits to her left.

Hearing house after house being sold at the auction, Taylor prays and hopes until suddenly, she hears the auctioneer yell, "Next up for auction is 2583 Desert Sky Drive!"

Hearing her address, Taylor tells herself, *Remain calm, stay cool! Ouch, the baby kicked. Okay, I'll bid.* "Two hundred thousand dollars!" she shouts.

"Start low, a minimum bid," Alex whispers into her ear.

"We've got $200,000. Did I hear another bid?" the auctioneer calls out.

A lady standing behind them bids, "$300,000!"

"What is she doing?" Reagan asks, looking behind her and seeing the bidder. "Hey, that's GiGi Walker. She's a real estate mogul."

I'm screwed. "$325,000," Taylor bids, and then looks at her friends, who are looking at her with wide eyes, mouthing, "Low, Tay, low!"

Cutting off the bid-low coaching session, Gigi Walker bids again. "$375,000."

"What's she doing?" Alex snarls.

"I don't know." *But she's not taking my house.* Taylor begins to raise her hand again.

Cutting in, Reagan says, "Go low, go, low. Remember, think Suze Orman, Dave Ramsey, only buy what you can afford, remember? You promised your husband."

Cutting Reagan off, Taylor inches her bid up by five dollars and bids, "$375,005."

"Wow, you showed her!" Alex jokes.

Taylor wrinkles her nose.

Reagan nods. "Good job, Taylor Ray. Stay within your means."

Gigi Walker bids, "$400,000," obviously realizing that her competitor is inching behind her with bids and perhaps wanting to end the game.

Wailing, wanting her house, Taylor bids, "$400,001."

"Did you just increase your bid by one dollar?" Alex asks.

"I said low, Tay, but I don't know if that's going to work. Walk away," Reagan says.

Taylor does not give in. She continues to inch bid behind Gigi Walker. Ms. Walker bids $450,000, Taylor bids $450,001. Ms. Walker bids $475,000, Taylor bids $475,001, but also knows the next bid will be a leap, so Taylor turns to her friends.

Reagan speaks first. "Taylor, honey, I'm sorry, but your money has ends today. Remember, you promised Whit?"

"Yeah, I know you want your house, but I don't think you can continue crawling."

"Tay, I'm sorry, but you must walk away."

I made one million dollars with that scandal story. I gave half to Alex. Taylor looks into Alex's eyes and says, "Alex, you do have the story money. I let you in on the deal because it was your story, but I really need the money, and we made one million dollars and—being fair, can't you pick up where my cash ends today, please?"

Taylor tunes out everything around her and focuses only on Alex's lips. She waits on words.

Alex is silent, thinking, then she says, "Tay what—"

But then the auctioneer yells out, "Sold!"

Taylor turns and looks at the falling gavel. At once memories and dreams fly away in her mind.

Embracing Taylor, Reagan says, "I'm sorry, but you have the baby. Whit is willing to work on your marriage. Taylor, trust—"

"Hush!" Taylor breaks the embrace and ends the discussion. *I don't want to hear your faithful, look on the bright side words!*

"Okay, all right, you're right. We're no victims here. Let's go approach this Ms. Gigi Walker. I have an idea, come on!" Reagan grabs Taylor's hand and leads the way.

Walking, in unison, hand-in-hand, the women approach Gigi Walker. Reagan takes the lead. "Ms. Walker—that is your name, right?" She speaks in a calm, nice voice.

"You're correct, and you are?" Ms. Walker extends her hand, but then she pauses and takes it back. Observing the women closely, Ms. Walker sighs. "Dear, my, you're the low bidders. Why ever would you engage in a game of cat and mouse?"

"Ms. Walker, I'm sorry, but she's pregnant!" Reagan says.

"And that's my house you stole," Taylor says.

"Dear, my, I wouldn't say stole, even though I'll admit, I did purchase this house at a bargain. I'd appraise this one at more than $1.5 million dollars," she declares, glancing at a spreadsheet.

"Well, that's my house you stole," Taylor says, repeating herself.

"Sweetheart, I didn't steal your house; I purchased your house. Your circumstances I do not know, but this is a deal and this is business, and if you'd handled your business appropriately, you wouldn't be here standing saying I stole your house."

"Why, you!" Taylor begins.

"Miss, really, she's pregnant, she needs a house. You are a real estate investor, right? Make a deal," Reagan says.

"You're correct. I am in business to make money, so make an offer. Clearly, selling your house back to you would be a quick and easy profit, so let's deal," Gigi Walker says.

I only have $500,000 cash.

"She wants a lease to purchase option, with the purchase price being $500,000," Reagan says.

"No, this is worth more."

Taylor sinks.

"I'll give it to her for $505,000," Ms. Walker offers.

Lifting her head and her shoulders, Taylor shouts, "Are you serious? I mean really, oh my thank you!" Taylor jumps for joy.

— 𝒥 —

Returning to the present, Reagan breaks the silence when she asks, "Taylor, how's everything with Whit?"

"Horrible! He's livid."

"Still?" Alex asks, sitting up.

"Yes, he's sticking around, but only for the baby. He won't look at me."

"I'm so sorry. I thought you were going to counseling. Do you want to come to my church and meet my pastor?"

"No, thank you. We're seeing a counselor, a spiritual counselor even. But you know, even with counseling, rebuilding trust is hard," Taylor admits.

"You live together, right?"

"Yes, again, for the baby. He doesn't want to miss one moment. But he stays downstairs, and I'm upstairs."

"I'll keep praying for you, Tay. Your marriage has to work."

"He's committed. He doesn't believe in divorce. But we don't know how to fix this. I really do think he hates me even though he doesn't want to, even though he wants to love me. I never knew this could be so hard."

"How does that work? Living in the same house, not speaking to one another, but then being there for one another?"

"Alex, one day at a time," Taylor answers, but then she trails off and starts thinking about a few weeks ago, when the baby kicked. Whit sat with his ear to her stomach. He smiled and talked to the baby.

Returning her mind to the present, she adds, "He's so close to the baby growing inside of me, but he acts as if we are strangers. We're working, we'll keep trying." She vows to make their marriage work, one way or another, somehow.

Wanting to change the subject, Taylor asks, "What about you, Reagan? How are you holding up with Jackson being, well—?"

– 9: –

Reagan smiles, peace envelops her as she looks out into the deep blue sea. "I'm at peace, and I'm forever hopeful. I pray relentlessly without ceasing for a miracle each day."

"But Jackson, I know he's stable, but how is he?"

"He's going through the chemotherapy, every other week."

"Is the chemo working?" Alex asks.

"His doc got all the cancer out, and the chemotherapy should work! He'll survive, I know, I trust, and I'm faithful."

"You're certain? Doesn't he have at least one year of chemo treatments?" Alex asks, as if unconvinced.

"Yes, I have a feeling. God will answer my prayers."

"Here we go," Taylor mumbles, but then adds, "But since you're talking, you go on, Reagan."

"Yeah, talk your religion about you," Alex adds.

"See friends, this much I know. *While darkness may exist for a season, dawn does break equally for all daily.*"

Suddenly, interrupting the flow, the women hear the music again. "Is that band singing 'Celebration' again?"

"Is the band following us?"

"Yep, looks like that's a cruise line or something?"

"The band's on a cruise?"

"Is that the only song they know?"

"Who knows, but I'm not running. I don't care. I know we'll be fine," Reagan declares.

Shrugging their shoulders, Taylor and Alex smile and say in unison, "What? Girl power!"

"Call the power what you want—Girl power, universal powers, positive energy, positive thinking, your choice, but I know we can stand strong together, because we're friends, right?"

"Right!"

"Yep!"

"Wait, looks like this is the countdown," Reagan says. In unison, the women countdown: "10, 9, 8, 7, 6, 5, 4, 3, 2, 1—Happy New Year!"

Interrupting the cheer, someone yells, "Ouch!"

"What?"
"Something's in my toe?"
"What's in your toe, a seashell?"
"I—I don't know, it's hard and rigid!" She reaches down to her toe and picks up the large object.

Bringing the sparkling object closer, the women shout, "Wow!"
"What, a diamond?"
"And can you say huge diamond?"
"Yep, I heard there were diamonds here."
"I know, I think miners mine for diamonds here."
"But who knew?"
"We'd find a gigantic diamond in between our toes on a beach in Africa?"
"I don't know, but hey girls, should we make a pact and start mining?"
"No, this one's enough. Things are looking up!"

And the symphony plays on sand on balance.

CPSIA information can be obtained at www.ICGtesting.com
Printed in the USA
LVOW090758250512

283184LV00001B/64/P

9 780985 001902